Huck Out West

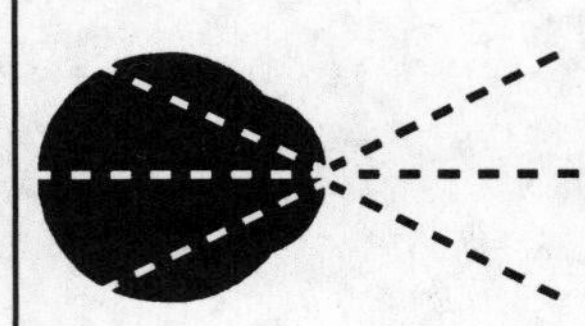

This Large Print Book carries the Seal of Approval of N.A.V.H.

Huck Out West

Robert Coover

WHEELER PUBLISHING
A part of Gale, Cengage Learning

GALE
CENGAGE Learning

Farmington Hills, Mich • San Francisco • New York • Waterville, Maine
Meriden, Conn • Mason, Ohio • Chicago

Wheeler Publishing Large Print Western.
The text of this Large Print edition is unabridged.
Other aspects of the book may vary from the original edition.
Set in 16 pt. Plantin.

LIBRARY OF CONGRESS CATALOGING-IN-PUBLICATION DATA

Names: Coover, Robert, author.
Title: Huck out west / by Robert Coover.
Description: Large print edition. | Waterville, Maine : Wheeler Publishing, 2017. | Series: Wheeler Publishing large print western
Identifiers: LCCN 2016058024| ISBN 9781410497277 (softcover) | ISBN 1410497275 (softcover)
Subjects: LCSH: Finn, Huckleberry (Fictitious character)—Fiction. | Sawyer, Tom (Fictitious character)—Fiction. | Large type books. | GSAFD: Western stories. | Adventure fiction.
Classification: LCC PS3553.O633 H83 2017b | DDC 813/.54—dc23
LC record available at https://lccn.loc.gov/2016058024

Published in 2017 by arrangement with W. W. Norton & Company, Inc.

Printed in the United States of America
1 2 3 4 5 6 7 21 20 19 18 17

For Georges Borchardt,
trail boss and fellow outrider
for close on half a century.

"He had a dream," I says,
"and it shot him."

Mark Twain, *Huckleberry Finn*

CHAPTER I

Just how I found my poor bedeviled self standing over a gulchful of expired trees, staring down the barrel of a prewar flintlock fowler toted by a crazy old cross-eyed prospector bent on dispatching yours truly, Huckleberry Finn, if not off to some other world, at least to the bottom of the mournful gulch below us, is something you ought know about on account of it being a historical moment — or ruther, like that decrepit shotgun pointed at me, a PREhistorical one. I warn't so afraid of the old buzzard shooting me as I was of that rusty musket going off of its own cantankerousness and fatally abusing us both. Pap used to wave one of them cussed things around, blowed off his big toe with it in a drunk one night, then give me a wrathful hiding afterwards like I'd been the one who done it.

I'd only went prospecting with Deadwood that day because he wanted company and needed watching after, him being the sort to mosey off and get et by wild bears out of pure unmindfulness. If I'd knowed we'd be a-finding gold, I'd a stayed down in the tepee, because there ain't much worse can happen to a body than getting rich. All gold is fool's gold, and I warn't in that neighborhood on its account. Drawed out by Tom Sawyer's stories and still here long after he'd upped and gone, I'd spent nigh half my life in the Territories, working one job or t'other. I was sometimes homesick for the Big River, but I mostly got used to the Territories and they got used to me, neither of us giving nor asking much, a way of easing through time that suited me when the world 'lowed it.

Making camp in Lakota country warn't legal, but the tribe had took me in a few years ago when I got snakebit and cured me of it, and so I had lived and hunted with them a spell and learnt something of the way they jabbered. It was the Lakota brave Eeteh who found me, all swoll up and near dead of rattler pison. He sucked the pison out and throwed me over my horse and took me to their medicine man, who poulticed me with prickly-pear and poured ammonie down my throat, which was worse'n dying.

The Lakota was mighty warriors and they

did not like white folks like me. I
deathly afraid of them and would a r
away if I could a run at all. It was Lakota
braves who'd ambushed poor Dan Harper and his fellow troopers and left them so full of arrows they looked like pin-cushions, so I reckoned they was just fattening me up for supper. But in the end they was good to me and I come to find them tolerable friendly, if maybe a bit quick to take a body's head-hair off. They was heathens like me, though they had some foolish notions on the side they'd got from chawing dead cactus that I could only smile at and chaw along with them.

I even had a Crow woman for a time, till she couldn't stand me no more. She had been took during a Lakota raid and was used around some before they give her to me, probably as a joke. Kiwi didn't have no nose and was at least half as ugly as me, and she was considerable inscrutable, not because she was a native, but due to her being a woman, whose species are by nature beyond my misunderstanding. They also give me a horse, probably a joke like Kiwi because nobody could ride him, but he took me on a grand adventure and I stayed with him the whole time, and we ain't hardly left each other since.

was having about the same kind of ith his tribe as I was having with im and me got on and we trav- ner after that whenever we could. s how it was that when the tribe, in their hunt for the disappearing buffalo, ported their lodges up into high Wyoming Territory, not far from the wagon trail where I'd met Dan, I trailed along, even though I knowed it was deathly bad luck to return to where a friend had got murdered. And it was. Because of Eeteh's turncoat Lakota brother, that ornery fancypants general found me up there again. General Hard Ass is what his soldiers called him, or else General Ringlets for his long curly hair which he lathered with a cinnamon oil that smelt a mile away. He was really only a colonel, but everybody called him general, because he wanted them to. He was on the warpath against the Lakota for what they done to some of his soldier boys and he wanted me to set a trap for him. Maybe I should a done, but I didn't.

If the general asked you to do something and you warn't of a mind to, you was inviting yourself to your own hanging party, specially if you messed his plans. So I followed Eeteh's sejestion and busted straight for the Black Hills, where I knowed the general was less than welcome. Hanging was as good as I deserved for the wicked thing I done, it was an out-and-out doublecross, but I was already black with sin, so I seen no reason not to add one more wrongfulness to the list and skaddle out of the hangman's reach. The Black Hills was sacrid to the Lakota, but Eeteh says the only Great Spirit that could be found there was what was stilled up by an old hermit whisky-maker residing in the Gulch, and that's where he'd look for me.

When I rode Ne Tongo into the little hid-away cluster of unpainted broke-down shanties and raggedy tents at the edge of Deadwood Gulch, nigh to cricks too fast and shallow for rafting, but prime for fishing — there was even a patch of sweetly clovered meadow beside the crick for Tongo to graze on — I knowed I was at home. A place I could take my boots off all day long. It was the rainy season, so him and me settled into a comfortable cave in the hills above the crick, shooed the bats away, and waited for Eeteh.

This was a few seasons back, before everything got so lively, when there warn't no town, just the Gulch, not no saloons nor churches nor women, nor not no gold, nothing to trouble the peace, only a few hairy old bachelors, one of whom, old Zeb, cooked up home whisky and sold it by the ten-penny glass in his front room which was the only room his dirt-floor shack had, except for a little tack-on shed where he kept his still and yist mash. His shack was the X on the map Eeteh drawed me. Zeb was the only body in the Gulch actuly producing anything, the others mostly living off of hunting and fishing and fruit and the few vegetables they growed or dug up. "Most a these lunkheads ain't producin' nothin' except what drops out their rear ends," Zeb says.

Zeb hailed from somewheres further down the Big River from me and Pap. He might not a been all white. He come west with only his old rags, his copper worms and pot, and a dona jugful of his pappy's yist mash, stirred up in buckets on his pappy's back porch, a stinking muck Zeb loved so much he called it his mother. Zeb was not a vilent man though he was said to have shot a few fools reckless enough to mess with her, and he kept a fierce mastiff named Abaddon who would chaw a body's leg off if Zeb give him leave. Zeb was a loner who didn't hardly talk to no one and then it was most like Abaddon's growl, but he was proud of his whisky like a fiddler is of his music. He didn't have no upper teeth, so his white-bearded lower jaw with its yaller teeth poked out under his nose like a cracked plate for it. He limped round like one peg was shorter'n t'other. Zeb's local clients was mostly luckless prospectors, chasing doubtful dreams like gamblers do, their profession one I'd never took to heart on account of it being such pesky hard work.

The prospectors warn't legal nuther, but there warn't many of them and they was tolerated by the Lakota on account of Zeb's whisky. They was all crazy about it. They mostly got sold by white traders a rubbagy whisky made out a black chaw, red pepper, ginger, and molasses, but Zeb never done that, and they appreciated it, Eeteh specially. The whole name they give Eeteh meant Falls-on-His-Face, and he always done his best to live up to it. He rode a piebald pinto the tribe give him. It had a peculiar hip wiggle the tribe thought was funny, though it could still outrun most a their other horses. Because of the pony's comic walk and pied colors, Eeteh called him Heyokha, which meant Clown, or Thunder Dreamer, in the Lakota tongue.

When he found me there, he fetched along my buffalo-hide lodge-skins and pipes and what-all else I'd left behind when me and

Tongo took to our heels. We cut and trimmed some lodge-poles and hoisted a tepee by the crick, leaving the cave to the bats, and set down to enjoy Zeb's brew. Eeteh told me the treacherous brother who'd set General Hard Ass on me had got throwed out a the tribe, but that might not a been a good thing, because the rumor was he'd took up scouting for the general.

Me and Eeteh helped Zeb trade his liquor to the tribe for buffalo meat and for the maize and barley he needed to richen up his whisky mash, as well as for blankets, hides, pelts, rawhide rope, pots and pipes, and other goods to trade with emigrants passing through. Zeb shared the meat with me and Abaddon, and he give me stillage for Tongo. The main occupation in the Gulch was lazing around and stopping by the bar in Zeb's shack every night, nor else a-jawing with Eeteh down at my tepee, smoking our pipes and sharing a jug. The Gulch was mighty peaceful and about as close as one could get in this world to the Widow Douglas's fancied Providence.

Well, this is a story with a fair number of years and persons in it and I've already took a wrong turn and got a-front of myself, so let me go back and tell you about me and loony old Deadwood and his antique musket and that fateful rock with gold in it, and then I'll try to give out the rest of it. His name was the same as that of the Gulch, but whether he'd got his name first or the Gulch did is in generl disputation. He says his pap, who was a Canuck trapper just passing through, give him his real Christian name which was Edouard, but his mam, who was part Pawnee — Deadwood's a mongrel, but who ain't — couldn't announce it proper. Others say that she changed it a-purpose because she judged that all he had betwixt his ears was like what laid at the bottom of the Gulch, and everybody thought that was comical and it stuck. Which might a gave others the idea of how to name the place, or anyhow that's how he likes to tell it because he says it gives him first dibs on anything found here, gold or whatsomever.

Well, now he'd found that glittery yaller rock, which I knowed as soon as I seen it was a powerful bad-luck sign, and he had got it in his mostly empty head that I was going to hire me a slick lawyer and steal his claim. To be sure that wouldn't happen, he'd raised his gun, took my rifle away, and got ready to shoot me, saying he hoped I was all right with Jayzus and all them other holy folks.

"Put that consounded thing away, Deadwood," I says. "You know I ain't no prospector."

"Well, maybe you ain't and maybe you is, but I cain't take no resks. I was borned here, ain't nobody else got rights, everything here is mine."

"Did I ever say it warn't?" Deadwood only shrugged his shoulder bones and cocked the musket. I was in a tight place and knowed I had to conjure up something quick like what Tom Sawyer would a done. "Now listen to me, Deadwood. You can go ahead and shoot, but just so's you're not disappointed, I'm bound to tell you that I set that rock there. I been feeling sorry for you being so low-spirited, and I done it to cheer you up. I don't know if there's more and I don't care, but if you shoot me I can't show you where I found it. You need me, and not only for finding gold. If you didn't have me around, who else would you have to listen at all your bullwhacky?"

"Awright then," he says with a cross-eyed scowl, lowering the gun but keeping it cocked, "show me. And no dad-burned monkey business."

At first I couldn't think where to take him and just set off walking. Then I recollected that old bat cave above the crick where I lived when I first come to the Hills. By luck, him and me was already on the path up to it, and it was fur enough off that I'd have time to ponder my strageties, as Tom called them.

The way the land humped up here was right peculiar, like something inside had tried to shoulder its way out. Back in school they learned us about the jeanie-logical ages. I didn't much credit it at the time, though when the widow said it went against the Good Book, I thought there might be something in it. I'd seen things hove up out on the desert, naked things carved by the wind into the strangest shapes, but here the hills was smothered over with wildflowers and big trees and was full of flying and scurrying varmints, with lots of dark damp places that smelt full of secrets. As the climb got steeper, the blackjack pines had trouble hanging on, which accounted for all the mortified trees down below us, though Deadwood says it was a mighty hurry-cane done it. He says the hurry-cane picked him up and hoisted him over into the Wyoming Territory, and what with all the buffalo stampeeds and scalping parties he had to fight his way through, it took him nigh two years and a half to get back from there.

"It was in here I struck the rock," I says

when we come to the cave.

"You set right thar en don't run off," Deadwood says, thinking my thoughts for me. "Ef you do, I'll hunt you down'n shoot you, even ef I do find gold in thar."

I lit up my stone pipe and sunk back on a granite outcrop, outweighing my choices. I didn't know where that rock he found come from, but not from inside that cave, where there warn't nothing but a dirt floor carpeted over with bat droppings, so if I wanted to stay I'd have need of a good story, and he might shoot me anyway just out of exasperation. I could run away — Deadwood's head didn't work too good, it's likely he'd forget to chase after — but I'd have to leave the Gulch just as I'd growed customed to it, and I could knock into that general again out there and wind up like all them misfortunate Santees in Minnysota.

All of a sudden, whilst I was still studying over my perdicament, Deadwood set to whooping and hollering in the cave. I was afraid he might a found a bear, or a bear found him, and I was on my feet, ready to tear, but he come out a-dancing with a big potato sack. "Looky here, looky here! Better'n gold! Money! Heaps of it! And other stuff, too! Look at this gold fob watch!"

"I know," I says, though it was news to me just like the rock was. I warn't the only body who'd holed out in that cave. "I seen all that. But it warn't mine, so I only kept the rock. Robbers, I reckon. Better leave it be."

"Ef they're robbers, they're most prob'bly hanged by now. I say, finders keepers. I'm a-goin' to buy me a jug from ole Zeb to celybrate. Ef you tote the poke, I'll 'low you t'come along."

Chapter II

So we done that, Deadwood not losing the opportunity at Zeb's to show off his rock to all the loafers there. How did he find that when nobody else had, they wanted to know. "Cuz I been here since afore time begun," says he, "and I knowed where it got hid." They asked him if he'd struck a seam, and he squinted, his eyes closing down on his nose, and says, "Yup, but I ain't talkin'." Though of course he warn't doing nothing else. After a few more swallows from the jug, that lode would be solid gold a mile wide and long and a hundred fathoms deep, but strangers and greenhorns couldn't see it if they was standing on it. For the price of a jug, he wheedled Zeb out of his raggedy old black vest so's to have a pocket to plunk the fob watch into. Deadwood says the watch was give him by the owners of the Pacific Rileroad. "I was out thar to show 'em how to spike up them rile things and they gimme it in reckonition."

"That must of been that golden spike I heerd tell about," Zeb says with a wink to the others. "You prob'bly stole that, too."

"Maybe. I ain't sayin'," Deadwood says, looking mysterious, and they all laughed at that.

Deadwood couldn't never resist a good brag. He liked to say he'd helped old Dan'l Boone, who'd got lost, find his way into Missouri, had learnt Jim Bowie how to handle a knife, and when he was just a pup, had went surveying with General Washington. "They credited him, but I done all the dern work." When I said I thought that gent lived in the last century, he said then maybe it was his younger brother. That lady liar Sarah Sod who Tom was always going on about couldn't hold a candle to Deadwood.

The only person could match him lie for lie was my Lakota friend Falls-on-His-Face. Eeteh was mostly a happy loafer like me with a particular hankering for Zeb's whisky and a generl dispreciation of the harsh ways of his tribe which, to hear Eeteh tell it, was nigh as ugly as the sivilization I'd lit out from. They got a Great Spirit that bullyrags them worse'n Moses and sets down what fundamentals they can and can't do, mostly can't. Eeteh says he never paid no attention to none of it, he couldn't see no advantage about it, and for that he took a power of whalings until Coyote learned him how to act a fool. Everybody laughed at him now, and they was always playing mean jokes on him, but they never whipped him no more.

You don't cross Moses and his holy gang without you get a hiding or struck with leppersy, but the Great Spirit hadn't no choice, he had to live with Coyote and his mischief. It was more fair. I ain't never seen him, but Eeteh says he has been to hell with the tricksome cretur to gamble with the dead, has helped him build a fire in a river bottom so as to catch cooked fish, and has walked the sky with him. The stars up there, Eeteh says, are like stones in the river and you have to hop from one to the next. It's scarier than a river, though, because if you slip you fall up into the black night and never stop falling. The tribe don't know whether to believe him or not, but just like the folks back in St. Petersburg living their own crazy lies, they're afraid he might be right, and so they give him his space and some attention. Deadwood warn't so lucky.

To be sure I couldn't butt in on his claim, Deadwood left me out of his yarns, which I took as a good thing because I didn't want no share of the trouble his crowing was bound to land him in. Our old neighbors was used to Deadwood's stretchers and was mostly too muddled up with Zeb's brew to be a worry, but rumbustiouser elements been moving into the Gulch who didn't know him. Some of them was there in Zeb's shack that night and they was already closing in on Deadwood in their grim friendly way. It looked like getting out might be a sight more harder'n getting in was.

I laid my rifle across my arm like I was thinking about maybe shooting somebody just for the heck of it and said we had to get back to the fort whilst there was still enough light to follow the mountain trail. I asked Zeb for some feed for the panther so's it don't bite my head off when I get back. Zeb was feeling flush with the windfall the barter of his antique vest had fetched him, so besides the feed sack he throwed in a couple of lumps of sugar. Deadwood was having a grand time and warn't easy to shift, but I remembered him not to forget what Dan'l Boone once told him, and that confused him enough to stumble out after me with his jug and gunny sack.

"What'd he say? What did Dan'l Boone say to me?"

"He says, Deadwood, he says, when strangers start a-crowding in, it's time to pick up and move on. You got them greedy boys all in a froth, showing them that rock a yourn, and now they want it, and they look ornery enough to try'n get it, any which way. I reckon you best stay with me tonight, and hope only we don't get followed."

"Dad-burn it, I ain't humpin' myself over no mountains t'bunk down with a blamed panther!"

"Well, stay and get killed then. But just so's you know, them mountains is all downhill from here and my panther has got better things to chaw on than smelly old prospectors."

He glanced back over his shoulder. There were three of them hard-looking strangers standing in the doorway, watching our way and talking together. Deadwood fetched out his fob watch and squinted his cross-eyes and studied it a moment. "Well, awright then," he says.

I throwed his gunny sack over my shoulder and walked us towards his shack until we got hid into the woods, shadowy now with the sun lost in the branches, then I made a quick turn down to the crick and hurried along it upstream to the tepee, moving faster'n suited Deadwood, grunting and complaining about his rheumatics behind me. There's a sad creamy glow about twilight that smooths off the edges and mashes thoughts and things together, like memory does when it's let loose on its own. It's the time of day when I most find myself thinking about the faraway river town where I growed up and about all the things I done there and the folks I knowed, most specially Tom Sawyer, who always had a lively idea of what howling adventure to try on next. Long time ago. Felt like a hundred years or more. So many awful things had happened since then, so much outright meanness. It was almost like there was something wicked about growing up.

Deadwood was weaving about, having oversampled, and was panting like an old dog when we reached the tepee, so I set him down by the woodpile with his jug and sack and went to feed Tongo the forage Zeb give me, letting him nubble the sugar out of my hand. I was glad to see him and he was glad to see me, bobbing his big head and snorting like as if to say so.

It was the tribe that give me the horse, about the same time they give me the woman. They come in the same parcel. I mostly got on better with the horse. My old horse Jackson had been with me since our Pony days, and if you counted up the miles, he'd hoofed it round the world a hundred times and at least thirty times flat-out. He was plumb knackered. I'd named Jackson after an island in the Big River where my life took a change because, with me and Tom setting out on our western adventures, it was a-changing again and I wanted to mark that. The tribe cooked Jackson up and et him which they said was doing him a great honor. When I named the new horse, Eeteh says to the others, "Ne Tongo," and they approved of that and give him a few baptizing slaps on his croup, and I approved of it, too.

That horse was a grand adventure, and I named him after the Big River, what the Lakota called the Big Water, thinking about the grand adventures me and Jim'd had on it all them years ago. We'd brung Jim out west with us when we'd run away, Tom and me, but we shouldn't never a done. When we hired on as riders for the Pony, we didn't know what to do with him. The war hain't yet started up, and though Jim was a free man, the bounty hunters didn't always mind such particulars. Sometimes we had to pretend he was OUR slave, and we always had to be on the watch-out he didn't get stole. The Pony Express Stables, however, was hiring only skinny young white orphans like me and Tom, and though Jim was surely an orphan, he come up short on the other requirements. The station-keeper said if we wanted the job, we had to get rid of him. I says we can't leave Jim behind on his lonesome, we have to look for another job. But they paid fifty dollars a month, which was more money than a body could tell what to do with, and Tom says we hain't no choice, and he sold him to a tribe of slaveholding Cherokees. "It's the right thing to do, Huck," Tom said after he'd gone and done it. "Jim's used to being a slave and he's probably happier when he has someone telling him what to do. And besides, they're more like his own kind." I knowed Tom was surely right as he most always was, but it made my heart sink into my wore-out bootheels to see Jim's grieved eyes that day. I waved at him and he looked at me like he was asking me a dreadful question, and then he was gone, with a rope round his neck. Tom bought us new riding boots with the money.

I opened the smoke flap in the tepee and stirred up the fire, and then took my pole down to the crick to catch us some supper. Dusk's half-light is always prime for fishing. Hardly before I'd begun I had me a handsome black crappie close to a forearm long to go with the half-dozen panfish on my morning trotlines, some of them still snapping their tails about in a kind of tragic greeting when I hauled them up. I know it don't make them happy, but it seems only fair for us fellow creturs to give up our bodies to others' appetites. I don't want to get et by mountain lions, but I wouldn't hold it against them.

I larded up a frypan and set it on the fire, throwed in some salt and the cleaned fish, and set back to enjoy an evening pipe. The Lakota had gave me a carved stone pipe which was soft and smooth and warmed the hand. I kept it in the tepee where I wouldn't lose it. It was what I had for good luck when the world was mostly throwing bad luck at me. It was such moments as made me feel I'd finally come to the right place. Plenty grub and an easy life, ain't no bad thing, as that humbug king we traveled the river with was like to put it.

At the same time, I misdoubted it could last. Though I didn't know it at the time, Deadwood's unlucky find would make sure it wouldn't, but you had to be blind in both eyes not to see there was already changes happening. The Gulch when I first slid into it felt like it was fixed here forever, but it warn't. There was always new fortune-hunters riding in, discovering their way to the whisky in Zeb's shack, and there was ever more and more of them, prowling the hillsides and crick beds. Some had staked claims, others just swarmed round to see what they could steal. They was tramping up the place and every day it looked ever more wore down and sivilized. These new folks warn't near as friendly as the old ones. Of course they was just like the old ones, warn't no beauties in the Gulch before them, only these new ones hadn't got rectified yet by failure and disappointment. And none of them was reckoning with Eeteh's people when their dander's up. For the Lakota, these scoundrels was all trespassing. Any fool could see, rough times was a-coming.

I'd just pocketed my pipe and took the fish off of the fire, when all of a sudden there was a muffled gunshot and a ball ripped through the tepee one side and out t'other, missing me by a whisker. Deadwood was screaming. "HALP! HALP! I been SHOT! I'm DYIN'!" I grabbed my rifle and dove under the cover at the rear, rolled over towards the woodpile, firing into the woods above us. I couldn't see nothing, so I listened as hard as I could, but I couldn't hear nothing neither because Deadwood was still thrashing around and howling and groaning pitifully. I shushed him, warning him he'd just draw more fire, but he yelped more louder'n ever.

"MY POKE! MY POKE! THEY'VE TUCK MY POKE!"

I always had enough trouble finding my way back to the tepee at night, even knowing where it was, so I was surprised that them new-comers had somehow tracked us here in the dark. Well, they hadn't. Nobody had. It turned out that Deadwood in his drunk befuddlement had rolled onto his old fowling piece and set it off, sending that shot through the tepee. He was laying on his coin sack. When I finally dragged him and his truck inside and stirred up the fire for a look, I seen there was a hole burnt in his new vest. He was likely burnt and bruised under the hole, but he warn't bleeding.

"Did ye git any of 'em?" he groaned.

"Get who?"

"Why, them dern robbers that was attackin' me! I lay I musta ruint at least six of 'em."

"I don't know about them, but your shot near took my ear off. Look at them holes in the tepee cover."

"That warn't me, it was them robbers. That just shows you they was out thar. But where was you when I needed you? I had to stand off that whole pestiferous gang alone!"

"Deadwood, I know it won't do no good telling you, but there warn't no firefight. You rolled over on your gun and set it off."

It was so, it didn't do no good. He carried right on. I could see he was contriving up a new tale for the loafers at Zeb's. When I says if he killed some of them, maybe we should go look for their bodies to bury them, he says, "No, they'll of drug 'em off by now." When I asked him where was the bullet hole if he got shot, he says his old ribs is so petterfied the bullets just bounce off. But then he groaned and his eyeballs crossed till they most joined together, like he was trying to stare backwards into himself. "But they shore do sting!" he wheezed. "Hurts worse'n the time I got shoved off of Pike's Peak by a claim-grubber!"

He was drunk enough to not feel too much pain, but sober enough to smell the fish and he et a couple of the panfish, bones and all. I was hungry and the crappie I'd catched was near as tasty as a Big River catfish, and it washed down smooth with Zeb's prime whisky.

"Them robbers, you know, they may come back looking for their truck," I says.

"Well," he says, "ef they do, maybe we can foller 'em, see where that rock come from."

"Maybe you should look right where you found it."

"But you put it thar."

I'd disremembered that. "Well, you always say I'm lucky, maybe the right place just come to me."

He pulled the gold fob watch out again to study it. I knowed that watch face didn't mean nothing more to Deadwood than higher-cliffs, so I asked him what time it was. "I dunno," he says. "It ain't that kinder watch. It's tellin' me other things."

"Maybe it'll tell you where to find the gold you're looking for."

"Maybe." His eyes was sliding together again. "Right now it's tellin' me them robbers is all dead . . . or else they . . ." And he fell back on the potato sack like he'd dropped there from a high place and set to snoring. His snores was outrageous loud, but I allowed they'd at least scare the wolves away. There warn't room for two of us in there, so I went down to the pasture and snuggled up to Tongo.

Chapter III

Next day we found Deadwood's shack tore up inside and out. It was always a wreck, but now it was a proper first-rate wreck. Them boys had gave it a powerful rummaging, even busting into the walls, and there was a bullet hole in Deadwood's straw tick where his head would a been. Pretty soon the scene had drawed a pack of loafers, so of course that set Deadwood to telling them all how he beat off a gang of desperados with his bare hands. "I think it was Jesse's boys," he says. "I heerd 'em braggin' about pottin' Jayhookers." He showed them the bullet hole in his bunk and they asked him how he didn't get killed. "Well, I was too dern fast for 'em, warn't I?" he says. "I ducked, and they only jest nicked me." As proof, he showed them a scar under his chin where his whiskers warn't growing, which he once told me he'd got from a Comanche arrow when he was riding with the Texas

Rangers.

There'd been some nights at Zeb's when knives and guns come out during the fist fights, Zeb had to sick Abaddon on a few reckless drunks, and some prospectors had went out in the morning and never come back, but that bullet hole was a dismistakable signal that the sivilizing of the Gulch was hard under way. Soon there'd be more people shooting at each other and then laws and lawmen getting mixed up in it and me and Big River would have to move on again. Tom was just the contrary. The law was like a rousing adventure book to him and he reverenced lawyers so much he went off to become one, even though he hated nothing worse'n doing what he ought to do. Well, he was smarter'n me. He knowed you had to learn the law if you wanted to stay outside it and out of trouble at the same time.

It was up in Minnysota that Tom made up his mind to give over cowboying and take on the law. Becky Thatcher was the daughter of a judge and maybe she give him the idea how to set about doing it. Before that him and me was mostly adventuring around without no thoughts about the next day. We run away from home all them years ago because Tom was bored and hankered to chase after what he said was the noble savages. At first they was the finest people in the world and Tom wanted to join up with them, and then they was the wickedest that ever lived and they should all get hunted down and killed, he couldn't make up his mind. Some boys in a wagonload of emigrants we come across early on learned us how to ride and shoot and throng a lasso so that we got to be passing good at all them things.

That story turned poorly and we never seen what was left of them afterwards, but ending stories was less important to Tom than beginning them, so we was soon off to other adventures that he thought up or read about in a book or heard tell of. Sometimes they was fun, sometimes they warn't, but for Tom Sawyer they was all as needful as breathing. He couldn't stand a day without it had an adventure in it, and he warn't satisfied until he'd worked in five or six.

Once, whilst we was still humping mail pouches back and forth across the prairie on our ponies, I come on a rascally fellow named Bill from a-near where we hail from. He was also keen on adventures and he was heading back east to roust up a gang of bushwhackers in our state to kill Jayhawks over in the next one. The way he told it, he had a bunch of swell fellows joining his gang

— that Jesse in Deadwood's yarn was in it, and Jesse's brother and some others — and he wondered if Tom and me might be interested. With the war betwixt the states starting, there was gangs forming up and making sport a burning down one another's towns, which seemed like sure enough adventures, not just something out of books, so maybe we was looking in the wrong place. But when I told Tom about it the next time we crossed up at a relay station, he says he allowed he'd just stay out west and maybe get up a gang of his own, because he couldn't see no profit in going back. But I knowed that warn't the real reason. The real reason was he couldn't be boss of it.

It was while we was on one of his adventures in the New Mexico Territory that Tom got the notion to go watch the hangings in Minnysota, a notion that would change everything. The Pony Express company had suddenly gone bust the year before when the cross-country tellygraph come in. We never even got our last paychecks, so we paid ourselves with ponies and saddles, which was how I got old Jackson, who warn't old then, but still young and fast.

We was both broke, money just falling out of my pockets somehow, whilst Tom was spending his up shipping long tellygrams back to Becky Thatcher. He wanted all his adventures wrote down like the ones he'd read in books and she knowed how to read and write and was the sort of body who would be impressed by his hifalut'n style and not have nothing else to do, so she got elected. She couldn't write back to him because there warn't nowheres to write to, but that warn't no matter, there warn't nothing she'd have to say that would interest him.

Riding, wrangling and shooting was what we done best and our backsides had got so leathery toting mail a body could strop razors off of them, so we hired on to guard wagon trains and run dispatches and handle horses and scout for whichever armies and exploring parties we come upon, and we had a tolerable good time of it. Back home we was Rebs, I guess; out here we mostly worked for the Union, though we warn't religious about it. Fact is, that time back in the New Mexico adventures we started out scouting for the Confederals, who was trying to cut a route through the Territory to California to get at the gold and silver; but we got misdirected and ended up scouting for the Union army instead and having to shoot at our most recent employers. Tom thought that improved the adventure considerable, adding what he called a pair a ducks, which Becky, if he wrote to her about it, maybe understood better'n me.

One a the Union colonels was a hardshell parson who carried such a strong conviction about the afterlife that he believed in shipping all his prisoners off there to populate it, sending along with them all their ponies, mules, grub, garb, weapons and wagons, just so's they'd feel at home when they got there, he says. He needed plenty of shooting and burning for this holy work and we was volunteered to supply it. Tom was a good soldier and done as he was told. I warn't and didn't always and didn't then. So I was oftenest in trouble while Tom palled around with the bosses. And it was while he was setting down with the parson over fresh roasted horse meat and the colonel's private sin supply, as he called his jug of whisky, that Tom learnt that they was laying out intentions up in Minnysota to hang more'n three hundred Sioux warriors, all at the same time. The parson thought this was the splendidest notion since the Round Valley massacres and Tom says it was something he had to see.

Tom loved a good hanging, there warn't nothing that so lifted his spirits, and he never missed one if it was anywheres in the neighborhood, not even if it was an out-and-out lynching, which he says was only a kind of participatery democracy. I warned him about getting too close to them things, some day they may decide it's his turn, and he says, "Well, if that happens, Huck, I'll only be sorry I can't watch." And then he grinned under the new moustaches he was growing and says, "But you're invited, Huck."

The notice of that quality hanging party up in Minnysota had Tom so feverish he couldn't set down, lest it was in the saddle heading north. "Just think of it, Huck! Over three hundred injuns all swinging and kicking at the same time! It'd be something to see! You could say you was THERE!" I druther be able to say I warn't there. Gallows always make me feel powerful uncomfortable and clumsy, like I might stumble and fall into one of them scratchy loops by happenstance. But Tom, like always, had his way, and soon Jackson was saddled up and we was making the long trek north.

Tom was afraid we'd be late and miss everything, so we clipped along at a fair pace, but it warn't nothing like galloping across the plains. Winter was a-coming on, there were north winds and snow, worse weather than I ain't never struck before nor since, not even in the Black Hills. We heaped blankets on us and on our horses and shoved our chins out and blowed up at our noses to keep them from freezing and dropping off. The days was ever shorter and seemed like nights, even at noon, and we didn't always know, famous scouts that we was, where we was or where we was going.

The people along the way was good to us, though. They fed us and our horses and let us sleep in their barns and pointed us towards the hanging grounds when we was misdirected. They all said they wished they was going with us, and told us horrible stories about what them filthy heathens had done to them and to people they knowed, and some of the stories was maybe true. They was all good Christians and said they prayed they'd hang every last one of them red hyenas, they was just pisoning the earth.

Then come the bad news. They was only going to hang thirty-nine of them; the President had let the rest off. The people was madder'n blazes. The President and his spoilt wife was living high and mighty off in the east somewheres and couldn't understand the feelings out here. They said they ought to make room on the gallows for that ugly string a bones. They was sorry they had voted for him. He had let them down and ruined their Christmas.

It was Tom's opinion that the President was a bumbler who ain't got the brains nor the guts for the job and who was only against slavery because it won him votes. And now that he'd stumbled the country into a war, he was too dumb to know what to do next. When I says that it seems like everybody wants to shoot him, and that'd be a pity, Tom says, "Well, that's just what makes this country so exciting, Huck. Just like in the time of King Arthur, and all them kings in the Bible."

"Was that the same time?"

"Almost. We was born too late, Huck. This is what we got."

I agreed it warn't much and sejested we turn back and go where it was warmer, but Tom wouldn't have none of it. It was still the biggest hanging ever and he wanted to be there, though you could see he was awful disappointed.

When we finally rode in, the sun was already gone down. Tom trotted us straight into town, afeard we might a missed it. A monstrous big gallows stood plumb in the middle of an open square betwixt the main street and the river, and there were crowds with lanterns milling about it in the dark, but the saloons was all closed and everything was stiller'n it should oughter be. There were candles in some of the windows. People was dressed up in their Sunday best and some of them was singing happy church songs, but we was pretty sure it warn't a Sunday. Tom was anxiouser than I'd seen him since we left the New Mexico Territory. He was sure we'd fetched up there too late and he was pegging at me for always moving too slow. "You don't have no respect for the BUSINESS of the world, Huck," he says. When he asked if the hangings had already happened, though, they called him a damfool and said you don't hang even injuns on Christmas Day. Christmas Day! We didn't know that. "Happy Christmas!" they said, and we said it back. Tom looked mighty relieved. "After sun-up tomorry," they told us. "We're stayin' up all night to git the best places."

We was most about starved, cold to the bone, and dog-tired. We couldn't a-stayed up all night if we was ordered to nor else face a firing squad. Tom was carrying a letter for the preacher of a church in that town, signed by THE FIGHTING PARSON, which described Tom as a hero in the noble battles against Rebs, Savages, and Unbelievers, and me as his stable boy, and the preacher welcomed us and fed us a hot stew with something like meat in it and blessed us and prayed over us in his quavery way and let us sleep under our blankets on church pews. He lived in a little room off of it. It was my first time in a church since I was held captive by the Widow Douglas and her sister Miss Watson, churches comforting me about the same as gallows do, though I felt a surge a spiritual gratefulness when I was able to stretch out at full length for a whole night. It warn't unlike the widow's notions of salvation. Tom stayed up to write another inmortal tellygram for Becky Thatcher by lamplight, but without no help from his stable boy.

The next morning, Tom was up and out well before the sun was, but I waked slower and stayed for bread and coffee with the preacher by the light of his whale oil lamp, setting at his rough-hewed pine table with him. He was scrawny and old, fifty year and more, with stringy gray hair down to his shoulders and dark pouches under his eyes like empty mochilas. He had a way of talking about Jesus and his friends like they was close kin of his, and praying come more natural to him than breathing done. He wore a raggedy black suit and peered over bent spectacles festooning the tip of a nose so thin and bluish it looked like a dead man's nose.

He seen that I warn't in no hurry to attend the day's revelments and, after mumbling a few more praise-the-Lords, he let it out that he'd preached against the hangings and all his congregation had upped and walked out on him. He knowed he shouldn't a done it, and he was sorry about it, but he couldn't help it. One of his deacons told him he resked getting lynched himself and he should best get out a town. He would a done, too, but he didn't have no place to go. He'd been waiting for them to come after him ever since and was scared to answer the door when me and Tom knocked the night before. But he was glad that he done so. He wondered now if maybe we could stay and help protect him. He couldn't pay nothing, he says, but he would pray for our souls three times a day, or even up to six times, if we wanted.

I told him we'd be leaving before them poor devils was even cold, and he shuddered and muttered that it was an ungodly thing they was doing, and the baby Jesus only a day old. He said them fellows and their families was starving to death. The federal agents wouldn't let them have no food without the govment paid them and the govment was too busy and broke fighting a war, so they could just starve, they didn't like them anyway, and it would be the govment's fault. Them poor people was always getting pushed around and most didn't have no place to live no more. Finally, they got desperater than they could stand and they fought back and, when it was over, hundreds of Santee Sioux was taken prisoner and put straight on trial by the army without no lawyers nor jury, not even no one to translate for them so they could know what everyone was yattering about. As the preacher laid open the story, his nose flared up in splotches and a kind of sparkly light come into his pale blue eyes. You could see there warn't no hope for him.

The little town set on a shallow river like a shrinked-down version of St. Petersburg back home. The walk to the middle of it shouldn't of took more'n a minute, but there was thousands of people to squeeze past on the streets. The night before, the streets was frozen mud. That morning, with all the tramping of them, they was just plain mud. It was the most people I ever seen clumped up together in one place. Some of them was locals, but most warn't. A few was looking scared, others angry, most was laughing and cussing. The saloons was all shut till after the hangings, but most everybody was carrying flasks under their coats, which they sucked at from time to time and whooped for the pleasure of it. They was having a grand party. I hain't seen nothing like it since in that river town when everybody come running to watch old man Boggs get shot dead by the Colonel.

The gallows was a giant open box with nooses hanging like Christmas ribbons, ten to a side, and it was set on oak timbers eight foot high so's there'd be room for the bodies to drop without hitting the ground. It also give everybody all the way down to the river a good view when it got light enough. It was the lonesomest thing I ever seen. It turned out from people talking that another prisoner had been pardoned, so there was a spare halter for whoever wanted it, and folks was volunteering each other and shoving them towards the gallows and hee-hawing. They said they better hurry and string up the rest of them devils, or they'd all get off and go back to killing and raping decent white folk again.

I didn't have no trouble finding Tom. He was standing on a special raised platform next to the gallows hobnobbing with the quality. Now and then the crowd let out a big cheer and the man standing alongside of Tom in a black swallowtail coat raised his top hat and smiled and waved at everybody, and Tom he smiled and waved, too. Tom had trimmed his moustaches and scraped his cheeks clean. He was wearing his slouch hat and doeskin shirt and was smoking a seegar somebody must a gave him. He looked a western gentleman all over. When he took notice of me, he made a sign to come up and join him, but I shook my head. I seen all I wanted to see. He said something to the chap in the hat beside him and stepped down off of the platform, the slicked-up spurs on his boots shining bright as new silver, and made his way over to me. The crowd respected him and opened up to let him through.

"Huck! Where you been? It's about to start! I got us the bulliest place to watch, so close you can almost reach out and touch a body a-hanging there. But you got to come now. It's starting up!"

I could hear them, somewheres further off, making some awful racket which might a been singing. "I seen you up there with all them high hats and was wondering what lies you had to tell to get invited."

"Lies! Huck, how you talk! I only let them know we was famous scouts and injun fighters from out west and showed them the parson's letter and I mentioned that you was the legendry H. Finn, breaker of wild horses, and all that was nearly mostly true."

You could see the prisoners by then, past the caps of the soldiers standing in two lines leading to the gallows. They was tied up and wearing what looked like rolled-up muslin meal sacks on their heads, which give them a comical aspect. They warn't moving too slow, but they warn't moving too fast nuther. Their faces was painted and they was singing to beat the band, but you couldn't hardly hear them because of all the hooting and hollering of the crowd.

"Who's that big-bug beside you up there, the one been collecting all the cheers?"

"Why, that's the persecuting lawyer, the one who got over three hundred savages sentenced to death. And they would've hanged them all, too, he says, if we didn't have such a weak injun-loving President. He says the heathen Sioux has got to be slayed to the last man and anybody who'd spare them is an enemy to his race and to his nation. That fellow ain't had to shoot nobody nor get shot at, but still he's the famousest hero here today. Ain't that something?"

"If that's him, he warn't nothing fair. Them people was getting badly misused.

And they warn't allowed no lawyers nor no —"

"FAIR! Stuff! You've clean missed the POINT, Huck! Ain't NOTHING fair, starting with getting born and having to die. THAT ain't fair. But a body can't do no more about it than them poor condamned injuns can. You can only live out what you got as fierce as you can and it don't matter when or where it ends." The prisoners was being marched towards the steps up to the platform. They was still chanting and singing their "hi-yi-yis" and the crowd was still trying to drown them out with whooping and cussing. Some was hollering out church songs. They was all round us and you couldn't hardly hear nothing else. "Besides, Huck, they're only injuns, who are mostly all ignorant savages and murderers and cannibals."

"What? They're all cannibals?"

"Ever last one of them, Huck. Come on now, it's —"

"You sold Jim to cannibals?"

"Well, wait, there's two kinds of injuns, the ones that keep slaves and the ones that's cannibals." The prisoners in their white nightcaps was starting up the steps, and folks was growing quiet, letting them sing if they wanted to. "But hurry! This is HIS-

TORY, Huck! You don't want to miss it!"

"Tom? Huckleberry? Is that you?" It was Becky Thatcher, completely out a nowheres, pushing through the thick crowds. It took a moment to reckonize her because she'd growed up some and warn't sporting yaller pigtails no more. Tom's jaw dropped like its hinges was broke, and I s'pose mine was hanging, too. "My laws! How you boys have CHANGED! All that FACE hair! That long stringy beard makes you look a hundred years old, Huckleberry!"

Tom had hauled his jaw back up, but he was struck dumb. He probably hain't never planned on his audience visiting him head-on. He turned and walked off without nary a word. Up on the gallows they was unrolling them muslin bonnets into hoods that covered their painted faces. Some of them was holding hands.

"Tom! Wait!" Becky called out, and went chasing after him. I should a stayed and watched, like Tom said, but that extra noose and the drumrolls was giving me the fantods.

Chapter IV

Deadwood and me hadn't got to the end of the bad luck fetched up by that consounded rock he found. I told him to throw it away or handle it off to one of them strangers in Zeb's, but he give a snort and says I must be plumb loco. It was mighty hard to learn him anything. Jim, who knowed most everything about luck, told me that both good and bad luck has a way of smearing itself round in the generl neighborhood, and one of the certainest ways to shut off the good luck is to be too close with what you already got. Like Deadwood in Zeb's that night with his jug, clinging to it like a cub to its mother. If he'd a showed a little more unstingeableness, maybe things would of turned out different. Of course if he'd let go of it, them scroungers in Zeb's would of made short work of it, and THAT would of been bad luck, so it's hard to calculate. I'd need Jim to cipher it out.

I'd come to the Gulch to hide out from that general who was set on stretching my neck, but I judged I was safe in the Hills because the Lakota was after him for all the bad things he done to them — Long Hair, they called him, naming him by the scalp they wanted — and he surely warn't such a fool as to come back here again. Well, I was exactly wrong, for one sunny morning there he was, sassy as you please, dolled up in his red cravat and silver stars and shiny knee boots. He was riding in with his calvary boys, a whole army of them, their blue coats sliding in out a the deep green pines, fields a flowers tickling their horses' underbellies.

The general had an Indian brave scouting for him. The brave's gaze was flicking about, looking for someone. Me. It was Eeteh's rascal brother. The tribe had throwed him out after his treachery up in Wyoming, and here he was, riding with their worse enemy. I laid low, peeking out through the gaps in Zeb's plank walls, ready to skaddle if I had to. There was other loafers scrouched down at the gaps, so I warn't the only one had got on the wrong side of General Hard Ass.

Deadwood's bragging had spread round. The general says he'd heard about a yaller rock somebody found, and he'd like to see it. A couple of loafers went running off and come back dragging Deadwood who was hollering out all the cusswords he could think of until he seen the general, and then he shut up. The general asked to see the rock and Deadwood says he ain't got it no more, somebody stole it.

The general smiled down at him under his drooping moustaches. I reckonized that smile. It was what I seen when he told me what I had to do and what he'd do if I didn't. All by my lonesome with nobody's hand to hold. "If you no longer have the rock," the general says, pulling out his revolver and pointing it at Deadwood's head, "I have no further use for you. You have exactly one minute to steal it back." And he cocked his revolver.

It had growed ever so still. In the silence, the revolver click was like a mountain cracking. There warn't nobody breathing. Maybe they was counting. It was like that moment of the three drum beats up in Minnysota just before the floor of the platform dropped away. Probably less'n a minute went by, though it seemed like a century before Deadwood finally reached into his pants pocket and pulled out the rock. A soldier pried it out of his gnarly fist and handled it up to the general. The general holstered his revolver, hefted the rock to judge its weight, and showed it to his officers. They nodded and the general dropped it into a leather pouch hanging from his saddle.

"That's MY rock!" Deadwood yelped. "I found it! I own it!"

"You own nothing," the general says softly. Everywheres there was the smell of cinnamon. "Not even your poor sad arse." The old prospector stared up at him defiantly and the general, still smiling his sorrowful smile, stared back, until Deadwood, cussing to himself, turned and stamped away. One of the troopers shot his hat off, and they all brayed like mules. He'd at last took my advice — or had my advice took for him — and had passed the bad luck on, but he hadn't got shut of all of it. There was worst to come.

The general was right to want to hang me. When you done something as wrong as I done, you can't expect no better. A body who hires himself out to generals has a bounden duty to do what he's asked, even when it ain't his druthers. Dan Harper, that young soldier I met on the wagon trail, learned me that, though I most likely already knowed it. The general had trusted me and I let him down. I won't say it was the shamefullest mistake I ever made, I made so many there ain't no smart way to rank them, but it's clean at the top for the troublesomest. When I done it, I set myself up for everlasting ducking and running, and what was worst, it was probably a mistake I couldn't stop making over and over. Can't you never learn nothing, Huck? Tom would say. The years rolling past just seemed to pile on more stupidness.

When I turned my back on Tom and history all them years ago, I seen the Minnysota River a-front of me, and it called me down to walk it a stretch like rivers do. It still warn't yet noon and, soon as the hangings was over, I was aiming to saddle up and light out whilst there was still daylight, but Tom was having a high time and I misdoubted he'd want to leave till he'd lined out a few more adventures.

I felt comfortabler down by the shore. A river don't make you feel less lonely but it makes you feel there ain't nothing wrong with being lonely. The Minnysota was a quiet little wash, near shallow enough to walk across without getting your knees wet, but a flat-bottom steamboat run on it, and it was setting out there then with a passel of whooping gawkers on it, watching the hangings through spyglasses. It had started freezing up at the shore, and soon walking across it would be all a body COULD do.

Past the steamboat landing, the shore was low and woodsy like a lot of the islands in the Big River back home, and it got me to thinking about other ways a body might blunder through life. By piloting a riverboat for a sample. That would be ever so splendid, and just thinking on it lifted some my sunk spirits. But probably I warn't smart enough. Well, I could do the loading. Folks running away from the war was saying the whole river back home was on fire and the bullets was flying like mosquitoes in August, but in this nation a body can get shot anywheres, and getting shot on the river beats getting shot in the desert every time.

The day warn't hardly more'n begun when I got back to the church, but it was already growing dark and puckering up like it might snow some more. The preacher warn't around. Maybe he was hiding somewheres from all the right-minded townsfolk. I found a morsel of bread on his pine table and, though it was at least a week old and worse even than the hardtack we got fed at the army forts, I borrowed it and went and stretched out on a pew under a heap of blankets to gnaw on it.

The next thing I knowed, Tom was setting there talking to me. I judged it was Tom. He seemed more like a spirit, appearing so sudden like that and in such a place. He had a candle, and the light from it made his face come and go. "What I wanted to tell you, Huck, is that there is two kinds of injuns," Tom says, if it was Tom. "There's the ones who slaughter white folks and roast them for supper, and there's the ones they call friendlies who ain't cannibals. The friendlies respect the white man and try to act just like him, which is why some of them keep slaves and eat with forks, and lots of them is even Christians." I believed Tom like I always done, but I didn't believe him. I was glad he come back, but I didn't know why he'd waked me up to tell me that. Then I seen the others. Becky Thatcher. The preacher. Tom's horse. "Huck, I'm gonna leave you for a time," Tom says.

It turned out him and Becky was getting hitched by the preacher, and me and the horse was the witnesses. Tom was giving the horse to the preacher as pay for marrying them, and him and Becky was taking the steamboat upriver the next day on its final journey of the year to connect up with the big riverboats headed down towards St. Petersburg. "You can come and see us off," he says.

The news shook me up considerable, but I done my best not to show it. Neither me nor the horse didn't say nothing, though the horse wagged his head about like he was looking for the way out. Well, he'd never been to church before and he didn't know how to act proper. It sure warn't the place to be dropping what he was dropping, but he didn't know that. Becky had bought some beer with her pappy's money to celebrate the wedding with and after the preacher had went and took the horse with him, the three of us set there in the church and drunk it. She'd also found some doughnuts and jelly somewheres to go with it. The hotel was jam full, Becky said, but a gentleman give up his room for them. She was staring at Tom like he was the most amazing thing she ever seen.

"You missed something great, Huck, when you left," Tom says. "One a them injun braves starts yelping out that if we found a white man's body with his head cut off and stuffed up his own backside, he was the one who done it. And he beat his chest with his tied-up fists and somehow got his britches down and wagged his naked backside at everybody. Ain't that a hoot?" Becky was blushing and excused herself to step outside a minute and Tom leaned close and says, "I learnt something here, Huck, about the law and how it makes some folks poor and some folks powerful rich and famous. I want me some a that power, Huck. Judge Thatcher will learn me. I'll come back and I'll find you wherever you are and we'll have adventures again. But they'll be better ones."

When they'd left, I blanketed me and Jackson and we headed south.

CHAPTER V

When me and the general first crossed trails, Tom Sawyer had been gone east some five or six years. Though he said he'd come back out and find me, he never did. I allowed he must a forgot. I seen a pretty girl who looked like Becky some years later over a-near a Wyoming trailhead, and if it was her, I judged that Tom was like enough there, too, but he didn't show himself.

When he left, I carried on like before, hiring myself out to whosoever, because I didn't know what else to do, but I was dreadful lonely. I wrangled horses, rode shotgun on coaches and wagon trains, murdered some buffalos, worked with one or t'other army, fought some Indian wars, shooting and getting shot at, and didn't think too much about any of it. I reckoned if I could earn some money, I could try to buy Jim's freedom back, but I warn't never nothing but stone broke. The war was still on, each side chasing and killing t'other at a brisk pace clean across the Territory, and they both needed a body like me to scout ahead for them, watch over their stock at night, pony messages to the far side of the fighting, clean their muddy boots and help bury the dead, of which there warn't never no scarcity, nuther boots nor dead.

Out in these parts both armies warn't tangling so much with each other as they was with the natives, who kept getting in their way like mischeevous rascals at a growed-ups' party. I was riding generly on the Northern side because that was where I found myself. They called theirselves abolitionists and what they was mostly abolitioning was the tribes. Every time they ruined a bunch of them, they ended up with herds of captured ponies, and somebody had to put saddles and bridles on the ones that warn't summerly executed and break them in the white man's fashion, and I could help do that. I s'pose I was having adventures like before, but without Tom to make a story out of them, they didn't feel like it. They was more like a kind of slow dying, and left me feeling down and dangersome.

Fetched low like that, I fell in with a band of robbers, though I didn't want for nothing to rob, except maybe a shot a whisky or a beer. I'd been hired on to guard a stage-coach from the east on its way up the Oregon Trail to Frisco, hauling a load a mail-order brides for gold miners who'd struck it rich out there, but I fell dead asleep just when the coach was set upon by a masked gang. When the shouting and hallooing begun, I couldn't hardly think where I was or even who I was. The bandits yelled out they don't kill women, it ain't in the books like that, so everybody could just leave their money and julery and weapons and run away and tell everybody they'd been robbed by the Missouri Kid and his murdrous gang, the Pikers, though if anybody wanted to stay and get shot, they could do that.

Whilst the Pikers was busy collecting their riches, I mounted old Jackson, ducked my head, and slid in with the others, but the ladies was mad at me for not trying to save them and they give me away. The bandits grabbed me off of Jackson and tied me up, and when the others was galloped off, they begun arguing about what to do with me. Some of them wanted to write a direful warning on my backside with their sheath knives and hang me from a tree for a lesson to passing strangers, others wanted to ransom me for money. "He won't ransom for two cents," one of them says, "and his butt ain't big enough to carve even half a cussword on it. I move we jest shoot him." They was all finally agreed that was the best way, and the Missouri Kid he cocked his pistol and asked me what my name was so's they'd know what to write on my gravestick.

When I told him, the others all laughed because of how long it was and hard to spell, but the Kid he staggered back like he'd been smacked in the jaw and says, "HUCKLEBERRY FINN! I cain't BELIEVE it! Is that really YOU behind that raggedy beard, Huck? This is MOST AMAZ'N!" He pulled off his mask to show me a gashly face with a broke nose and one eye whited over and a thick black beard sprouting round a loose scatter a chipped teeth. "It's ME, Huck! BEN ROGERS! Don't you 'MEMBER me? We was in Tom Sawyer's robber gang together, back when we was jest mean little scamps!"

He untied me and give me a happy punch on the arm. Ben Rogers! It did feel good to find someone I knowed out in all that miserable wilderness, even if he was a bandit and a body couldn't hardly reckonize him. "Gol DANG it, Huck!" There was tears in Ben's good eye. He says he's been so horrible lonesome for me and Tom and all the others from back home he most couldn't stand it, and he begged me to travel with him and his boys for a spell. He says the Pikers only rob from the rich and give to the poor, specially poor orphan children, but they don't know nobody poorer'n what they are and they ain't met up yet with no orphans before me, so they mostly give it to theirselves so's not to waste it. "C'mon, Huck! It'll be jest like old times!" Ben says I don't must do nothing I don't want to, except promise to bury him if he gets killed and be sure to tell everybody back home about the Missouri Kid and what all he done. He says I can add a few stretchers if I want to, and I says I could do that.

So I become a highwayman and me and Ben Rogers rode together for a time, working the Platte River emigrant trails with his Missouri Piker gang, and I helped hold up the sort of wagons and coaches I used to ride shotgun for. Ben and me talked about the fun we had in the old days back on the Big River, and he told me all his adventures since then, saying I should maybe be writing some of them down whilst he could still recollect what he just said. He says he lost the eye when an old prewar pistol backfired on him, but I could say it was because of a fight he got into with a hundred Mexican bandits along the Rio Grande. He says he ain't never been there, but he heard it was as mighty as the Big River and twice as muddy.

I ain't had no adventures since Tom left, so I told him about me and Tom riding the Pony Express, which made Ben whistle out his beard and say it was the most astonishing thing he ever heard in all his born days. I told him about the Fighting Parson's righteous slaughter of the tribes and about riding northards in the winter with Tom to see all them poor Santees get hung. Ben says he wished he'd seen that, and I says I most wished I hain't.

One evening, when the Pikers was holed out on a woodsy island in the middle of the river, me and Ben moseyed off a few miles away to a saloon that I knowed from the Pony days to have a drink and buy some bottle whisky for the others. There was thousands a birds a-fluttering through the twilighty air, making a body restless, and fish was a-jumping and plopping in the still river like they wanted the birds to pay them more mind. The saloon was fuller of loose women than I recollected, and Ben, scratching his black beard, says he had a weakness for their kind and he warn't leaving till he'd got close acquainted with at least six of them. Serviceable ones ain't easy to come by out in the wilderness, he says, so a body had to store up a few extra to fill in for the off days.

We had a good time that night and was tolerable tight when we rode back, Ben personating a Big River steamboat and its bells, making wide turns on his horse and singing out a load a ting-a-ling-lings and chow-ch-chow-wows, the wolves and coyotes yipping and howling along with him, elks blowing their whistles. On the island, though, there warn't nobody singing, nor howling nor whistling nuther. All Ben's gang had been murdered by a rival gang. The rivals was called the Boss Hosses and all the corpsed bodies had horseshoe nails hammered into their chests or backsides. Ben cussed and wailed and fired off shots into the trees around. Then we left the island and went back to the saloon because Ben says he has to dunk his sorrows. One of the two rival gangs was Union, t'other Confederal. I disremember which was which, but it probably don't matter none.

We still had some swag left, and Jim had been worrying my mind, so I sejested we go see if we can buy him back from the Indians who bought him. Ben didn't know who Jim was and, when I told him, he says he ain't going to resk his neck for no dad-blame nigger slave. I says it was Tom's idea of a bully adventure, and maybe we might could even turn a profit off of him. Ben still warn't convinced, but he finally agreed when I told him how friendly the Cherokee maidens was. Mainly I s'pose he was scared and sadful after the massacre of his gang by the Boss Hosses, and just only didn't want to be left alone. I reckoned after he met Jim, he'd like him like I liked him and would forgive him and wouldn't want to sell him back into slavery again.

Ben Rogers warn't no cleverer at hanging on to money than what I was and by the time we fetched up at the border of the Cherokee Nation, we only had two dollars left. We spent one of them on a bottle a whisky to carry along like a gift, and that left us just a dollar. Ben says it warn't near enough and he wanted to go spend it on more practical things like women, but I reckoned a dollar might buy us an elbow or an ear and they could maybe borrow us the rest.

The Cherokee Nation warn't a tribe a feather-headed natives in wigwams. They was all Southern gentlemen, living very high off of the hog. They wore puffy silk cravats and stiff high collars and growed magnolia trees and tobacco and had slaves picking cotton in their fields, though I couldn't spy Jim amongst them.

The chief come out from his white mansion in his creamy pants and black frock coat, and I raised my hand and says, "How!" and give him the bottle a whisky. He took one taste, spit it out, and throwed the bottle away.

Ben yelped in protest and run to pick it up. "Tarnation! Who the blazes does that dang barrel organ monkey think he IS?" he roared. I tried to shush him up, but he went right on cussing and hollering and calling that Indian every name he could think of.

I didn't know no Cherokee, so I says to them as clear as I could, "Me looking for slave negro name Jim."

They all busted out laughing. They took my dollar and passed it around like a joke, give it back to me. "We only accept Confederate money here," the chief says, gripping his coat lapels in both hands and peering down at me like a judge. "You boys abolitionists?"

"No, sir! That slave belonged to my family back on the river, but he run off on us. My pap and uncle sent me and my cousin out here to try and hunt him down."

"Well, you're out of luck," the chief says.

"We judged he was a runaway and there might be somebody like you turning up to claim him, so we sold him to some white bounty hunters, and they put him in chains and carried him off east."

A little Cherokee girl about twelve years old was smiling up at Ben from behind one of the tall white pillars of the chief's big house. "Hah!" Ben says. "There's one!" She squeaked in fright and run away and Ben went a-chasing after. I yelled at him to come back, we was going now, but he cocked his good eye at me over his shoulder and shouted, "You can see how spunky she is, Huck! Won't take me a minute!"

"You'd better rein in your cousin," the chief says coldly, fingering the little gold cross hanging round his neck.

"That won't be easy," I says. "He suffered a dreadful head wound at Vicksburg a-near where our families' plantations is, and he's been crazy like that ever since. You can see how he was half blinded by it. I hope, sir, you can forgive him his trespasses."

"I can, but her father probably cannot."

He couldn't. He clove Ben's head in with a tomahawk. They brung the body, throwed it over his horse, and chased us out of there with war whoops and horsewhips and gun shots.

So I rode out in the desert and dug a hole for Ben's remainders and told the hole I'd let everybody back home know about the Missouri Kid. If I ever got there. Then I rolled him into it and kicked some dirt in to cover him up and went back to killing buffalos and guarding wagon trains. My bandit days was over.

Chapter VI

Nookie told me about the bad man whilst we was taking a bath. Baths warn't something I was partial to, but she done things with her spidery fingers that made them more favorable. It was like sometimes she had an extra pair of hands. Maybe she used her strange unregular feet with the wiry little toes. She could do most anything with them, including licking them like a cat or lacing them behind her neck. But they warn't so good for walking. I done more baths with Nookie than all the rest a my life piled together. I knowed they could do a body harm, so I been cautious to mostly stay away from them, but I ain't sorry for the ones I had with Nookie.

Her painted tin tub was just big enough to stand or set in, with a little ledge on one side. I never seen nothing like it before, generly using rivers and rain to get wet in. Nookie would squat at the edge with me raired up on my knees in the tub and sponge my backside with a soft squshy soap she made herself, and then she would crawl in at my feet when it was the other parts' turn. She made a whiny sound whilst she done it, which was maybe Chinese singing. She says she was muddytating. The tub was made for one body to set in, but we was so skinny there was room for both of us, so when she poured warm water over me to wash off the stink of the soap, she got in, too.

Then it was Nookie's turn. Helping Nookie soap herself was one a the comfortablest things I ever done. The Widow Douglas always used to learn me that it was better to give than to receive. You couldn't credit nothing the widow said, but it was maybe true about baths. Of course, there warn't much of Nookie to wash, we was both slathering up skin stretched tight like wet wrapping paper around bones, and hers was most like bird bones. If she'd been bigger, maybe it'd seemed less agreeable. "You rike my bluzzer, Hookie," she says, looking sorrowful at me. "He skinny, too."

When Nookie called me Hookie, it sounded like cookie, both our names did the way she said them. She says it was the bad man who named her. She told him her real name, but he couldn't never learn it. He told her Nookie was what her name meant in English or some other language. "He say, I am Rooskie, you are Nookie. Is only time I hear he laugh. Zen he hit me. Har-r-r. Like he mad bout sumssing." She says Nookie was sort of like her real name, but when she told me the real one, it warn't nothing like. It was more like a bee in her nose. I couldn't learn it neither.

She says her brother was "a Chinaman coo-leee," which seemed mostly a way to die before you catched old age. She says all the men in their village come to America on the same ship they did. Things in China was "so-o-o ba-a-a," she says. "Many trub-oh." Women was s'posed to stay back to take care of the old people, but their mam and pap was killed in the troubles, and her brother didn't want that to happen to her, so he brung her over with him. Girls warn't allowed on the ship, so she had to pretend she was his little brother, though she was older'n him, and she worked alongside of him in the mines and on the railroad till they found her out, and since she warn't legal, they done with her whatever they wanted to.

She says when her brother asked for water one day and got hanged as a troublemaker, the rail boss took her away and misused her every which way he could think of, then handled her over to the bad man who was working for him. The bad man horsewhipped her naked just for fun till she thought she was going to die, but he didn't have nobody else to beat on so he kept her alive in a box in his lean-to and fed her potatoes and berries. She says he warn't American, but wanted to be, so he joined the army to become one. Also it suited him. He liked shooting and hurting people. He dragged her along with him on his way to the war the first day or two, but she slowed him down, so he unloosed his orneriness on her till he was wore out and then he left her there to die on the trail. She hoped he'd get killed in the war, but now it was ended, she was afraid he might come back looking for her. "If I scleam at bad man, Hookie, don' come herrp me!" she says. "Lide way fast an' don' come back!"

I was mighty surprised. "The war's over? I didn't know that," I says.

"Rong time yestidday," she says. "That nice plesident, man kirr him, too."

I warn't paying much mind to the rest a the world after I buried Ben Rogers. Except for saloons, I didn't need the world and it didn't need me. For beer money, I hired on with emigrant trains and wagons, taking on work wherever I could find it, me and Jackson drifting generly northards, and it was up a-near the Oregon Trail where I found Nookie, or she found me. Chinese ladies warn't in much demand, but she'd struck a little abandoned sod cabin to move into and, like me, she didn't have many wants. I seen her setting cross-legged outside her cabin in the sunset and she seen me and motioned me over and give me something to eat and we started having baths. She said she asked me because I was so skinny, but she was skinnier.

Her telling me the war was over made me think of Jim. Nookie didn't know who won the war, and when I asked others, they just laughed at me or punched me if they thought I was making fun. Which was how I calculated the North must a won. So I reckoned maybe Jim was free now. This cheered me up some when nothing else did, except maybe Nookie's baths.

Then one day I come back from leading some people in funny hats over to the Mormon Trail junction and found her cabin all busted up and Nookie gone. She'd left her tin bathtub behind. I waited two or three days, but she never come back, so finally I washed myself in the tub one last time, thinking how she done it, and struck out for the Bozeman trailhead to look for work as a scout and guide. There was forts being built along the trails up there to protect the cows and emigrants rumbling through, and it didn't take me long to know the trail and the tribes along it. The worst was the Lakota Sioux. It was like they was born angry. I was deathly afraid of them. Them and snakes.

It was in one of the forts I met Dan Harper. Dan was a Union soldier, a Jayhawker from Kansas who had volunteered for the army in a fit of patriotics, but the war betwixt the States was over before he got to kill nobody, so they sent him out west to destroy Indians instead. He was lonely like I was, so him and me we spent a good while just setting over our pipes and jawing. I told him I knowed a Harper back in St. Petersburg who wanted to become a robber but who probably took up loafing like everybody else, and Dan says he might a been a relative, it was a sizable clan, but he'd only been to Missouri once and that was to burn down a town full of Rebs. He says it was fun at the time, but he didn't know what good it done. He hoped I didn't have no relations there, and I says I didn't have no relations nowheres.

I told him about Tom Sawyer and Ben Rogers and Nookie and her muddytatings, and he told me about a fat lady in Fort Laramie who could crack nuts with her bottom. I says I didn't believe that, and he says he don't neither, but that's what they say. When I told him about Jim, he says he ain't never knowed any Negro people up close like that and warn't sure he wanted to. They didn't have none in the town where he growed up, even though they was abolitionists. I said about Nookie's brother stopping work to ask for more water and getting strung up with five other Chinamen as a warning to the rest of them, and how white folk come and cheered the hangings and shot the dead bodies for sport.

"Leastways they was already dead," Dan says, and he tells me the worse thing he ever done was when they catched some Indians and the officer made them throw them live off of a cliff. " 'Le's listen at 'em yell!' the officer shouts, but the Indians didn't yell. The silence was awesome scary. Finally, the officer he begun yelling for them. YI-I-I-i-i-iee . . . . And then we all did."

His fort was on Lakota land and the tribe was cranky about it, so their warriors was forever attacking it, and Dan had shot and killed a few of them, but he warn't bragging about it. "Of course they're bothersome," he says. "These lands was their'n and we're bullying in and taking it all away from them. If they was doing that to us, we'd be bothersome, too." I told him about hiring on to shoot buffalos up in these parts not long after the war was over, and he says he got ordered by a general to do that, too, but he didn't like it.

"I didn't neither," I says. "It was like killing bedrolls. But it don't matter, they was only cows."

"No, they warn't, Huck. We was killing the Indians. They can't live without buffalo. They use them for food, clothes, their tepees, soap, plows, thread, ever blamed thing. They burn dried buffalo shit to stay warm in the winter. They use their skins, their bones, their skulls, their horns, even their guts and ballocks. The little Irisher general he says, 'Kill the buffalo and you kill the Indians.' And that's what we was doing, the whole derned point of it."

"Well, he's a general, so I guess he knows."

"I guess he don't."

When I told him about the Minnysota hangings and what the loony old preacher said, Dan says he was maybe crazy, but he was also brave, standing up like that against everybody else. "When you're living with a mob of other people, it's hard not to fall into thinking like as they do, and then you ain't YOU no more. It's like when you're in the army. You could rightly say everybody else in that town was crazy except the preacher. When we burnt down that Missouri town and killt all them people, I felt like a cloud had come down and sucked me up into it and it warn't me that was doing the awful things I done."

I was learning a lot from Dan. He was younger'n me, but he knowed more. There was some in the fort, he says, who didn't like him for the things he said. They called him an injun-lover. Some a them was wearing scalps on their belts and they liked to get him down and rub his face with them. "That ain't the pleasantest thing, but it don't change what's true and what ain't." Tom he had a way of talking like the books he read that sometimes beflummoxed me, but what Dan said mostly made tolerable good sense even if he was a Jayhawker, and we started looking forward to my passing through the fort with one wagon train or nuther, so's to set back and smoke and jabber into the night.

Dan didn't have no appetite for the army life, and we reckoned we might ride together when he was freed out of it. I says we could go up into the northern hills where the fishing and hunting was prime, and Dan says maybe we could go exploring down the Colorado canyons where nobody ain't never been before. We was full of notions like that and they was all smartly better'n the lives we was stuck in. Dan's bulliest idea was to join a circus, where we could do bronco riding and fancy shooting and lassoing tricks. "We can even set up our own circus if we can't find one'll take us. We can get some Indians to join with us and we can have some pretend fights and then be friends after." I was most excited by this notion and I begun practicing on the dogs and pigs at the fort.

But then one day, when I was guiding some wagons bringing supplies up the trail towards the fort, we got set upon by a passel of wild whooping Lakota warriors storming down on us, painted up like demons out from the Widow Douglas's end-times Bible stories. We was overnumbered, so we abandoned the wagons, set off some gunpowder to back them off, jumped on our horses and humped it out a there, making straight for the fort, arrows flying about our ears and off our backsides and those of the horses. A garrison was sent out to drive off the war party and fetch the wagons back and the captain took Dan with him. Then, another patrol was sent out later to bring back the bodies.

I went to where Dan was laid out with the others. They was all shot up with arrows and scalped and tomahawked, and some was eating what before was betwixt their legs, a most gashly and grievous sight. The Lakota had fooled them by disappearing, then popping up again further on, beguiling them over and over till they was trapped too far from the fort for help. Dan's chest and belly was full of arrows like a porkypine's, but there warn't no blood. It was like as if all their arrows had been shot into a dead man. Laying on his back. "If I don't come back, they'll say I was deserting and they hadn't no choice," he said. I could a turned him over to see if there were bullet holes in his back, but I didn't do that. Other soldiers was watching me like they was considering over something, so I packed up that night and drifted back southards and took up the cowboying line, and not long after, found myself marching through the snow with General Hard Ass.

CHAPTER VII

When Dan got himself massacred, I felt like I'd hit bottom, but the bottom was soft and ashy like Nookie's soap and I only kept sinking deeper and darker, like there warn't no end where misery could take a body. I ended up working for Texas ranchers, wrangling their spare horses whilst the cowpunchers was drovering the cows along. I got paid less'n the others, and it was a desperate hard life, but on the trail nothing cost nothing, and it beat shooting Indians and their ponies. And I was comfortablest around horses. Tom always tried to learn me about nobleness from the books he read, and fact is, horses has a noble side and human persons don't.

As the railroads growed, the ranchers borrowed old Indian trails to river crossings and cut some new ones, driving longhorns up through the tribal lands to the new Kansas railheads so's they could be carriaged to their last rites out east where the main beef hunger was. The natives that was in the way didn't like it and so sometimes them and their ponies had to get shot just like before, but cowpokes ain't settlers, and the tribes was mostly pleased to let us ride through for a dime a head and two-bit jugs a whisky for the chiefs on the side.

Moving two or three thousand cattle over all them woesome miles warn't no Sunday-school picnic. We rode slow, not to burn too much meat off of the beeves, pasted to our saddles for upwards of eighteen hours a day in all kinds of weather, with nothing for grub some days but bread and coffee. There were boils and blisters to tolerate, ague, dispepsia, piles, and new-monia, plus rustlers and rattlers, trail bosses and wolfpacks, prairie fires, hailstorms, and stampeeds. A crack of lightning and the cows'd go thundering off like they'd et too much locoweed, and sometimes under sunny skies for no reason at all other'n to aggravate the cowhands. Some days it rained like it warn't noway going to stop, the mud slopping up so deep the poor creturs resked getting stuck and had to be cruelly lashed to keep them plodding ahead, whilst other days it was so dry and dusty, riding drag at the rear, where I generly was, was worse'n getting buried alive under a pile a filthy potato sacks.

Some of the range hands went crazy on account of the horrible moan of the wind, the awful emptiness, and the way the sun seemed to eat a body alive, but I growed customed to it and it suited me. The desert seemed as lonely and sadful as me, so we got on in a family way. I owned my saddle, my guns, my hat and bedroll, bought back when I was earning extra riding for the Pony, and I had old Jackson to get me about. There warn't nothing else I wanted, including being somewheres else, without it was back on the Big River, and maybe I didn't want that neither. Since Dan Harper had got killed, I had the blues down deep, but I reckoned I'd never not had them, and I'd growed customed to that, too.

In my desperate low-spiritedness, I'd took up some of Pap's habits, so when I warn't on a horse I was likely in a saloon if there was one about, and there most surely was, for they was common as sagebrush. They was rough but easeful places where a body could generly find a plate of hot biscuits and bacon and maybe a loose woman or two, which I'd come to appreciate in my lazy and nonnamous but mostly grateful way. And one night in a saloon up at the northest end of the Chisholm Trail, after I'd just been paid off by the cattle ranchers and turned loose for the winter, a drunk army officer holding up the bar beside me set to blowing round about his general, calling him a mean low-down poltroon who didn't give a hang about his troops, who wore out them and their horses till they all got sick and died whilst he was kissing bigwigs' behinds and perfuming himself and chasing the ladies. "When his own soldiers got ambushed by savages, he warn't even man enough to go back and try and rescue them!" he roared out with his fist in the air, and then his eyes crossed and he keeled over, busting his head on the bar as he dropped.

His friends come over and dragged him away. "Delirium tremenjus," one of them says, a scraggly little chap in fringed buckskin and pinned-up slouch hat. He picked up the drunk's beer and finished it off, then with a twitchy wink stuffed a plug in his whiskers. This gent, who called himself Charlie, says he's a scout for that selfsame general, and when he asks what I was doing in this hellbegot town, I says I'd just rode in with a herd of beeves. "So you're prob'bly out of a job," Charlie says, knowing all about it. "Our wrangler at the fort catched the choler and ain't no more, so they're a-looking fur somebody new. You any good with hosses?" I told him what I could do, but also that I warn't interested in nothing to do with soldier types, and he nodded and spit a brown gob on the dirt floor and squshed it with his boot and bought me a beer and struck a lucifer to light my clay pipe by and somehow, one thing stumbling along after t'other, there I was next day in an army corral trying to set a rumbustious young mustang. Tom is always living in a story he's read in a book so he knows what happens next, and sometimes it does. For me it ain't like that. Something happens and then something else happens, and I'm in trouble again.

This time the trouble come from the dandified curly-haired general with the red silk noose at his throat, watching me bust the bronc. The horse was a wild mustang with a white star in his forehead and a long thick tail that swopped the dirt when he reared. His belly was swoll from the free grazing life, the difficultest trick being to cinch the saddle round him, but I had him roped and hobbled and snubbed to a corral post, so in the end he didn't have no choice. When he was bridled and saddled, I freed him from the ropes and, twisting his ear to keep his mind off of ought else, grabbed the saddle horn and sprung aboard. He was a feisty cretur and done what he could to buck me off him, but I finally wore him down and rode him to a standstill. The general nodded like I done what I was s'posed to do and says to get some horses ready, we was going to take them for a walk.

It was already darkening up into an early night, and Charlie had just come riding in to declare a snowstorm rolling our way — "Like dark angels on the warpath!" he says — so I warn't sure I'd heard the general rightly. But he was soon back and a-setting his horse in his bearskin coat and shiny calvary boots, and he fetched out his sword and stabbed the low sky with it and give the order and we all slung on a cartridge belt and marched off into the blow. I was still on the pony I'd broke, so I left Jackson in the stables so's Star, as I'd come to call him, could work off some of his excess belly. He was still a-quivering like he'd catched a fever, but he did not reject my company.

That night I learnt why his troops called him General Hard Ass. We was marched all night through a power of swirling snow and nobody warn't happy. It was so cold, a body couldn't think two thoughts in a row. The troopers I was riding with was a hard lot, with every other word a cussword and scalps of all sizes strung from their belts like fish on a trot-line. They liked to brag what they done to the native ladies before they took their hair off. Or whilst they was taking it off. Some of them was former runaway-slave hunters, now chasing down natives whilst still lynching ex-slaves whenever they could snatch one in the neighborhood. There warn't no bounty profit in ex-slaves no more. They said they done it for honor. Which is about the worse reason for doing whatever except, maybe, passing wind.

The officers was all riding up front with the general, so the troopers felt free to cuss him out behind his back. But they was scared of him, too. They wanted to run away, but they knowed he didn't tolerate it. Back as a Union officer in the war, he was already famous for hanging deserters and he had not give up the practice.

A beefy character name of Homer was riding alongside of me, his bushy red beard peeking out through the snow heaping up there. He had a squeaky bark when he talked that minded me of people I knowed from the Ozarks back home, and when I asked, he said he might of been from there or thereabouts, but he was born a rambling man and place didn't stick to him. As for the general, he says he was a dirty low-down liar and a fraud. "He ain't even a general, only just a cunnel, he dresses like a floozy, and a hatefuller bully I hain't never seen. He shot deserters without no trial and wouldn't let doctors tend the wounded nor drug their pain whilst they was a-dying. I was there. I seen it. They court-martialed the weasely shite-poke, but here he is, sporting about free and easy, whilst the only officer who ever had the guts to stand up to him has been wholly ruint!"

"I think I met that sad fellow in a saloon," I says, and Homer he says, "Well, he was a hard drinker, but he was the straight-shootingest sumbitch I ever knowed, leastaways when he was down sober."

Whilst Homer was trumpeting on ("I'll rip that hard-ass cunnel apart with my bare hands if I ever catch him alone by hisself!"), I fell asleep in the saddle, waked from time to time by the snow and Star's restlessness. My head weighed down and kept bouncing off my chest. My limbs didn't have no feeling in them and my thoughts was all muddled up. There was a moment when me and Dan was in a circus, and it seemed like the realest thing ever. We was way up on a high icy platform skiddering about, and Homer was up there, or else it was Tom, trying to push Dan off. Their feet went out and they both dropped away, and I was a-dropping, too — I come to with a start, nearly falling off of the horse, and when I looked around, I couldn't think at first where I was, only that it was dreadful dark and cold.

"Who was that Dan feller you was yelping about?" says someone beside me. It warn't Homer there no more, it was General Hard Ass's whiskery scout Charlie.

"A soldier I knowed who got killed."

"By injuns?"

"Maybe. Maybe not."

"Which tribe done it?"

"They said it was the Lakota."

"You and the general got that sadfulness in common, then," Charlie says. "He lost a young officer in a ambush, the boy and all his party. They was a-bringing the general a dispatch, but they got entirely massacreed instead. All them sweet boys with their glistning headbones on show, it warn't a uplifting sight." Charlie's whiskers was white with snow like I s'posed mine was, except his was painted with tobacco drool. "Them injuns was also Lakotas. Lakotas and Cheyennes, palling together in their heathen devilment. We gotta larn 'em they cain't do that. It's like larning your dog not to shit in the tent — the stupid creturs cain't think fur theirselves, so you hafta swat 'em now'n agin to make the rules stick." Charlie took off his slouch hat to knock the snow off of it and unpin the floppy front brim, then he set it back on his bald dome, tugging it down to his ears, and he touched his forehead and shoulders like some religionists do for luck. "They's a pack a them shameless Cheyenne butchers camped just up ahead. They think night-fighting is unsivilized, the iggorant sapheads, so they won't be especting us. We'll catch 'em with their breechclots down."

"Theirs is a sad life," I says, thinking about what Dan said.

"Yup," says Charlie. He leaned over to spit into the snow. "And it's 'bout to git sadder."

When I asked him what happened to Homer, he says, "That dang blowhard run off with some other mizzerbul buggers. I gotta go catch 'em and hang 'em, nor else shoot 'em if they take a vilent dislike to the rope." He peered over his shoulder, twitching like he often done, and he made that good luck sign again. "Fallen angels," he says. "Ain't nuthin more wickeder." It had got dead quiet with only the *push-push* of the horses plodding in the snow. "The general was mighty inpressed by your bronc busting, Hucklebelly," Charlie whispers. "I told him you was planning to join another cattle drive in the spring, but he wants you to stay. He's took a liking to you. You're a lucky feller."

"Why don't I feel lucky, Charlie?"

"Well, it ain't easy when your arse is froze," he says with a grunt, and him and four others turned and struck backwards into the snowfall.

What happened a few minutes later come to be called a famous battle in the history books and the general he got a power of glory out of it, but a battle is what it exactly warn't. Whilst me and Star watched over the spare horses, the soldier boys galloped howling through the burning tents and slaughtered more'n a hundred sleepers, which the general called warriors, but who was mostly wrinkled up old men, women, and little boys and girls. I seen eyes gouged out and ears tore off and bellies slit open with their innards spilling out like sausages.

When I turned my head away from the distressid sight, there was General Hard Ass a-setting his horse behind me. "Sorry about your soldier friend," he says. Nothing on his face seemed to move when he spoke, except his frosty moustaches, a little. "Maybe this will help you feel that some justice has been done." Under the stony cheekbones, there was a thin sneaky smile on the general's face that seemed like it was chiseled there. "After we're done punishing the Cheyenne," he says, "we'll go after the Lakota. I promise. Now come along. There's something I want you to do."

The tribe had roped up near a thousand ponies and what the general wanted was for me to shoot them all. It seemed such a rotten low-down thing to do. They was good ponies and hadn't hurt nobody. I says I could herd them all back to the fort, but he reckoned I couldn't, and anyways there warn't no use for horses broke in Indian-style. "They're enemy weapons," he says, "and they must be destroyed."

He rode off to roust me out some extra shooters and to tot up the numbers of the killed and captured natives. There warn't no wounded ones. They was all summerly dispatched, which he said on such a night was an act of mercy. Whilst he was busy with that, I loosed up the corral ropes best I could, trying to think what Tom Sawyer would do to stir up a restlessness. He'd like enough have thought about it back at the fort and fetched along a pocketful of black pepper, but I ain't so smart as Tom and didn't have no pepper.

The soldiers the general volunteered me come over from the blazing lodges, wiping their knife blades off on the seats of their pants and sucking from flasks of hard liquor. They was a most horrible sight to see. There was blood all over their hands and faces and bellies, and their shirttails was out and their eyes was popping and their teeth was showing and they was snorting and wheezing like they'd run a mile. They didn't waste no time. They was all fired up and set right to pushing their hot gun barrels against the ponies' heads and sending the piteous creturs crumpling to their knees. It was too many for me, I couldn't stand it no more, but I couldn't see no way out.

Then, all of a sudden, Star took to bucking and kicking and I don't know if I set him off or the flames from the camp did or if he done it himself, but the next thing all them horses was busting through the loosed ropes and bolting in all directions. I was hanging on to Star's neck for dear life, scared of falling off and getting tromped in the stampeed. Some of the soldiers did get stomped on, but others further off was shooting at the runaway ponies, and some got away but most of them was murdered.

Star warn't rearing and kicking no more,

but he was trembling all over, and his eyes was wild. I stroked his sweaty neck with my gloves and talked quiet in his ear, trying to steady him. I felt like him and me was drawing close and understood each other. General Hard Ass come over on his horse through the smoke and stared hard at us for a moment, and then, still smiling his frozen smile, he raised up his pistol and shot Star in the head. He looked down at me where we'd fell and says to get on one of the horses I'd led here, we was going back to the fort.

The snowflakes was still a-drifting down in the early morning light, falling on hundreds of dead ponies and dead Indians and smoldering tepees, as we got back on the trail we'd laid down on the snow going there. I was shaking and needed a pipe, but it was too cold to take my hands out of my gloves, and my teeth was clattering so, I'd a likely bit clean through the pipe stem.

On the way back we passed a lonely stand of froze-up cottonwood trees where the deserters was hanging. Homer, being a stout fellow, hung lower'n the others, and the snow had shook out of his thick red beard. Homer always said place never stuck to him; instead, it was him who'd got stuck to place. Their horses was standing round looking downhearted and guilty and half-froze. The officers ordered me to gather them in with the others and take them to the fort, whilst they cut down the bodies, and I done that.

I was scared and ashamed and only wanted to run off somewheres and hide when we got back, but it was late November, which ain't never a good time for setting off nowheres. Soon as spring come, though, I lit out. The army life warn't for me. I knowed that before, but I'd forgot.

Chapter VIII

That was the summer I become an ornerary Lakota Sioux. I'd been awful afraid a that tribe since they ambushed Dan Harper's patrol to death, and from what people was saying, I warn't even for certain they was human altogether. Yet, the next thing a body knows, there I am, smoking, hunting, and drinking with them, even living in one a their buffalo-skin lodges with a native woman.

But the trail to that life warn't a straight and easy one. When I left General Hard Ass's fort that spring, I'd rode northards, aiming for the old Dakota Territory where I'd found work before, because if I signed onto another drive from out a Texas, I'd only end up back where the general could take a-holt of me again. He warn't customed to people taking their leave without his say-so. Only look what happened to poor Homer. I warn't no deserting soldier boy, I was only hired for a spare wrangler, but it warn't reliable the general respected the difference. If the general took a notion to hang a body, he generly just went ahead and done it.

I left fast and early without telling nobody. It was Charlie who set me running. He come by the stables one evening to talk about the scouting life. He says he reckoned I have a talent for it, and that might be useful because him and the general was having some difficulty between them. Charlie was twitchier'n he commonly was and it took him some time to get it out, but it seems the general warn't crediting his scouting reports no more. "Well, it's his funeral," Charlie says spitting through his whiskers. Charlie says to keep it quiet, not to make the whole place go crazy, but what he seen out in the desert was some Cheyenne braves fixed to the ground by their navel strings, and he tried to warn the general about that, but the general wouldn't pay no heed. "I seen 'em," he says. "They was taking their feed direct. It's why they cain't be starved out, and why killing 'em don't do no good. I lay them damn savages has made some kinder pack with the devil. I reckonized one of 'em as an injun I destroyed personal. He still had a red line acrost his throat where I took his head off, and there he was, back on his feet and sucking up strenth and meanness straight out a hell. It's why them heathens always gather up their dead. It ain't to bury 'em. They take 'em back and plug 'em in agin." Charlie told the general the only way they could win the war against them was to hack out all their navels and burn them to a crisp and scatter the cinders, but the general says he didn't think he was going to do that, and only give him a mean sneaky look like he himself was in cahoots with the devil. "So they might be needing another scout any time soon," Charlie says, and I don't say nothing, but soon as he was gone, I packed up.

I'd broke in more wild mustangs at the fort by then, and I wished I could a rode one of them out so as to let Jackson track along as only a packer, but I couldn't resk getting chased down as a horse thief on top of what-all else they might want to hang me for. So the poor old fellow got loaded up with me and a pack saddle and everything else besides, my bedroll, tent, guns, powder and percussion caps, a sack of feed and enough vittles for a couple of weeks, plus a few handy trail supplies borrowed from the fort, like tin cook-pans, matches, spare shoes for Jackson, and clean army socks for me without no holes in them. I'd won a few two-bit racing bets with Jackson back in the days when we'd just left the Pony, he was the fastest animal I'd ever rode till then, but he'd slowed considerable over our years of hard traveling and was become more a moseyer than a galloper. He hung his head mostly, looking ever so mournful and low-spirited, and he let out a snort from time to time to show how disgusted he was with everything. His snarled mane hung down like knotted rags betwixt his eyes, which was always oozing something like tears, making him even sadfuller-looking. Him and me was two of a kind back then. Sometimes we just laid down together in a lonely place and moped a while.

We slid out at the streak of dawn, and that first day we put as many miles as we could betwixt us and the general, plodding along well past sundown. Jackson never complained. He wanted out of the army life bad as I did. The moon showed itself, one of them big fat ones with a pale face on it, and the open prairie we was passing through glowed unnatural round us like a ghost of itself. There warn't nobody else out there, we was all alone, just a speck hardly moving in all that huge lighted-up emptiness, companied by the creepy night music, somewheres far off, of owls and wolves. "It's like the end of the world out here," I says to Jackson, and my voice scared me, so I didn't say nothing more.

Finally, when the night sky was blackest, the moon brightest, we come upon a glittery water hole with a few skinny trees and dry shrubs loitering round it. I knowed the water could be pisoned, but there warn't no bones or skulls I could see and we was mighty thirsty, so we pushed our snouts in and drunk our fill. We was too tired to keep on going on. We settled onto a patch of bunch grass alongside of the water for Jackson to nubble on and for me to spread open my bedroll and empty it out. I was too sleepy to strike a fire, so I peeled a potato and et it raw, then rolled myself into the blanket, dreaming of a hot breakfast of coffee, bacon rind and beans in the morning.

I dropped off so hard I didn't know nothing till I waked up with the sun in my eyes and my belly fretting from emptiness. What I seen when I could see was that we'd had visitors overnight. Things was chawed up and scattered and all my vittles was gone. I couldn't tell how big the varmints was, but we was probably lucky all they wanted was the vittles. What it minded me of was that, no matter what it might a seemed like in the moonlight, we warn't never alone by ourselves out there. Even that lonesome prairie was a-swarm with living creturs, and nary a one of them that warn't desperately hungry.

Then I seen, far off on the horizon, varmints of a familiarer sort. Dust was raising up from a train of covered wagons, pulled by oxes and slowly rolling my way. I could make out people walking longside, women and children amongst them. I gathered up all my scattered goods what warn't ruined and rolled them into my blanket and tied it up, filled my canteen from the water hole, loaded up Jackson again, and rode out to meet them, hoping they might have some corn-bread or jerky for a poor wayfaring stranger.

There was a white-bearded gent setting the lead wagon, and when I drawed close enough, he tipped his black hat at me and shouted, "God bless you, sir! Who are you and what's your business out here?"

"Huckleberry Finn, sir. I'm heading up Fort Laramie way to look for work," I shouted back, touching the floppy brim of my own crumpled hat, whilst keeping my eye on the fellows walking along with their rifles out. The women and children looked scared to see me.

"Why, that's where we're a-going. Ain't you pointed the wrong way?"

"No, sir. You must a left the trail. Fort Laramie is over your shoulder."

The old fellow looked back like he was trying to see it somewheres off on the bare horizon. He was setting beside a little old lady in a white sun-bonnet, smiling kindly at me behind her wire-rim spectacles. A couple of the bullwhackers come over to palaver with them. They called him Reverend. They looked up at the sun and done some pointing and calculating, and then the old fellow hollered out, "How many days we got to go, you reckon?"

"For me and my horse, a week maybe, but for your wagons, at least three."

They all give themselves a sad look. "You ever been up thataway?"

"Yes, sir, I've got some practice," I says. "Rode that stretch for the Pony Express, then scouted some. Helped move a herd of breeding cattle up into the Montana Territory. They know me at the forts."

"The Pony Express! Do tell! We was thinking about maybe preceding on Montana way. Are you a shooter?"

"When I got to be."

After the reverend and his followers had got their heads together again, he says,

"Well, maybe you could join us. We're only jest pore Christian missionaires, a-looking for the Promised Land. We don't have no money, but we got enough breadstuff to feed you and your horse as fur as Fort Laramie."

I warn't untempted. I was most about starved and there warn't much to hunt nor fish for out there, but I says, "That's mighty kind, mister, but I'm dead busted and I need to earn some money. I think I best get on to Laramie as fast I can."

The reverend raised his hand like to say wait a minute, got a nod from the others, and says, "Well, we can offer you nine dollars and free grub for the three weeks. If you'll also hunt for us."

"That ain't Christian, Ezekiel," says the old lady beside him, wearing her sweet smile like the main argument. "You should pay him twenty dollars like you done that slicker you hired who got us lost."

"Hush, Abigail."

"You got family, son?" she asked.

"No'm. I'm an orphan."

"There. You see, Ezekiel?"

Abigail was still smiling. Old Ezekiel seen he was beat. "All right, then," he says, and he gives a grumpy little shrug. "A dollar a day up to twenty, payable when we get there." Their wagons was moving mighty slow and the general's fort warn't all that far away yet, but I'd been ready to take the nine dollars so as to get fed, so I nodded. "Which way you reckon we should go?"

"Best aim up towards Fort Sedgwick and the Oregon Trail," I says, pointing, and they all swiveled around. I knowed that border stretch well because of the plague of desperadoes and warring tribes that habited the region back when me and Tom was riding through it for the Pony. Our home station up at Horseshoe Crick warn't no Sunday school nuther, but that Julesburg relay station a-near the Nebraska line was a dreadful wild place. We had to keep our heads down and push fast as we could so as to dodge all the murdrous road agents and Indians. Even the stationmaster was a bandit, so we had to keep our routes secret from him not to get waylaid by his own boys. I was always scared, but there warn't nothing made Tom so all over happy as heeling it through there when the bullets and arrows was flying. "The mail must go through!" he would yell out, laughing like crazy. He wrote down what he done every day in a little purpul notebook, adding a few stretchers and some things people told him, and he read it to me whenever we was in the same place at the same time. He called it "The Wild West Adventures of Tom Sawyer and His Trusty Sidekick Huckleberry Finn." Huckleberry was pretty stupid, but with Tom Sawyer's help, he done interesting things. "The railroad stops a-near there now," I says to the missionaires, "and there's outfitters and trading stations where you can rest your bulls and stock up for the rest a the trip."

"Any Indians?"

"Yes, sir. You'll find them whichever way you go. The Lakota killed some folks up there a few years back and burnt a couple of towns down, but mostly they ain't much bother."

"We ain't afeard. It is our mission to bring them pore ignorant savages to the loving booz'm of our Lord Jesus."

I seen they was a group who had their own milk cow and chuck wagon, so whilst they was struggling to wind their oxes around, I walked over to see if the cookie couldn't find me a biscuit or at least some coffee. He was a tall Negro fellow with curly gray frizzle above his big ears, and when he turned around, my heart jumped in my chest like a poked frog.

"You looks dog-hungry, Huck honey," Jim

says with a big gaptooth grin on his face. "What you says to a stack uv flapperjacks?"

CHAPTER IX

Well, I ain't never been more joyfuller surprised. I give Jim a big hug, I couldn't help myself. He'd took on a few pounds and give up some hair and teeth, but it was old Jim his own self! I begun crying and Jim he was crying, too. We hugged again and some a the emigrants was watching us like it was a scandal to them, but we couldn't give a dead rat what they thought. "Lawsy!" Jim says. "I never jedged to lay eyes on you agin, chile!" At that moment, we was all by ourselves on the Big River again.

Jim offered me to stow my rubbage behind the chuck box to ease up Jackson's load, and let me hitch the old fellow alongside, so I done that whilst he was cooking up the flapjacks, the two of us blattering away without stopping. We both had a thousand things to tell. I told him about the Pony and Tom and Becky and about Ben Rogers and Dan and General Hard Ass, and he told me about life with the Cherokee and the wicked slave owner he got sold to and how the reverend and his missus saved him and set him free again and how he got lost but Jesus found him somewheres and fetched him home again.

I tucked into his flapjacks and told him they was the best thing I ever tasted since before we all come west, and he spread his gaptooth grin again and cooked up another stack. It was like when we was back on the river and Jim was waking me up with a catfish fry. I showed off my own gaps and let out a little whoop. It just popped out. I was feeling mighty peaceful. Even if the general come to hang me, I could die a contented man.

I told him how I went looking for him at the Cherokee Nation to try and buy him back, but they says he was sold already to some bounty hunters. Jim says them traders parsed him on to a white slaver downriver from where the war was happening, and even if he was a freedman, he warn't sad to get sold back there because it warn't fur from where he last seen his wife and children, and he was worried about them. But his new owner had a mean streak a yard wide, and he treated him real bad. Jim pointed to his missing teeth and raised his shirt to show me the welts on his back. "He warn't nuffn like ole Miss Watson. She uz a considable sour ole thing, but she never k'yered to harm a soul." I says I was nation sorry and tried to tell him it warn't me who sold him, but he only smiled and says, "S'awright, Huck honey, nemmind. I'se free now'n I done found the Lord. I forgives you."

He told me how the reverend and his missus had bought him and freed him and led him to Jesus, because that was what the reverend done for a living. Folks still bossed him around and he had to work for next to nothing, but the missus wouldn't 'low nobody to beat him nor call him names no more, he was only just Jim, and that made him comfortabler. The reverend took him to go looking for his family and says he'd buy them, too, if he could, slaves was going cheap by then, but all three of them had got sold to some miners heading to the gold fields in the Montana Territory.

He still hoped to find them, though, and he 'lowed Jesus'd help him out it he didn't sin no more. "I ax him ever night, Huck. Ain' no magic dat genlman cain' do." He asked me if I'd found Jesus yet. I says I warn't looking for him, and he says he warn't neither, Jesus just kinder slid up and knocked him off of the stool he was setting on. "I reck'n'd 'at he was agwyne to fetch me off to de yuther side, so I run fer de reverend, en he tuck en rassled wid my sins for mos'n hour en arter dat Jesus'n me was bes' frens."

When the war was ended and all the slaves was freed, the reverend and his missus told him he had their blessing if he wanted to leave, but as they was fixing to go preach out west, he asked to join along with them so's to search out his family. I told Jim I wouldn't leave him till he found them, and I meant it, but at the same time a sadful feeling leaked in on my happiness. The adventures I'd had with Jim were the wonderfullest I ever had, but they was over. If we found his wife and children there wouldn't be no more. It'd have to be the best one.

The missionaires had got their animals and wagons faced around in the right direction, so I went back out to lead them up towards the Trail. Their ox-drawed wagons lazed along inch by inch, nubbling away at eternity, which would a suited me fine if the general's fort warn't still so close by, so I done what I could to hurry them along. The missionaires was heading out to spread their fancies amongst the heathen tribes, and maybe pocket some gold and silver for the faithful whilst they was at it. They was guilty of a power of camp-meeting praying and singing whilst they was rolling along and they was all teetotalers, but other ways they was decent enough and, after what they done for Jim, I took a liking to them.

They was also hunting for the fountain a youth which they'd learnt was out here somewheres, and they thought if they could find it, it would do them all a sight of good. Jim he had a vision, they said, that it might be up in the Montana Territory somewheres, and they asked me if I ever heard tell of it out thataway. I hain't, but I kept quiet, s'posing Jim might be conjuring up visions that could help him try and find his family. I warn't looking for no such thing myself. I had about the same conviction towards such notions as I had towards prospecting for gold — even if it was there, it warn't something a body wanted. Them people was forever down on their knees yelping about crossing over out a life's miserableness, they couldn't hardly wait, so wanting to put it off with a soak in a water spout seemed like a counterdiction, but I didn't say so.

In the inbetwixt times, when I warn't jawing with Jim, I saddled up Jackson and rode out ahead to scout for water and game. I seen a jackrabbit and shot it and took it back and Jim skinned it, but there warn't many varmints out there volunteering theirselves for Jim's stews. I was also scouting out for natives, and I seen some, but mostly only in my head. They was hanging from a scaffold, or lying dead or half-dead in their burning tepees, or being lined up and shot for target practice. I couldn't shake them out no more'n I could Ben Rogers with his skull split open or Dan with his bellyful of arrows.

Though the ride was bumpy, the reverend's missus mostly kept to her seat on the wagon, setting there on a stack of pillows like the Queen of England, whilst the reverend he got down and walked along with everybody else. He generly took to praying with one or another of his congegration, sometimes with several at the same time; he couldn't stop himself no more'n Charlie could stop his twitch. Jim says Brother Ezekiel was some sorter Babtis', and on that account, we never passed a river nor a water hole, where he didn't push somebody's face in it. Jim commonly helped him out and sung a few songs and preached a little.

Once when I was walking by their wagon,

old Abigail stops me and says like she was scolding me, "You was friends with black slaves?"

"No'm. Only Jim. We rafted down the Big River together. He was running away then, and I was a runaway, too."

"Well, he's free now."

"Yes'm. I'm mighty grateful for what you and the reverend done for him."

"He says it was you sold him to the Indians. Someone called Mars Tom told him that. Mars Tom told him you was pore and didn't have no education nor scruples, so a body shouldn't blame you, and he don't."

"It warn't me who sold him, mum."

"No, I reckon not." She smiled politely. "You're running away from something now." She don't say it like she was asking a question, but it was one, just the same.

I was hired to guard the wagon train as well as guide it, so it wouldn't give her no confidence if I says I was running away from Indians or bandits. Woman troubles was not in my line and I couldn't say I was running from Pap, because I already told her I was an orphan. Finally, I says I warn't really running away at all, I was only a hired horse wrangler, but I warn't happy with the work and I up and left.

"Who was you employed for?"

"Well . . . the army, mum. But I warn't never a soldier. I warn't deserting. I was only changing jobs."

"Did the officers say you could?"

"No'm. I didn't ask."

"So they could still come and take you away."

"Yes'm. But I don't reckon they'd bother. I ain't nobody."

"What was the soldiers doing whilst you was minding the horses?"

"Just army things, mum," I says.

"Killing Indians?"

"Sometimes."

"Did you kill any?"

"No'm. I warn't asked to do that."

"What was you asked to do?"

I seen I was in a tight place. She was setting me up for trouble with the general. Probably his soldiers was already on the way. She was still staring my way under her white sun-bonnet with her kindly smile pasted on her face like a last judgment. I dug hard for an untroublesome answer, but she warn't a good audience for stretchers, so finally I just let it out. "He told me to shoot all the Indians' ponies, mum."

"Did you do that?"

"No'm. But others done so."

"That must've caused you some trouble."

"Yes'm."

"So you left. You felt like it was the righteous thing to do."

"No'm. I was only scared."

Even whilst we was talking, I could see them coming, just as I had suspicioned. Three fellows in soldier blue with their brass buttons glinting in the sun. I shot for Jackson, but seen I'd noway reach him and unhitch him in time, so I jumped into an old covered farm wagon to hide out. I could hear them galloping up and asking loud if anyone had seen a scrawny runaway passing by. I was so afraid I couldn't hardly breathe. "Might a been two of 'em together."

"Why, yes, we seen one," the old reverend was saying. "A skinny young chap with a long thin beard. He was right —"

"But that was some miles back and they was both heading t'other way," says his missus, butting in. "They crossed by and begged for something to eat and drink. They was right hungry, as my husband was about to say. We done our Christian duty by them both and sent them on their way."

"Both — ? But, Abigail — !"

"Don't try to cover up for them, Ezekiel," says Abigail. "Always tell the truth, it's God's way. There WAS two of them, but they was so skinny they only jest weighed together like one. If they turned sideways in the sun, you couldn't hardly see them at all."

"Did they say where they was going, ma'am?"

"One of them said something about jining the Mormons so as to load up on a passel a fresh wives, so I lay that's where they was aiming."

"That's what my father is going to do to me, sir," whispered someone in the wagon with me. I most jumped out of my skin. There was a pretty girl with big sad eyes setting in a dark corner. Her hands was roped together. I whispers back that I was nation sorry for busting in on her like that, and she says it don't matter, it was a thrill to be visited by the famous Pony Express rider. But her chin was quivering. "My father has brought me out here to sell me to the Mormons for some old man's extra wife," she says. And, without making no noise, she begun to cry. "I feel so all alone!" she whimpered, the words half stuck in her throat. "I need somebody to help me!"

"A crazy little fella with a twitch, ma'am?"

"That's him."

"Him and Charlie must be traveling on-sweet, Buck."

" 'Pears like it, Rafe. Makes it easier. Catch one, catch both. But we got to turn round t'other way."

The bound girl was silently sobbing. It most broke my heart. I couldn't hardly look at her eyes without busting out myself. She had dark coiled ringlets at her temples, little dimples in her cheeks, soft unpainted lips that was all a-trembly. She was the prettiest thing I ever seen.

"We don't hold no truck with Mormons," Abigail was saying. "Hope none a you fellas ain't one."

"No, ma'am. We're all Christians."

"Well, I'm right pleased to hear it. We're set to hold a prayer meeting. I hope you boys'll stay and pray with us."

"Uh, no thanks, ma'am. We'll be pushing on. Got to catch them two renegades and deliver 'em to their rightful punishment."

"Well, God bless you, then," she says. "You boys take care. Mind the rattlesnakes."

When the soldiers had galloped off, the missionaires broke out in loud argufying over what the reverend's missus had done and said. Some says it was treason and blastemy and she could get them all hung and outlawed from heaven, others that you couldn't never trust them bluecoats and Sister Abbie was a hero and a saint to stand up to them like she done. They was talking about me, too, but I couldn't hardly hear them. There was a loud whumping in my ears. The young girl was telling me in her soft weepy way that I had to help her run away, and I got to go with her to protect her in the wilderness.

"Say, where is that fellow?" someone was asking, and the reverend he says, "Let us pray for guidance."

"We can go where you took the bleeding cattle," the girl whispered. I mumbled what they was really called, then wished I hadn't, because she wanted to know what THEY was and how they done whatever it was THEY done and why. She looked at me with such a sweet timid smile, tears running down her cheeks, I couldn't think how to answer, though the widow would a wanted to wash my head out with soap if she'd knowed what was a-roaring through it. The girl set to telling me then how her cruel father would rope her wrists to her ankles, push her on her knees, face down and naked, and thrash the highest part with a horsewhip. She cast her eyes down shyly. I didn't know where to look. "He's wounded me most awful," she breathed. "I can't show you now, but when we're alone . . ."

Outside, the holy hallooing was winding

down. I knowed that meant I'd have to go, and that's what the young girl whispered, touching my hand with her bound ones and fairly melting my bones. "My father will be coming back now and he is a mighty hard man." But I couldn't move. I was desperate for something, but I didn't know what.

"If I pin my white hair ribbon on the back flap, it means it's safe for you to stop by," she whispered. She bent forwards and kissed me on the cheek, damping it with her tears. It warn't much but it was something never happened to me before. "Now hurry! Here he comes!"

I didn't know where I was, but I knowed I had to be somewheres else. I slipped out the back, scrouched down for a second betwixt the big wagon wheels, then scaddled over to Jim's chuck wagon and crept inside. I laid down behind the chuck box in all the gear I'd stowed there, touching my cheek where her wet lips had been and feeling marvelous sick, till the others found me. Love. I knowed then what it was and knowed I was most ruined by it.

CHAPTER X

After that smack, all I could think about was that pretty girl and her plan for us to run off together from her monster father. I passed back and forth behind her wagon, my eyes peeled for the hair ribbon. I didn't even know her name, but I couldn't think who to ask without drawing trouble down on the both of us. I tried to recollect what Tom said about distressid damzuls and what you was directed to do when one landed on you. I judged it probably warn't the properest thing to squeeze them, but I didn't want to do nothing else. Such thoughts was making me feel dreadful restless and uncomfortable, but whenever I rode out to ca'm myself, I rode straight back in again and went a-looking for the ribbon, aching all over.

I done what all I was hired on to do, pushing their wagons off in the right direction each morning, guiding them and scouting and hunting for them by day, and then helping them set their wagons at night to circle round their livestock. Whilst they was into their nightly religious rollabouts, old Jim yelping away amongst them, I unyoked and scrubbed down their oxes and done the same for Jackson. But it was like some other body was a-doing it all. People asked me questions and I couldn't think what they was asking.

For the first time ever, I wanted that money Judge Thatcher was holding for me so's I could buy the girl away from her pap and the Mormons like the reverend and his missus bought Jim. I was mighty grateful to that lady for saving me from them soldier boys, and whenever I passed her wagon I bowed my head and touched my hat brim, but if ever I sneaked towards the back of the girl's wagon to spy around, I knowed that old lady's eyes was on me, and could judge what was laying on my mind.

Jim was watching me, too, but like a friend watches a friend, and I reckoned he was a body I could talk to, so one night when we was having our usual gabble under the stars like we always used to done, I asked him if he was ever in love, and he says, "Sho. Mos' all de time."

"Did you ever get in trouble?"

"Awluz tried to." He grinned his grin, then he closed up and shrugged. "But, praise Jesus, not de kiner trouble dat you is in, chile."

I heard him and I didn't hear him. I didn't have no time for it. I had to go see if that white hair ribbon was on the back of her wagon. It still warn't. I'd begun to s'pose she'd forgot me. And then one night, there it was, pinned to the drop curtain at the back of her covered wagon. It most made me jump. I'd been wandering the circled wagons, thinking about her and practicing what I'd say when I seen her again if ever I did, but I disremembered everything with that ribbon blazing up the night. Her little roped hands poked through the flap like a puppet's, one finger beckoning. When I drawed nigh, I could hear her pap snoring. She didn't show herself, but whispered behind the flap that we couldn't wait till Fort Laramie to run off because her father had learnt about some Mormon traders up ahead who steal babies and buy young girls to use for wicked purposes. "Oh sir, I'm so afraid!"

So was I, but I dasn't show it. I warn't generly so desperately needed by somebody, specially a pretty girl, and for certain I ain't never run off with one. But I was needful, too. My whole distracted rubbage of a life had got some sense to it all of a sudden. If I warn't the hero she judged I was, then I would have to fashion up such a person out of my own head and set him out to play the part. "Just tell me, miss," I says in a low growl like I heard men do in saloons, leaning on their elbows, and then my throat snatched up and I had to clear it and start over again, though it warn't a growl this time, more like a squeak. "Just tell me when you want to go . . ."

"Oh! I love you, sir," she says with a little gasp. "You're so brave and good! Everybody has spoke about the famous Pony Express rider and all they've spoke is true! I've watched you set your horse so masterful and handsome and twirl your lasso and talk so manly to the others. You're just the sort of western man that I've been dreaming of." Her pale little hands disappeared behind the flap, and when they come out again, they was holding a shiny cloth which she begged me please to take. "It's the only nice thing I have left in the whole world. I want you to keep it for me."

It was a pair of silky drawers edged at the knees with lace. I ain't never held such a thing in my hands before. It was slippery as a live fish and I had to grab on to it with both hands.

"My father won't let me wear such finery and says he'd use them for greasing the wagon wheels, except they're my only dowry. When he's drunk and acting mean, he still might do that, just in spite. I hope you can take care of them for me till we're far away from here." The drawers was like oily water and kept sliding through my fingers before I could catch a-holt. I was afraid I might fail her before we even got started. "Now, please, sir, can you help me cut these ropes? There's some tied round my ankles, too."

I was able finally to get a grip onto the lacier bits and stuff the drawers deep inside my shirt so as to give me a free hand to fetch out my clasp knife. My fingers was as useless as mule hoofs, though, and I dropped the knife twice before I could reach for her rawhide ropes, and then I dropped it again. "Give it to me," she says, falling out of patience, and I done so, just as her pap snorted loud in his sleep and shouted out some cusswords. "Oh no!" she gasps. "He's waking up! RUN!"

I bounded back to my sleeping tent on all fours like a scared rabbit, the drawers oozing out of my shirt and scrapping the ground under me. I crawled in under the tent and laid there, my heart pounding like it was looking for a way out through my breastbone and feeling most putrified with disgrace. I felt like that stupid Huckleberry in Tom Sawyer's wild west yarns. Why can't you never do nothing right, Huck? I could hear him say. I slid her drawers under my head and lit up my pipe and sucked on it a while, but I couldn't sleep. I didn't know if I could ever sleep again. But then all of a sudden I did.

I startled up from a beautiful dream about running off somewheres with a pretty girl. I was ever so happy and feeling lucky for the first time in my life. Then I recollected it warn't a dream without everything was. "I love you, sir," she said. It was so strange and unregular I couldn't take it in when it popped out of her. Now, laying there in the dark with the soft chorus of snores all around, I could hear her clear as if she was laying alongside of me. "I love you." It sent a shiver down my back and made me set up to catch my breath.

I restoked my pipe, tucked the silk drawers under my shirt again, and went for a walk. It was the middle of the night and a million stars was out and it was ever so still and grand. Starlight on the river makes a body feel at home. Starlight on the prairie is dustier and generly makes a body sadful and lonesome. But on that splendid night they was lining out the amazing adventure that me and the girl was starting up that didn't have no end to it. Only the lonesomeness and sadfulness was ending.

The hard part, I knowed, would be leaving the wagon train without them catching us. We'd have to pack up in secret and sneak out when nobody warn't watching. Her father was expecting to get rich off of her and might ruther shoot up his property than lose it, and for certain he'd aim to hang me as a common thief if he catched me. And we'd have to borrow another horse from somewheres. Jackson couldn't even walk with two riders on him. But these problems warn't no consequence. My hands was inside my shirt and the drawers was sliding and slithering betwixt my fingers. I'd find a way.

I warn't alone in my restlessness. I come across one of the bullwhackers also out studying the stars. He was sucking from a canteen and he don't ask me if I want some, he only took it off of his shoulder and handled it to me. I took a swallow and it near knocked me over. He says it was made out of chokecherries, crab grass, rubbing alcohol, and cactus figs, with some molasses throwed in to soothe up the bite, and while I was still wheezing, he took the canteen back and poured down a gulletful. He says him and his missus warn't members of this congregation, but had joined up back at the railhead on the Missouri border. His druthers was to hurry along on horseback, but his missus had a trunkload of fancy dresses and julery and some quality furniture, so he'd had to buy an old farm wagon and rig it up. He seen that I warn't part of the holy beseechings neither, and judged I might could use a drop. He offered me the canteen again, and I says I did have a considerable longing, but I warn't certain I could survive another jolt of that brew.

"What you got there, sport?" he says, squinting. "Is that your guts spillin' out?"

It was the silk drawers on the move again. I pushed them back in one side and they leaked out t'other, all a-shivery like they was alive. "It's a poultice for my buboes," I says, "and there's too much grease on it."

"You got buboes on your belly?"

"That probably ain't how they're called. That was my pap's name for them. Of course, he didn't know nothing." I shoved the shifty drawers in with both hands and, to change the tune, I asked him why he was a-going west. "You a prospector?"

"Y'might could say so. I been minin' a deep gully and I ain't got to the bottom of it yet." He let loose a mighty belch like a steamboat blowing out its chimbleys, then took another swig. "I met Blanche in Nawlins where she was a workin' gal. She says she wants to get to Frisco and I says I'd take her there but she'd have to marry me first. So we got hitched and we been on the road ever since. Blanche she is a hellion, but I cain't live without her. I cain't live with her, I cain't live without her, it's like a question without no answer."

"I've knowed ladies like that out here in the Territories," I says, still trying to swallow down that first swallow. "But mostly I've took up with the older ones who is generly of an easier disposition. I got me a real girl now, though — back home, I mean — who's most awful sweet and beautiful, with big eyes and little dimples in her cheeks." I could see her wagon across the way and I had a powerful hankering to go over and crawl into it. "I can't stop thinking about them dimples."

"I know what y'mean, scout. My Blanche has got dimples, too. Nothin' like 'em for rousin' a man up. Who's watchin' over your gal whilst you're gallivantin' round out here?"

"Don't no one need to. There's only me. She said so. We've laid out a plan to run off together."

"Only you, hunh? Wisht I could say the same. I had to shoot a man in Arkansaw for messin' with Blanche, and I cain't really say fer sartin it was his misdoin'. But why run off? Why not jest go home to your cherry'n hook up?"

"She's got a mean pap who keeps her locked up and beats her most severe."

"Hm. That old bugger should oughter have his ballocks tore off. Unless she's like my lady. When I jined up to the wagon train, I seen that these was religious people and Blanche she warn't of the same style. I didn't want her leading all these pore rubes into tentation, so I keep her tied up in that wagon over yonder where she cain't git in mischief."

He laughed and raised his leg and passed some wind and offered me the canteen again, but what he'd said had just took the tuck all out a me. I turned and upchucked vilently and stumbled back to my tent and throwed myself inside it, him a-laughing drunkenly and shouting out something about my buboes.

I laid there all night worrying this awful news and feeling so desperate sick I dasn't raise my head. Was his Blanche and the young girl the same person? I couldn't patch them up. I kept seeing her pretty face, the tears on her cheeks, her little hands bound up so cruel, her innocent smile. Well, maybe not so innocent. If she was the bullwhacker's missus, she was a married woman and a hellion and a lady of the night and a bareface liar, there warn't no use to deny it. But the worse of it was, even if she was, I still wanted to run off with her. The way she looked at me, nobody'd ever done before, even if it was pretend. Maybe if I went on pretending, she'd go on pretending, and we could live a pretend life like that. Warn't that how most lives was? Just look at all Tom's yarns.

And maybe she and that fellow's Blanche WARN'T the same person. The more I studied about this, the more certainer it become that there was TWO girls tied up somewheres in this wagon train. Both girls having dimples warn't the commonest thing maybe, but it warn't the unpossiblest neither. I begun to feel a sight better.

When the sun come up, I could set up without commencing to heave again. Jim, seeing how I was, throwed some leaves and roots in a pot and boiled them up for a tea that settled my wobbles better'n a doctor could a done, and I says so and he grinned and showed his gaps and says he's been palavering with Jesus about me to see if he can't unloose a blessing on me.

I got busy setting the wagon train off towards the trail to Laramie, doing my chores, and considering the direction me and the girl was going to take and all the things we must do to get ready for running off. Like finding that other horse, for a sample. I thought I might catch a wild one and break it, and I rode Jackson out ahead of the wagon train to hunt for one. I didn't find no wild ponies, but I did roust up a herd of antelope, and I chased one down and shot him for supper. I throwed him over Jackson's back and walked him back to the wagon train, feeling more taller'n usual and hoping she could see me. Everybody was mighty pleased and Jim set to turning the carcass into steaks. I felt a grin coming on, but I kept it off my face because she might be watching and I knowed heroes warn't the type to let one loose.

Whilst I was out there, I seen a fresh stream out ahead, so I led the emigrants to it to set up camp for the night, and they was thankful for that, too. They jumped right in, clothes and all, and splashed around, and hollered out their thanks to me and God. I pulled my tired feet out of my boots and give them a soak. I was mostly browned and roughened up by the long travels, but my feet was soft and white, and wanted the air, so I give it to them.

During the missionaires' prayer meeting, whilst I was standing in the stream scrubbing down Jackson, I told him when me and the girl ride out of here, we was going to have to cross some mountains and he'll have to move pretty fast. Was he ready for that? He raised his head up and down like to say yes, then he snorted and shook it like to say no. He was suffering the same counterdictions as me. Believing something and not believing it. Like them missionaires when they're praying. Seems so natural when you're rolling round in it, shouting at the sky, so strange when you ain't. Them's the thoughts that was rattling through my head when that bullwhacker come a-reeling past, let off one of his chimbley-blowing belches, tilted back his canteen to empty it, and crawled up into the girl's wagon.

Jackson's shiny wet back looked bald and black in the fading light, most of his hair there plain wore off. His head was down in its usual sadful mope, though I knowed these baths pleasured him. When I washed his legs below the knees, I seen he needed new shoes. I hain't been paying enough heed to the old pony and I told him I was sorry for it, and was aiming to do better by him. I laid the damp blanket over his back to soothe him and we stepped out of the water. I says to him things may not work out here. Him and me might be moving on. He raired no oppositions. People was passing by on their way to their tents and wagons, exchanging God blesses. When they'd gone and the night had settled in, she come sneaking over.

"My father's been drinking. He's sound asleep. We have to go now, sir. I can't take no more." Her tearful eyes was pleading so, my heart was near broke. She was so beautiful there in the dusky light I most couldn't stand it. Her hands was free now. She had my clasp knife in one a them and she touched my face with t'other. "Please, sir, I love you. We have to hurry." But it was too various for me. I warn't no Tom Sawyer.

"I ain't going, Blanche."

Her eyes squinched up a little. "It's my father! I saw you talking! He's been lying to you! He only pretends to be my husband so he can do to me the awful things he does!" I reached inside my shirt to give her back her silk drawers, but she wouldn't take them. "You PROMISED!" She was still beautiful, but she was more like a cat with its tail up than a pretty girl. She looked like she didn't know whether to kiss me or claw me. What she done was snatch the drawers from me, slash them with my clasp knife, and throng them on the ground. "YOU SKINNY STRING A PUKE!" she yelled. Her face was twisted up now with fury and disgust and she warn't so pretty like before. "YOU GODDAM LUMP A CRAVEN GANGREENY MULE SHIT! YOU AIN'T WORTH A WET FART IN A HURRY-CANE!" She ripped her blouse away from her shoulder and throwed my knife down with her tore-up drawers. "HELP! RAPE! MURDER! HELP!"

I yanked up Jackson's picket and jumped aboard. I could hear the bullwhacker roaring out his wife's name. As I ripped past the chuck wagon, Jim hollered out and tossed me my rifle. "I'M TERRIBLE SORRY, JIM!" I hollered over my shoulder. There was gunfire, screams, things falling over. "COME BACK HERE!" the bullwhacker bellowed, adding a string of ripe cusswords. "I WANNA TALK TO YOU!" And then his guns went off again.

I could a stayed if I wanted to, but I didn't want to.

Chapter XI

One night after I come here to the Gulch, me and Eeteh was out on a ridge, our moccasins off like usual, listening to the katydids and smoking a pipeful of something that was like tobacco but that warn't tobacco. It was spicier with an extra nudge to it that eased along our talk like the sweet melon-cholical way a river flows, following whatever banks it strikes on, pushing this way and then that, and picking up some leaves and tree limbs and other rubbage on the way.

We was passing tales about when we was little, him here in the Hills, me on the Big River. Mostly we talked about all the bad things that happened, and how we sneaked through them best we could. Eeteh says that both of us growed up too early and missed a lot, so really didn't grow up at all, just only got older. I says that's probably better'n growing up and Eeteh was of the same opinion. Eeteh spoke passable trading-post American and by then I'd lived for a time with his tribe, so we gabbled away in both languages at the same time, hashing them up agreeably and understanding what we was saying near half the time.

I got to telling again about how me and my friend Tom finally just upped and run away one day without telling no one, and Eeteh says he always wanted to do that, too, but the only friend who thought like him got caught and beheaded by white bounty hunters when he was out fishing. If he busted all on his lonesome into places where mostly white men was camped, they'd shoot him or lock him up, and if he crossed into where other tribes was, he could end up a slave or a human sacrifice. I didn't know they done that, I says, and he says they did, some did. I sejested we could try Mexico where he'd match right in. I didn't know nothing about it, but the Mexicans I'd met was mostly thieving rascals, liars and loafers, so we'd be comfortable in their company.

That somehow led us to talking about the generl stupidness and meanness of the whole human race, and what a body was to do to survive amongst the vicious creturs. I guess our jabber was booming along out in the mainstream by then, even if we was still dragging all the old rubbage with us.

I told him about the murdrous Fighting Parson, the Minnysota hangings, and General Hard Ass's slaughter of all them families whilst they was sleeping. I says it was enough to make a body shamed of the whole human race. Eeteh nodded and showed me a scar he says he got from his own brother Rain-in-the-Face, and he told me then about the day him and his cousins tried to make a warrior out of him by fetching him along to the massacre of a wagon train of emigrants from the east. Settlers was swarming into the land of the Great Spirits like a mortal fever, his brother said, and to make the land pure again, the white devils had to be killed or drove out, ever last one of them. And all the nation, even fools, was obleeged to help do that. Them particular emigrants took to praying ruther than fighting back, and that throwed his cousins into an awful rage because they thought the emigrants was using magic against them, so they emptied out their guts, scalped them, and spiked them on spears stuck in the ground. Eeteh says he turned away from the sickly sight and his brother shot an arrow into his side. "He can kill me, Hahza, but only want hurt. Remember me who I belong."

I asked him when that was, if I was already living with the tribe, and what the settlers looked like. But stead of answering, Eeteh says how Coyote taught him the trick of seeing without seeing. He says Coyote took him to where the Great Spirits was celebrating their Every-Hundred-Moons People Slaughter. "I think more often," Eeteh says, peeping out through the long black stringy hair hanging in his eyes and over his shoulders, "but Coyote call it that." When him and Coyote got there, the Great Spirits was already hard at it, there was burnt and chopped-up flesh everywheres, and Coyote says to him to stare straight into the middle of it and tell him what he seen there. It was horrible, but he done what Coyote asked and told him what he seen, and Coyote says that's not the middle, keep staring. So he done that and Coyote says that's still not the middle, look harder. Eeteh says he was looking as hard as he could and he kept naming things and Coyote he kept saying that's not the middle. Eeteh stopped like it was the end of his story, and relit his pipe. I asked him did he ever find it, the middle? He shrugged, shook his hair out of his eyes, took a pull on his pipe, let the smoke curl out through his heavy nose, and says, "No middle, Hahza. But I look so hard, middle not only nothing I not see."

I understood Eeteh pretty good, but Coyote was trickier. I thought we might be having difficulties by consequence of the different kinds of words we spoke, because after all Eeteh's talk I still didn't know nothing. But I judged it wouldn't do no good to ask again, he warn't going to say no more about that wagon train. Maybe he'd just made it all up to answer my own stories, you couldn't never tell with Eeteh. But though Coyote taught him how not to see nothing, I was seeing too much. There warn't no warrant for me to s'pose the wagon train in Eeteh's story was the emigrant missionaires I was traveling with, but there warn't no warrant not to, and my head was spinning in that direction, seeing things I most wanted not to see. I was specially worried and feeling bad about Jim. I had broke my promise to him. The worse thing is he probably forgive me.

It had been a whole flock a moons, as Eeteh would say, since I bolted that wagon train without even no time, except for a last desperate shout to Jim to say goodbye. The first thing I noticed galloping off that night was I didn't have no boots on. They was old and tattery with rundown heels and holes in the soles, but they was the only boots I had and I didn't have no money to buy new ones. I shouldn't never have took them off to wash my feet, but I done it and there warn't no taking it back. I never wanted nothing on my feet, but a body couldn't live out there without boots, so I was in a pickle, as Tom's Aunt Sally used to say. But it was my fault, like it most always was. I shouldn't noway have kept them boots. They was the ones Tom bought me with the money from selling Jim.

I didn't have no saddle neither, only the damp blanket I'd throwed over Jackson's back after I washed him. It was like the old fellow was half-naked. He'd had that saddle since we left the Pony, and he wore it most days all day long till time to get washed and bedded down. We was both mighty uncomfortable without it, but we had to keep going. The oxes was slow, and even if the old pony didn't have much left in him, the wagon train couldn't catch us, but that rageous bullwhacker might try to chase me down and shoot me, if he could find him a horse and knowed how to ride one. I hoped that leastways I was shut of love once and for all, though that pretty hellion with the drippy cheeks had stirred up feelings that still clotted my chest like higher-up gas cramps.

Clouds kept the moon hid and there warn't no stars out to guide by. We was moving in the dark through grasslands that rolled off tedious and lonely in all directions, not knowing where we was going, just only away from that wagon train. In the middle of the night, my thoughts begun to float about, and when the old pony slowed to a mosey, I fell to sleep on his back. And soon as I did, there she was again, down on her knees and knuckles, sirring me in her sugary whisper, beguiling me all over again. It was a kind of nightmare and jolted me awake, but every time I closed my eyes, she come back like them devil women who drive all the widow's saints so crazy. Can you help me, sir? I thought it was the widow who was the crazy one, but now I knowed better. One time when I come to, I seen that Jackson had stopped and was sleeping standing up, and we stood like that for a while, dozing off together with half-open eyes, until I thought I heard horse hoofs behind me, and I startled up and we pushed on again.

At dawn, the thick clouds slowly lighted up a-front of us, then more paleness spreading round, signifying we'd been a-wandering east all night, so I bent Jackson northards towards the old beat-down emigrants' trail. There was a few stray open-range cows scattered about, sejesting we was nigh water, cows needing barrels of it every day not to keel over and donate their bones to the landscape. There was also one human person out there, a scruffy fellow with a black beard, but he was dead, laying with his hands crossed over his belly and a sign pinned to his shirt that said HOSS THEIF. One of the unluckiest things a body can do is hive a dead man's boots, specially those of thieves and murderers, but they was near my size and they was just crying out for needful feet like mine. I did not want to get shot as a BOOT THEIF, so I pulled them off him fast as I could and we hurried away, aiming for some rock formations I'd spied up ahead, rairing up on a low hill all by theirselves in the early morning light like giant thumbs and fingers.

Bad luck can chase a body for years before it shows itself, but it can also strike a body down on the spot. This was most like what happened. There was a little stream below them stone pillars. I drank my fill and picketed Jackson near it, then pulled on the boots and walked around a while to get customed to them. That horse thief's feet was bigger'n mine; I'd have to stuff some rags in the toes. I clumb up the little rise to the tall stones to see what I could see, and there in the valley on t'other side was an Indian camp. I most dropped in my tracks. They was all painted and feathered up and they was howling and stomping around like they was on the warpath, or maybe they was just praying in their savagely way. I went running back to the pony, hoping nobody seen me, but I warn't watching where I was going and I trod straight on a rattlesnake nest. There was a *bzzzt!* at my heel and a sudden burning pain behind my knee and down I went, trying not to holler out.

I knowed I was in desperate trouble. My leg was paralyzing up fast and the loose boot on it warn't loose no more. I was so scared I most couldn't think. I reckoned it was all up for me. And then, if things warn't worse enough, one a them wild painted-up Indian warriors come at me and ripped my pants away with a knife and stabbed me in the leg. I thought he was going to scalp me, and I worried what that might feel like, but he leaned right in with his teeth where he cut me. I recollected what Tom said about them all being either cannibals or slave-holders, and I seen that this one was a cannibal who liked his meat direct off of the bone. I tried to fight him off, but I didn't have no strength left. And then I didn't have no thoughts left nuther.

The first thing I seen when my eyes was opened was a grim old rip wearing a horned buffalo skull on his head, shaking some rattles and mumbling over me. It was steamy hot, minding me of the widow's stories about where bad boys go when they die. Firelight was flickering on the domed hides above and somewheres there was a thumping sound, or maybe it was my own heart pounding, if I still had one. Then I seen that stringy-haired cannibal setting there, beating softly on a drum of stretched hide, his legs wrapped round it. I couldn't feel nothing in the leg that got snakebit, so I allowed he must a et it. I was dead or dying and I only done it to myself, I couldn't blame nobody else. I shouldn't never have smouched nothing off of a dead horse thief, least of all his boots. When I done that, I stepped right into his bad luck. I knowed better, but knowing better don't always help. Maybe it don't never.

The buffalo head seen me stirring and tried to shovel a spoonful of something from out of a clay bowl into my mouth. It looked like it might have shriveled fingers and deer scuts in it. I thought I might still be alive and he was trying to pison me, so I clinched my teeth against him. A big native woman without no nose reached down and slapped my face. I held the old man off, but after the demon woman whopped my jaws a couple of licks, I decided I likely WARN'T alive, so it wouldn't do me no harm to take it even if it WAS pison. It was even horribler'n I thought it would be, but I begun to feel a little better. My leg had swelled up and was a nasty color and it was hurting again, but leastways it was letting me know it was still there.

I warn't feeling too steady, so I closed my eyes again, and when I opened them, I was in a tepee and that cannibal with the long black hair was setting beside me. He was smoking something sweet and give me a pull off his pipe. He told me his long Lakota name and it was all a jumble to me, but the last part was "Eeteh," and he says to call him that. He pointed to the lady who'd been slapping me and says she was now my wife. I didn't know how that happened, but he says she'd be taking care of me, so maybe it come with the job. She also had a long name like Eeteh's that I couldn't never learn, but the first part was "Kiwi" and that's what I called her. I was slowly getting my senses back, and knowed better what'd been happening. I thanked Eeteh and he shrugged and give me another pull on his pipe.

CHAPTER XII

It took some while to clean out the snake pison, and meantimes, me and the tribe growed comfortabler with each other. None of them was happy I was there, but they seen I was mostly harmless, and I was Eeteh's friend. I warn't so afraid a them as before, though life with them warn't never easy. They was forever pegging at a body to join them in jumping around and beating on theirselves as a way of putting their Great Spirits in a good mood, and there were more dismal strictions than when I was trapped in a house with stiff-necked old Miss Watson. Eeteh had calculated how to duck the warrior life by becoming a kind of clown, so they seen me as one, too. They used me for laughs, and there warn't much Eeteh could do about it because they treated him the same. The no-nose lady was one joke and the horse was another. As Eeteh says, nobody'd ever managed to ride neither of them without considerable bruising, and most everybody had tried.

Kiwi was a Crow lady the tribe had captured in a raid. She come with her nose still on, was took as the fourth or fifth wife of one of Eeteh's older brothers to help with the weaving and back packing, then got her nose clipped for cheating on him, or else just for being difficult. She'd been living ever since with a couple of cranky old Lakota women, in-laws of some sort, and she was mostly glad to be shut of them. She didn't speak no American, but she was good at sign language, specially when it included a whack or a punch. I generly stayed out of her way, sneaking off with Eeteh for a smoke and palaver, or setting outside the lodge in my new breechcloth, deerskin leggings, and moccasins, thinking about how Tom Sawyer would a wrote about this adventure and how he would make it turn out. I don't think he would a thought up what happened next.

Somebody decided I should ought to pay more attention to Kiwi, and ordered up a love potion from the medicine man. Like enough it was them two old busybody women who done it, but it seemed everybody knowed about it. When the medicine man come to see me in the lodge, most a the tribe had already gathered round outside. He warn't wearing nothing but an old tattered elk hide and elk antlers on his head near as tall as he was. He pointed to where my old snake wound was and then at the potion. It warn't hurting no more so I tried to shake him off, but he started hollering and wailing fit to bust. The tepee cover was rolled up and the people all round was shouting and carrying on like the wild savages that they was. Kiwi warn't far away and I was afraid she might start swatting me again, so I swallowed the potion down. The medicine man begun to grin and then everybody was grinning.

It was near as fatal as the rattler pison. My eyes stopped working together and my tongue flopped out and I broke into blisters from my neck to my knees. An awful itch was killing me and made it hard to keep my leggings or breechcloth on. I warn't able to set nor lay down, I could only yip and whinny and kick out and bounce around like a startled-up rabbit. The medicine man started bouncing with me, and then all the others, too, kicking out when I kicked out, bouncing when I bounced, and fairly laughing their bones loose.

I thought I seen that wagon train hellion coming after me. She was kicking and bouncing like the rest, but she was also dead still and tears was running down her pretty cheeks. Her nose was there and it warn't there. Please help me, sir, she says, and she reached out with her roped hands to scratch my itch. Then she give me a blow that flattened me out and she jumped on me and all the others piled on top as well. The itch was driving me crazy and my eyes was wheeling around on their own, so I can't say what happened after that, but it tired me most to death. I warn't able to get up and walk again for three days.

When they took me to ride the horse, I reckoned it was another mean joke, but Eeteh says even if it was, the horse was a gift and I couldn't not take it without making the whole tribe mad. This animal warn't no half-pint cow-pony. He was a big dark stallion, fifteen or sixteen hands tall, and so wild they had to fence him apart not to sicken the herd with his contrariness. They kept him in a corral made a poles and brush, and when I stepped into it, he raired up over my head and snorted and punched his hoofs at me like to box my jaws. I ducked back, feeling about six inches tall.

He come with just a cinched pelt on him, no saddle or bridle, he wouldn't tolerate them. What they wanted was for me to sivilize him by breaking his wild spirit. All I really wanted to do was open the gates and set him free, but that warn't a choice I had. The tribe liked to say they warn't crippling the animal when they broke it, but was welcoming him into the tribe as a trained warhorse and a fellow hunter, and I had to think like they thought. Which was the way the folks back in St. Petersburg most thought about me.

The first thing was to lasso him round his neck and choke him out of his wind, throw him to the ground when he stopped fighting back, and get a halter on him. They call it gentling, but there ain't nothing gentle about it. I thronged my lariat at him a dozen times, but he was ripping around the corral like the very nation, ducking his head under the rope when I flung it and whinnying like he was laughing at me.

There warn't nobody else laughing. Maybe the tribe was hee-hawing on the inside, I thought, but on the outside they was stiff as wooden totem poles. Then I seen it. The fear. They could a done to this horse what they done to old Jackson, but they was scared to. This stallion warn't entirely of this world, that's what they was thinking. Medicine dog. God dog. There might be dreadful consequences far beyond the eating of him. So this warn't just a joke, then. They was using me for something else. I felt like one a them human sacrifices Eeteh was telling about.

When I finally lassoed him, I did wish I hadn't. He hauled me right up off my feet. I was flying behind him, trying to get my feet under me whenever I landed, not to bounce on my belly. I must a made a most comical sight, but there still warn't nobody laughing. Eeteh come to help, grabbing onto the rope, and together we slowed the horse enough for Eeteh to somehow snub him to a post. The horse raired and pulled back with all his might like to bring the whole corral down, but the rope held and tightened round his neck. Both me and Eeteh suffered a power of mighty kicks, but we was finally able to cross-hobble him, roping his forefeet to a back foot. He stopped fighting us then, and just stood there snorting and looking sadful. I felt bad about it and hoped he wouldn't hold it against me.

Eeteh give me a thin rawhide thong. I'd watched the Lakota warriors on their horses, so I knowed what it was for. I had to loop it like a bridle over the horse's lower jaw without getting my arm et, or I wouldn't stand no chance of getting up on him so's I could be throwed off again. He whipped his head round like he was trying to break my arm with it, but I managed to get the thong in his mouth and pulled tight round his neck.

There warn't no stirrups to jump into, no saddle horn to grab. That warn't the tribe's style. I kicked my moccasins off, grabbed the rawhide thong and a handful of his mane, and swung aboard — and flew right off again, clean out of the corral. When that horse bucked a body, it was like what a cannon done to a cannonball.

I decided I'd just take my licking and admit I was well beat. I was only a clown, I could do that. I stepped back in, knotted his mane round one fist while he was twisting and jumping round, pulled myself up on his back, dug in with my toes and told Eeteh to let the horse free, but before I could even get set, I was flying out of the corral again, scraping my stern on the fence posts as I sailed across them. A circus clown couldn't a done it better.

I warn't feeling too brash when I staggered back in. I wanted to go set in front of the lodge again without doing nothing, but I knowed the tribe was all still waiting for me in their stern-faced way. I allowed getting throwed three times would have to be enough fun for everybody. I hoped I could live through it.

The horse was a-galloping around free now, so I crawled up on the corral fence, waited for my moment, and jumped on his back as he thundered past. He tried to buck me off, but this time I hung on no matter how he ripped and tore and cavorted around. One minute I was up in the clouds, the next I was dropping straight to the devil. I don't know how long it went on for, but it was the scariest and joyfullest ride I'd had since me and Jim, clinging to our raft for dear life, went a-booming down the Big River in a raging thunderstorm all them years ago.

Then all of a sudden the horse stopped in his tracks. He was still nervious-kneed and all a-tremble, but he dipped his head and snorted like to say I could please to get off if I wanted to. The army would a clapped me, but the Lakota they was silent and stony-faced like always. Maybe it was because I'd spoiled their joke, or maybe because they already had a notion what was going to happen next. The horse he suddenly raired up and sent me skiddering down his back, leaving me hanging on only by his mane and the thong — then away he tore like a house afire! He galloped straight for the corral fence and ripped clean through it, whacking it down with his mighty hoofs, poles and brush flying everywheres! I ducked the flying rubbage and hung onto the big stallion's neck with my eyes squeezed shut, too scared to let go.

He was on a tear, but he warn't bucking no more, only galloping, and by and by I was able to peek out at where we was going. We was pounding over a desert, but when I peeked again we was suddenly splashing through a river, then tromping a wheat field, and next on the grasslands, scattering herds a buffalos and yelping coyotes. I had to scrouch down when he run through a low forest, not to get scraped off, then pull my knees up as we raced through a narrow gorge. We hammered in and out a mining and cow towns, Indian camps and army forts. There were gunshots a-plenty, but I judged we was safe, the bullets couldn't catch us. We was going faster'n I never went before, even when riding for the Pony or shooting down the Big River in a storm.

We run all day and when the sun started to set out a-front of us, the horse barreled towards it, like as if he wanted to go where the sun was going. Or maybe he was racing against it, seeing who'd get there first. It was dropping behind a mountain, and we clumb up that mountain wonderful fast, though we didn't catch it. There was a lake up there and the horse held up for a long drink. Betwixt swallows, he shook his big head like he was disappointed, and looked all over the sky to see where the sun had gone. I was thirsty, too, but I couldn't resk getting left behind if I crawled down.

The moon was rising ever so peaceful over the lake in a sky all speckled with stars when we started back down, and I was just setting back for the dreamy ride, when we was suddenly moving flat out again, ripping through the night like we'd ripped through the day. But I warn't hanging on to his neck no more. I warn't scared. I was leaning into him, urging him on, slapping his shoulders and haunches, feeling him under me like a part of me. I didn't know where we was, but I didn't care, so long as I could stay with the horse. I ain't never been happier. I didn't want the night never to end.

We run all night and some a the next day. The rising sun ca'med the horse's excited spirit and by and by he slowed to a canter and then to a brisk walk. He seemed mighty pleased with himself. Maybe he reckoned he'd won the race after all.

There was a river up ahead, glittering in the morning sunlight, and I walked him over to it. I found I could do this with nothing but my knees and a little tug on the thong. We got down into the water up to his withers and freshed ourselves up. I nearly drownded on the Big River back home, but I didn't. Instead, I come to love the river, though the river never loved me. That's how it was with this horse. Ever so splendid and mighty, but indifferent as running water.

Even when it was wet, his coat warn't a shiny dark, but one that was murky like a secret or like a river at night, witch-dark as Jim would say, and it had lighter flecks like when shore lights glimmered on the Big River's surface. I knowed his name then.

We moved towards the sun as it rose up over us, and directly we could see the tribe's encampment. It was scattered out over the plains like pointy pegs on a giant cribbage board. Hundreds of horses wandered among the lodges and in and out of them. It was a welcome sight, but it warn't home. I didn't have none. Wouldn't never.

I was saddle sore without no saddle, beat out and well broke in even if the horse warn't, but I was setting tall and easy as we entered the camp. They come running out of their lodges to meet us. They all wanted to touch the horse, as if they warn't for certain he was real, and the horse snorted and shook his head and scared them. They wanted to know what I had seen on t'other side. I says it was mighty lively. They nodded very solemn at that, though I didn't know what I meant and I didn't know what they meant nuther.

Later, Eeteh says he was glad I come back, but he didn't expect me to, so he told them when we went tearing off that we was going to the land of the dead. Coyote was disguised as a horse and he was taking me there to show me the sights. Now they'll ask me what I seen there, he says, so I should think up what stories I could tell them. I don't have to make nothing up, I says. I really was somewheres else.

Chapter XIII

When the general left the Gulch and went back east with Deadwood's glittery rock, he wrote up about it and took the credit, though it was really the loony old prospector who set off the Black Hills Gold Rush. Not that he had no profit in it but a tale or two. It swept right over him like that hurry-cane of his, but this time it didn't pick him up, it knocked him down. A body has to live in one to know why they call it a rush. One day there's a few shaggy sad-eyed loafers setting in a shanty sucking up home brew and wondering how the heck they'll ever get back home again and what they'd do if they got there, and the next day there's a million people stampeeding in and crowding up the crick shores and hillsides, claiming one patch or nuther with handwrote wooden stakes and fighting each other over them, and then another million comes piling in right afterwards with their wagons and pack mules to try to make money off the first million.

I'd waked before sun-up that morning and had set out my trotlines and clumb up on Ne Tongo with a couple of whisky-jugs and rode out through the hills to the tribe's lodges to do some trading for Zeb and have a smoke with Eeteh and maybe some a them fried turnips they're so proud of. But the lodges warn't there. Only ashes from small cooking fires spotted about, a few still smoldering like the tribe had packed up and left in a hurry.

I warn't certain what made them decamp like that, though I could guess, and when I rode back to the Gulch I seen I guessed right. There was tents and lean-tos and wagons and mules and people swarmed up everywheres, with more rolling in every minute. And noise. The Gulch was the silentest place I'd knowed since back on the Big River deep in the night, and now there was hammering and clanging and sawing and horses whinnying and donkeys hee-hawing and all manner of shouting and cussing and arguing, a general lunatic hub-bub. Everybody wanted to get rich but only a few would, if any, so they warn't polite. I heard the crackle of gunfire going off some-wheres, sounding like a prairie brush fire, and I knowed it warn't the last I'd hear.

When I reached my tepee, there were three raggedy men squeezed into it, frying up a pan of fish which I reckoned come direct off of my trot-lines. The tepee was smoky because they hadn't opened the tent flap above the fire. One of them had a black eyepatch and a row of gold teeth like he was doing his banking there, and another with a wooden leg was smoking my stone pipe. They was all three sporting scars got from fights or from getting catched thieving. Peg-leg's greasy hair hung down over his ears which was both cut off. Their guns was close to hand, but they seen the rifle I was carrying and where my finger was.

"This yer tent is occupied," Eyepatch says in the snarly way like old Pap used to talk. His black hair was tied into a knot at the back and hung to his shoulders like the tail of a pony. He wore a black bandanna round his head and gold loops in his ears like a river pirate, and his shirt was black. All he lacked was his pal's wooden leg. All three was trying to look like they warn't about to jump for their guns the moment I blinked. "That's right," I says, "I live here." They says they judged it was only some damn injun's and was surprised a white man, if I WAS white, was living such savage ways.

"But we left you a corner over there by the back flap, chief. It ain't exceedin' clean, but it's all yourn." They laughed a mean laugh at that.

"Oh, I ain't staying," I says. "I don't use it no more, not since my brother Jacob died in here. It don't feel right."

"Your brother? What was wrong with him?"

"He got the pox and there warn't no doctors round here to cure him from it, even if they could of. It was dreadful to watch him go. He screamed all the way t'other side."

"Pox? You mean, small — ?"

"Warn't nothing small ABOUT it! Jake had the gashliest sores you ever seen, all bubbling up from head to toe like hot springs, and he spitted up green stuff that had something crawling inside it. It most made me down sick to see my own brother in such a woesome state. His only relief was sucking on that pipe you're smoking." Soon's I said so, Pegleg warn't smoking it no more, only staring at it through his tangle of greasy hair like it might shoot him. "His birddog Ranger wouldn't leave his side and the poor cretur catched it, too. It let out a nasty drool like Jake's and its eyes filled up with pus so's it couldn't see. Him and Jake they died at the same time, the dog's paw on my brother's chest. It was ever so sadful. I most wish you'd been here to see it. They was a-laying together, right there where you're setting." The one setting where I was pointing jumped up and brushed off the seat of his pants, mumbling something around the two or three brown teeth left in his mouth about how he s'posed at least the fish fresh from the crick was in good health, and I says they probably was. "Jacob used that frypan for a spittoon as he was a-dying, but I rinsed it off in the crick and drownded most a them crawly things." Thinking about that poor faithful dog a-dying by its master, even though there warn't no such animal, had set my eyes to watering up, and that done it for them, they was all three out of there on the double, spewing out the fish they'd been chawing.

The rest of the day, I kept Tongo with me lest he get stole, walking him by his rawhide thong through the strangers crowding in. Tongo wouldn't let nobody but me ride him, but a body who'd got throwed or kicked might be mad enough to want to shoot the horse that made such a damfool of him, so I didn't plan to let him never out of my sight. As we walked along, I explained to Tongo what was happening, so as to get him of a disposition to give up his pasture and move on again, and he shook his head from time to time and snorted. He didn't like the looks of things, nuther.

The fortune hunters was still rolling noisily into the Gulch like they was coming to the circus, most of them tearing off into the hills with their picks and pans and wooden stakes. One country jake carried only a pitchfork and a big wheelbarrow for toting all the gold he was going to dig up like potatoes. He was wearing muddy brogans and a floppy straw hat just like the ones I used to wear back in St. Petersburg, and he looked a fool like I must a done. I couldn't let the tepee out of my sight and had to go back down there from time to time to make sure nobody else warn't thinking about moving in. It looked like poor old Jacob was going to die a thousand deaths before the day was done.

Most of the new emigrants was heading out to mine the cricks and hills, though some was setting up to mine the miners. A stout man with bushy yaller whiskers put up a sign saying he was a banker and also a dentist at a dollar a pull. One chap come hauling in an old shackly wagon all weighted down with painted signs, mirrors, doorknobs, pump handles, and fancy wall clocks, even some hinged doors and old chawed-up hitching posts, which he says he'd cleaned out from a deserted mining ghost town. There was lots of wagons filled with borrowed truck like that. It was like the towns theirselves had hitched up their pants when they got left behind and had went chasing after their restless townsfolk.

By the middle of the afternoon, even with many of the prospectors out digging and panning, the Gulch was filled up to near half as big as St. Petersburg and twice as ugly, and it got ever thicker and nastier by the hour. A body could learn more cusswords in five minutes than in a lifetime back on the river. There warn't no women around, so the whole camp become a public outhouse. The banker-dentist with the yaller whiskers had set out a plank table and added a new sign saying he was also offering a friendly game of cards. The ghost-town scavenger was nailing up a storefront, startling up all the birds and people was shooting them. Under the falling birds, a long bony man in a black stovepipe hat come riding in with a wagonload of pine boxes which looked like they might probably be coffins, and folks stepped out of his way and let him pass.

Word had got out that General Hard Ass's famous chunk of ore had been found by

Deadwood, and each new arrival dragged the old prospector out to show where he found it, and so he was famous in his way but he warn't happy. I lettered a wooden sign that claimed him the spot, and most everybody respected that, like enough because they didn't believe the rock was really born there and he didn't nuther. Most of them looked up into the hills above the Gulch, trying to cipher out where it might of fell from. Some of them offered him a share of their stake if he could fetch them to the source. One of the old loafers passed by and asked Deadwood with a wink at the others to show them another rock from that giant lode he struck. "No, I ain't taking no resks," he says. "I put 'em all where that bandit cunnel can't find them. I done a good job of it. It'll take me more'n a week to find 'em myself."

The sun scrunched down behind the hills like it dreaded to see what was going to happen next, and throngs of prospectors, empty-handed and feeling grumbly, begun drifting back, scowling round to make sure nobody had beat them to a find. It was early spring and still chilling down when the sun dipped. Open fires was built in the streets and birds and small animals was spitted over them. You had to watch where you walked not to stomp on the heads and innards being flung about. The plank bar in Zeb's shack was crowded round with gruff sweaty men toting picks and shovels like battle-axes, a bonanza for Zeb maybe but not for his old regulars, who couldn't even squeeze in the door and was apt to get a drubbing if they tried too hard. The prices had shot up, but Zeb, surrounded by ornery bands of strangers fighting each other for custody of his goods, did not look all that happy, even if he was getting rich.

Deadwood was setting on a three-legged stool outside Zeb's shack, studying his fob watch from time to time in the half-light, popping it open, snapping it shut, and regaling the drunks with his stretchers. Deadwood was about all what they had for entertainment, and sometimes they spotted him a ten-penny glass of whisky or a dribble of whatever they dug out of their saddlebags — "To grease up his wheels," as they said. As me and Tongo passed by, they was asking him how the hole in his vest got burnt. He says it happened when he was defending the Alley-mo, his gun getting so hot he had to drop it in his pocket to cool it off and it set the vest on fire. But then Davy Crockett sent him off to find Sam Houston and bring back help, which was how him and them other fellers lost the Battle of the Alley-mo and all got killed. "Ole Davy was a passable tale teller, but he warn't worth a mouthful a cold ashes as a cunnel. He's got a plague of ornery Messykins flooding over the wall, and what does he go'n do? He sends his best dern shooter off shaking wild gooses."

"You purty good with a gun, Deadwood?" someone asked.

"I was handy. They useter call me Dead-Eye Deadwood. I got stories wrote in books about me."

I'd wanted to let him know about my new brother Jacob and his tragic disease so's he didn't speak to the contrary, but it warn't no use, he was wound up for the night. I seen Eyepatch and his two pals looking me over like they was measuring me up for one a them pine boxes, so me and Ne Tongo headed back down to the tepee to see what vittles they might a left us for supper and to consider what we was going to do next. "Tongo," I says, "we got no place to go and we got to go there." He snorted like he understood, but like he warn't no more pleased than what I was.

Who I found in my tepee this time was Eeteh, setting in the shadows and sampling from one of the jugs I'd laid aside for the tribe, his tomahawk in his lap. I was ever so glad to see him and I told him so. I told him I'd went looking for him with that jug and found everybody gone, and he says he was glad I didn't get there sooner because they was so tore up about all these stampeeding white folks they might have scalped me on the spot.

"Even if I was bringing them whisky?"

Eeteh nodded. "All crazy," he says, looking up at me through the stringy black hair hanging loose over his face and shoulders from under his headband. All the tribe wore long hair, they allowed it roused up their spirits, but the others kept it braided. Eeteh didn't like nothing knotted up, and let it hang long and snarly, like mine. He never wore no eagle feathers in it, because they was tokens a killed enemies, and he never killed no one that he knowed of. The vest he wore was really an old fringed and beaded buckskin shirt that a cousin was wearing when he got killed in a battle. Eeteh tore the bloody sleeves off and worked some porkypine quills into the beadwork, which he says is who he is. Needley. "Tribe on warpath, Hahza. Want guns, no whisky." Hahza is my real name in Lakota. When Kiwi first heard it, she busted out laughing and give me a punch where it hurt, and that set the whole tribe off laughing, except for Eeteh who said that his name was also a joke for everybody, so for him it meant the same as "brother." Eeteh had brung along some buffalo jerky and we chawed on it, while sipping at Zeb's liquor. "Long Hair," he says. "Want war."

"I know it," I says. "When he rode in here, he had a thousand calvary boys with him, and I judge they ain't far away, just itching for something to shoot at. It's all too many for me. The general ain't spotted me yet, but I don't aim to let that happen. I'm riding out soon's I'm packed up."

Eeteh nodded and says he wants to go with me. He says the tribe with its glory fancies was driving him as crazy as they was, and Coyote told him that him and me had to leave before it become our fate to shoot at each other. But he says we wouldn't get far if we didn't find some guns for them because that's what they sent him here to do, and he don't want to think about what they'd do to him if he didn't at least bring them back a few rifles. "They give me money. Silver." He held up the soft leather pouch and jangled it. "Help, Hahza."

I studied hard about that, chawing slow on the jerky. I knowed it was a most shameful and low-down thing to do, and I could get hung for it and wouldn't have nothing to say to my defense, but I was lonely and scared and I needed Eeteh's company. He was the first proper friend I'd had since poor Dan Harper, and Eeteh was scared, too. It had been whilst I was feeling ever so mournful about Dan's killing that I first got in trouble with General Hard Ass. I run away, but he found me again, and after what I'd done, he'd want to hang me, so I didn't really have nothing to lose except my ruputation and that was considerable ruined anyways. I'd never learnt how to do right and it warn't no use to try to learn me now. "I seen wagonloads of them for sale today," I says. "And Zeb has took in guns on credit for his whisky. I reckon they'd be cheap. I could take them up to that cave where I first lived with the bats till you come."

"No. If they see you, bad trouble," Eeteh says, giving me the pouch. "Leave guns in here. Go way. I find them."

Chapter XIV

After Eeteh left, I couldn't fall to sleep. I tried hard, knowing how pesky tight the next days was going to be, but it warn't no use. I was too a-jitter. I was hearing all manner of rustlings outside the tepee like there was a mob of emigrants creeping round out there trying to see who they could rob and kill. Coyotes, wolves and wild bears would a been more welcomer; they was only hungry. It was cold, spring slow a-stirring up in the Hills, but I dasn't light a fire and set the lodge cover aglow like an invite, so I shivered under blankets with my rifle across my knees and drunk more whisky just for the warmth in it, feeling most miserable.

The Gulch's easeful stillness was also gone, another unspiriting thing. Sounds was more muffled down by the crick, but there was still a power of sawing and hammering and hollering and cussing pouring down from up where Zeb's old whisky shack was, and where a whole new town was suddenly festering up like a rash of warts on a toad's back. There was shouts and twinklings of kerosene lanterns in the hills around and along the crick shore, and gunshots was going off everywheres like strings of firecrackers. Eeteh's people could hear the racket, too. I don't hold to nothing sacrid, but I knowed how they felt about the Hills — it was like how I felt about the Big River — and so they was suffering and resenting and a ruckus was a-biling up.

Mostly, though, I couldn't sleep for thinking about what was going to happen next. I'd growed comfortable in the Gulch, but it was plain ruined and was getting ruineder by the hour. It was filling up with something that was alive and looked human, but that warn't human. Something older'n meaner. People was wearing it, but like they was wearing their grandpaps' noses.

Even worst, General Hard Ass was close by, and he couldn't be happy till he seen me dangling. I had to get to somewheres he wouldn't find me, but running away from him, I could as easy run into him like I done before, and if I did, mercy warn't in his alphabet. I couldn't be comfortable again till we crossed into Mexico, if we ever did. I warn't sure they talked American there, but

I'd cipher out their blatter like I done with the Lakota. And at least I'd be with Eeteh and not so lonely no more, and that was good, but thinking about all that couldn't let me sleep, too.

Tongo was snorting in a nervious way, fretting just like I was, so I took a blanket and the whisky and my rifle and went out and rested against him. Laying there under the open sky, I didn't hear strangers sneaking about no more. Maybe the rustlings I heard was only how the breezes blowed on the tepee cover. We'll be all right, Tongo, I says, and stroked his trembly neck. I don't know if he believed me or not — if he was like me, he didn't believe me — but he was breathing in his ca'm steady way again, and directly I begun to ease up, too.

When I rode back to the tribe after that amazing adventure Tongo took me on, me setting native fashion a big wild horse who didn't seem so wild no more, my ruputation raised up considerable. They treated me more solemner and fetched me buffalo meat and wild bird eggs and give me a bear-claw neckless for good luck and a beaded buckskin shirt like Eeteh's vest, though without the porkypine quills. His warchief brother Rain-in-the-Face give me a pipe with a stone bowl carved like a horse's head, but more like a spirit horse from t'other world with its mane flying behind like a war bonnet and its toothy jaws dangersomely a-gap.

The Lakota call their horses medicine dogs, meaning they got some kind of unnatural powers. That's too many for me, but it's true that Ne Tongo warn't like any horse I'd ever rode before. I thought I knowed everything about horses and riding, but all I really knowed before was my saddle. I had to learn horse all over again from Tongo.

Tongo never tolerated nobody else to ride him, so if I warn't on him, he was wild as he ever was. Some of the braves was jealous and pushed at me to take a turn, but he throwed or kicked anybody who tried him, and they warn't always happy about that. One of Eeteh's brothers decided I warn't worthy of a horse like Tongo and claimed him for himself. He shoved me away and made to mount him, but Tongo galloped a few yards, stopped, and bucked him heels high into a cactus patch, making the whole tribe laugh. That brother blamed me and turned against me, and in the end he turned against the tribe, too.

They all wanted to know what was so lively about t'other side, so with a little help from Eeteh I unloosed a few friendly stretchers about dancing with the dead, and got to know Coyote better that way, though I'd still never met him nor warn't likely to. For the Lakota, Eeteh says, the next world was just like the one we was in, which was a considerable improvement over harps'n angels. Except IF it's like this world, Eeteh says, he don't know what they do with all the enemies they kill. Maybe there was another next world for them that gets killed twice. And so on . . .

So I told them how Coyote and me met up with all the dead chiefs in their splendid lodges and went to their wild parties and et and drunk with them, though it was like eating and drinking air. The dead was all having a most joyful time, but when me and Coyote tried to join in the fun, they warn't really there, just pictures of them that could talk to you, but didn't have no surfaces you could lay your hands on. Being dead looked like a lot of fun, but they told us we warn't ready for it. They laughed at our meatiness and sent us back to this side again. I did kiss one of the ghosty maidens, I says, and felt her lips for a minute, so maybe I was half-ready, and the tribe give me a few haws for that.

Kiwi, who thought all the Lakota was crazy and me worse'n all them together, left me not long after that and moved in with the two old tyrants again, or maybe the joke was over and they made her do it. The tribe had plenty young widows of warriors who was killed in battle or in ambushes by settlers and soldiers or just betwixt theirselves — even the games they played for fun was mighty rough — and these widows come to my lodge from time to time to take care of me. They sometimes wanted to make a family, but I warn't never a family man — Pap had cured me of that — so I didn't let none of them move in. Some of them did try to ruin the lodge by cleaning it up all over, but it warn't hard to mess it up again after I'd chased them out.

I traveled with the tribe for many seasons, mostly hunting down the last of the buffalo herds, having about as good a life as I ever had. Me and Eeteh, we spent hours talking and riding together, sipping whisky, and beguiling ourselves by matching up Coyote against the Great Spirits, tripping them up and making clowns like us out a them so's they'd be more tolerable. Eeteh, who don't believe in nothing, not even Coyote, says it was Coyote who hitched him up again to his spirit side and helped him to see and hear with the eyes and ears of his heart. "Laughing all we have, Hahza. No Great

Spirits. Only laughing." I amenned him and laughed and raised the whisky-jug at him, then drank from it and passed it over.

Leaning there now against Tongo, I was just sinking into a muddled doze with my eyes open but not seeing nothing, my thoughts not thoughts no more, just pictures, mostly of me and Eeteh or of them young widows, when a crunching noise and a curse over by the tepee startled me up again. I grabbed my rifle and hunkered down and stared into the dark trying to make out who it was and what they was doing over there. There was a dark shape thrashing about a-near the opening like a wounded bear and I took aim at it. "Dag NAB it!" it cried out. "Somebody HELP me!"

I lowered my rifle and went over to give old Deadwood a hand. When I lifted him to his feet, he just sunk down again. "It's the dern rheumatics," he whimpered.

"You're so blamed drunk, Deadwood," I says, "I'm surprised you was able to find your way down here." The old prospector mumbled something about worrying about me and coming to protect me, but a body could see how lonely and scared he really was. I lifted him inside and wrapped him in a blanket. There warn't much of him, just pointy bones with dry skin stretched over.

"I'm cold!" he says, shivering. "Cain't you set a fire?"

"Them new rapscallions up there mostly ain't been round long enough to know where I'm living at, Deadwood, and I ain't setting out a lantern for them. Many of them's worse'n road agents, they ain't even prospectors, just pure robbers and murderers, but you already know that." Which give me a notion about collecting the rifles Eeteh needed without having to let out who they was for. "Some of us is joining up a vegilanty gang to do something about them varmints, Deadwood. We need good shooters like you, so we'd be honored to have you in the gang." This chippered him up some. "I'll be gathering up rifles for the shooters. But it's a secret and you mustn't tell no one." Which was like telling a mosquito (I'd just got bit) it mustn't bite no one. You can slap at it (I done that), but it's always too late.

To give Deadwood a little more to think about, I sejested a secret signal for who's a friend and who ain't, knowing he'd get it mixed up and tell everybody. "Just show them your fob watch. If a body don't ask you where you got it, that's a clue they're in on the secret and you can tell them about the rifles. But if they do ask, watch out, don't let on about the vegilanty gang. Just tell them that the railroad bosses give you the watch, like you done before."

"Railroad bosses?"

"You know, like you was saying."

"What was I saying?"

"For helping them spike the rails together on their new train tracks."

"Oh. The RILEroad bosses. Yup, I prob'bly done that. It's why they gimme this fob watch." He showed it to me.

"And one other thing I got to tell you about, Deadwood. My brother Jacob he come a-visiting and he died of the pox here in the tepee."

"Your brother — ?"

"You recall Jake. The tall skinny baldy with wire spectacles."

"No front teeth?"

"That's him."

"He was your brother? I didn't know he catched the pox."

"Sure, you remember, Deadwood. He broke out in all them runny green sores from head to foot. You SEEN him. It was horrible. Both him'n his dog Ranger."

"His dawg?"

"They was laying dead right there where you're setting." Deadwood stared down in alarm at the ground betwixt his legs. "But it's all right now. They both got buried proper up on the hill and everything in here's all cleaned up."

Deadwood worried this over. I could see he was already remembering Jacob into his yarns. I reckoned to take the tepee cover with me when me and Eeteh lit out, and Deadwood, I knowed, wouldn't even notice I was gone. He'd only miss the tepee and make up stories about who lived in it and what outrageous things they done. "Afore Jake got ruint by the pox," he mumbled, though his voice was so slurry you had to've heard the yarn or one like it a thousand times before to understand a word of it, "me'n him useter do shootin' contests." His eyes was closing, and he was snoring and mumbling at the same time. "He'd throw a silver dollar in the air'n shoot it'n afore it come down I ud . . . I ud . . ."

I left Deadwood sleeping in the tepee and walked down to the crick to wash some cold water on my face. Deadwood's snores might keep wild beasts away, but human beasts was likely to get drawed to them, so I'd have to keep awake. The next thing was to find some rifles for Eeteh and stow them in the tepee. Zeb is always up hobbling round before dawn, so I reckoned I'd start there, maybe get it all done before the sun come up.

Chapter XV

Whenever Widow Douglas grabbed me and scrubbed my face, she called it washing my sins away. She always said that some day we'd have to pay for our sins. The widow didn't have no sins, so I judged it was only her way of bullyragging me. But paying for sins is like getting the bad luck a body deserves for doing what he oughtn't done, like handling a snake-skin or stealing a dead man's boots. So when the tribe and me packed up our lodges a few seasons ago and struck for the Montana border to chase after the few small buffalo herds still remaining, I should a reckoned on bad luck because it was partly my fault the buffalo was extinct-ing. My soldier friend Dan Harper had told me that long ago, and I hadn't forgot, I only hadn't cared to remember.

Before we struck northards, the tribe sent one of Eeteh's brothers to scout out what the calvary was doing, and he come back with the news that General Hard Ass was marching his bluecoats south into Comanche territory, so our route was clear. That seemed like good luck, but though the troops was maybe marching, General Hard Ass warn't. I didn't know that then. I was feeling light and easy. But we was heading up towards where Dan got himself killed and that was even a worse thing for luck than handling snake-skins, specially when Eeteh told me it was most likely his own cousins who laid the trap for Dan's patrol. Learning that was like bad luck was already happening. When I asked Eeteh if he was there, he says maybe, and then he don't want to talk no more about it.

We was many days on the move and finally set up camp in a grove of cottonwood trees on the banks of a river in the Wyoming Territory, up a-near the Montana border, about a half day's ride to the fort where Dan was a soldier. Me and Eeteh was volunteered to scout the area, and as him and me was moving through a deep gully, he says this was where it happened. But he warn't with the others. He didn't want to kill nobody nor get killed, he says, so when he come on a dead soldier in the woods — he showed me where — he stayed there and killed the dead soldier again, shooting all his arrows in him so he couldn't have no more to shoot. His brother come to examine the body and when he seen what Eeteh done, he hit him in the chest so hard he couldn't breathe and he thought he was going to die.

"Did the dead soldier have any bullets in him?"

"No see. He your friend, Hahza. Sorry."

"No, it's all right. If Dan saved your life, even after he was dead, he'd a been happy to hear it."

In mining and cow towns and in settlers' villages along the railroad and wagon trails, I often done the trading for the tribe, having the natural words for it. When we was settled in Wyoming, I done the same, and in a saloon up there where I'd gone to buy the tribe a parcel of whisky and cured tobacco, I come on General Hard Ass's old scout Charlie setting a barstool, his scrawny back to me.

Charlie had bolted from the army same time I did. His travels hadn't treated him kindly. He looked well fried by the desert sun and he didn't have no more meat on him than old Deadwood, just skin and bones and rags, that's all he was. His whiskers was bushier'n before, but I could tell him by his twitchiness. I warn't sure what kind of luck it was to meet up with him, but I judged it was most probably bad, so I set about to do my business as quiet as I could and sneak off before he seen me.

Charlie was telling the drunken loafers in the saloon about things that happened to him out on the desert, and the loafers was hooting and snorting and spurring him on. "I seen the mother a God out there, boys, nekkid as a jaybird and scratching herself," Charlie says, scratching himself. "I was a-dyin' a thirst. She lemme suck her tits'n saved my life. I been a true believer ever since."

"Haw! What kinder tits did she have, Charlie?" one of the drunks asked. "Big 'uns or small?"

"They was like buckets," Charlie says, and the loafers all hee-hawed. Charlie swung round to grab up his empty glass and seen me. His eyes looked like black pin dots in the middle of his thick brows and whiskers. "Why, I be damned! If it ain't Huckerbelly Finn! I'd got wind you might show up. You come jest in time to rise a glass with me!"

"It's the middle a the day, Charlie, I don't —"

"I thought you was dead, Huckerbelly!" He waved one of his knotty sun-burnt fists at the barkeep and struck up two bony fingers. "And who's t'say? Maybe you IS dead! I seen a power a mortalized bodies up bouncin' round a late, like they's a big party jest a-waitin' to happen. Only last week I was drinkin' in here with Aberham Lincoln, who's been expired nigh onto ten years. You member him? Ole honest-to-God Abe! He was settin' right where you're settin', stovepipe'n all. It's the gospel truth! He was feelin' low-spirited on accounta the desprit sinfulness of the nation, and was gittin' well soaked t'fergit his stately keeres."

"He was a good man, I reckon," I says.

"Better one now he's dead." The barkeep set the whiskies down and told me I owed him for both of them. Charlie don't have no money, he says. "Dyin' improves EVERbody," Charlie says, downing his drink in a single swallow. "Killin' a body is a means a doin' 'em a favor."

"Well, don't do me no favors, Charlie. I ain't looking for improvements." I took a sip and felt it burn a hole clean through me. When I could talk again, I says, "You ain't down at the fort no more?"

He grunted, twitched around at the others, ducked his head, and leaned close. He smelt like something dead, like he'd already joined that big party that was a-waiting to happen. "You recollect that saucy jig dancer sung all them smutty songs?" he growled.

"The Irish girl with the red hair?"

"Yup, that's her. Was. The Whore of Babylon got inside the pore thing and it was my Christian duty t'free her up, warn't it? She had friends who was most prob'bly also infested with demons, and purty soon they was legionin' up agin me, sayin' I was a heartlust murderer, when I was only doin' the best I could to save her black soul from etarnal dangnation. So they didn't give me no choice, I was obleeged to leave them parts in a hurry." He twitched his shoulders and thrust up his horny paw to ask for two more, but I shook my head at the barkeep. Charlie was likely disappointed, but his pin dots warn't very expressive. "So, who you workin' for now, Huckerbelly?"

"Whoever'll hire me."

Charlie stuffed a wad of chaw into his cheeks. "Still wranglin' hosses?"

"Sure."

"The general's in a fort a-near here now and I heerd tell he was a-lookin' for scouts and wranglers."

"You mean General Hard Ass? Near here?"

"That ain't his name, but, yes, that's the cocky SOB I mean, and I mean that complimentry. He took over a fort up here a coupla years back, and he's killt slathers a injuns so's to keep the emigrant wagons rollin' through. Killin' injuns is a gift he's got. He stopped in for a quick snort one day and he says some injun he's got workin' for him told him you was on your way here." Charlie let fly a gob of chaw in the generl direction of the spittoon. "Cain't trust no dumb injun a course. But if I seen you, I'm obleeged to tell you he might have work for you."

I had to get this news to Eeteh and the tribe, so I give Charlie the rest a my drink, good-byed him quickly, and had just went to settle up for the whisky and tobacco, when I seen a pretty lady, dressed ever so grand, coming towards the saloon's swinging doors. I blinked twice to be sure. Yes, it was Becky Thatcher! I grabbed up my change and goods, but by the time I reached the doors, she was gone. Maybe she seen me, maybe not. She warn't so schoolgirl-looking like before, but even fancied up, you could see she was still a St. Petersburg girl. So, if she's out here, I allowed, Tom Sawyer must be, too, and I was most roused up by this possibleness. Her classy outfit made me think Tom'd struck it rich. I judged he was trying to find me, but didn't know I was traveling with natives. I couldn't hardly wait to spread him my adventures.

When I got back and told Eeteh about the general, he cussed in Lakota and says it was that brother that my horse throwed in the cactus. He was the one done the scouting for the tribe and must a lied about Long Hair. Eeteh reckoned his brother was trying to land me in trouble with the general, so I should stay in the camp till he found out more.

But I was desperate to see Tom again, I'd been dancing about ever since I seen Becky, so I pulled my hat down over my eyes and rode Tongo back into town looking for them. I didn't find nuther one. Who I found — or who found me — was General Hard Ass. Me and Tongo was resting by a stream, cooling off from the midday heat and calculating where to look next, when I smelt the cinnamon. I looked up and there was the general setting his horse over me, fitted out proud in his red neckerchief and his pressed uniform with its shiny brass buttons and epolets. "Well, well," he says. He was sporting a broad-brimmed cream-colored slouch hat with the brim turned up on one side and fastened to the crown so's he could sight his rifle whilst galloping along. His rifle was slung across his lap and he warn't hiding it. "Our deserter."

"I ain't a deserter," I says. I got to my feet

and so did Tongo. "Sir." He was still setting a mile above me, his yaller hair curling over his shoulders. "I ain't never been a soldier. I'm just a plain cowboy wrangler and I only set out to sign on another cattle drive, like I said I'd do. I asked Charlie to tell you."

"If you work for the army, son, you're IN the army."

"But . . . well . . ." I had to think up something fast but my brain was froze. I was scared for me, but more for Tongo. Seeing that rifle resting there made me think about Star and how his days ended, which I knowed was how he wanted me to think. We was in trouble. "I was in trouble, sir," I says, but I didn't know yet what trouble I meant. I couldn't use Charlie's story, because it was likely the general already heard it. He was staring down on me, waiting for more. "There was a man wanted to kill me."

"What for?"

"He kept his lady hog-tied in a covered ammunition wagon and give her wrathful hidings there. He thought I'd been messing with her."

"Were you?"

"No, sir. Not exactly. I was only trying to help the lady in her distressidness." The general smiled benignly. "She was sweet but she had a dirty mouth. When the man started shooting, I lit out."

"I see. You disappointed me, Finn. I had high hopes for you. But I can understand how circumstances might have interfered with your judgment." I was dressed mostly in cowboy clothes to do the shopping, but I was wearing my beaded buckskin shirt and had my bear-claw neckless on for luck, and the look he was giving them things warn't a friendly one. "But you can redeem yourself. You're traveling with Indians. I assume you were captured while running away. No white man would voluntarily live with savages."

"No, sir. I wouldn't never think of it."

"In fact, you're living with a squaw. I'm told Kiwingya is her name."

"No, she —"

"It's all right. Sometimes it's a practical thing to do." I warn't sure how he knowed all this, but I could guess. "I once had a squaw myself. She was a princess of some sort and was kindly and serviceable. But I'd have happily had her disemboweled and fed to the wolves if that had been a convenient example to others, and I assume you'd do the same."

"I hope I don't never need such samples, General. But I anyways don't live with her and the tribe no more. She throwed me over and turned the tribe against me."

"I'm sorry to hear that, Finn. I have something for you to do, and it might be useful if you were still living among them. You'll have to go back to them and make amends."

"They're awful mad at me. They won't let me back."

The general was giving Ne Tongo a long dark study. I took hold of Tongo's rawhide thong. "I think I recognize this stallion," he says. "He's one of the animals that got away during our attack on the Cheyenne, when you couldn't control your own horse. If so, he's army property and you, in effect, are a horse thief."

"No, sir. Wild Bill give me this horse back in Abileen. Roped it himself up in the Utah Territory. He says it was the wildest horse he ever seen, and when I broke him, he bought me a whisky and says I could keep him. You can ask him."

"I will. I know Bill well. What's the horse's name?"

"Big River, sir. Mostly I just call him River."

"When you were talking to him just now, he had a different name. An Indian one. And he has been broken the way the natives do it, not like I watched you do it for the army. Why do I get the feeling, Finn, you're not being honest with me?"

He was right, I was unloosing one bareface lie after t'other, and if I could a thought up another one, I surely would a let it out, but before I could roust one up, the general he says: "You're an American, son, those savages aren't. You mustn't betray your own people. That's treason."

My crimes was a-stacking up. There warn't no more sand in my craw. I could only hold onto Tongo and try not to show how guilty I was.

"We're going to lure the Lakota warriors into a cul-de-sac and destroy them, the same way they murdered your friend Corporal Harper and his brave army unit. I also had a young friend in that garrison who was killed. And while the savages are chasing us, their camp will be vulnerable to attack, so it too will be destroyed and all who are in it. That's what's going to happen, Finn. And you're going to help. You'll return now to the tribe and when we need you, you will be informed and you will lead them to us and us to them." He smiled down at me. "That's an order, son." He didn't have to say no more. I knowed what they done to deserters, traiters, liars and horse thieves. General Hard Ass took another long hard look at Tongo, touched the wide brim of his hat and, still smiling his cold fixed smile, slowly rode away.

Chapter XVI

Riding Ne Tongo up to Zeb's shack in the dark before dawn, I felt like I was returning back to the beginning of my story without going nowheres. Zeb's was where me and Eeteh met up when I was running away from General Hard Ass three years before, like now I was still running away from him again. What was the same was the running. Started back on the Big River, running from Pap. Ain't never stopped.

When the general catched me up in the Wyoming Territory, I didn't know where to go. I'd told the general that the tribe was mad at me and throwed me out, so if I went back to where they was camped in the mountains, and Eeteh's pesky brother snitched to him, he'd see I was lying. Of course that wouldn't change nothing, I was already a low-down liar in the general's books, heaving stretchers at him by the muck-cartload, and him knowing it. But what if I led his troopers there? Maybe, I thought, looking back over my shoulder, he was only letting me go so's I could do that, reckoning on my stupidness. So I dasn't go back, but if I didn't, Eeteh wouldn't understand why. He might even calculate I'd been captured and stumble into trouble trying to find me. It was like one a Tom Sawyer's pair a duckses.

The first thing I had to do was get word to Eeteh somehow. Maybe he'd know what to do. When him and me wanted to call out to each other without nobody knowing, we always hooted back and forth like owls, so I was listening everywheres for his hoots and I was who-whooing myself, best I could, but I didn't hear nothing back. Me and Tom mostly me-yowed and I was naturaller at cats. They was more like family. Eeteh says my hoots might be exact, but they warn't made by any owl he ever heard in these parts. "Then it's the hoot of an emigrant owl," I says. "That way, you'll know it's me."

It was resky, but when it got dark and I hain't heard from Eeteh all day, I rode Tongo up onto a rocky slope in hooting distance from the camp, done my emigrant owl who-whoos, and this time Eeteh was pretty soon hooting back. I was toting the whisky and tobacco I'd bought in the tavern for the tribe, so when he clumb his pinto up and found me, we settled into some boulders high up on the hillside under the moon to drink and smoke a pipe or two, happy we was both still alive, but not for certain how to stay that way.

Eeteh had thought I was already completely dead. He says that pestiferous brother told everybody he was scouting for the tribe and he seen Long Hair and his soldiers grab me and drag me off to be shot. He was all alone, he couldn't do nothing about it. He even said he heard the firing squad before he sneaked away. The brother drooped his head down and says he was terrible sorry about it. I says the general found me all right, but if that sorry brother was watching, he didn't stay around long enough to see what happened next. Eeteh says that he didn't see nothing, he just set the general on me, and cut. It's what the low-down liar fetched the whole tribe there to do, he didn't care about what trouble he was dragging them into. Eeteh was madder'n I never seen him, and says that brother don't belong in the tribe.

I told Eeteh all the general said, how he declared me guilty of an awful sight of hanging crimes, and how he wanted me to repent my wickedness by leading the whole tribe into a death trap. Eeteh nodded and sipped his whisky and says the tribe and me should move separate to the Black Hills, which warn't fur off, and where the army warn't allowed. The tribe can send out a decoy to lead Long Hair and his troopers the wrong way, he says, and then, whilst his calvary is a-chasing ghosts, they can haul their lodges over there. He told me about the whisky-maker in the Gulch and drawed a map on birch bark how to find him and says he'd look for me there when the tribe finally reached the Hills.

So that was how it was I first come to the Hills, which for me, till now, was more like home than home was. Soon as Eeteh got nearby, he brung me my lodge-skins and helped me cut some poles and set up my tepee and move down out a the bat cave where I'd been living. Tepees are the changeablest kind of a layout for living in. They make a body feel at home wherever they are. I'd stayed with the tribe for a few years, moving round, and could a gone back with them again, but they seen I was a Hard Ass magnet, and was afeared a me being too close. I was also a little wearied of them and their peculiars, so both Eeteh and me was agreed it was best to abide in the Gulch on my own.

When old Zeb first seen me and Eeteh together, he hired us to do his trading with the tribe, and that made it easier for Eeteh to come and go when he wanted to. It was the best time of my life, and of Eeteh's, too. The Indian-hating emigrants hadn't arrived yet, and we could set around in my tepee and drink and jabber the night through. Zeb needed grains for his whisky-mash, and meat and fish for himself, turnips, hog nuts, berries, whatever other food the tribe gathered, and he also traded for things he could sell to emigrants passing through. All in all, Zeb was doing tolerable well, he was the richest man in the Gulch, though back then that warn't saying much. Now, everybody was going to be rich in the Rush and old Zeb maybe the richest of them all. I worried Eeteh's money pouch wouldn't mean beans to him.

It was a cold damp morning and I had my chin tucked down in my buckskin shirt. It was too dark to see nothing, but I could hear the noises of others up sneaking about, stumbling over the bodies lying in the cold mud, cussing back whenever one of the bodies got stepped on and let out a nasty bark. There was an awful stink like everybody was just dropping their pants wherever and doin' their producin', as Zeb would say, and it made me push my nose deeper into my shirt.

Then, just as me and Tongo was pulling up to Zeb's shack, somebody kicked me in the head and knocked me slap off of the horse into the mud. I sprung up and swung my rifle round in the dark, trying to see who done that. And how. The emigrants in their sivilizing fever had chopped down most of the trees thereabouts, but one out a-front of Zeb's was still rairing up, and something long and lumpy was a-hanging from it. It was so dark, I had to get right under the muddy farm brogans to see that it was that country jake in the floppy straw who come to the camp with just only a pitchfork and a wheelbarrow. I judged it must be desperate bad luck to get kicked in the head by a dead man, specially one who was wearing your own hat, and I begun to feel worried and shaky about the rest of the day ahead.

Abaddon, Zeb's cantankery mastiff, was a-guarding the door, but him and me was old pards, so he only wagged his tail and grinned his devil grin whilst I scratched his pointy ears. Inside, Zeb was already set to work by lamplight on a new batch of liquor. His shack was always in ruins, but it was ruineder than ever. Them strangers piling in last night had wrecked everything that could still be wrecked. "It got purty mean," he acknowledged, scratching his chin. There was a heap of rifles, pistols and other goods like saddles, spurs and even britches and boots, over in a shadowy corner behind the plank bar, things Zeb had took in exchange for whisky. There was also blood on the dirt floor. "Year's wuth a whisky. Swallered in a night. Tried t'shut the shack down afore that happened, but they shoved a gun in my face."

"I've had trouble down at the tepee, too."

"Some tough-lookin' jackasses come askin' to buy up my stock'n close the place permanent, sayin' they'll be tearin' my old shack down t'build somethin' fancy with whores'n gamblin', and I kin work fur 'em. But I ain't stayin'. I don't work fur nobody. And after yestidday's rush, I ain't got no stock left to sell. Jest the mother. They ain't gettin' that over my dead body," he says, jutting his jaw further out under his nose like he was daring a body to argue with him, his yaller bottom teeth showing like scattered nuggets.

I asked him about the tree decoration out front, and Zeb says, "Shootout over the last jug a whisky. One of 'em killt t'other one like usual. Committee formed theirselves up, mostly stewed pards a the loser who was a-layin' there with his mouth open. They poured some whisky in it, and when it only filled up like a cup, they says the winner'd committed murder, which they declared t'be a hangin' offense. They was generous, though. Let the feller have a slug a the whisky he'd fought over afore stringin' him up, then drunk the rest to his mem'ry."

"It was too dark to see clear, but it looked like he still's sporting his old straw hat."

"Heerd one of 'em sayin' that accordin' to the laws back home, where they had hangin's ever week, it was reckoned the most sivilized thing t'do."

"All this sivilizing is too many for me and Eeteh," I says. "We're moving on, too. If you want, we can scout for you. We're a-going to Mexico, and we'd be happy to have you and your mother as company all the way, if you wouldn't care to join along."

"I'm headed thataway, but I'll prob'bly jest go on back home on the river, now the war's over," Zeb says, staring off like he was already a-pulling in there. "But I could use a coupla guns breakin' out a this hellhole'n some help totin' the provisions."

I says we can do that. "But me and Eeteh we can't leave till after sundown."

"Me nuther. Cookin' up a new batch. More like injun whisky. Givin' it away free.

Git the whole camp fallin' down stone drunk. Then heel it out." Injun whisky was brewed from black chaw and pine sap and hot peppers and wood alcohol and other worse pison. Zeb never done that. Seeing him go against his principles only showed how horrible things really was. He give me a list of vittles for the road and of rubbage to add to his devil-brew, if I seen them laying round free, and then he flung me a worried look, his bottom teeth chawing on his flabby upper lip. "This dern stuff rots the head cheese, Huck. Turns some people desprate crazy."

"I'll come watch your back, Zeb. First, though, I need some a them guns piled up over there. I'm organizing a, you know, a vegilanty gang." I showed him the soft leather pouch Eeteh give me. "I can pay."

"Don't give two hoots who or what they're fur," Zeb says, seeing through me like everybody else done. He pocketed the pouch without looking inside it. "Jest need the money t'set up a new still somewheres."

"How many will that buy?"

"All of 'em. Any left, they'd jest git stole anyways. If it warn't fur Abaddon, they'd awready got stole back. And I don't want no extry guns layin' about tonight when the craziness sets in."

As we was piling the weapons into grain sacks, I told Zeb about my "brother Jacob" so's he don't blunder up my story, and Zeb says somebody asked about him last night. "Feller with an eyepatch."

"You didn't tell him nothing?"

"Don't know nothing."

We settled the sacks over Tongo's back, and him and me set off downslope to the tepee, easing wide round the hanged man, floating there like a creepy shadow in the darkness. It was still nightish, but not like pitch no more. There was just enough dismal light to make a body feel they might was being watched. Through a gun sight. To get to Zeb's in the old days, you had to walk through a woods. Now there was only a couple of lonesome trees still standing, leaving his shack set out on a wide muddy clearing clogged up with emigrant wagons, parked higgledy-piggledy. The bodies laying in the muck was starting to stir, cussing and snorting and trumpeting out their backsides. Some warn't getting up, and didn't look like they probably never would.

Down at the crick, there was a scrawny young prospector in a round stiff-brimmed black hat hammering a stake into the shore below my tepee. I didn't say nothing, I just walked towards him with my rifle cradled in my arm. He had a few black hairs blooming on his upper lip like he was thinking about growing a moustache but couldn't made up his mind about it. Under it, he muttered something that warn't American, pulled up his stake, and planted it further upstream. I fired a shot off into the air, and he picked up his stake and moved further on. I warn't about to shoot nobody over land I was fixing to leave behind, but I couldn't allow nothing to bother getting the guns to Eeteh, so's we'd be freed up to go.

In the tepee, I dug a shallow hole next to the fire and laid in it the guns, still in their grain sacks, covering them over with an old tribal blanket Eeteh give me. I cooked up some fish for breakfast, then I scattered a few fishbones and ashes from the fire on the blanket so's it'd look like it'd always been there. With charred sticks from the fire, I drawed a skull and crossbones on the tepee hide outside, and wrote POX! PISON! above them and CONDAMNED! below.

By the time I was done, the sky was commencing to lighten up and a ceaseless commotion of banging and yelling was a-rumbling down from above again. I let out my emigrant owl hoot and heard what might a been an answering hoot somewheres far off, or maybe I only wanted to hear it. The day was still just a-dawning, but prospectors was already swarming up and down the crick shore and through the hills, staking claims, fighting with each other. Sometimes a gun went off.

To give Eeteh time to collar the weapons, I hiked Tongo back up to the emigrants' camp, where things was so thickening up, there warn't hardly no room to pass through. More covered wagons and overloaded freighters and prospectors on horseback was still stampeeding in, there was a long line of them out into the hills far as a body could see, and new shanties and lean-tos was cropping up like cheatgrass. There were streets now of a sudden, though there warn't no pattern to them, lined out any which way by the tramping boots and hoofs and the wagon tracks. Storefronts with signs on them was raising up at the edges of the tracks, most of them without nothing behind them yet but gumbo. If them emigrants had come here prospecting for mud, they would surely all been rich.

Traders sold straight from their tents and wagons or set up rough lumber on barrels and laid their wares out on them in the street, or on the new wooden sidewalks being slung up so's to be able to move around without sinking knee-deep in the muck. There was everything for sale from shovels and skillets to wooly underwear, picks and tin lanterns. A power of rifles and shotguns and six-shooters was being bought and sold, too, and axes and hatchets and mean-looking knives. That rawbone coffin-maker in the black stovepipe hadn't stopped sawing planks and hammering boxes together since he got here, and he still didn't have none left over.

There was rumors gold had been struck upstream, so regiments of fortune-hunters was charging out to scrouge for it. There warn't no law about any of what was happening; it was a bully's game. They was so eager to race out and grab up the gold, they mostly just left their wagons where they stood, offering up vittles and bottle liquor a-plenty for borrowing, and swarms a loafers was sneaking about doing that.

Others was prospecting for gold off of the prospectors. That fat little dentist-banker with the thick bush of yaller whiskers was now setting in front of a map he'd drawed and was announcing himself as a land surveyor for folks who wanted to know for a dollar where the gold was before they went rattling off into the heathen wilderness. Swarthy fellows was peddling burros and pack horses, herding them through the muddy streets. Sawyers and carpenters and millers hung out their shingles. I heard a baby cry, so families was starting to elbow in, too.

A beardy slack-jawed chap was pushing the country rube's ownerless wheelbarrow, offering it up for sale. As he slopped along, somebody thronged a dead body in it. He looked the body over in his meloncholical way, slowly scratching his hairy jaw. Then, when he calculated he couldn't profit by it, he tipped it out and pushed on again.

There was a small crowd of loafers a-wanting to get into Zeb's, being persuaded off by Abaddon. When Abaddon first snarled me up against a wall, I thought I heard Zeb call him a bad 'un, but then I learnt it was the name of some devil, and he did have the snout and temper of one. Zeb didn't hesitate to sick Abaddon on robbers and vilent drunks, and not every one a them had two working legs afterwards.

One of the old regulars leaning on a wagon next to the stone path leading up to the shack says he's heard about a vegilanty gang I was banding up and he'd like to join it if we was passing out guns because he ain't got his no more, Zeb does. He says he was told that members of the gang got to take a blood oath, and he was ready to stick himself and do that, so I seen Deadwood warn't only spreading the word, he was tossing in a few of his own. "Tonight, at Zeb's," I says, "special vegilanty whisky. For free. Let the others know."

Deadwood his own self warn't far away. He was telling everybody who wanted to listen about his shooting contest with my brother Jacob. "We set out to see how long him and me could keep that silver dollar up in the air by shootin' at it," he was saying. "First one missed lost the dollar, though it didn't hardly look like one no more. More like that chunk a the moon I struck here when I was a young'un, and first got famous." When he seen me, he took his gold fob watch out of his vest pocket and raised it up and blinked both his crossed eyes like two winks at once. "We didn't nuther two of us miss," he says, pocketing the watch and returning back to his audience again. "But ole Jake he finally won on accounts of I run out a dern carteridges."

Those rumors of plasser gold in the crick was spreading round, so me and Tongo went where I could keep an eye on the tepee. What I seen was smoke a-pouring out of it. I rode down there with my rifle and pistol cocked: it was Eyepatch and his pals again.

Wooden claim stakes was springing up along the shore like jimson weeds, including a new one sprouting in Tongo's pasture. The smoke warn't from a cooking fire. They was trying to burn the tepee down.

Eyepatch snarls for me to get out, I'm trespassing on their claim. "I ain't making no fuss about that," I says. I'd helped the army burn down enough native villages to know the lodges burnt slow, but I couldn't resk losing that hide cover, and I needed to know if the guns was still in there or if these rascals had already smouched them. "Ain't a prospector, and don't never aim to be one. But you'd best douse that fire."

"We got a ordnance to burn it," Eyepatch says, "it bein' a mortal hazard."

"Who give you that ordnance?" I says, both fingers on triggers.

"We done." His gold teeth and the loops in his ears was glinting in the morning light. He didn't seem to think I'd shoot him and he was probably right.

"Well, my brother's buried in there and you're spreading his pox all over the Hills by setting smoke a-flying out from that sick tent."

Pegleg frowned and lifted his neckerchief over his nose. "Why the hell didn't you tell us that in the first place, chief?"

The fellow with the scattered brown teeth says I'm a goddam liar and drawed his pistol, so I was obleeged to raise mine and fire off some damage to his hand, adding to all the old wounds he was already wearing like a thief's campaign medals. The other two's hands was twitching, but they warn't taking no chances. "He's a shooter," Eyepatch snarls with a mean grin.

"I'm going to put out that fire and move my brother's remains off of your claim. Him and me are going to be traveling soon. I'm a-taking him home. If you want to stay and watch, you got to come in there with me and help me dig him up."

"If it's so damn dangerous," Pegleg says, "why're YOU goin' in there?"

"I got the impunity from tending Jacob. I catched the pox, too, but I only broke out in freckly spots. There ain't pus leaking out a more'n one or two now. I can show you if you ain't scared of drawing too close." They didn't show no signs of wanting to do that, so I says, "Zeb's stilling up a special whisky to welcome folks to the Gulch tonight. It'll be for free, so they're already getting in line. Maybe I'll see you up there later."

"Awright, you carry on, chief," Eyepatch says, holstering his pistol. The one who drawed on me was still moaning and cussing and clutching his wrist. “C’mon, Bill, le’s go git you doctored up.”

“How you going to do that?” whined Bill. “There ain’t no doctors.”

“There’s a dentist turned up. He prob’bly can do it. Git them bones shifted, chief. Pronto. We’ll be back.”

I watched them move up the slope till they was near out of sight, then ducked inside. It was all tore up in there. I grabbed up the blanket to beat out the fire, and I seen that the guns had been took. It was just what I was afeard of. Eyepatch and his gang had got to them first. Our plans was ruined.

But then I seen the eagle feather.

Chapter XVII

They was all having a grand time up in Zeb's that night. Pap would a felt right at home. It only took one swallow of Zeb's special brew to melt a body's brains and knees, and two was good enough for delirium tremens. Of course Pap would a got in a fight with everybody, even if he couldn't get his feet under him, but that was part a the revelment for Pap, maybe the importantest part — and it was just the sort of climacteric Zeb was aiming at that night so as to make our escape from the camp without resk of nobody on our tails. Zeb's mastiff Abaddon was penned up and mighty unhappy about it, growling out something betwixt a snarl and a whimper all night, but Zeb didn't want the dog to chase nobody off before he'd soused them up.

That yaller-whiskered banker-dentist turned land surveyor was there and he was the most popular man in the shack. Zeb's bar was just a plank set on two hogsheads, and Yaller Whiskers was standing there, alongside of a chinless character with long droopy moustaches spread round a set of mule teeth. Mule Teeth was showing off a speck a gold, which he says he come on that day by following a map he bought off of the surveyor. The speck probably warn't worth ten cents, but you'd a thought the fellow was become a millionaire, and now everybody wanted to buy a five-dollar map from Yaller Whiskers. There was some who'd already bought maps who hadn't struck nothing. "They warn't maps, they was more like newspaper cartoons," one of them says, and Yaller Whiskers spit through his bushy beard and says, "Well, you prob'bly warn't readin' 'em proper, son, so you messed out the punchline." They asked the millionaire over and over where he'd staked his claim, and he smiled round his big teeth like a king and slurped and unloosed a handsome heap a lies.

Some was complaining to Zeb about that hanged hayseed still blowing in the wind out a-front the shack, saying it warn't an eddyfying sight and couldn't be no good for business. Zeb says business right now was most all he could handle, but they was free to go cut him down if they warn't afeard a being ha'nted by him after. Several was willing, saying ghosts don't scare them none, except maybe spinster ghosts who was knowed to be the vilest sort, but they didn't want to lose their approximity to the free whisky whilst it lasted, undrinkable hell-begot bomination though it was.

One of the emigrants fetched along a homemade fiddle and he was a-ripping away on it, yelping out songs he'd thought up about the awful Silver War and about lonesome, whooping, dogie-driving, and dying cowboys. Some a the drunks was yelping and yuppeeing along with him and some was bawling and some was cussing the memory of their trail bosses and the wretchid lives they had. I remembered the lonesome part, but the rest was mostly sentimentery hogwash. I wouldn't be unhappy to go back to the cowboying trade, but I wouldn't be specially happy nuther.

Then the chap got to singing about young women in calico frocks and Sunday bonnets, and that got the drunks to hooting and hollering and in generl misabusing theirselves. One of them tied the sleeves of a sheepskin jacket round his back to make a kind of skirt out of it, and he commenced to prance around like a prairie nymph and then strip himself off one thing at a time, like I seen the ladies do in saloons down in Abileen. They was all awful excited. If a real woman had turned up, she wouldn't a stood a chance. All the loafers was roaring and clapping and haw-hawing until the dancer was start-naked, and then they booed him and asked him when's the last time he washed that nasty thing.

"When I felled in a river," he says, "back in '68."

Eyepatch crept over through the crowd, stepping on the bodies that had already got knocked down by Zeb's vegilanty whisky, his earrings and gold teeth a-glinting in the lamplight, and asked me with his everyday snarl if my brother was moved away yet. I says that Jake was out a the ground and laying down there in the tepee under a blanket. His two pals was watching me from across the shack. Pegleg was chawing a plug, and nuther him nor Bill was drinking. "I promised to help out Zeb tonight, and when I'm done I mean to pack Jake off to a proper burial back home. Him and me'll be gone by noon."

Eyepatch says they seen an injun sneaking around down there.

"Yes. He's watching over the body so there don't nobody come too close and catch the pox off it."

"Ain't the bugger apt to catch it hisself?"

"Probably, but he's only an ignorant savage. He don't know nothing about poxes and I ain't telling him."

Eyepatch and his pals was too sober, and I knowed we'd have to keep a sharp lookout for them when we pulled out with Zeb. When I says so to Zeb, he says I should take care. "Them rapscallions is afeard a you'n yer gun, and there ain't nothing more dangersomer than a skeered killer."

Deadwood was uncorking his stretchers in the middle of the shack for any loafers tight enough to listen at him, and showing his fob watch at most every opportunity, popping it open and closed, though now there warn't no point. He was presently telling about when he scouted for Louie Clark. He says Louie asked him to bed down a princess name of Porky-Hauntus to have her learn him the secret tunnel through the mountains to the ocean. "She took me in thar and showed me more'n I never wanted t'see, and when I come out I was ten years younger, boys, but limp as a dern noodle till I'd growed back them lost ten years."

Zeb had richened up his brew with a gallon of homemade black rum donated from one of the emigrant wagons I passed by earlier, plus some store hair slick, a bowkay of chili peppers, a pot of crabapple jam, some powder that Zeb tasted and said was most like rat pison, and other useful rubbage that had turned up in prospectors' wagons and saddlebags. One of the drunks says he reckonized the sweet muddy taste as out'n his own rum jug that was stole that day whilst he was off staking his claim, and before I could move, he'd drawed his pistol on Zeb and says he was going to kill him dead, and other guns come out round the room. But the drunk had been sampling Zeb's mulekick all night and his eyes rolled back of a sudden and his pistol dropped and he stiffened up and keeled over, and everybody put their guns away again.

But it was a sign of how the party was hotting up. There was knife-throwing games and rassling and fancy shooting contests that could easy turn vilent. A bespectacled chap in a black derby hat had borrowed an old army drum from somewheres and was a-beating on it, adding to the racket. Some of the boys, wearing scraps and tatters of blue and gray uniforms, was already doing some pushing and shoving and cussing out each other's generals. It wouldn't take long. That long bony coffin-maker come through the door, took one look around, and went back to hammering boxes together.

I'd been thinking about our leaving all day and couldn't hardly wait to get started. I had loved the Gulch, but it was most ruined now by this plague a grabby emigrants. As a haven for loafers, it warn't one no more. It was time to go.

Eeteh he was ready, too. He was down at the tepee, hiding out from all the Indian-hating emigrants and watching over our goods, waiting for Zeb and me. I'd left Tongo with him and I was glad of it, seeing how ugly things was turning in the shack. Everything except the lodge-skins was packed up down there and ready to be grabbed on the run. The reward for killing Indians was rising up every day, so Eeteh was restless that we had to wait for Zeb, but he was happy about traveling with the old whisky-maker and his magical mother, who he said Coyote was planning to marry. He says the tribe was proud about what we done and they maybe warn't happy we was going, but they wouldn't try to stop us. They might even give us an escort if we asked them. He says they wished I was the chief of my tribe, though they knowed my tribe was too stupid to think of that, and I says, yes, they was stupid, but I ain't the chief a nothing and won't never be, and he nodded at that and lighted up his pipe and I lighted up mine.

Before I left him to come up to Zeb's, he told me another Coyote story. There was a time, he says, when things was going poorly for Coyote. He had the earache, the toothache, the bellyache, and monster boils under his tail, but the worse thing was the rash of pustulous sores that broke out in his crotch. His wife was disgusted when she seen them and left him to go live with Snake, but he couldn't a done nothing with her anyways. A woman come to take care of him, but she pisoned him with an evil potion that left his innards twisted wrongside out, and then robbed him of all his money, tobacco, and spirits. He knowed that Snake had powerful medicines and "speak great wisdom," as Eeteh put it, so he decided to go visit him. Snake might a s'posed Coyote was a-coming to kill him on account of the cheating wife, but by then Coyote was so sick he could only crawl like a worm (Eeteh imitated this), so Snake laughed and took him in and doctored him and talked to him whilst he was getting cured. The peyote that Snake et give him visions of the beginnings and endings of things, and those visions led him to concluding that nothing mattered in the world no more and everything, even boils and pustules, was funny. Coyote laughed along with him, and then when he was well again, he killed both Snake and his woman and cooked them up with prairie onions, wild mushrooms, and buffaloberries, and et them, saying he hoped Snake got the joke and didn't take revenge whilst he was passing through. Eeteh was telling me this story in Lakota, and I had to stop him now and again to ask him what some words meant. I had the feeling that whenever I done that, he was changing the story a little.

Things was a-biling up now in Zeb's shack. Folks was turning testy and old Zeb was nerviouser'n I never seen him. The drummer in the derby was pounding the skin of his insterment like he was trying to bust it, and the fiddler was scratching his strings and screeching away through his nose like something of his'n down below was a-getting twisted. A new emigrant come in wearing a string a black-haired scalps on his belt, some of them with their ears still on. He knocked over a drunken loafer who was in his way and opened up his pants and let fly against a wall. One of Zeb's regulars took offense at that and was just sober enough to take aim and shoot the emigrant's pecker off. That crazied the new emigrant so, he fetched out two six-shooters and he might a hurt somebody if the others hadn't stopped him dead with twenty or thirty shots before he could start blasting away. "Thanks, boys," Zeb says, crawling out from under the bar plank. "Some people ain't got no manners."

With guns going off, them who had give up their weapons the night before was worried they didn't have nothing to fire back with. They wanted to know when the vegilanties was going to get armed up. Zeb says he put the vegilanty guns in a safe place on account of he didn't want no more weapons here tonight, but some a them had got stole. Eyepatch's pal, the one with the scattered brown teeth and bandaged hand, says it must a been the injuns. They was on the warpath and scrouging for weapons. Zeb says maybe, but he don't think so. "All these here wagons rollin' in has skeered the breechclots off a them heathens. No, I warrant it was prob'bly somebody in the camp what collared 'em. Somebody maybe right here in this shack tonight."

The drunks didn't have much reason left and was most open to sejestion, so they begun staring around at each other in a suspicioning way. Best they COULD stare, for most of them warn't focusing too good. Some says they reckonized the guns others was carrying as their own, and fights broke out. Some joined in only because they couldn't get out a the way. Things was a-darkening up pretty quick.

"It was injuns," Eyepatch says, glaring at Zeb with his one eye. "We seen them crawlin' outa the crick over on t'other side this mornin' and scamperin' away. We fired some shots and chased 'em off and maybe might a killt a couple."

"That must a been when you was trying to burn down my tent," I says. "I hid some of the guns in there for Zeb, and when I got the fire out so's I could see, they warn't there no more. You never said nothing about Indians." Eyepatch started up like he'd set on a cactus. Mean murmurs started going round. Eyepatch's two pals Bill and Pegleg was already out the door.

Zeb was holding back a final jug of his vegilanty pison and he fetched it out now. One of Zeb's old regulars beside me took a swig and near choked to death on it. "This wretchid forty-rod ain't like Zeb's likker at all. It's wuss'n runny dogshit," he says, staggering around and wheezing like he's got a burr in his throat. "Shore got a kick, though."

The fiddler was still torturing his music box. He was too drunk to do more'n snort a loud racket through his nostrils over'n over that was s'posed to be singing but warn't a near neighbor to it. It was enough, though, to set two men a-dancing together. One of them was wearing his vest like an apron, but both was still sporting black hats over their beards and they was dead serious. There warn't much room in the shack and there was bodies all over the dirt floor, but they went kicking out just the same, and the others made room for them and pulled the bodies out of the way and clapped them on, and some was grinning, though most was church-going solemn like the dancers.

Deadwood was so drunk he couldn't hardly stand, but he wobbled and wove amongst the two dancers, his eyes crossing and uncrossing, a ten-penny glass a Zeb's brew in one hand, spinning his fob watch on its chain round and round with t'other. The old regular a-near me says Deadwood should oughter hide that gewgaw and keep his head down not to get it shot off. "See them two rough old dead beats over there by that Yankee drummer?" I seen them. Pock-faced fellows with squinty eyes peering out from under slouch-hat brims, dressed in white shirts yallered with age and tattered black waistcoats. One a them had his long hair knotted at the back like a horse's tail. They warn't drinking, only chawing and spitting. "Highwaymen t'hear 'em talk. One of 'em says he reckonized that fob watch from a stagecoach holdup and was a-wonderin' where was the rest a their truck."

"I could tell Deadwood," I says. I been afraid of them robbers turning up, and here they was. I had to haul Deadwood out somehow. "But he don't listen."

"I know it," says the old regular.

Just then one a the drunks stomped over betwixt the two dancers, pushed the "man" away, and set to dancing with the "woman." The "man" pushed him back and they got in a fight. Another emigrant stepped in and took the "woman" for his own partner, and then all three of them was at it. The "woman" just watched haughty-like, then danced with the next drunk to claim him. Others was fighting over what was left in the special jug or over one insult or t'other. There was a generl wild-eyed bust-up winding up. Next to me, Zeb leans onto his short leg and whispers, "We got to go now! I ain't got nothin' more to hold 'em off with!"

"Let's go get Eeteh," I says.

Punches was being throwed all around, and they was kicking out with their boots and clubbing heads with whatever come to hand. Some was going crazy with the whisky and was down on their hands and knees, screeching and bawling, and others was rolling round and round and screaming that devils had got a-holt on them. The drum was still getting banged somewheres by someone, but there warn't no rhythm to it. The plank bar crashed over and drunks tumbled over it. I looked for Deadwood to pull him out, but he seemed to of used his head for once and was already ducked out. Nor else he was one of the bodies on the floor that everybody was falling over. Eye-patch was gone, too. I worried that him and his pards might be down at the tepee again where Eeteh was all alone. I had to whack a few of the drunks with my rifle butt for me and Zeb to shove through and make it out the door.

We hurried over to where Abaddon was penned and found him laying dead with his throat slit. Zeb groaned an awful groan and fell down to his knees and hugged the dead dog and bitterly cussed out whoever done it. Then, his eyes still tearing up, he unhitched his mare and his old packhorse, and we struck for the tepee. His goods was already packed up on the horse, and the saddlebags on the mare I was leading was loadened down, too. His stinking bucket a spent mash, the precious whisky-mother that give it its special taste, was sealed up inside a box with leather straps made for it by the coffin maker. The brawl was spreading outside where all the wagons was parked and the country jake was a-hanging, so we ducked down through a dark tangled ravine back a the shack towards the crick and tepee below.

About halfway down, I heard a most woeful moan and fetched up short. I thought it might a been a wild animal and I spun around with my rifle pointed at it, but it was Deadwood a-laying there in a patch a moonlight, looking half-ruined. His face was just raw meat, he was a-bleeding round the ears, and at least one of his arms was broke; a leg, too, looked like. He didn't have many teeth before, now he didn't have none. "Deadwood! Who done this to you?" I asked. He couldn't talk, he could only groan. Anyways I knowed who. His fob watch was gone. Looked like his jaw might be busted. He needed a doctor, but there warn't none anywheres I knowed of. Unless Eeteh could help. I started up my emigrant owl hoot.

Zeb limped up with the packhorse behind me. "We don't have no time for this!" he says. You could still hear the hollering and the guns popping, but not so loud down here. "If that damfool's in trouble, it's trouble he's made for hisself! WE GOT TO KEEP MOVIN'!"

"It was the fob watch, Zeb. Them robbers reckonized it. It's them that's done this. I told Deadwood to show it, so's we could get everybody up to your shack tonight. He done it for US! And he ain't got nobody else to help." I could hear Eeteh far off answering me. I let out some more urgent hoots.

"We AIN'T takin' that crazy old liar WITH us!"

"No, we ain't. He's anyways too beat up to travel. He might not even make it through the night. But we can't leave him here to die where they throwed him!"

Me and Eeteh kept on hooting, and soon he was down in the ravine and crawling up. Zeb was still complaining, and when Eeteh took one look, he says he don't know no medicine powerful enough for the mess Deadwood was in. "Zeb right, Hahza. We leave now."

"You know some things that might help," I says, staring into his black eyes, shining out from behind their curtain of ropy black hair like from behind hanging vines. "You and Coyote. You know." Eeteh shrugged and looked down at the old prospector. "Leastways we can try to set what's broke and carry him back to his shack where he can rest more easier. After that he can take care of himself."

Eeteh sighed and shook his head. "Is right thing to do, Hahza," he says solemnly in Zeb's language and mine. "Is wrong thing to do. But I do what you do." Zeb grunted irritably.

"You're pulling a slow packhorse, Zeb," I says. "You can get a head start." I took off the bear-claw neckless I was wearing under my shirt, and give it to him. "This is for good luck, Zeb. It ain't done me no favors, but maybe it'll work for you. Watch you follow that back trail like we said, so's we can find you. Me and Eeteh will settle Deadwood and catch you up before dawn."

Zeb looked like his spirits was sunk in his boots, but he dropped the bear claws in his jacket pocket and clumb up into the mare's saddle. He reached into his saddlebag and give me a small flask a that black rum he'd used for the vegilanty brew. "I was keepin' this for the road," he says. "But Deadwood's gonna need it more." Then, leading the packhorse behind him, he trudged off slowly, climbing up into the dark.

Chapter XVIII

Whilst we was setting Deadwood's broke bones in the moonlight, using sticks and branches tied with rags tore from the shirts of emigrants laying dead-drunk in the mud up the hill above us, Eeteh got to telling the story of how Coyote tricked Time. Deadwood was favorably busted up, but he warn't feeling no pain. He didn't know where he was and he probably wouldn't never know again. His nose was squashed and Eeteh had molded up a new one, pushing his fingers up the nostrils to press the inside papery bits back together. We scooped up mud and grass to make a cast for it.

When Eeteh was resetting Deadwood's toothless jaw, I sneaked back up to Zeb's to pry the bar plank out from under the drunks who'd fell over on it. Things was still pretty crazy in there, but sinking towards a generl stupidness. The hooting and hollering and gunshots was mostly moved outside where it warn't so crowded up with bodies.

We strapped Deadwood down to the plank like a litter, and betwixt the old prospector's scrawny shoulder blades, we stuffed a shirt I'd hived off of a fallen emigrant. We stripped off his filthy old coat and pants, leaving him in a kind of handmade union suit he probably hadn't took off since he put it on, and begun trying to do something about his busted bones. It was slow work, stretching all the bones apart and settling them back together best we could, then splinting and bandaging them up, and time was exactly what we hadn't got near enough of. Which was why Eeteh was gabbling on about it. We was both scared, but we neither of us was trying to show it.

Eeteh says that Time used to be lost in empty space and nobody growed old, until Sun and Moon come along. Sun and Moon they worked for Time. Time was the boss. He could talk to you, mostly just to push you around, but you couldn't talk to him. There warn't no stars yet and Moon was always either shining or not shining, so there was only two days in each month and they flew by, tick-tocking back and forth like Deadwood's fob watch. People growed old so fast they didn't hardly have time to get born before they was dying. It was how

Time wanted it. Dying warn't a particular concern a his and he didn't have to learn to count past two.

Coyote was feeling very sad about it, Eeteh says, so sad he thought he might kill himself to stop growing older, but he was a coward as bad as we was and couldn't make himself do that. He reckoned the only other solution was to stop Time or at least stretch him out somehow like we was doing to old Deadwood.

Time kept Sun and Moon apart, they lived in separate lodges and warn't noway allowed in the same one together. Only one a them was let out into the sky at the same time, though Moon sometimes lurked about like a shy ghost in Sun's sky, wishing Sun would look her way. Wishing didn't do her no good. Sun was only in love with his own self. This was before Coyote sent Turtle diving down in the ocean to bring up earth for people to live on, Eeteh says, so the world was still slopped over with water, and Sun spent all his days smiling down at his own reflection. He would a kissed it if he could. Moon stared at her reflection, too, but only because her sky was dark and there warn't nothing else to look at. Her reflection was pale as death, a-floating in pure blackness, and it only made her feel more lonelier'n ever.

I says I thought it was Duck dove down. Eeteh, making a sling out a some loafer's muddy shirt, says he didn't know for sure if Coyote ordered Turtle down or else it was Duck or Water Beetle or Muskrat, or even if he went himself, like Kiwi always said. Kiwi was a Crow and Eeteh reckoned the Crows knowed more about the beginnings and endings of things than the Lakota done, so he thinks maybe Coyote swum down himself. I says that either way it sounded like right down bullwhacky to me, even though it warn't near so foolish as the stories folks back in St. Petersburg took stock in, declaring them to be the Gospel Truth, and Eeteh says stories is stories and got their own rules about the truth.

The tribe was most always all asleep when Moon was let out in the sky, and people never even seen her, Eeteh says, easing Deadwood's shoulder bone into its socket with a crunchy noise, but Coyote he stayed up and watched. We put the broke arm in the sling and strapped it to his chest and Eeteh set about working on the fingers. They was most all busted. Sun was proud like a warrior chief, Eeteh says, and he lit up the water world like it was on fire. He lorded it over everybody and didn't need nobody else. But Moon she was lonely and sad and was always chasing after Sun, Coyote seen that.

Eeteh made a little ball out a mud and leaves and fitted Deadwood's fingers round it, pinching each bone carefully into place. It was like he could see Deadwood's bones with his own fingers. The problem, Coyote judged, was dawn. It there warn't no dawns, people wouldn't have to die no more. So he stitched up a curtain of rain and fog so's Sun couldn't see himself on the waters no more and nobody couldn't see him. That was how clouds and rain begun, Eeteh says, wrapping a rag round Deadwood's balled hand and settling it into the sling. His hair, hanging loose and tangly from the headband, kept getting in his face, but he let it.

Then we set about working on the busted leg, which was a good sight harder. Deadwood was a sinewy old bird, and pulling his leg bones apart to refit the broke ends was most more'n we could do. We needed eight hands, not only four. Sun was terrible lonely, Eeteh went on, grunting from the stretching work, and he went hunting around for that bright face he admired so. He couldn't find it. It had plain disappeared. But Sun seen a face looking like it, Eeteh says, only ghostlier and sadder and beautifuller in a less showy way, and he could not only look at it, he could kiss it, and he knowed then he warn't never going to be lonely again.

We was both straining hard and could feel the bone pieces fitting back. There was a little click like maybe the bone ends was coming together and maybe they warn't. Maybe they was only breaking off worse. Meantimes, Eeteh grunts, reaching for the splint, Time kept stubbornly plodding on, too stupid to be able to change his ways. Like most a the Great Spirits, he didn't really have no brain of his own. Without Sun and Moon to help, he was lost and fuddled and didn't know where he was.

It was desperate hard work, but we somehow got Deadwood's thigh bone put together and the splint tied up and we set to work on the lower part, while Eeteh, stubborn as Time was, kept on with his story. Moon knowed twenty-eight ways of hugging and kissing, Eeteh says, and she learned Sun all of them, showing him a different piece of herself each time to rouse him up, and then she learned him them all again, and all over again, and again, and that was how the stars was born and the year was made. If she'd knowed a hundred ways to do that, then months would have been even longer, and lives, too, Eeteh says, but she couldn't think up no more. Sometimes she made Sun think up one of his own, and they added that in, but mostly he choosed things he used to done by himself when he only had his own reflection to stare at, and he let her do it to him, and that's how the Spirit Road got made. "You have better name for Spirit Road," Eeteh says.

Then one day, Moth was out nibbling at the world like that pest always done if you didn't watch him, and he et a couple a holes in the curtain. Time seen then who was behind it and what they was doing. He tore up the curtain in a furisome rage and throwed Sun and Moon back in their own lodges. Time was the boss. He was stupid maybe, but he didn't give nobody no choice.

We didn't have none nuther. The trees around us was commencing to show theirselves more like pictures than shadows, and that meant that dawn'd be a-breaking soon. We had to clear out before that happened, so what was done was done and we couldn't do no more for the old man.

We throwed his old rags on top of him, picked up the plank with him strapped on it and scuttled in a hurry down the ravine, alongside of the crick, and up to his shack.

The hollering and groaning and gunshots was all stopped. Fog was a-rolling in and, except for the distant rumble of snores, it was so quiet you could hear toads burping and the far-off howls of wolves. The moon was swimming in the fog and glowing in her grievous way, and Eeteh, looking up at her as we clumb, says that after Time broke them up, Moon went on showing herself in twenty-eight ways as a meloncholical rememberer of the beautiful time when they done them all together. Sun could see her from his lodge on t'other side the world and he was grieving, too, though every day he got up and pretended he warn't, not to give Time no satisfaction. I says I most wished he'd show a little more spine and not get up today.

When we set Deadwood down on the floor, his eyes peeped open in their bruised sockets. Both of them was staring in panic at the mud cast on his broke nose. One of his eyes swiveled round to look up at me. He yelped horribly and passed out again. "He's a-going to blame us for what happened to him," I says.

Eeteh nodded, pointed to the old prospector's head. "Many strange bumps," he says, pointing.

"Must be where all his lies is lodged," I

says. "You think he'll live?"

"No."

"Me nuther. But Deadwood's got one good advantage. He don't worry none about it." I set out Zeb's rum flask for him and some corn-bread crumbles from my vest pocket, and me and Eeteh struck for the tepee and the horses down below. There was already light leaking into the sky, so we was heeling it as hard as we could put. We heard somebody beating a drum, and we unfurled our heels and run all the faster, trying not to make no noise.

Then I heard people shouting — *"Help! It's old Zeb!"* — and my heart jumped up amongst my lungs. I turned and shot towards the shouting without thinking what I was doing. Only that Zeb was in trouble. Somebody hollered out my name, asking for help. Behind me, Eeteh called out: *"Hahza! Stop!"* Men was riding in on horseback. That chap in the goggles and black derby was slowly banging his army drum. One of the horses was carrying a limp body over its back. With white hair hanging down. His back was full of bullet holes. It most froze me. *"It's Zeb! He's been murdered!"* The man riding in front was Eyepatch, wearing his black headband and raggedy black shirt with a silvry star on it that looked cut out of a tin can. Riding longside him was his two pals and them two pock-faced robber varmints who'd crippled up Deadwood. Flashing his mouth of gold teeth, Eyepatch raised up a finger and pointed straight at me. I turned to run but there was a stampeed of human varmints all round me and they grabbed my beard and hair and throwed me to the mud and give me a most powerful thrashing and there warn't nothing I could do.

Chapter XIX

Gulch history got made by 'lowing me the novelness of a trial, but they didn't lose no time in their charging, convicting and condamning drills. After my licking, they hauled me up out a the mud and got right to it. Dawn warn't even completely broke. They was dragging me straight to the tree where that country boy was a-dangling, but Eyepatch stopped them and says that warn't sivilized, they had to give testimony and take a vote, and THEN hang me.

Eyepatch he was the persecuter, his pal Bill whose hand I shot was chairman of the jury, and his other pal Pegleg, who was earless and couldn't read or write, was who they give me like a lawyer. Yaller Whiskers was the judge and the jury was all the scoundrels left over, mostly sick red-eyed emigrants just raising up from the mud or crawling out a their shackly wagons, not knowing what they was s'posed to be doing or even where in creation they was, but madder'n hell. To keep order in the court, Eyepatch hired on them two ugly pock-faced robbers who nearly done old Deadwood in, and they watched over the trial doings like turkey buzzards with clubs in their claws and their hat brims down over their beaks.

One a the robbers raised up his gold fob watch and says it's time to get the blamed thing over with. Bill told his jury to ca'm down or he'd see personal to them being horsewhipped. There was some loud cussing in objection to his pronouncement, some declaring it was just as toothless as he was and stunk even worse, but Bill fired off some shots into the air with his good hand, and that settled the matter.

Eyepatch shoved a thumb in his waistband and raired back and declared that I was an arched crinimal who was on trial for the gashly Bear-Claw Murder. He held up my good-luck neckless and says they found it fastened like a noose round old Zeb's throat, his both eyes popping their last pop, and all his traps and his packhorse stole, and he asks me if the neckless was mine. I says I give it to Zeb for good luck, and he says to shut up and answer his question: Was it mine? I says it was, but — and he cut me off again and says it didn't bring nuther of us much luck, did it? And them loafers all had a good hoot.

I was in a tight place. Zeb's killers was my accusers and judges, but if I raired a fuss and said so, Eyepatch'd just laugh and turn the others loose on me. They was only looking for an invite, feeling monstrous sick and unhappy. I couldn't spy half a friend among them.

"And whar did this string a heathen julery come from, genlmen a the jury? Why, from them filthy iggorant Sooks who the killer has been pallin' round with! You want to know whar your vegilanty rifles has got to? Ask them war-pathin' redskins that give him this neckless in thanks for all he done for 'em! Finn ain't only a cold-bloody murderer, genlmen, he's a traiter to all white Christians everywheres! He's a traiter to YOU'N ME!"

His rising voice had all them rapscallions roused up and it warn't sure he could hold them back if they took after me. Already I was getting punched and kicked by the nearest ones. Worse, Eyepatch was right in parts, I couldn't deny it. Helping Eeteh the way I done so's we'd be free to leave together was a low-down thing. Ain't never done a low-downer thing. But what was the low-downest of all was I warn't sorry for it. I would hive them rifles for him all over again. I only wished I hain't been such a fool as to go and get caught. That was the most low-downest thing I done: letting Ee-teh down. I was feeling terrible worried and sorry about him, but at least they warn't passing his head around like a trophy, so maybe he got away.

"And that ain't ALL!" Eyepatch says. "Him and his brother and his dog catched the POX and they didn't TELL no one — did any a you ever hear of it? NO! Them flat-heads went on recklessly spreadin' their mortal sickness round THE WHOLE TERRITORY! They wanted everybody to catch it like they catched it theirselves! Now the brother is dead, the dog is dead, only this KILLER is still a-kickin'! But, genlmen —" he looked around at them all with his glittery one eye — "he only's got JEST ONE KICK LEFT!"

They was all a-whooping and hollering for justice and saying they had to hang me NOW! They had a terrible itch in their pants and couldn't wait no more. Yaller Whiskers had a hammer for a gavel, and he was belting a stump with it like he was trying to split it for kindling, and yelling for them to just hang on, ding-bust it, they'll all get their chance.

"And even THAT ain't all!" hollered Eyepatch above the ruckus. There still warn't much light in the sky. The day was slow at waking up like it was afraid to open its eyes. "He also shot our jury boss when there warn't no warrant for it and ruint his hand so bad the pore man cain't even pan for gold no more! Jest look at it! Hold it up thar, Bill! Ain't that the horriblest mess you ever seen? If Finn ain't been such a bad shot, he would a killt him, cuz he's a natural-born crippler and killer! Why, jest last night he give our feller Gulch citizen Deadhead an unmerciless hiding that peart nigh destroyed the ole rip!"

"That ain't so!" I says, though I knowed better than to say nothing at all. Huck, I says to myself, you ain't never going to learn.

Eyepatch he only smiled his cold gold smile at me and signaled to his jury chairman to go for Cross-Eyes. They fetched the old toothless prospector on his plank and set him down and Eyepatch pointed at me and asked him if I was the one who give him his awful thrashing. Deadwood raired his head an inch or two and aimed one or t'other of his crossed eyes at me, groaned and nodded, and he fell back and they carted him away again. “I cain’t hardly believe how any human person could be so despicable crool and mean!” Eyepatch says. “Such a varmint don’t DESERVE to live!” Them two robbers was shaking their heads sadfully, like they couldn’t believe it nuther.

If all them red-eyed emigrants reckoned I was the one who beat up Deadwood, they also reckoned I doctored him afterwards, because when they seen that his bandages was ripped from their own missing shirts, they shouted that if they catched the new-monia and died, there’d be even more murders to hang me for. Others was cussing me out for pisoning Zeb’s whisky, saying I was the worse killer since Ulysses Grant, nor else Robert Lee, they warn’t all agreed which one was prime.

Eyepatch says Zeb was toting some a that pison in a fancy box which probably his killer hid there to be shut of it after he stole everything else. When they smelt its horrible stink, he says, they poured it out so’s it wouldn’t harm nobody never again, hoping only it didn’t kill off all the trees.

“You oughtn’t a done that,” I says. “That was his mother.”

“Sure it was,” says Eyepatch, “and you’re my sister.” And they all fell about snorting and hee-hawing.

I asked Pegleg why he don't point out the bullet holes in Zeb's back which was what killed him, and he spit a gob and says, "What bullet holes?" The old whisky-maker's body was still a-drooped over the mare's back and them holes was in plain view.

"You can see how desprate he is, yeronner," Eyepatch says to Yaller Whiskers with a meloncholical smile, fingering his badge, "unloosing bare-face lies like that to try'n save his wretchid hide whilst losing forever his pit-black soul."

The jury thought that was the splendidest thing that they ever heard and they clapped their hands together in testimony of it, leastways those of them that warn't back to sleep again or throwing up or drifting off to attend to the biling disturbance in their bellies, grabbing their guts and holding up two fingers to ask Bill's permission.

My lawyer he stuffed a plug of chaw in his jaws and says I should ought to plead guilty. I says I warn't guilty a nothing and I ain't saying I was. "The defender says he's guilty, Judge," Pegleg says, and Yaller Whiskers rapped the hammer down on the tree trunk, and says there ain't nothin' for it, I got to be hanged till I'm completely mortified, the trial was done and over.

They swarmed over me again. I thought I was about to join that rube in the tree and my heart was in my throat, but they fetched me along to Zeb's shack and throwed me in it. The chinless mule-toothed prospector who struck the gold fleck the day before was posted at the door with an old shotgun, looking like he'd only made it partways into the new day and warn't inclined to go no further. His moustaches hung like sad stringy curtains around his big front teeth.

The old whisky shack stunk more'n it commonly done, not only of sick and privies and stale whisky like always, but also from a couple of carcasses laying about and starting to go off. They'd stay there till somebody decided they wanted the shack for theirselves, and then they'd get throwed in the woods for the wolves to supper on. Which was where I was headed. Wolf vittles. My feelings was sunk low and such thoughts warn't of a nature to raise them up again.

CHAPTER XX

Mule teeth was soon tipping back in a chair, taking a snooze, the shotgun leaning against the wall, and I judged I could walk out past him and just keep on going. He half opened one bloodshot eye under his floppy hat brim and seen me calculating. "I know what you're thinkin'," he drawls from under his two monster teeth. "I don't sejest you try it. I don't give a keer, one way or t'other, and I ain't goin' to stop you, but they's a posse a hongry bounty hunters out thar jest a-waitin' for sumthin live to shoot at." He raised the other eyelid halfway up and struggled slow to his feet like his bones was made a lead. "C'mere. Look at behind all them wagons and trees. See 'em?" I seen them. All watching my way. "I don't reckon you done what they say you done, and I'm nation sorry for you, but there ain't nothin' I kin do, nor not you nuther."

"It warn't me who killed Zeb. It was that

one-eyed persecuter and his pals who done it."

"I know it," he says, sinking dozily back into the chair. He slurped noisily and says he judged the Cap'n was setting to take over here, him and the judge together, and my hanging was their ticket for that, so it didn't matter whether I done nothing crinimal or not. Mule Teeth was right. The rule a law warn't about such matters. Eyepatch and his pals was rich now after robbing Zeb, and they was calculating how to use the law to get richer. Mule Teeth says that like enough they was the ones who robbed all my goods, too, because there warn't nothing left down by the crick except the tepee poles.

Mule Teeth called Eyepatch Cap'n on account of that's what he was in the Confedderal army in the recent troubles. He lost his eye at the Battle of Shiloh, and he come out west after that to help the Rebs cut a trail to California through the New Mexico Territory to where the gold was. Leastways, that's what Mule Teeth says that Eyepatch says. Me and Tom was scouting down there for the Rebs back then, so, until we got lost and ended up scouting for the Union instead, us and Eyepatch was maybe traveling together. But though I seen plenty one-eyed bandits like old Ben Rogers, I ain't got no recollection of any long-haired one-eyed captains. Lying come easy to Eyepatch. Most probably he was a plain deserter, living off of robbing and killing like other ordinary runaway soldiers.

When Mule Teeth warn't drowsing under his hat, him and me talked away the morning. It was my last one and it seemed as how there must probably be liver things to do with it, even penned up in a smelly old shack, but I couldn't think of them. It was just only a morning like any other morning and it slipped by like they all done.

The bounty hunters was still outside, watching the open door, hoping I'd make a run for it, so I held my nose and stayed back in the shadows in case them fellows' fingers got itchy. I could a broke out and got it over with, dying the way Dan Harper died, but I warn't brave enough. Maybe, if Tongo was out there waiting for me, I might a took a chance. Nobody mentioned a wild horse down where the tepee was, so maybe he was with Eeteh or maybe he run away to live wild again, but I was scared for him, and for Eeteh, too.

Mule Teeth told me about having to pay extra for prostytutes on account of his teeth, and asked me what it was like to kiss a woman because ain't none a them ever allowed him to do that. I says I ain't done much kissing neither, because there warn't nothing romantic about most a the women I knowed, except for one maybe, and my Crow wife she didn't have no nose and was uncomfortable about a body getting anywheres close to the area.

"You had a squaw?"

"For a while, till she cussed me out one day and walked out a the tepee and never come back."

"You lived with injuns? That's innaresting," he drawls and slurps again. "They say a squaw's business runs sidewise 'stead of fore'n aft. Is that how you found it?"

"No, just ordinary," I says. I was worried to know more about Eeteh and Tongo, but this didn't seem the right way to get at it. "Old Man Coyote, though, had a wife with one that was like the mouth of a coiled-up snake that swallowed you down in like a whirlpool."

"That must of been fun. But who was Old Man Coyote?"

"They have stories about him. A friend told me."

"Injun friend?"

"Fellow who used to help the owner of this shack trade with the tribes."

"The one you murdered. Or they say you did."

Out a-front the shack, men was hacking away at the foot of the hanging tree, making the dead country jake jiggle and dance on his rope like a puppet till his straw hat fell off. Mule Teeth says they was chopping the tree down to knock up a gallows there. "The persecuter and the judge reckon it ain't possible to sivilize a place without you got a proper insterment to hang a body. The coffin-maker's busy a-buildin' it, so you still got a little time. Wisht I could find somethin' to help you pass it better, but we pretty much drunk the camp dry last night, and I'm anyways dead sick from it and ain't got no stake left to buy nothin'. Don't even have a dang chaw to share."

I asked him what he done with the gold fleck the yaller-whiskered land surveyor helped him find. "I give it back to him," he says. Yaller Whiskers was setting up a table in the street and there was already a line of emigrant prospectors waiting to buy one of his hand-drawed survey maps. "The judge only borry'd it to me to set out his bonyfydies, as he called 'em, so's he'd fetch a fair price for his maps." Yaller Whiskers was drawing pictures fast as he could, but newcomers was rolling in by the minute, he couldn't keep up. He was finally only putting a few marks down on each page, and yelling cusswords whenever a body complained.

Meantimes, the tree with the rube still hanging in it got cut down and dumped upstream in the Gulch where all the other dead trees was. The coffin-maker had already built sections of the new gallows, and now he set to hammering it all up together where the tree had stood. A lantern-jawed picture-taker in a billed cap and black frock coat was setting up his camera in front of it.

The bran-new street out a-front was so packed with emigrants, wagons, horses and oxen, you couldn't hardly move. The men was all excited and grinning ear to ear about the chance of watching a body get stringed up. Fingers was pointed at me in Zeb's shack. They didn't know who I was nor what I was s'posed to be hanged for, but that warn't no matter. Eyepatch was right: the gallows was going to make the Gulch more sivilized-looking.

A preacher come to see me about my soul, and how I could save it by fessing up to murdering old Zeb even if I ain't done it. It was that chubby land surveyor-banker-dentist-judge Yaller Whiskers again, only now he was a preacher. There warn't nothing that fellow couldn't do if he set his mind to it. He was wearing the hanged man's floppy straw hat which was the same color as his bushy whiskers. With his dusty clothes, he made a body think of a small round haystack with eyes. He wanted us to pray together to some of the same dead people the Widow Douglas and her sister Miss Watson was always carrying on with, and see if we couldn't strike a deal with the Lord about my soul before I danced the hempen jig, as he called it, and flew off to Providence, or some place even more unpleasanter.

"Praying ain't never worked for me, Reverend," I says, "and I ain't got no soul to barter with. Maybe I used to have one, but if I did, it got drownded on the Big River, nor else it was stole by a couple a royal bamboozlers like yourself who didn't have none a their own."

The preacher he got a little hot under the collar then like he done when he was a judge and says he won't be talked at so disrespectable. He says he should a sentenced me to a hundred lashes besides only getting hanged — he would a gratefully laid on the lashes himself, before, during or after the hanging. He was going to go right now and fetch his horsewhip to the ceremonials, in case he got a chance to use it, and, given my rascally nature, he allowed he surely would.

The more Yaller Whiskers carried on, the madder he got. He remembered me of old Pap when he went to ripping and cussing like all fury, swearing to cowhide me directly as he got sober, and that made me smile, which made Yaller Whiskers so sore, he whiffed his pudgy fists around a-front my face till his cheeks was red and he throwed the rube's straw hat at me and kicked at my knees and yelled, "What're you laughin' at, you goddam sneak-thief injun-lover?"

Then he ca'med down and picked up the straw and set it back on, saying he was sorry, and he went back to being a preacher again. Sin always got him riled up like that, he says, he just didn't have no tolerance for it. But he had to learn himself more Christian forbaring, it went with being a man a the cloth, he says, though he probably didn't know no more'n I done what cloth he was talking about.

It was nigh noon. Yaller Whiskers and Mule Teeth tied my hands behind my back and took me by the elbows and walked me out to the gallows, tromping through the gumbo and the thickening crowds. All the busy hammering and sawing and hollering stopped when we stepped out a the shack, and people begun running towards the gallows, pushing and a-shoving to get the upfrontest places. I warn't customed to being much noticed of a rule, but they was all gaping at me and didn't want to look at nothing else. Some was laughing or shouting out cusswords, but most was only staring with their eyes wide open like they was trying to eat me with their eyes.

That army drummer was at it again, banging out a march, and we was stepping along to it, the crowds opening up as we come on them. Eyepatch was a-waiting for us by the gallows in his black shirt, his black bandanna knotted round his head, his gold teeth and earrings and tin star glinting in the midday sun. He looked like he might a washed his hair for the grand occasion, nor else he only greased it. His pals Pegleg and Bill was standing longside him, Bill with a nasty three-tooth sneer on his face.

The lanky coffin-maker in the tall black hat was there, looking monstrous proud of what he'd made. One of his empty body boxes was propped up against the contraption, and the picture-taker was aiming his camera at it. So I warn't going to be throwed into the Gulch, after all. I was going to be a famous murderer and bandit with white eyes and a stretched neck, laying in a pine box. Maybe they'd even get to see me back in St. Petersburg.

The preacher he says he'll ask for mercy because of middle-gating circumstances, if he could think of any. Though I knowed it wouldn't make no matter, I hoped Mule Teeth might furnish some. "We fetched you the prisoner, Cap'n," Mule Teeth says, and when Eyepatch asks him if I repented of my vilence whilst he was guarding me, Mule Teeth says I did not. "Fact is, Cap'n, he bragged about it, goddamming everybody and you in partickler. He's a liar and a traiter and he pals around with hoss-tile hucksters. Got a squaw with a business that sucks a body in like quicksand." That done it. Like my mean old Pap used to say, it's the ones who talk lazy and drawly you got to watch out for. Eyepatch nodded. It was all up for me.

It was earless Pegleg who took over then and led me up the steps. The drummer had stopped his pounding and was commencing a drumroll. The drumroll was scary, but warn't near so as the wooden peg knocking loud and hollow up the stairs ahead a me. Whilst climbing them, I recollected that crazy Indian in Minnysota who Tom said dropped his pants and wagged his naked behind at all the gawkers. I wished I could do something owdacious like that, but I was too scared and downhearted. I didn't never want to die, and now that it was happening I didn't want it more'n ever.

There was a powerful lot of steps to climb. The picture-taker in the long frock coat had moved his camera on its long skinny legs and was watching me through it. That chap with the fiddle was twanging away sorrowfully and whining through his nose something about jumping off into the other world. I was thinking about Ne Tongo, who won't understand what happened to me or where I went off to. How do you explain that to a horse?

From up on the platform I could see all the tents and lean-tos, the muddy streets, the half-built shanties and storefronts, the long line of incoming wagons stretching back into the hills. Many of the new-comers was hopping out a their wagons and running towards us with big grins on their faces. Others was galloping in on horses. They didn't know what was happening, but they didn't want to miss nothing.

Pegleg stood me onto the trapdoor and fitted the scratchy rope round my neck. "Kin I have the next dance?" he asks with a mean grin. I warn't able to grin back. I was feeling desperately lonely and wished there was somebody to hold my hand. But I was all alone. Did you ever notice, Eeteh says to me one day, how making a world always begins with loneliness? The Great Spirits could invent all the suns and moons and rivers and forests they wanted, but it warn't never enough. They was still lonely. There warn't nobody to talk to and nothing was happening. So, they had to make us loafers to kill so's to liven up the passing days.

One of the arriving emigrants was galloping in on a high white horse with a passel a friends behind him. He was fitted out in bleached doeskin and a white hat, with white kid gloves and a red bandanna tied round his throat, gleaming silver spurs on his shiny boots. He had big bushy moustaches ear to ear and long curly hair, twinkling eyes. Puffing on a fat seegar. Coming for a laugh. "HANG HIM QUICK!" Eyepatch shouted. Pegleg drawed his pistol with one hand and reached for the lever with t'other and I dropped. My throat got snagged and then there was a shot and I kept on dropping, landing hard on the ground under the gallows. Then more shots, and Pegleg come falling through the trapdoor and landed on top of me. That seegar-smoker must a shot the rope!

Only one man I knowed could do that. He was grinning down at me from his white horse. "Hey, Huck," he says, flicking some ash off his seegar. It was Tom Sawyer! His own self!

Chapter XXI

Tom Sawyer always did know how to throw on the style. Except for his ear-to-ear moustaches and fancy white duds, he warn't changed a whit. Eyepatch and Bill broke off on a run, and Tom flung out a rope straight off of his horse and lassoed both of them with one throw and hauled them in. Everybody cheered and howled and clapped their hands like they meant it. The two pock-faced robbers was heeling it out through the crowds with the plump yaller-whiskered judge, but Tom hollered out "GRAB THEM DESPERADOS!" and the emigrant miners snaggled them and rassled them to the mud and give them a few licks just for fun. Then they fetched them up to the gallows, and Tom's pals tied them up.

"We don't have no bull pit yet to lock them in," Tom says with a sadful look. "If they're guilty, I allow we'll just only have to hang them." Everybody says, "Yay!" They was all pining for a hanging. But Eyepatch warn't of the same opinion, and says so in so many usswords. He pointed out Zeb's shack where they'd held me, and Tom put on his boss's face and give Eyepatch a long look and nodded and posted a guard with a rifle in charge of keeping them all in there. The guard was a big fellow named Bear with thick black brows and a warty nose, and he warn't the sort that a body'd care to argue with.

The ropes was cut off my wrists and I was helped to my feet. I was wobbledy and my throat hurt. My heart was still a-thundering in my ears. But I was standing in a world that still seemed real, or mostly real.

Then Tom jumped onto the gallows platform direct out of his saddle. He told the crowd his name and they all give off a mighty cheer. He pointed down at me, and, in a big voice so's everybody could hear, he says, "There stands afore you the daredevilest rider of the famous Pony Express, one of the greatest heroes of all our country's injun wars, and the best scout and horse wrangler I ever knowed ANYWHERES!" They was whooping at every word he says. "The legendry Huck Finn and me rode together at the battles of Glorieta Pass and Sand Crick, Circleville, Skull Valley and

Skeleton Cave, and HUNDREDS MORE! He saved my life I don't know HOW many times! He was the best pard a body COULD EVER HAVE!" I warn't none too pleased with his stretchers, but I ain't never been so happy as I was to see Tom Sawyer again, so I just grinned and let him blow. I was still his pard. He said so. "He has been holing out here in the Gulch because Sitting Bull HIMSELF is after him! And not for no reason! Huck Finn has took more'n three hundred injun warrior scalps, and five of them was CHIEFS!" These emigrants was new arrived and didn't know nothing, so Tom could say whatever he wanted to. "And that's NO SITTING BULL!" Tom hollers out. Maybe he didn't say "sitting." The miners all roared and hooted and stormed and haw-hawed. It was a first-class show. Nobody could spread himself like Tom Sawyer when it come to unloading a speech in the grand style. "Huck Finn was born modest, so he'll try to say it ain't so, but DON'T YOU BELIEVE HIM! Them thieving scoundrels was trying to lynch a NATIONAL HERO! They don't deserve NO MERCY!"

They cheered Tom and they cheered me, too. He raised up his white hat and waved it at them, winking down at me. He might a been elected king right where he stood, if kings warn't gone out a style. He held the hat up long enough for the picture-taker to get his photograph. His moustaches was the happy sort and made it look like he was always smiling. When his hat was lifted off his head, I seen his long curly hair was sneaking back on top towards the shiny place at the back of his scalp, and that was a sad thing, to think that even Tom Sawyer was a-growing old.

He declared he was sent here by the govment in Washington as a federal overmarshal with a legal jury's diction over the whole Territory. I didn't know what an overmarshal was, but I didn't doubt but what Tom would learn me. "The United States is a-going to take over this Territory to itself and kick out the blastemous cannibal redskins — who ain't even completely HUMAN!" he says. "And from here on, the American army is a-going to protect ALL legal emigrants and miners! WHEREVER you want to go!" They was all cheering like crazy. "I tell you, friends, there ain't going to BE no more injun massacres nor no more mob trials nor lynchings nuther! Everything is going to be LEGAL and on the UP'N UP, accorded to the BOOK! The AMERICAN book! Highwaymen and hoss-tiles and claim-jumpers will be PERSECUTED! Everything's going to be like it OUGHTER be! We're making the first ever perfect nation out here and there ain't no damn injuns going to stand in the way, nor not no kings nor no sentimentery Quaker tomfoolery nor foreign bankers nuther! It's going to be a paradise on earth where everybody's RICH and nobody's trying to take away what's rightfully YOURN! It's the new ELDERAYDO!"

Then Tom set about putting things in order — and people let him do it! They was grateful and done what he said! He ordered Pegleg to be laid out in the box meant for me to have his picture took. He pointed to a naked hill a ways off with a pine stand at the foot and says that will be the Gulch's burying place, but that Pegleg warn't good enough for it. He says they should take off the wooden leg afterwards and save it, and handle the body over to Doc Molligan for his scientific purposes. He ordered up new nooses for the scaffold and vittles for the prisoners. He says he's using his own money to pay for them. He announced an election for mayor-govner of the Gulch and himself as a candidate, and everybody yay'd again and elected him on the spot and he says he was honored to serve.

He borrowed the land surveyor's pine table standing there in the middle of the street and set up what he called the first legal claims office. "All previous claims is dull'n void," he says. The miners who'd already staked some claims warn't happy, but Tom asked me who was here before the Rush begun. I pointed them out, and Tom he give them first dibs on their old claims or new ones for free, so they was well pleased. "But only one free claim each, the rest has to be paid for with goods or money, just like everybody else. There's lots of deserving folks has come to the Gulch and more is on the way. Caleb here is a licensed court reporter and official recorder of claims and deeds, and he'll make sure everything's fair and square and that all the right words get used."

Caleb, a scrawny gent hiding his balditude under an orange too-pay, with stringy whiskers on his chin and a Colt revolver on his hip, nodded solemner'n a preacher at a tomb-laying, and set down behind the table alongside of a bespectacled assistant, spreading out his charts and maps, the prospectors squirming and scrouging to get in line. Knives and guns was quickly out, but Tom's other pals took the weapons away, breaking arms when they had to.

I begun to breathe again, and I told Tom about the old whisky-maker who'd been murdered by Eyepatch and his gang and who was now laying dead up in the shack. Tom says he'll be the first registered resident of the new graveyard, and he ordered up a proper funeral for that very afternoon, with Caleb's goggled assistant Wyndell doing the preaching, that being one of his trades on the side. There was objections from some of the emigrants who'd got deathly sick on Zeb's vegilanty brew and was still not getting over it, but those that was here before all agreed that old Zeb was a genius legend and rightly deserved the honor, never mind he also near killed them all. They missed him and his mother, they says, more'n their own mothers, who they didn't even hardly remember, and whose hearts warn't never so pure.

Tom bought some corn-bread and grilled wild pig sausages at a food stall in the main street. People cheered him wherever they seen him, and he tipped his white hat at them. Sometimes he grinned, but he tried not to. I et one a the sausages he bought and Tom et the rest. "You don't weigh no more'n you done in your Pony days," he says. He asked me who it was discovered the gold here that the colonel wrote up about, so I told him some of what had happened and took him to see Deadwood.

With the trees cleared away, Deadwood's old shack seemed closer into the middle than it was before. New streets was winding every which way around it, with tents and shanties popping up alongside of them like locoweeds. The streets was jam full of wagons, animals and restless miners, lugging picks and rifles. A blacksmith had set up a forge and smithy. Saw-logs was stacked up in the mud, and loafers was setting on them. The ghost-town scavenger had a sign on his new storefront that says he has pump handles, a pitchfork, gold pans, guns, and used pants for sale. The Gulch was already a town and everybody in it was strangers.

Deadwood was laying in his union suit on his old straw tick. The union suit looked like something his mother might a wore long ago. He'd took off his splints and slings before things had got healed, and I was sorry to see it. His arms and legs now angled ever which way. The shack was mighty fragrant, which was probably why nobody warn't bothring him. When Tom seen his awful injuries, he got madder'n the devil. "Who DONE this to you, old man?" he barked, his dander up. "I'll see personal he's HUNG for it!" The old prospector lifted his working arm and pointed a feeble finger at me.

"Me and a friend found him in a ravine after he'd took his hiding," I says. "He was ruined with drink and he thought we was busting his bones stead of setting them. Them two pock-faced robbers you got penned up in the old whisky shack is who done it to him."

"He stole the watch them rileroad bosses give me," Deadwood whimpered faintly out the side of his crooked jaw, his bruised cross-eyes trying to find Tom. Without no teeth, nothing come out clear. "I don't know now what's a-goin' to happen NEXT!" He sounded like he was fixing to cry.

"He was showing off a fob watch all night from some truck them two robbers stole that he found in a cave," I says, "and they wanted to know where the rest a their loot was. The old fellow ain't got no real memories left, so he didn't even know what they was talking about. They might a killed him right out, but probably they was having too much fun beating on him."

"Robbers, eh?" says Tom. He was grinning in an ornery sort of way. He settled a seegar butt in under his moustaches and went over and made Caleb into a judge. Then he turned the claims table into a courtroom bench so's Caleb don't even have to get up out a his chair. The photographer come over and took his picture.

Tom set the drummer in his black derby to rattling away, and ordered the two robbers be dragged out of Zeb's shack. They seen straight off what was about to happen, but their ankles was roped together and when they tried to run, they could only hop and fall down. All the men in the street was laughing at the sight and hollering out friendly cusswords, and then tripping them up so's they'd fall again.

As the crowds gathered, Tom stubbed out his seegar, put on a pair a wire-frame spectacles, set his hat straight over his scowl, and declared that the two prisoners was notorious murderers, highwaymen, skulduggerers, army deserters, blastemers and perverts. He says he has been tracking them for months and has been appointed by the American Congress to bring them directly to justice.

"We ain't perverts," one of them says, and the other says, "We ain't none a them other things nuther."

Tom peered over his eye-glasses and laid into them then with slathers of insofarases and wherefores, and though they couldn't cipher out whatever he was talking about, they knowed it was going against them. They was both badly marked up, the sad stories of their lives carved into their hides like gravestone writing, scars drawing half-hid pictures of past crimes in their black beards. You couldn't hardly tell them apart in their raggedy shirts and black waistcoats, except one of them had a gray ponytail hanging down to his bony shoulders, whilst t'other's neck was sunburnt and bare.

Tom named all the scores a people they robbed and killed, including, with a sober wink at me, his Aunt Sally Phelps. I ain't heard that and it made me terrible sadful to learn it. He swore in one of his gang members named Oren as a maternial witness to a famous Oregon Trail robbery and murder near Julesburg, which was one of the wickedest places we had to ride through when we was working for the Pony. Tom described it to a T. Oren hooked his thumbs in the straps of his bib overalls and called the killings that he seen "the terrible Devil's Dive Massacree," and says he lost his dear old pap on that dreadful occasion. "The old man was riding shotgun for the stagecoach and he throwed up his arms in surrender, but got croolly blowed away by them wicked buggers. That there," Oren says, pointing, "was his fob watch."

"Well, I guess we don't need to wait for justice no longer," Tom says.

"Wait! I ain't done nothin'!" Ponytail yelped.

"Of course," says Tom, stroking his jaw and looking at one of them, then t'other, "we can't be sure which one of them done the actul killing."

"I never done it! HE done it ALL!" screamed Ponytail, pointing at his partner.

"What are you saying, you snivelin' low-down back-stabber?" says t'other one. "We warn't even there!"

"I seen him! I SEEN HIM!" screamed Ponytail, his pointing finger all quivery. "Look! It's HIM'S got the fob watch! HE murdered 'em all!"

"Consarn it, you traiterous bloodthirsty liar!" yells Redneck. "It was YOU done all the killin'! I says to take pity, fer God's sake, spare them pore innercent people! But you cain't wait t'cut their throats!"

"You lined up all them men and boys and shot 'em like they was bottles on a stump, you mizzerbul hyena!"

"It was YOU done that, you filthy piece a ratmuck! 'Member that lady whose belly you carved open jest to see what her dang innards looked like?"

Wyndell and Oren had already tied the

robbers' legs and elbows together and raised the two of them up on the scaffold platform. Wyndell was laying a prayer on them, but they warn't listening. They was back-to-back, but still screaming at each other over their shoulders, and never stopped even when Tom fitted the ropes round their necks. It warn't my intention to get them hung — that warn't my intention for nobody — but that's what happened. The rope burns on my own throat was tingling and I could feel again that fall into nothing, when I turned my back and heard the robbers drop. Somebody grunted. Might a been the robbers theirselves.

Chapter XXII

When Tom was gone east, there warn't no way to tell one day from t'other. They just went a-slipping along like drift logs on the Big River, and near as dark. But now Tom was back, and the day was alive again, lit up and frisky. In less'n one of them, he rescued a pard from a lynching, showed off his shooting and lasso tricks, got himself elected mayor-govner of Deadwood Gulch, thought up a bunch a new laws, captured gangs a thieves and murderers, tried and hung some robbers, organized a funeral in a bran-new burying ground that he conjured himself, and let fly an amazing yellocution for an old whisky-maker he never even knowed.

And he warn't done. Once Tom Sawyer set off adventuring, a body couldn't hold him back. Whilst we was still lowering old Zeb into the ground — Zeb only had one gold tooth and, before they closed his box, I seen he didn't have that one no more nuther

— Tom asked me what happened to the traps and scrotum bag full a money stole last night from the old fellow? I says that probably his murderers has it all, and Tom says, "If so, they ain't parading it. Le's go find where he got killed while there's still light out!"

Tom was in a sweat to do that right when he was still thinking about it, he couldn't rest till his doing catched up to his thinking, so he signaled Wyndell to hurry up his amens and get to throwing in the dirt — "He ain't called Wyndy for nothing," he says — and next thing we was on our way. Tom decided to take along one of the murderers to show us what they done with their plunder. He chose Bill because he judged he'd crack quickest once he was away from the others, and with his shooting hand ruined he warn't likely to cause no trouble. Tom and Bear tied Bill's hands behind him, set him on an old mule, and slung a rope round his scrawny neck, which Tom says was to remember him of the meaning of life. Tom clumb up on his big white stallion Storm, who he says he named Spirit a the Storm after a famous pirate ship he once read about. He give me a skittery young pony the same style of our Express ponies, and the three of us rode the back trail out from the camp like Zeb done the night before.

After setting the saddle a while, I growed customed to it, but it warn't comfortable. I was missing Tongo badly and worrying about him, and Eeteh, too. I didn't know if they was alive nor dead. Them two was what I had like adventures, and I wanted to brag to Tom about them and go with him to look for them and rescue them if they was in trouble, but after what he said up on the gallows, I was afraid he might be disappointed with me and go away again. I was ever so happy he was back, I didn't want nothing to spoil it, so I didn't say nothing, not yet.

As we was moving slowly along, watching for what we could see, I says to Tom I was nation sorry to hear about his Aunt Sally.

"What's wrong with her?"

"You know, them two robbers that KILLED her!"

Tom laughed. "Aunt Sally's still kicking, Huck. She's got almighty old and cranky and she can't remember five minutes ago, but she can still haul off and give a body a rememberable larruping."

"But the robbery, the massacre — !"

"Aw, Huck, there warn't no such. We made it all up. I thought you seen that. I set the whole yarn down in Julesburg just so's you'd have a laugh. Ain't you got no sense a humor?" He bit off the end of a fresh seegar, and leaned away from Bill to spit it out. "Maybe we can round up forty of these scoundrels and get them all to fessing up to one awful crime or nother like them robbers done and set a new one-day hanging record," he says with a grin, lighting up his seegar. I was also grinning, but I didn't know why.

I reckoned the murderers had been waiting for the old distiller and begun following him as soon as he crumb out a the ravine, but they might of chased along behind him for a time till he got further alone. That would of give Zeb time to do something with the money and goods he was carrying after he heard the robbers back of him, so I kept my eyes peeled for hiding places. Bill had his head down and warn't giving no sign. When Tom poked him with his rifle barrel and asked him what they done with all their booty, he cussed and says there warn't none.

"Must of been the Cap'n who murdered the old fellow," Tom says to me, but loud enough for Bill to hear. "He's the one's got money in his pockets."

"He's the one," says Bill. "But he ain't got nothin' in his pockets except holes to push his fingers through to claw his itches with."

We passed an old oak with a bole hole in it. On a hunch, I stuck my fist in, hoping only there warn't no rattlers coiled up inside, and I fetched out some pocket watches and a string a black flea-bit scalps, some with dried-up ears on them. "Well, at least we ain't rode out here for nothing," Tom says with a laugh, pocketing the watches and settling the scalps over his saddle. Bill didn't look happy at what he seen. "You judge these was the whisky-maker's?"

"He was packing along any goods he could barter with. I reckonize them scalps."

I asked him where was Pegleg getting buried, and Tom says he ain't. He says the doctor desecks them. "I think Molly also eats them, the mushier parts anyhow, like their brains, livers, and oysters. The old sawbones calls it going to market." I says I hope I don't never need his close attention. Tom says Doc first went west with some settlers who got caught up a mountain in a long winter snowstorm and was obleeged to eat each other, nor else starve to death, and he developed an appetite for it. But he's a good doctor. He was dislicensed as a doctor for doing unlegal favors for the working girls.

We come on a roughed-up patch on top of a ravine with hoof marks tromping on other hoof marks in the mud. "Probably happened here," I says, and Tom set his see-gar in his jaws and clumb down off of Storm.

A chill breeze struck up and the sun sneaked behind a cloud and I felt something cold and wet on my neck like getting licked by a ghost. But not Zeb's ghost. Abaddon's. How the dog sometimes greeted me when I give him a hug. I seen again his slit throat and horrible smile, and it give me the shakes so bad I had to slide down off of the pony before I fell off.

We could see some a Zeb's goods scattered about in the ravine below, so we hobbled Bill's mule and crawled down to look around. It was mostly just Zeb's old rags and spilled vittles, but I did come on his yist-mash bucket. It was still half-full of muck, with maybe enough live yist left in the stillage to seed a new batch, so I hoisted it up and toted it along. I says it was Zeb's mother, and Tom says, well then, we can charge them with mattresside. "We can bile them in oil, if we got any. That's what the books say."

Tom raired his nose and sniffed. "I smell something else," he says, and he crawled deeper down in the ravine. "And here it is!" he shouted from the bottom.

It was already turning dark down there, but when I crept closer I seen it: the carcass of Zeb's old packhorse with Tom's fist up its backside. "Hah! We hit a seam, Huck!" He pulled his arm out and held up what he found in there: Eeteh's soft leather money pouch, even fatter'n when Eeteh give it to me! "Filthy LOO-ker," Tom howls with a moustachioed grin, his seegar bobbing.

"How'd you ever think to poke around in there?"

"Well, I asked myself what I'D do if I was being chased by robbers and wanted to hide my goods. I s'posed they'd take my horse and everything else, except maybe this old rackabones, and there warn't many other places I could hide nothing on or in him." There was a small crick down there, and Tom scrouched down and washed the bag and his arm off in it. "You'd have to be crazy to dig for treasure up a packhorse's arsehole," he says, and winked up at me again. He says he don't think Sarah Sod ever thought of that one.

When we crawled back on top, we seen that Bill's mule had somehow kicked free of his hobbles and was meandering sluggishly on down the trail into the dimness. Bill, still bound, was pushing the mule on with desperate grunts and humpings. I felt ha'nted again by Abaddon and seemed to hear him snarling like he done before he took a chaw on a body's leg. Tom was counting through the money in Eeteh's pouch as if he didn't care no more about Bill. Maybe he was letting him go free. No, he warn't. Without really looking at him, Tom turned and shot him, then swung up on his big white horse and begun to head back to the camp.

"Wait!" I says. Bill was a-laying still and lonely on the trail, the loop of rope loose round his neck, his arms tied behind his back. Abaddon's ghost had stopped snarling, though my neck rope burns was itching again. "Don't you want to see if he's dead or not?"

"He's dead."

"But why'd you have to do that?"

"DIDN'T have to. But he was stealing our mule. Better'n taking him back and hanging him for it, ain't it?" Tom was watching me, a sad smile on his face. "He's a hard case, Huck. He tried to lynch you. And he'd do it again if we give him half a chance. We ain't doing that."

"But you said everything was going to be LEGAL now and on the UP'N UP!"

"And so it is and will be, Huck. Now, if you want to help, you can go get that mule. We'll lead him back where we borrowed it."

The mule was wandering on down the twilit trail, but I give a pull on his bridle and he swung back to go our way without no fuss. Bill was facedown with his hands tied behind him and a hole in the back of his head. I picked him up and slung him over the mule's back. Tom don't say not to. He only says to untie him.

"Let me tell you a story, Huck," Tom says on the way back to the camp. "There was an injun tribe in a mining town down in the southwest where I was working like a lawyer. The injuns warn't doing nothing, except just being ugly to look at. They didn't belong. So a few local business fellows hired up a mob of Mexicans to go with them to the injun camp and kill them all. It was a dreadful slaughter, mostly of women and little boys and girls. You may a read about it. They clove their heads open with machetes, emptied out their bellies, shot all their animals, burnt their tepees, stole their julery, and peeled off scalps to sell in the market. Baby scalps was specially profitable. The businessmen come home to the mining town, bragging about the killing they done and showing off their scalps. They got arrested and charged with organizing the massacre, so's, you know, everything'd be on the up'n up." Tom's seegar had went out, so he lit it up again. "I got hired as their lawyer and it took some smarts, but I got them all off scot-free."

"But warn't they guilty?"

"Of COURSE they was guilty, Huck. You ain't paying ATTENTION! I'm telling you about the UP'N UP. The law is amazing. Like magic. I was famous for what I done. They made me a judge after, and one a them business fellows he become a govner or some such crinimal." He seen me shaking my head, and he shook his and says, "Trouble is, Huck, you never growed up. You're still living in some dream of a world that don't exist."

Jaws was dropping and everybody was staring when Tom rode back into the camp with all them scalps dangling from his saddle. When people asked, Tom didn't say nothing, he just pointed at me. He walked Storm over towards the picture-taker, smiling steady, and waited for him to get his camera ready and take his photograph.

We left Bill and the mule off with Bear and, on the way down towards where my lodge was, we stopped at Deadwood's shack to give him back the fob watch. Deadwood set to crying, he was so happy.

"That old slant-jawed sourdough looks part injun to me, Huck," Tom says as we continued on down to the crick, and I says, "We're all mixed breeds, ain't we, one kind or nuther."

Tom raired his head and scowled down at me in an unpard-like way. "I ain't," he says.

Whilst we was gone, Tom's pals had pitched up a large army tent for us where my lodge-poles'd stood. It was big as a horse shed. There were cots and blankets in it and mirrors and washstands and even a bottle a prime saloon whisky from the States setting on a table like a little soldier at attention. "It's very grand," I says, and Tom he shrugged and says he favored a hotel better. I favored my tepee better and was lonely for it, but I didn't say so. It wouldn't a fit Tom's style.

Outside, there was a fire snapping away with an antelope spitted over it. Hog nuts, prairie turnips and wild onions was slow-roasting in the coals. Tom fetched the whisky along, took a long pull, and handled me the bottle. It warn't the equal of Zeb's home brew, but on a day that seemed'd never end, it was most welcome. Bill laying there on the trail with a hole in his head and Tom's story about the up'n up was still festering up my thoughts, but the whisky eased them away. The sting of the rope burns, too. The birds was doing their day's-end bragging and, far off, a body could hear coyotes howling in their soft sadful way. It was nigh as peaceful as rafting down the Big River. I felt like Deadwood felt — like I'd got my fob watch back.

Down by the shore, near some smaller canvas tents that Tom's pals was living in, there was a couple of fellows working a big sluce box to pan for gold. When Tom went down to talk to them, I judged he was aiming to chase them off, but he offered them a swig from the bottle and waved me to come on down. "Show him what you got there, Peewee," he says. "See them specks there in the drag?" With the night settling in, it was hard to see nothing at all, but the specks did let off a peculiar spark. "Them's colors. Plasser gold. Might be the richest gravels in the crick. You may be a millionaire, Huck."

"I'm sorry to hear it," I says. I grinned back when they all laughed, but it warn't a joke. Them gold specks was telling me that the day's good luck might be fixing to change back again.

CHAPTER XXIII

That night, me and Tom laid in our cots smoking and sipping bottle whisky by lamplight and gabbling for hours. We talked about when we was boys on the Big River and all the mischief we done, about the ha'nted house and the graveyard and the awful things we seen there, about our adventures when we run away to ride for the Pony, then everything we done since. It was just like old times and we was both feeling mighty happy. "This is great," Tom says. "Everything's going to be just like before, Hucky! I promise!"

Tom told me about how St. Petersburg was emptied out now, leaving only the losers behind. "Ain't nothing happening there," he says. "The place is dead." I says that sounds perfect, and told him about the lonely cattle trails I rode after he was gone and about the wagon trains and the hellion and the bullwhacker. Tom roared with laughter and says, "I'd of liked to've had THAT gal working for ME!"

Tom wanted to know everything about this place he was now mayor-govner of, and I told him what all I could think of, but there warn't much left that hadn't lost its trueness. Most people in the Gulch had only just got here a day or two before, and more wagons was rolling in every minute, erasing everything that used to be. But Tom wanted to hear it all: about old Zeb, the pioneer miners and the Lakota tribes, about Deadwood, General Hard Ass, the yaller rock. "Warn't worth shucks," I says. "Felt more like a cork ball than a stone."

"Blossom rock, Huck. They call them floaters because you throw them in the water and that's what they do. Sure-'nough sign a gold ore." Tom always knowed things I never heard of. Eeteh had a story about Coyote throwing a rock into the water and saying if it didn't sink, everybody'd live forever. Too bad Coyote didn't know about floaters, he could a saved the whole world. "I bet when the colonel come and took the rock from the old cross-eyed sourdough, the first thing he done was heft it."

"That's right. He done that."

"Where there's a floater, there's a seam. Ever hear of somebody finding one?"

"People's scratching about for something like that, but I never seen it nor went looking. I s'pose a seam's something like a stitch in the ground?"

"Well, you could say so. Though sometimes it's more like a stitch in the side."

"I know what you mean. That's what all these emigrants piling in has been like for me." I told him about finding Eyepatch and his two pals in my tent that first morning and how I chased them out with a story about a brother who died in there from the pox. I says I was trying to think up the sort of lies Tom Sawyer might a told. Tom laughed and says I ain't never been a slouch at stretchers myself. The Cap'n was one a the low-downest bad men he ever struck, he says, as mean and ornery as they come, but what he had was STYLE. "It's there or it ain't, Huck, you can't grow it." He says he made him think of river pirates back home, though he couldn't name none who actuly had an eye patch, so maybe he was only thinking about pirates he'd read about from books.

"You recollect how little Tommy Barnes come to your robber gang meeting dressed up like a pirate?" I says. "He had a wire ring in his nose, a birchwood sword, and a paper hat with a skull and crossbones inked on it!"

Tom snorted. "But then the cry-baby wouldn't prick his dern finger for a blood oath!"

"Ben Rogers said he should oughta walk the plank for that!"

We both laughed, thinking about little Tommy Barnes. Tom drunk from the bottle and passed it across to me. There were wrinkles round his eyes now, and sometimes a kind of sadfulness crept in, even when he was laughing. "Well, Tommy Barnes ain't no more, Huck. He enlisted into the Union army to get the bonus they was offering, then deserted and volunteered at another recruiting station with a different name for another bonus. He come home to St. Petersburg bragging about that, picking up girls by throwing his extra money round. They pretty soon cleaned him out, though, so he tried to enlist for a third time somewheres else and got caught. They accused him as a deserter and a bounty jumper and shot him with a firing squad." What I seen in my head was half a dozen leather-headed bullies with field rifles aimed at a little cry-baby in a paper pirate hat who still peed his pants. I felt the jolt of it when they fired and says I was dreadful sorry to hear it and passed the bottle back.

Tom he only laughed again and says that Tommy Barnes was a hero for half the town who thought Yanks and Rebs should both go to hell. He took a long drink from the bottle, and by and by he says, "My old pal Joe Harper, though, he was a genuine hero. The Shucker of Pea Ridge, they called him back in St. Petersburg after he shot a general up there. They made him a corpral major and loadened him down with medals, and then he got killed on Graveyard Road in Vicksburg, leading a ladder assault on a stockade. I allowed all them medals made him slow afoot. I was there when they fetched his body back up the river by steamboat. They raised money in town to make a statue of him. I give them four bits."

I says that I met up with a young soldier out here with Joe's family name, and he's dead, too. All Tom had to say about that was that, if he was dead, he didn't care to know him, and he handled me the bottle and relit his seegar.

Joe Harper was the boy me and Tom run away with to Jackson's Island to live the pirate life, and we thought back on that a while. Tom says he still had some cutlesses and a pirate flag that he borrowed from a museum, thinking he might give up the West some day and go to sea like a pirate, and says maybe we could do that together. I says great, let's go. Jackson's Island was where I learnt both him and Joe to smoke. It made them dog-sick, and that give me a laugh. But I showed them other things, too. They didn't know nothing about living in the rough, just like I didn't know nothing about school and church and all them sivilizing concerns. I done most a the work, but it warn't LIKE work. I was Finn the Red-Handed, and I ain't never been happier. Joe and Tom they was running away from home, but I didn't have no home to run from and none to go back to. I was at home right there on Jackson's Island. They was looking for buried treasure. For me, the treasure was out a-front of our faces, plain as sun and water. I took a swallow a Tom's whisky in memory of it and of old Joe Harper. And of Dan Harper, too.

Our stories was all mostly sorrowful ones about old pals dying and I didn't know if I should tell him about Ben Rogers getting his skull clove in for chasing after a little Cherokee girl. But I did, and Tom he says, "Good for old Ben. Way a chap OUGHT to go, not in some stinking war. I hope he done the little heathen's privates some serious damage before they massacred him, so's he never died in vain." I was going to say what we was doing in the Cherokee Nation in the first place, and about how famous the Missouri Kid's bandit gang was because I promised Ben I would, but Tom blowed a lungful a seegar smoke up at the tent roof and says, "Ever smoke opyum, Huck?"

"I don't know. Maybe. I had a Chinese lady friend who give me something for my pipe that was mighty relaxing."

"That was probably it. I mostly only lay with white women as a rule, but one night in Tucson I ain't got no choice. Half the girls was sick, the other half was already bought and bouncing, and all that was left in the crib was a scrawny old Chinese granny, who was maybe a hundred years old. She drugged me with opyum and sent me down what she says was eight folding paths to heck-stasy. The opyum left a body feeling dead with its spirit floating over it. I was scared, not having no control over whatever was happening next, and sometimes what she done hurt like blazes, but in the end it was most amazing. I ain't even reached the fourth folding, when I'm geysering like old Yallerstone. She says she learnt the trick from Confusion. Was it like that for you?"

"No, Nookie was more interested in giving me baths." Even then, laying there in Tom's tent, I could feel her spidery hands on me. "She spent a considerable time at it and when I asked her what she was doing, she says she was muddytating."

"Muddytating on what?"

"On my backside, mainly."

"Hah! Is that all you done?"

"No, but it's what I most remember." I also seemed to hear her screams when the bad man come back and grabbed her away. I never actully heard them, I was guiding emigrants out on the trail, I only seen the ruins afterwards, but still they ha'nted me, and they was ha'nting me now.

There warn't many girls and women in my life. Mostly, I ducked and run. It's what I told Tom to do, too, but he didn't pay me no heed. He up and married one. I took another swallow and passed the bottle over and asked about her, and he says Becky wanted babies, so he left her back in St. Pete, doing that. "I got things to do in this world so long's I'm in it, Huck. Ain't got time for family. Don't believe in it. Ain't it funny how people think they're creating up something new, when all they're making is more miserable copies of themselves?"

"You just a copy?"

"Hope not, but I can't say. I never knowed

my pa and my ma died young. I allow I mostly made myself. I surely ain't no copy of Aunt Polly!"

We laughed, thinking about his crotchety old Aunt Polly, and the way she'd grab a body by the ear and crack his head with her thimble, though I was also thinking about Eeteh and whatever happened to him when I run the wrong way this morning. Nobody never mentioned him nor the horses all day, so I could hope he was still alive and I might find him again. I so wanted him and Tom to be friends, but Tom still thought about Eeteh's people like he thought about Injun Joe.

"You remember my old girlfriend Amy Lawrence?" Tom says, and sets the bottle down on the ground beside his cot. "Well, I seen something of her again when I was in St. Pete. Amy ended up marrying Johnny Miller, Gracie's brother, and after he'd got his virgin tumble, Johnny left her. Him and her pa both headed west on the same wagon train and ain't neither one never been seen since. Like my pa. Or, well, like you'n me, ain't it? Adventuring's more natural to a fellow than homebodying. Amy's just a ten-dollar whore now, though she don't call herself that. That's a heap a money, I know, but she's worth it. She ain't so pretty like before, but she's got some new angles, and she throws in a home-cooked supper with her and her ma, who sleeps in the same room as Amy when she ain't doing business, and sometimes when she is."

I says about seeing Becky not so long ago over in Wyoming, and he grunts and says she must a run away again. I seen he don't care to talk about her, so I asked him, if he was out here all this time, why he didn't come looking for me, and he says what am I talking about, he ain't STOPPED doing that since he rode back here with his new law diploma in his mochila, but I didn't leave no tracks nowheres. He finally reckoned I must a give up and gone back east, so for a while he stopped looking. Then he got wind of me wrangling horses for some general in Abileen and he went inquiring round, but he couldn't find nobody who'd ever heard a me. "Later, I run into a crazed desert rat in a doggery north a there who was one peculiar fellow. He claimed he knowed God personal and played stud poker with him on Fridays. He recollected somebody called Huckerbelly, but he says that fellow got hanged by the general as a deserter and a godless reprobate, and if he didn't, he shoulda. It cost me three whiskies to find that out, and it warn't exactly the news I was scrounging for."

I says I got in deep trouble with that general and I was still hiding out from him, and Tom says that was plain dumb. "Generals is all ignorant windbags to a man, so full a their stupid selves their eyes get squshed shut to the world around them. Ain't one a them worth a peck a wormy apples, but they all got power. HANGING power. You got to mollycuddle 'em and get all you can off 'em."

"It's too late for mollycuddles. He means to hang me. I'm aiming to run away to Mexico."

"Mexico! Aw, Hucky, don't be such a knucklehead! Them cussed greasers is worse'n injuns! They even SMELL worse! That cactus juice they swill makes them crazier'n wild dogs with their tails on fire! And twixt here'n there ain't nothing but trouble. You can't get there alone!"

"I was hoping you might go with me."

"Me!"

"They got mountains of gold down there. And silver."

"They got gold and silver here. And Mexicans ain't like injuns, Hucky. Injuns is setting round in sad little half-naked gangs, just hankering to get sivilized at the end of a rope or out the barrel of a gun, but Mexicans is a whole damn country. You'd need an army and a bunch a lives."

"Well, you can live with folks without trying to whup them."

"No, you stay here. I'll take care of you. Don't worry about the general. I got a way with generals. I can set out an appeal against him. Won't be easy to win, but the law generly works by who a body knows, and I know everybody. Some day, the calvary'll go after the Mexicans again, and next time it'll get done proper. That's when we'll go there. Mexico will be just another American territory then, leastways till all the gold's gone. But first we got to get shut of all these wretchid hoss-tiles."

"You used to say they was the most wonderfullest, giftedest, hospitablest people in the world."

"Well, I was still reading books. I've growed up since then."

"What's made you hate them so?"

"I DON'T hate them, Huck! I ain't got NOTHING against them. Only, we're building something grand out here, ocean to ocean, and they're in the way. Some day, we'll make statues of them, like they was our own heroes. First, though, we got to kill them all."

"All this killing, it's too many for me," I says. I was getting very sleepy and my eyes was closing. It had been a monstrous long day. I was still worrying, but I'd have to do the rest of it tomorrow.

"Stuff! I don't know what else humans is GOOD for, Huck," Tom says, and yawns. "A hundred years from now, you and me'll both be dead and forgot and people'll still be killing each other. This is OUR killing time."

"If it is, everything just don't seem to mean nothing, that's all."

"Don't nothing MEAN nothing, Huck! How could it? Two and two don't MEAN four, they only IS four, that's all. I worked out a long time ago that, no matter what you do or think, you DIE and it's all wiped away. Your brain rots and your thoughts, wants, loves, hates, simply ain't no more. Others may borrow your thoughts, but you won't know that, you're gone like you never was. What we got is NOW, Huck, and now is forever. Until it ain't. So, you can't worry over nothing except putting off the end a your story as long as you can, and finishing it with a bang. Bekase nuffn doan mattuh, as old Jim would say, no SAH!" Tom stubbed out his seegar butt in the ground beside his cot, blowed the lamp out and sunk back into his pillow. "Y'know, Huck, when I first got me some money, I went back to buy old Jim away from them injuns. I felt bad about what we'd done to him. But Jim smiled at me with all his teeth and says he ain't going. He was become a Cherokee medicine man and had more wives than Sollerman. He says he ain't never had it so good, and he thanked us for what we done for him."

"Are you talking about Jim?"

"You remember how he always knowed when it was going to rain? Even when the sun was out in a blue sky and blazing away? Well, Jim waited till one hot day the signs was all lined up, then he got all them red-skins into a rain dance. It warn't nothing like their own dance, but he got everybody dancing like him, and down come the rain." Tom laughs sleepily. "They always done it Jim's way after that," he says, "and some-times Jim jumped in, but only when he was pretty sure there was rain a-comin'."

I says it warn't like that, but Tom was already snoring, his moustaches rising up and down like the tail of a cantering pony. "I seen Jim," I says, "when I guided some missionaires north. That hellion was with them. Jim was their cookie. His biscuits and flapjacks was the best I ever et anywheres. He showed me the stripes on his back where his white masters, the ones before the missionaires, whopped him. They knocked out some of his teeth with whip handles. He was already free then, but they didn't respect it. He's free now again for the second time and a-looking for his wife and children. He's got religion and, with his big singing voice, they all listen to him." I was talking to the tent, filled now with Tom's snores.

Though I ain't slept in two days, I warn't so sleepy no more. I picked up the whisky bottle and stepped out a the tent. The fire under the spit was just red ashes now. The tents by the shore was all dark. I was hearing some owl hoots I judged warn't made by owls. They seemed to be coming from above the crick, high in the woods, from the direction of the robbers' cave where I first lived when I come to the Gulch. They was asking questions. Or the same question over and over.

I wanted to crawl up there, but Bear was setting guard outside. I handled him the whisky bottle and says it's a beautiful night and he guzzles and grunts and then acknowledges it is. I made an answering emigrant hoot to the hoot across the crick, and got a happy hoot in reply. Bear laughed. "Them owls is middling smart, Bear, they're famous for it," I says. I was ever so glad to know that Eeteh was alive and looking for me. "Out here in the Black Hills, they're so smart, they sometimes even answer back, like that one just done for me. Try it yourself."

Bear hooted, but there warn't no reply. "Like this, Bear," I says, and sent out another hoot. This time there was an answer. So Bear and me set about practicing hoots, and finally Bear got an answering hoot. "That's it, Bear! But watch out. That old bird may reckon you're his missing wife and come try to make you a mother." Bear laughed hard and tried again. I taught him happy hoots and watch-out hoots and see-you-tomorrow hoots, though he didn't know that was what they was. Sometimes he was answered, most times he warn't.

Bear says, "That was fun. But maybe I ought to shoot that owl."

I says that shooting owls was a sure way to bring on bad luck. It was worse'n black cats, touching a snake-skin with your hands, and looking at the moon over your left shoulder, all at the same time. "And owls ain't good eating. They're mostly all feathers and their meat has a high smell."

Then somebody did shoot, cussing the owl for the noise it was making. "Hey! Y'all shot my pal!" somebody else hollered, and next thing, they was all shouting insults into the night and shooting at each other.

"What did I tell you about bad luck, Bear?" I says, and him and me had a laugh about it, and that owl across the crick also let out a happy hoot. I left the whisky with Bear and stumbled back inside the tent. I couldn't hardly make it back to my cot.

CHAPTER XXIV

I was in a tight place. I'd crawled into an empty hogshead behind the slaughter-house and fell asleep and now I was stuck. Somebody must a nailed the lid on. Sleeping on the street or in the woods, I always waked up with the sun, but there warn't no sun in here. It was dark and hot and stunk a stale whisky. I couldn't breathe. I had to get out. Someone was waiting for me. Then I seen a way to crawl out, but somebody was a-holding me back and I had to fight him off. It was Tom. "Easy, Huck," he says.

The fat cannibal doctor was there, too, trying to pour something biling hot down my throat. He was devilish red-eyed and his grizzled face hairs sprung random and weedy on his fat jowls like a wolf's. "Willow bark tea," he says. "Drink up, boy. It's good for you."

"You catched a fever, Huck," Tom says,

his hand on my forehead. "You're burning up."

I was laying on my cot in the big tent in a heavy sweat. "Blame it all!" I says. I felt all quivery. "What time is it?"

"A little past noon," says Tom. "I come back from exploring up the Gulch and found my old pard thrashing away in a sorry state. Now, drink some a Doc Molligan's tea. It'll bring the fever down." Whilst I was trying to do that, Tom showed me a rock that looked like Deadwood's. "Turned up this morning down at the crick. It's mainly what we was looking for. I traced it back upstream. I think I seen the blowup where the old sourdough's rock might a broke off and fell from, then washed down here. But people was following me, so I had to act disgusted and walk on by. Others may a seen what I seen, though. Quartz is hard to miss. Caleb has staked a claim for us, it's ourn now, we got it legal, but we may have to shoot a few thieves and yokels who don't know where the claims office is. This ain't only plasser gold, Hucky, this may be the tarnal mother lode herself! If we can hang on to her, we're rich! Richer'n you and me can't never imagine!"

That warn't all Tom done that morning. Bear told me later that, first thing at dawn,

Tom led a posse out to defend some arriving emigrants from an attack by the tribe. Bear had fetched me some fresh water and was helping me drink it by holding my head in his big paw. Tom tried to roust me out to ride along, Bear says, but I was like dead. Nobody knowed yet about the fever, but Tom called Molly to come take a look. He says it must be the yaller janders, though he warn't sure. "There was wagons a-pulling in by the minute, and then suddenly there warn't," Bear says. "So us and Tom we rode out to see what was wrong, and we come on a wagon train being set on by the bloody Sooks. Folks was a-laying dead all over the place. 'Twarn't fair, attacking them innercent white folk like that! Tom he rode straight at them savages on Storm, his cremson bandanna flying and guns a-blazing, and they was most astonished and couldn't turn tail fast enough. Tom killt at least three of 'em and prob'bly hurt a dozen more. Now he's laying plans for a revenge raid on the tribe." Big Bear's black brows frowned down his warty nose so low, his eyes had to peek out from below them like they was hiding under a woodpile. "We're at WAR!" he growls.

Bear was right, the war was begun. I knowed that, even in my fever. Emigrants was still a-rolling in like they owned the place and battles was happening all across the Territory. There were rumors that Sitting Bull was gathering the tribes up in a big army, and the price on Indian heads was shooting up. Didn't matter who you killed or how, so long as they was Indians. I heard all that from my cot. I tried to get up, I needed to find Eeteh somehow, but I kept falling over. All I could do was crawl back up in my cot again, ready to die some more.

There was several days a-going by like that, and I couldn't really tell which was which. On one of them, Tom put on his white hat and led the settlers in a raid on the tribe. Everyone was amazed how brave Tom was, but this one didn't turn out so good. Two emigrants was killed and Bear got a pison arrow in his rear and was sick for a time with the jimjams.

Tom was spending most of his days at his new claim, so he moved out and let Bear have his cot, Oren taking over guarding Zeb's old shack, where Eyepatch and the judge was being bunkhoused till they could be tried and hanged. Bear was shouting out that scorpions and rattlers and mad dogs was after him. There was times he jumped out a the cot and throwed himself about like he was rassling with the wild things.

Everyone down at the shore was afraid he was going to bring the tent down, so they dragged him out into the open air where he could rassle with the trees. Sometimes he bawled like a baby and called out for his ma. Once, he screamed he was being pecked to death by owls.

When he'd swallowed enough a Doc Molligan's tea to ca'm down for a spell, he says that just THINKING about shooting that owl must a fetched him the bad luck. He swore never to think bad thoughts about owls again. He'd just quietly kill them all till they warn't no more. Doc come every day to what he called the camp horse-pistol and fed us both thin brothy soup. I hoped there warn't nobody's remainders in it. Doc warn't the only visitor. We warn't never lonesome. There was a passel a folks living down by the crick now, and one or t'other of them was dropping in on us most all the time, mostly to sample Tom's whisky. The crick was swoll up with the spring rains and getting harder to work.

One day when Bear was out rassling with the trees again, Tom comes in and sets on my cot and says he had more to say about Jim. "We was having such a good time that night, I didn't want to spoil it," Tom says. "But one day Jim's rain dance worked TOO good and the tribe got flooded. They warn't dressed proper and some a them drownded. They thought Jim may a done it a-purpose and that made them mad, so they sold him off to some missionaires passing by. Them holy rollers believed in saving souls by whopping folks and busting their teeth out. Jim got saved and become a preacher and they respected him like they ain't done before, but all he could eat afterwards was flapjacks and biscuits." Tom must a been half-awake behind his snores that night. He was telling awful lies again, but I let him.

The picture-taker come to see me after Bear'd got better and moved out. Somebody told him I was dead. When he seen I was still blinking, he says he already wasted a glass plate on me when I was on the gallows, so this time he'll wait. "I ain't feeling so good," I says. "Hang around ten minutes and see what happens." He drawed close to squint into my eyes and trace the rope burns. I opened my mouth and he peered into it and shook his head gloomily. "Meantimes, help yourself to a glass a Tom's whisky," I says. It was what he was waiting for. He was one a them lantern-jawed fellows whose grins split their faces. He set down with just such a grin breaking his face in two and turned his billed cap backwards and poured himself a glassful. "How long you been traveling with Tom?" I asks him.

"Since Yankton." He swallowed the whisky, poured himself another. "My workshop's thar. Mostly I done pitchers a dead people. Tintypes a dead babies is my famous speciality. If I get the little tykes quick enough, I prop them up like they was still alive. I keep straw dolls in the workshop to stick in their tiny fists. Old folks is mainly easier if they ain't got stiffened up, but they ain't as purty. I made pitchers a live people, too, but they warn't so popular." He showed me a photograph he'd took of Tom in his all-white rig with his hand tucked in his shirt, setting Storm like a general. He tucked a cheroot in his wide lips, lit it and smiled. "The Amaz'n Tom Sawyer he come'n found me there, and I been out on the trail with him ever since. I take his pitcher wherever he goes, fighting injuns and highwaymen and injustice and hunting for gold and hanging crinimals, but mostly when he's having a rest on his horse in his white hat and doeskins. He's the Sivilizer of the West, he told me so. He's making a famous book about hisself."

"When did he find out I was here in the Gulch?"

"Don't know. Since before I was with him."

I laid there, thinking about this. I remembered now that the picture-taker was there at the gallows that day setting up his camera, before Tom come a-riding in. "Why didn't he try to find me sooner? Why did he wait till I was most dead?" Well, I knowed why. It was how the story went.

"We was here in the neighborhood a couple a times," the picture-taker says, and helps himself to more whisky. "But I think he was aiming to surprise you."

"He surely done that. But he only give himself one shot. What if he missed?"

"Well, I'd of got my pitcher," he says with a thin wicked grin. He plucked some grains a tobacco off his tongue. "But it warn't likely. He's the Amaz'n Tom Sawyer, ain't he?"

A couple of nights later, Tom come back from working his claim and we set up smoking and jawing into the night again like we done before I got the fever. I was glad he was back because, when I was alone in it, the big tent give me nightmares. Sometimes I propped the bedclothes up to make a little tent inside the big one, and I slept better.

Tom says he may a misguessed the seam by a hundred yards or so. We'll all still be mighty rich, but probably richer if him and the others form up a consortion. It's something he knows how to do regular as a lawyer, and his partners all appreciate that. He may make himself president of the consortion. I says what the picture-taker told me, and Tom says, "I heard you was somewheres in this corner a the Territory, and come a-looking, but I couldn't never find you. Nobody even knowed who you was except one old miner who says, last he seen, you was off hobnobbling with the injuns and living in tepees. I was disappointed to hear that, but I s'posed you must of was scouting for somebody."

He lit up half a seegar and says he's been holding talks with the Lakota chiefs. "We smoked peace pipes together and they says we was all children of the Great Spirit, we shouldn't be killing each other, it warn't convenient. They fetched in a drag loaded with buffalo hides and says it was payment for the settlers that got killed. They was sorry it happened. They says it was some young bucks done it, boys being boys. They been punished for it. The tribe don't want to be called hoss-tiles no more, though I says that's exactly what they was. They says they was a free people living off roaming creturs like the buffalo, and they'd only starve if they was penned up on a reservation, so they can't go along with that. But they don't mean nobody no harm and says there's room in the world for everybody. I says that may be so, but not in these parts. They say this land is sacrid to them, and I says, then maybe they should have a gab about it with their Great Spirits, and see if they don't have other sejestions."

Tom picked up the whisky bottle and poured some in a tin cup and come over to my cot to see if I wanted any. I shook my head. "Even your eyeballs is yaller," he says, and crawled back into his cot. "Before them hoss-tiles left, they asked about somebody named Hahza," he says, sipping at the cup a whisky, "and finally I allowed they was talking about you. I think they wanted you to be there. I says you was very sick with the yaller janders. They muttered some injun words about that and rode away." He blowed some seegar smoke up at the top of the tent. "Who is this fellow they call Eat-A?"

"He's a pard a mine. He's a loafer and a drunk like me and he don't fit in with his people no more'n I fit in with mine."

"I thought I was your pard."

"You warn't around."

"Am now." He finished off his whisky,

stubbed out his seegar, and blowed out the lamp. "Palling around with injuns, Huck, is right down dangersome. You can't trust 'em. Remember what happened to them poor emigrants we met when we first come out here. You'll get your throat slit before you know it. And it ain't right. There's a war on."

"We made the war, not them," I says, recollecting what Dan Harper said. "We been bullying in and taking away everything they s'posed was their'n. They're only just defending theirselves."

"Well, from where they set, Huck, they got a point. But we ain't them. We got to stick with our own tribe, even if they ARE all lunatics. If we don't, we'll end up crazier'n any of them. You remember that poor preacher up in Minnysota? Even if he was maybe right, his rebel notions was turning him plumb loco, and in the end they probably got him lynched by his own congregation. These lands is become our lands, that's the story now, and it's only got just one ending. There ain't nothing them hosstiles can do about it, nor not you nuther."

"Tribes," I says. "They're a powerful curse laid on you when you get born. They ruin you, but you can't get away from them. They're a nightmare a body's got to live with in the daytime."

"I ain't never told nobody this, Huck. I don't know if I should tell you, but you're my oldest and best friend." He was talking in the dark. His voice seemed like different from the rest of him. "When my pa went west, I always s'posed he must of become a famous bandit or bank robber or at least a sheriff. When I was a kid, I probably told you stories about him that I made up. Mostly he got killed in some tragic way. I missed him awful, growing up. I reckoned in spite a my yarns he was still alive somewheres, so when I come west as a lawyer, I went looking for him. I finally found him in Baker City, selling used hats from a little wagon. Some a the hats had bullet holes in them. Warn't a one of them ever been cleaned. They was full a nasty little varmints crawling round." Them hats had somehow got in the cot with me. I was all over itching. "He was living with a fat two-bit whore who warn't no cleaner'n the hats. He warn't NOBODY, Huck! He didn't have no STYLE! He says he still loves Ma, and when I told him she was dead, he busted out crying. He was making me sick. I couldn't stand him. So I shot him. Had to shoot the whore, too, because she was watching. Left town that night. Ain't been back."

CHAPTER XXV

On Jackson's island, when me and Tom and Joe Harper run away to be pirates and didn't have nothing else to do, we laid on our backs at night, looking up at the stars, and Tom and Joe discussed about time and space. They couldn't agree if the two, if they WAS two, run on forever or if they didn't, and IF they didn't, what was on t'other side a them. Joe argued in the Sunday-school manner for sudden bust-out beginnings and horrible ends, and he says that heaven and hell was out there past where the stars run out. The stars, he says, was like a huge sparkly curtain that God slung up for privacy. What was he doing back there, I says, that he don't want us to see? GLORY, says Joe. It burns your eyes out. Tom says that bust-out beginnings and horrible ends was sure-'nough true about people, but the universe seemed more like a clock that had got wound up and then forgot, and people was just caught between ticks, which he says was the scientific idea about it. I says I couldn't see no advantage about arguing, it was most awful beautiful up there, all speckly and grand, and it was enough to only lay back and watch it. Joe says that was plain stupid and only showed how ignorant I was. Tom defended me, saying it warn't my fault, I hain't never been to school and learnt how to tell true from beautiful.

Now that Tom's growed up, time don't really happen for him no more. It's just always NOW, nor else nothing. That's probably because he's always at the center of everything. The Amaz'n Tom Sawyer. For a body out at the edge like me, watching time go by's like laying back and watching the stars. Mostly don't nothing happen, but now'n then a star falls and streaks up the sky for a second. And it don't matter if you seen it or not, it still happened. And will go on happening when you ain't around to watch. But Tom's right, I ain't never really learnt how to think proper. He'd probably say something crazy like stars DON'T fall, even though any fool can see them do it, and yet the Amaz'n Tom Sawyer'd be right again like always. It was too many for me, really. Tom was mountains smarter. I should give him all the thinking to do for me and him both.

I was laying on my cot, muddytating on all this, and wondering what Coyote would say about it, when Tom, suited up in his bleached doeskin, busted in like Joe's universe to roust me out. He wanted me to come to a meeting in the public square to talk about the tribe's peace offer. I didn't have no pep yet and I was still a ripe shade a yaller, but I could stand up without falling down, so he allowed I was well enough to come help him out. "I been thinking about it, and I AGREE with you, Huck, peace is BETTER'N war," he says, helping me to my feet and setting a hat on my head. "I BELIEVE in peace. I don't believe in nothing MORE! People have fun killing, but they don't care to GET killed, so that's how you make peace. But these emigrants is stubborn as mules. You got to HELP me. Come on. Le's go see what you'n me can do."

The crick shore was a-filling up. There were more tents, more people, more horses and mules, more fires, more smoke, more rubbage. The crick was wider and rushing faster like to echo the persons' rush into the Gulch. Peewee and the others was still panning for plasser gold at the water's edge, and they give Tom and me a nod when we passed by. There was a horse path now up to Zeb's old shack and we walked up it, climbing towards all the shouts and hammering. We passed some log cabins on the way with plank roofs and cooksmoke rolling out their mud-brick chimbleys. The forest that used to hide Deadwood's shack from Zeb's was mostly gone, but other shanties and tents and lean-tos had raised up round them, and the empty spaces between was full of wagons and animals. It warn't clear where any more could be squeezed, but they was still rolling in like the first day, you could see them far out into the hills. They wouldn't know nothing about what had happened. They had to learn everything all over again. If they wanted to. They mostly didn't. They only wanted people to move over and let them in.

The gallows out a-front the shack was bigger'n when I broke it in. There were nooses now for three necks and Tom says they may need more. The sad truth, he says, is that these new emigrants warn't all decent citizens, come to get rich in honest hardworking American ways. Fact is, many of them was right down thieves, swindlers, highwaymen, rabble-rousers, crooked gamblers, gunslingers, thugs and murderers, and they had to be weeded out like the hateful pests they was. "I can see where this country is going," he says, proud as pie, "and I can help it get there."

I asked him how many he'd hanged so far, and he says only about four a day, though some days was busier than others. I asked him if he thought they all qualified, and he says there might a been an exception or two, but he was pretty sure most of them did. "Anyways, Huck, EVERYTHING'S a hanging offense. Being ALIVE is. Only thing that matters is who's doing the hanging and who's being hung." The judge and Eyepatch warn't yet amongst the hanged pests. I could see them peering out Zeb's door over Bear's shoulders, Yaller Whisker's two eyes wide open and panicky, Eyepatch's one eye full of dark fire like a wild animal's.

We slopped over to the claims registry and Tom told Caleb and Wyndell to shut down till the meeting was done. Their pine table was moved out a-front the ghost-town scavenger's generl store onto a new wooden sidewalk hoisted up three feet off of the gumbo and the horse and ox muck. The store had a shingle front now and a new sign. At first, it was stocked mostly with secondhand goods left from disappeared miners, but now there were saws and hammers and guns and boots carted in from outfitting towns around. They fetched a camp chair out from the store and set me on it, and I was grateful for that. I was tired all the time now and the climb up from crickside had clean wore me out.

The raised sidewalk was high enough it give me a view of a sea of dilapidated hats. I couldn't hardly reckonize the place. It was becoming worse like a town every day. Now there were assay and law offices and grocery stores and tin shops and liquor dealers and a brewery and market stalls in the streets. Along with their fly-spackled meat, butchers was selling little leather sacks for gold dust. They was more expensive'n the meat on account of there was only two per cretur, and sometimes none.

The streets was mostly filled with men, young and old, skinny, bearded, dressed in black jackets and vests, dirty white shirts, wrinkled pants, but a few women now, too, spruced up in flouncy calico gowns. They warn't nothing to look at, but they was getting a power of attention. Their pretty clothes remembered me of Becky Thatcher up in Wyoming. I warn't sure she was doing what these women was doing, but I judged she probably was. I was feeling sadful and it made me feel more sadfuller.

Tom set at the table with his fancy white

hat and wire-frame eye-glasses on, along with Caleb and Wyndell and two or three others picked out by Tom, and the folks out front give them a big cheer. The picture-taker come and made everybody set still for a picture. Tom took off his spectacles, stroked his bushy ear-to-ear moustaches, and raired his shoulders back for the photo, then he put his specs back on, banged on the table with a wooden hammer and says they're all there to talk about the latest Sioux peace offer.

That set the crowd to hooting and cussing and shouting that it was time to kill all them filthy lying heathens, they was a tarnal nuisance, le's go do it now! "God give us guns, and we should use 'em, praise the Lord!"

Tom held up a white-gloved hand and says he understood their feelings, they was mostly his feelings, too, but peace warn't all bad, Jesus spoke pretty good about it, and they should at least give a thought to it. "You all know Huck Finn here as a famous Pony Express rider and one of the greatest injun fighters of all time, with more scalps than most of us got hairs on our heads!" Tom took off his white hat and patted his bald spot and the crowd broke out in whoops and guffaws and applauded all my scalps. "Out on the trail, Huck was our main bullwork against the savages till he catched a fever, and it's only since he's been laid low that things has got so worse out there. As a legendry scout he has considerable experience of the tribes. He has lived in their mist and has got to know their peculiar ways and he truly believes that they are pining for peace. He reckons it might save a lot of people from getting scalped and tomahawked if we can custom ourselves to the idea, so long as they don't want nothing else of consequence."

A stormy howl went up that peace was only another injun word for meanness and trickry. They was treacherous animals, the crowd yelled, who don't have no more idea what peace was'n a pack a wolves! "Look at the turrible mischeevousness Setting Bull and Crazy Hoss was up to right now! We ain't got no time for pap-sucking Quaker poltroons! Everybody should ride straight over to their dad-fetched camp and shoot 'em all, afore it's them that's swarmed up and done the killing!"

"Also they's a crick over thar and it might have gold in it!"

It was his own complice Oren who first raised the howl and that surely must a nigh froze Tom, but he only took his spectacles off so's he could see better and says it was easier to holler for war than to stop it once you cranked it up. "We thought that hellish conflictation twixt the States was cooled down ten years ago, but NO! It's still a-blazing away!" That shut up some a them because they was all strangers and couldn't be certain who was standing next to them, but others started cussing and bellowing like as if to set off the war again. People was listening to local ways a talking and was moving about, lining up sides like before a ballgame. Somewheres that fiddler had struck up "Dixie," and the drummer was bashing his drum and blowing on a juice-harp, trying to drown him out.

Tom stood up and slapped his hat down and they all quieted down some. "Yesterday is dead as a coffin nail, my friends!" he shouted. "Let the past bury its own dang dead, whilst we bury the bloody hatchet and act, act in the living NOW!" He started getting applause again. "We got to toil upwards in the night together through the mud and scum of things without no fear and with a manly heart! No damn ifs, ands, or buts ABOUT it!" They was all making a racket and cheering him on, though it warn't clear what he was talking about. Something he read in a book, maybe. "PEACE! There ain't nothing preciouser even if you got to go to WAR to land it! Ain't no man alive more keen on peace than me! Huck Finn KNOWS that!" He pointed at me and I jerked my head back like I'd been poked and everybody laughed and cheered again.

Caleb raised his hand. "Everybody here believes in peace, Tom. Jest look round. Them white folks out there is the most peace-loving people on earth. But how you going to git them bloody injuns to lay off massacreeing them?"

"Well, I s'pose, on account of it's their land, we could offer them to share out the gold as, you know, a kind of levy."

"But this AIN'T their land, Tom!" Caleb says above the loud boos. "It's GOD'S land! And we're God's PEOPLE, ain't we? We shorely ain't obleeged to share out our rightful wealths with no godless savages!"

Tom did look like he just took a punch to his soler plexus. Even Caleb! Just when he was finding his old voice again! "Of course, I ain't saying it wouldn't be a damn sight more peaceful if there warn't no hoss-tiles around," Tom says, "but —"

"It's like that fat little Irisher general says," shouted Oren, putting in his shovel. "The only GOOD injun's a DEAD injun!"

Bear hollered out something from the

door of Zeb's shack, but there was so much yelling and cussing and cheering and carrying on, he couldn't be heard, so Tom asked him to come up closer. He squeezed his bulk in with the crowd surrounding us and says, "You and Huck're acting in a most sivilized manner, Tom, and we all appreciate that and thank you for it! But them savages don't deserve it! Like you said yourself, they ain't even completely human!"

"Well, I have said that, Bear, and I do believe it, but I am prepared to change my mind if it ain't true, or if it's true, but inconvenient."

You couldn't hardly hear him. They was shouting him down again. He done his best but they was all against him. Poor Tom. He looked sadful and defeated. His best friends! He turned to me and shrugged.

Then suddenly, with Bear away from the door, Eyepatch and Yaller Whiskers broke out! Tom raired up with his gun and the judge spun around and throwed himself back into the shack and covered his head, but Eyepatch unfurled his heels and kept right on shoving. Tom shot — but MISSED! He only hit him in the LEG! Eyepatch stumbled and fell, staggered to his feet, limped away in a mad panic. Tom drawed a bead and emptied his revolver, but only hit him in the leg every time! Even Tom Sawyer warn't perfect!

We all stepped down off the raised sidewalk to go look at Eyepatch. He was laying in the mud, snarling like old Abaddon, his left peg ruined from the knee down. Tom reloaded his revolver and put the barrel of it to Eyepatch's head. Eyepatch spitted at him through his mouthful a gold teeth and throwed some mud at him. Tom grinned. "Sorry, Cap'n. That leg's a sickly mess. Bad case a lead pisoning. Don't leave us no choice. Go fetch Molly, Oren. Tell him supper's on."

Chapter XXVI

Eyepatch was lucky that Tom's aim was off that day, because it give Tom the idea of making him into a pirate stead of hanging him. The emigrants was probably more hoping for a hanging — some a them was so new they hadn't seen a single one yet — but they all cheered Tom when he brung down Eyepatch. They had a hoot at the rascal's sass and they was mostly happy to have him around to look at a while longer, specially when they learnt Tom's plans for him. Tom was also lucky for having saved Pegleg's wooden leg stead of burying it with him, if he ever did get buried, which just goes to show it was always good to hang on to such things as wooden legs in case a body needed them later. First, though, Eyepatch's shot-up leg had to get chopped and healed, so they dragged him off, howling and cussing, to Doc Molligan.

Whilst they was doing that, Tom and his

pals gathered round the claims table on the raised wooden sidewalk to talk about what Tom called their stragety. The others wanted to attack the redskins right then and there, hitting them with all they got, and bring the calvary into it, too. But Tom he didn't like the idea and says they ought to powwow again with the tribe first and see if they couldn't be learnt to be more friendlier if maybe they paid them some money or beads. Nobody thought this was a good idea, so Tom looked at me sadfully and shrugged and says, "What do you reckon, Huck?"

"I don't see nobody getting out a nobody's way," I says. "So, what I reckon is that something really bad is a-going to happen."

Some a the others yayed at this, judging something bad was good, but Tom only nodded and sighed like to say he done all he could, and he ain't been left with no choice. Tom says if they was meaning to attack the tribe, though he wishes they warn't, they should choose a day when the enemy ain't expecting it, like when it's snowing or hurry-caning or some Sunday morning before dawn. I says we should wait for the hurry-cane, but nobody else was of that opinion. Caleb he says he don't read the weather, so he don't know about snow in

June, but there was a Sunday coming up, three days away, and Tom says that should give him enough time. He says there's been troubles at the claim, he already had to shoot at some pesky claim-jumpers, and though he had business partners now, he didn't trust them, so him and Bear had to go make sure it didn't all get stole away from him. But if Caleb could plan out the attack and round up a proper Black Hills Brigade and make sure all the best shootists was there, he'd get back before dawn Sunday. He looked at me and winked over his bushy moustaches and says he knowed the greatest injun hunter in the Territories wouldn't want to miss a chance for a few more scalps, and he hoped I was out a my sickbed by then.

Then Tom put on his white hat and slung a lecture about gold and freedom, and how a body could stake a claim to them and keep the claims safe, which I warn't listening to. I was beginning to feel muddly and weak in the knees. After Tom had spoke, everybody got up and left except me and Caleb and Wyndell and a long line of miners waiting outside the claims registry office. Tom slapped my back before he stepped down into the mud and says I should go get some rest, I looked like a Chinaman with consumption. Somewheres further off, Eyepatch could be heard screaming and wailing and cussing the world and everybody in it. There warn't much out here to heal with, and most of it hurt like the blazes.

Whilst we was moving the table back into the office, Caleb says he ain't never seen Tom so charged up on peace-talking the savages, I must be having a bad influence on him.

"I hope I ain't held responsible for his bad shooting, too," I says, worrying if I could make it back down to the crick or not. "I been thinking about what if he'd missed the hanging rope and only shot me in the leg like Eyepatch."

"He wouldn't never a done that, though I cain't say he shouldn'ta," says Caleb flatly. He lifted up his orange too-pay to scratch his balditude, set it back down again. "Why're you such a favrit a his?"

"Been pards since we was little."

"Well, you ain't wuth it."

I had to find Eeteh before Sunday, but by the time I stumbled down the hill to the tent and fell over a couple a times on the way, I couldn't do nothing more'n flop half-dead onto my cot. I maybe waked up enough to hear some owl hoots, but I might of only dreampt them. I was pretty sure when Tongo come and talked to me about freedom and power, it was a dream, if it warn't his ghost ha'nting me. Tom's horse come in to join the palaver, and probably he warn't a ghost. Tom himself come back late and helped himself to a bedtime suck on a whisky bottle and says I should not go gallivanting off nowheres on my own whilst he's away. Gallivanting ain't my best trick right now, I says, or might a said, and the next thing I knowed it was morning and rain was drumming on the tent canvas and Tom was gone.

Everybody was staying in out a the rain, so there warn't Peewee or nobody else down at crickside. Tom and Bear was both away. It seemed like a good time to go search out Eeteh. I reckoned it best to start with the robbers' cave in the hills above, which was where Eeteh first found me living when I come to the Gulch and where some of his hoots lately seemed to of come from. I could go up there and send off some hoots a my own, and see what happened.

It warn't an easy hike, but I was rested up from sleeping most of a day and was feeling generly less peculiar. Before leaving the tent, I was even able to eat a dry biscuit dipped in fresh milk from an emigrant cow, and I pocketed a couple extra biscuits to munch on the way up. I still couldn't tolerate whisky, but I fetched along one a Tom's bottles in case Eeteh showed up. If he didn't, I could leave it behind for him like a kind of eagle feather.

It was a slow plod up to the cave. I warn't customed to it, my legs was rubbry, and my boots was soon heavy with caked mud, but climbing into the hills chippered me up considerable. There was a soft light everywheres and the rain was hushing down through the leaves and pine needles and the forest was ever so cool and lovely.

The cave stunk the same as it always done and thousands of bats was still hanging upside down in there, packed together, their wings shuttered up for their daytime doze, but I was glad to reach it. I was dog-tired from the climb and needed to set somewheres out a the weather and rest a spell. But first I stepped to the mouth of the cave to let out a hoot — and all of a sudden there was a hand smacked on my mouth!

The ROBBERS was back!

NO! It was EETEH! I was so happy to see him, I nearly shouted out, but he shushed me and led me to a chink in the cave wall where I could peek out. "Tu'wayuh," he whispers, pointing. There he was, the spy Eeteh seen, far off down the gulch, creeping through the woods with a rifle, peering up through the rain in our direction: Tom's heavy-bellied pal Oren.

"Eeteh!" I whispered. "They had a meeting! They're going to —"

He clapped his hand over my mouth again. He pointed at me, at himself. "Kho-LAH." Friends. Then he shook his head, pointing down at Oren. "Tu'wayuh shnee!" He grinned through the webby tangle of black hair that hung over his face. "Mah-kocheh!"

I nodded. We warn't scouting for nobody no more, not the Americans, not the tribe. We warn't belongers to none a that now. We was only pards, running off on our own to Mexico. It was dangersome, but staying here was dangersomer, and leastways we could watch out for each other.

Eeteh says the worse thing for him right now was Sitting Bull's army. The Lakota camp was full of strange warriors from other tribes, who don't respect a poor fool's privileges. They was forever slapping him about for not braiding his hair or for dancing when it warn't proper or for telling stories out a season or not wanting to cut himself in their war dance rituals, and his brothers was out-powered and couldn't do nothing to protect him, or didn't want to.

The others say they'll make a warrior out of him or kill him. They was all planning to move west directly to join up with Sitting Bull's army on the Heyhakha River. He says he ain't going with them.

Eeteh had brung me my stone pipe, the one with the carved head of a spirit horse on it that his war-chief brother give me. Feeling it in my hand remembered me how much I'd missed it. I fetched out the whisky bottle and biscuits, and thumbed tobacco from my vest pocket into the pipe bowl, feeling rich as a duke again. We watched Oren thrashing about in the wet bushes, looking for a way up. Eeteh uncorked the bottle, took a sniff, smiled, tipped it back for a swallow, then handled the bottle to me. It looked like melted gold and was a sore trial for me, but I handled it back. "Don't set well with the yaller janders," I says, and he looked closer at me and nodded.

"Ne Tongo?" I asked. I was scared to ask. I was missing that horse more'n I ever missed nothing before, and I was still afeard I might a seen a dead horse's ghost.

Eeteh says Tongo was a heap of trouble that night and wouldn't do nothing like he wanted him to do, but with a lot of tugging and talking and begging, he somehow got him and my goods back to where the tribe was camped. I was awful happy to hear it, and I says so, and thanked him, and then thanked him again, and struck a match over my stone pipe bowl. He says there warn't nobody could ride Tongo, not even himself, but the tribe treated him like a Great Spirit and he could have anything he wanted from them. The new braves riding in warn't so respectful, though, and they sometimes laid a whip on him when he didn't do what they wanted him to. He says Tongo don't have much to say, but a body could see he was restless to break out a there and shove for Mexico or wherever.

I drawed in some smoke, tasting the sweetness of it, my fingers wrapped round the warm horse head, and says I had a dream last night about Tongo. "Anyways, I think it was a dream. He come into the tent and nuzzled me to wake me up and says he wants to keep running like we done that first time, and never stop. He says a body is free till it don't want to be, and he ain't got to the not-wanting time. He says he hopes he dies before he gets there."

"Me, too," Eeteh says.

"Tongo announced some more things that don't make no sense, like freedom IS power, but he was jabbering in Lakota and neighing at the same time, I couldn't hardly understand half of it. Then Tom's big stallion Storm come in and says freedom without power is only a pretend freedom, and don't amount to beans, or horse words to that effect. Storm talked more like an emigrant. He says if you ain't got the power to hold on to freedom and use it, it ain't no bigger'n what a prisoner's got on his way to the gallows. Power IS freedom, he says. Tongo he snorted and says Storm should talk about freedom when he ain't hitched to a saddle. He says power don't help a body keep freedom, it only knows how to keep'n make more of itself. When a body is trying to hang on to power, he ain't free to do nothing else. Storm got mad and dumped a golden load out his rear end and says THAT'S what your FREEDOM is! Tongo done the same and says THAT'S your POWER! Tom come in by and by and drunk some whisky and give me some advice and I told him to watch out for the horse dung. He thought I was talking about his advice and says if I warn't so sick he'd go find some horse dung and make me eat it. Everything was ordinary except that Tom was laying about six inches above his cot. I reckoned he was just showing off."

Eeteh laughed and says he don't know who's Tom, so I remembered him that Tom

Sawyer was the friend I first come out west with, but hadn't seen in all these years after he went home to get married. I says how Zeb's killers catched me and tried me and was just hanging me from the new gallows, when Tom he come a-galloping in out a nowheres and shot the rope and the hangman as well. Eeteh whooped like it was the wonderfullest thing he ever heard, and then he says how scared he was when I got catched. I never answered his owl hoots for a whole day, and when I did it was mixed up with other hoots. Then he didn't hear nothing at all, except somebody trying to imitate me. When his brother come back from the powwow after the wagon train attack, he says I warn't in the camp no more. "He say Hahza dead."

He raised the bottle, shook his head and laughed. "TOM!" I clicked my pipe bowl on his raised bottle and says, "TOM!" right back and we both laughed and I took a deep puff to Eeteh's swallow. The bats was growing restless above us. "Me and Tom was boys in the same town, we played bandits and pirates together, run away together. There ain't nobody alive with more brains and gumption and plain level-headedness than Tom Sawyer. People love him wherever he goes and want him to tell them what to do, and so he does." I blowed more sweet smoke up at the fluttery bats. "Tom he wants me to stay now and help him run the camp. He says he can keep me safe from General Hard Ass. I ain't so sure about that, but even if he could, this place is plumb ruined for me. After my fever's gone, there ain't nothing to keep me here except Tom Sawyer himself, and I'm hoping I can push him to go with us."

Eeteh says it'd be an honor to ride with such a great shootist, though he hoped he'd make up his mind fast. Then he stared at me for a moment, and turned back to look through the chink in the wall again. "Who send tu'wayuh?"

Down below, Oren was moving his overalled belly from tree to tree. "I don't know. Tom probably. He's the boss now. He's off chasing a claim and, whilst he's gone, he's probably worried about me."

"Scout follow you, find me," Eeteh says. "Maybe try kill me." He didn't say nothing for a moment. He warn't smiling. "Tom . . . He bad man in white hat?"

"He does wear a white hat," I says. Tom led an attack on the tribe in that hat, I'd forgot that. Eeteh was the best friend I had for years. I felt like I already knowed him better'n I never knowed nobody else. But

Tom was my pard, always had been. I didn't want to leave neither of them behind. "Tom makes up adventures like he reads out a books, though he ain't scrupulous about the consequences, and he maybe does some things he oughtn't, but he ain't really bad inside. Life by itself just ain't enough for Tom. It ain't got no point and the way it ends makes him mad. So he contrives up these adventures to get him through it." I told him about the meeting yesterday, how Tom wanted peace with the tribe, but all his best pals was against him. "I never seen them buck him like that before." Eeteh nodded, thinking about that. He says he understands. He says his friend who got scalped by white emigrants warn't perfect, too.

There was so much we needed to talk about, but Oren was a-scrambling up closer. Eeteh says he needed to go where the spy couldn't find him, and he asked me to set outside to keep him busy while he slipped away. He handled me the whisky bottle. "Take it, Eeteh," I says. "It's yourn." He shook his head. He says the tribe expects him to tell them everything, so he don't want them to know we even seen each other. "I'll leave it here in the cave for you, then. I ain't s'posed to drink with what I got, so if they ask, I'll tell them I come up here to sneak a swallow now and then."

While Eeteh crawled towards the back of the cave with the bottle, I took my rifle and went out and set on a rock. When Oren seen me, he ducked behind a tree. "Hey, Oren!" I shot a branch off over his head. He made a little squeak like a mouse does when an owl grabs it. "You come to shoot me?"

"NO!" He peeked out with his hands in the air, his rifle pointed up to the sky. "I only come t'say hello."

"Well, hello, Oren," I says. " 'Bye."

"Tom sent me to pertect you!"

"From what?"

"Injuns. Bears. Coyotes. Whatever. Kin I come up?"

"I reckon. If you're careful." I kept my rifle pointed at him. He set his over his shoulder and clumb on up. He tried to keep his eye on me, but whenever he looked up, he slipped in the mud. His bib overalls was a mess. I wiped the rain out a my face and says, "A body'd have to be pretty stupid to be out in this weather, hey, Oren? Without they got something big to do, like tromping up a mountain to say hello to a sick old trail bum."

"So what brung YOU up here?" he grunted, pulling up onto the flat space a-front the cave. His muddy overalls was full of heavy breathing.

"Reckon I must be one a the stupid ones." He stood there, gripping his rifle, studying the cave mouth. Eeteh was right. He was come to kill.

"There's somebody in there," he says. "I kin hear 'em!"

"You scared a bats, Oren?"

"Ain't scared a nuthin!" He gritted his teeth and busted on in, blasting away into the darkness. And busted right back out again, chased by the furisome black flutter of a million squeaking bats. He dropped his gun and went shinning down through the gulch considerable faster'n he clumb it, swarmed about by distressid bats. You could hear him screaming clear to Jericho. There was a yowl and a crash through branches and then it was quiet. He must a struck where the gulch dropped away of a sudden.

Eeteh come out with the whisky bottle and done a wobbly little dance like he drunk too much. I asked him what he's doing and he says it's a rain dance. "It's already raining," I says, and he says he knowed that, but he don't trust his luck enough to dance a rain dance when it ain't.

He squatted by the rock I was setting on and tipped up the bottle. "I thought you was gone," I says. The bats was wheeling around overhead again, finding their way back to bed. Eeteh wiped his mouth with the back of his hand and says he was thinking about Coyote, how him and Snake was such good friends, had been since they was little tykes, but how a problem was growed up between them. Coyote made the world and all the creturs in it and he judged that give him the right to lay with any woman he wanted to. He could change his shape, so he could try on cougars and beetles, sandhill cranes and porkypines, and he laid with them all and always had a good time doing it. But when he took a turn on Snake Woman, Snake warn't happy about it, and he come to have a considerable less friendly attitude towards Coyote.

I says that I thought Coyote killed both Snake and Snake Woman and et them, and Eeteh says that he did, but that was a different story. I seen right off I was going to have some trouble with this one. I was also wondering, if Coyote made the world, how was him and Snake both tykes at the same time, but I knowed better'n to ask. I warn't made to understand everything in this world, and maybe not none of it where Coyote was concerned.

Snake, Eeteh says, had took a particular fancy to Lark's eggs and stole them whenever he got a chance. Lark suspicioned Snake was the thief, and says so to everybody, but he was a slithery fellow and she never catched him doing it. Snake felt Lark was being unfair in blaming him alone because he reckoned everybody in the nation was stealing her eggs. And that give him an idea. He told Coyote about how much fun it was to lay with Lark, and got him excited, and off he went, using the new wings he'd just put on. Snake called his pals together, specially those he knowed to be secret egg-smouchers, and says he was going to prove to Lark that it was Coyote who was thieving all her eggs, but he needed their help and he told them what to do and say, no matter what he done and said. They was more'n glad to find someone else to blame their crimes on. Meantimes, Coyote was having a most splendid time and so was Lark, who never had such a vigrous lover. They rubbed together in all the hundreds of ways that birds do, till they was both about wore out, and they fell off sound asleep. Snake come then and et Lark's eggs and dropped the broke shells on Coyote. Lark waked up screaming, and directly all the other birds was screaming, too. For them, stealing eggs and eating them was murder. All Snake's pals grabbed Coyote and netted him before he could fly away. The net was too fine even if he changed into a gnat, and too strong if he turned into an elephant or a buffalo bull. Some wanted to kill him straight off, but Snake says Coyote should have a trial fair and square and he invited any testimony. Most didn't know what to think, but Snake's pals say they seen him hiving the eggs and eating them, and accused him of also being too full of himself and of corrumpting the young braves with his ridiculous notions. Lark herself says how she was seducted by Coyote against her will, though she warn't widely credited, and Muskrat accused Coyote of making fun of the Great Spirits and not taking them serious. Muskrat was mostly right, and Coyote ain't got nothing to say about that. Snake defended his old pard by saying it warn't fair to charge a natural-born egg-sucker with thieving his own vittles, but Mountain Goat spoke up and says he warn't only guilty a collaring the eggs, he also was a liar and had a sick comical view of life. Life ain't comical like that, Mountain Goat says. It's an insult to the Great Spirits and to the nation. Everybody seemed agreed to that. Snake looked sad and done a little shrug, best a snake can shrug, like to say he was awful disappointed but he done all he could for his pard. Spider Woman crept up to Lark on her tiny toes and whispers she seen Snake steal the eggs and scatter the shells on Coyote whilst he was sleeping. Wait a minute, Lark says. I don't think Coyote done it! I think it was — Snake's tongue shot out from nowheres like magic and snapped her up. This lightning show of power scared some folks and convinced others that Snake was the boss they was looking for. Spider Woman skittered away not to get stomped on. Whilst they was all debating how to kill him once and forever, Snake Woman slid up to the net and whispered to Coyote to change into a snake, and she'd make a little hole he could wriggle out of and they could run off together. But the hole she made was too small and he got stuck. Snake's assassin pals was all waiting for him with knives and tomahawks and they chopped him into bits, then chopped the bits into bits, and thronged the pieces far out in the sky so's he couldn't noway be put back together again. And that's how all the other worlds out there got made.

I laughed. Eeteh always told comical stories. "Of course, he COULD be put back together, and that's how the next story begins. That lying sneakthief Snake is in trouble!"

Eeteh shook his head. He warn't smiling. He says it's the end of Coyote and his stories. There ain't no more. All stories now will be Snake stories.

It was an awful story. I don't know why he told it to me.

Chapter XXVII

I ain't quick at ciphering things out, but with Eeteh's help it finally come to me that there warn't going to be no attack on the tribe that Sunday morning. They was just trying me out to see if I'd spill their plans and rile the natives up into their warpaint. To do that, I'd need Eeteh, and they hoped I'd lead them to him. They hoped right. Eeteh was smarter, but they made a fool out a me. I warn't happy about that, so before dawn I holstered up and took up my rifles and went over to roust out Tom and ask him, tarNATION, pard, when does the danged Black Hills Brigade ATTACK begin? He'd got in overnight and was sleeping like a dead man. He was madder'n the dickens and roars at me didn't nobody tell me, dammit, there warn't no attack, it was called off. "Besides, you're still the color a week-old horse piss, Huck, you oughtn't to be going nowheres." And he rolled over in disgust and set to snoring again.

Later, when he was drinking coffee out by the spit and chawing on a cold mule-deer leg for breakfast, I asked him why he sent Oren chasing after me. "Clumsy numskull," he grumbled. "Fell'n broke his damn arm. Don't know WHAT the leather-head was doing up there, any more'n I know what YOU was doing."

"He says you sent him. To protect me."

"Well, Hucky, you do need protection. Sometimes you ain't got no common horse sense. Getting over-friendly with the enemy whilst a war's on, a war we ain't even winning yet, just ain't rattling smart."

"Seemed like Oren was up there to kill somebody. Hope it warn't me."

Tom sighed, took a sip a coffee, poured more from the tin pot resting in the coals. "You remember when I took Becky's whipping for her? It was in that old one-room schoolhouse a-front of everybody, a gloriful moment, which you ain't able altogether to 'preciate because you was luckier'n me and warn't never penned up and tortured in there. Ornery old Dobbins really laid on the hickry that day and Becky begun bawling for what she'd got me into, but she got pretty excited too, as she told me later, feeling a vilent tingle on her own bum whilst mine was getting publicly flayed. To keep my mind off it, I read all the signs in the room I could see from the position I was in, and one of them says KNOWLEDGE IS POWER. At the time, getting flogged by a schoolmaster, I took that as a mean low-down joke, but later it become a kind of golden rule for me." Tom tossed out his coffee and poured more and says, "That's what Oren was doing up there."

"What? Getting his backside whacked?"

"No, listen at what I'm saying, Huck. Knowledge is power."

"Well, I wouldn't know. I ain't had much a nuther a them things, nor really cared to have some," I says.

"Which is why you need me, Hucky. I know all we need to know and I got enough power for both of us. Without power, you ain't nobody, and you ain't free nuther."

"Your horse told me the same thing."

"My horse?" Tom rolled his eyes like he was talking to a crazy man. "You must of catched a bad dose a brain-fever on top a your yaller janders, Huck," he says. "I hope it ain't fatal. See Wyndy over there with goggles on, watching you? I got to spend some time at the claim. He'll be keeping an eye on you whilst I'm gone, so's you don't get in more trouble. Do me a favor and don't sick your bats on him." He give me a long look and then says he's been to the cave himself. "I found one a my own whisky bottles up there, mostly drunk."

"That was me. Don't tell Molly. The cave stinks because a the bats, but it's comfortable for me when I'm off by myself. Used to be where them two robbers you hanged stowed their plunder."

"Well, please to don't go up there no more, pard. I don't want no accidents to happen to you. When you've shook off the janders, I'm going to need your help. If you want whisky, help yourself right here in the tent. I don't give a hang if you want to make yourself sicker'n you already are."

"What kind of accident you reckon might happen?"

"Hain't no idea. But look at poor Oren. Who'd a guessed a bat attack?"

After what Tom said, I had to see Eeteh again, but, with Wyndell watching me all day long and sleeping outside the tent flap at night, there warn't nothing I could do, not even when Tom was away, like he mostly was. I couldn't even answer Eeteh's lonesome hoots. Wherever I went, Wyndy was right behind me. When I turned around to talk to him, he only smiled sadfully and waited for me to start moving again. I'd begun shoving things we'd need for our travels to Mexico under my cot, like tarpolins and coffee and tin cups and ammunition, but now it was harder to collar things, with him always watching me. I dragged him around through the whole camp, hoping he'd get tired, but he never did. I did. I still warn't over the janders.

Old grizzled red-eyed Doc Molligan says maybe I won't never be over them. On t'other hand, he says, maybe they'll go away tomorrow. Science don't know much about the yaller janders, he says. For sure, HE don't know NOTHING about them. He come by the tent most every day to help himself to a cup a Tom's whisky and jaw awhile about the horrible diseases and beautiful women he's knowed. Both diseases and women was always mysteries to him, he says, which was considerable better'n knowing too much about neither of them. A mistake he never made a-purpose. He often described them both by how they smelt and tasted. He called it his prog-noses.

Molly says carpentery's more his line. He says he sawed off the ruined part below Eyepatch's knee and strapped Pegleg's wooden one onto the stump, and the Cap'n was near as good as new, though he warn't a satisfied man. His prog-noses for Eyepatch ever being satisfied was the same as for my yaller janders. Not likely, but you never know. Dad-fetched mystery, like the rest of life.

Whilst leading Wyndy around the camp, I seen that Eyepatch's pal, Yaller Whiskers, had took over Zeb's old shack and turned it from a jail back into a bar again. If Tom wanted his jail back and Yaller Whiskers in it, didn't nobody have to go too far. It seems that nobody paid him any mind after Tom shot up Eyepatch's leg, so he just stayed where he was and set himself up back in business again. He somehow found a card table and four chairs and a used slot-machine, and there was already a line waiting for them. He had a new partner, a sleepy-eyed chap with a flabby upper lip hanging down over a tuft of Chinaman's beard, who ducked when he seen me. He was familiar, but I couldn't think who he was.

Toothless old Deadwood, jaw askew, was setting out front on a wooden chair in his filthy union suit, popping his fob watch open and shut, and telling folks passing by how he got so crippled up. Sometimes it was Indians, sometimes it was bandits, sometimes it was wizzerds or that hurry-cane that carried him off to Wyoming, sometimes just his rheumatics. They say the new town was going to be named after him, or else after the same thing he was named for, and he was monstrous proud about it. He'd right away that same night shook off the splints me and Eeteh put on him, so now one elbow and one knee bent up the wrong way and nothing else was exactly right nuther. Deadwood says out the side of his mouth it was that hurry-cane dropped him flat on his backside and scrambled up his bones. When I come towards him to say hello, he yipped and tried to run away. His limbs took him every which way at the same time, making him look like a daddy-longlegs running. "Outen the way or suffer the con-SEEquences!" he shouted as he banged up against Zeb's old shack. The loafers hanging round hooted and clapped.

When he hit the shack, both Yaller Whiskers and his pard was looking out and they both fell backwards to the floor like they'd been knocked over like duckpins. I reckonized the chinless sleepy-eyed pard now. It was Mule Teeth without his two front teeth. Must a pulled them out and shaved his upper lip to disguise himself when Tom was rounding up all the crinimals that day he come riding in. His Chinaman's beard warn't hanging straight under his nose, but was parked back a ways.

There was talk about the calvary riding thisaway to round up all the loose hoss-tiles and end the Indian problem once and for all. That set off cheers here and there as the word spread round. General Hard Ass was said to be leading them. Eeteh and me didn't have much time. I looked over my shoulder, but Wyndy was still dogging me. Once when I was telling Tom my troubles with the general, he says, "Hard Ass is the name of every general I ever knowed. On the outside they're hard as rock, but it's just a hollow shell. If you say something to them, you can hear your own voice rattle round inside."

The picture-taker come out and set up his traps on one of the wooden sidewalks, aiming them at the front door of the generl store. Tom was strolling behind the parked wagons in his white hat and doeskins, looking important, chattering quietly to folks as he passed them by. The drummer was with him, mumbling his drum softly. Then the drummer banged louder and Tom clumb up on the sidewalk, stepped a-front of the camera and raised his hat. Everybody hoorayed. "As I got to be away so often on vital govment business about the hoss-tile problem," he declares, "I'm today pointing a new deputy mayor-govner, a man who has already contry-BYOOTed to law'n order in the Gulch by setting up the first gallows, and who is himself a prime sample of redemption from a life a grisly wickedness: the famous Black Avenger of the Spanish Main, CAP'N PATCH!"

The front door of the generl store opened up and Eyepatch stepped out on his new wooden leg, fitted out in black like always, a gold-toothed smirk on his scarred face, gold loops in his ears, his one eye a-glitter with raw meanness. The crowd out front yelled and whooped. They could not get enough of the amazing apparition. His black shirt had been mended, his boot shined, his black hair combed and knotted at the back, and his moustaches trimmed. What was new was the wooden peg and the bear-claw neckless round his throat, the one the tribe give me for good luck, but that fetched me and Zeb so much bad. Two old-fashioned horse-pistols was tucked in his belt, and one a Tom's gleaming cutlesses was hanging at his side. The picture-taker asked Eyepatch not to move, and he didn't, snarling steadily at the camera lens till the picture-taker was satisfied. He LOOKED like a bad man and he WAS a bad man. I couldn't think what Tom was up to.

So that evening at twilight, whilst setting

around the fire after supper, having a smoke, I asked him. "He's the scoundrel who killed Zeb," I says. "Shot the old fellow in the back and stole that bear-claw neckless. If you ain't here, he's bounden to get into more mischief."

Tom didn't know what old fellow I was talking about at first. "Oh, the whisky-maker, you mean. Never knowed him, so I can't judge. What I need right now is to find a parrot or a falcon for the Cap'n to wear on his shoulder. I wonder if a chicken-hawk would be like enough? You know how to catch one?"

"Tom! He's a cold-bloody killer! After he murdered old Zeb, he tried to hang ME for the awful things HE done! You're making a hero out a the wickedest varmint I ever SEEN!"

"I agree he ain't no angel, Huck. Cap'n Patch was born bad, and he'll die bad. Can't help himself. Meantimes, though, I need a chest a gold doubloons to bury, so's he can dig them up."

"You got nothing BUT buried treasure out here. Let him pan for them dern specks. Hang it all, Tom, you ain't —"

"No, they got to be doubloons. Maybe I could knock out his gold teeth and CALL them doubloons, then hide them and make him find them."

"That name you give him — warn't that what you called yourself when we was kids together playing pirates?"

"Might a been. Not important. Don't even know what the heck a Spanish main is, but it's a powerful clever name for a pirate."

I could see it warn't no use. He had his mind set on doing whatever it was he was doing. I relit my pipe and laid back against a stone. I was smoking my stone pipe because I wanted to. Me and Eeteh was going soon. Warn't no reason to hide nothing. And it felt good in my hand. It was still early. I could only see one star. Twilights was peacefully long up here in the Hills this time a year. There was enough light that some of Tom's pals was still panning gravel at the shore, though they was wading deeper out now. Tom says I been setting on one a the richest plasser gravels on the crick, and he fixed up a claim from the year I first come here. I says he can have it. He also claimed up acres and acres a mud at the emigrant camp above, which he was planning to parcel out into lots once he makes it legal for it to be a town. Noises was drifting down from up there. A gunshot or two. Sivilization. I says he can have that, too.

Tom had been staring at my stone pipe

for a while and now he asked about it. I says it's the head of a spirit horse and it was give me by the tribe after I rode Ne Tongo back. Big River. So then he wanted to know about Ne Tongo, and I told him about the magic ride and all that happened after. It was darkening up some and a few more stars was showing. I was glad Tom was getting interested in my life, even if he warn't going to share it.

"Still got your old pony saddle?"

"No. Don't use none."

"What happened to the pony?"

"The tribe et him."

Tom clucked as though to say, that's savages for you. I grinned. I think I felt more at home with the tribe than even Eeteh done. "Where's the horse now?"

"Eeteh's watching over him till we leave."

Tom paused, thinking about that, and poured himself some whisky. "Is he riding him?"

"Can't nobody ride him. Just me."

"Do you think I could? Would he except a western saddle?"

"No, but you could try him without one like me. Don't think he'd let you, but mostly anything I can do, you always do better."

He sat up and turned to look at me. "You shouldn't go, Hucky. I need you. I can get the horse back for you."

"But what about Eeteh? There's a bounty on his head now. And the tribe's on the warpath. That don't work for Eeteh. He's lonely and scared like what I am." I could hear him now, if it warn't a real owl. It warn't a happy hoot. "Him and me can't stay. But you can come with us."

Tom had a thoughtful look on his face like he was considering that. Then the accident he was worried about happened. The robbers' cave blowed up. The explosion was deefening and sent rock flying all the way down into the crick. Might a been anything blowing up, but I knowed it was the cave.

Tom and everybody went running up there, and I clumb up, too, though I warn't running. I was scared at what I'd find. There warn't no cave, just a pile a rock, dead and stunned bats everywheres. There was a dead body all blowed apart, but it didn't have Eeteh's head. It had Peewee's. I judged he might a been sent to light the fuse, but Tom, who was poking about in the rubble like something might be found in it, says panning the crick for specks probably warn't fast enough for Peewee. He must a been looking for a shortcut.

There warn't no sign of Eeteh. The last thing I heard from him was that owl hoot.

If it was him. I had to hope I'd hear another, but I didn't think I would.

Chapter XXVIII

I walked up to the cave through the rain the next day to look around. Wyndell tried to stop me, but I pushed him away. Tom once said I knowed how to cuss and fight, but not how to get mad. Maybe he was learning me. The preacher had a grumpy look on his goggled face. He probably wanted to go report on me, but there warn't more'n one a him, so he only could follow me along. It seemed like it rained every day in the Hills. It was always sloppy and uncomfortable. It was like a wet picture of my squshed-down miserableness inside.

Before he left crickside that morning to go make himself richer, Tom says he's sorry to tell me, but he's afeard my friend is fatally expired. At the cave, Bear says the same. Him and a couple of others was trying to move the rock pile, but he says it was a most nation hard job, and they don't know if they can do it. Bear showed me a beaded buckskin vest, torn and bloodied, that they found under the rocks. Eeteh's. He says it was near some body bits, which was probably once part a him. "We ain't struck no more heads yet, only Peewee's, but me and the others're still looking. Don't hold much hope, but it don't matter. Jest only an injun. He prob'bly won't mind being buried right where he's at." He give me the vest when I asked for it. "Nice beadwork," he says. "Needs cleaning up, but it should fit."

If the body was dug out, I reckoned I'd put it in a tree in the tribal way. Bodies are set in trees so their souls can fly straight off to the next world without nothing to get in their way. In Eeteh's Coyote world there ain't nothing next and no souls neither, only a few comical ghosts, but I'll do that for him anyhow. We both been good at pretending. I was pretending now, jabbering in a quiet way with Tom and Bear, tolerating Wyndy.

Whilst I walked sorrowing along, heading back crickside because I don't know where else to go, I passed a small horse-drawed buggy, and the person inside called out, "Huckleberry! Huckleberry FINN! Is that YOU?" It was Becky Thatcher! "Get IN!" she says with a happy laugh and opened the door for me.

She give me a big kiss when I squeezed in and laughed again. There was a pretty smell about her and a most wonderful softness. "Tom ain't here," I says.

"I KNOW that, Huckleberry! It's YOU I want to see! It's been so LONG!" I asked if she warn't the person I seen, dressed up so pretty, in that saloon up in Wyoming a few years ago, and she says, "Aw, Hucky, those were my working clothes. I HATE them. Yours are prettier. I LOVE that vest, though it needs a washing. I was still chasing after Tom back then, and I was working that trail, waiting for him to show up on it. I supposed most everybody would, sooner or later. And there was no shortage of customers. Cowboys get lonely."

When she says the word "lonely," I felt the hurt of it and my throat thickened up. "You was riding with cowboys?"

"Oh, Huckleberry . . ." She sighed and touched my cheek. "I'd just started up my new profession. Cowboys are mostly only little boys, their pants full of ignorant excitement. If they also got money in their pants, I can generally do something about the excitement, and about their ignorance, too. I GUESS you could call it riding with them." She laughed and clapped her hand on my leg and I jumped. "Aren't YOU the ticklish one!" she says with a tittery little laugh. "All right. Let me tell you flat out, Huckleberry. Tom left me in St. Petersburg more'n a dozen years ago when I was six months heavy with our baby. I lost it and, when I stopped crying, I came west looking for him. A girl's not supposed to DO that, but I did. Sometimes I got close, but it was like he'd always catch wind of me somehow and move on. I ran out of money and hope and finally I met Dorie and started doing what I HAD to do or starve. I was just only coming to work that day when you saw me. I didn't want Tom to know, and I was afraid he might be with you. If he did turn up, I didn't know if I'd hug his feet or shoot him." She sighed. "Now, it don't matter anymore." She slumped back in the seat like she was thinking over about what she just said. "So, where've YOU been, Huckleberry? Did you come here to the Hills with Tom?"

"No, been here for a time. The Gulch was a most lazy and tolerable place till people like Tom come'n ruined it. Me and a Lakota friend helped an old whisky-maker trade with the tribe and move his goods, and we helped him drink them up, too. I was happy as I ever been. Then a crazy old prospector found a yaller rock and everything changed. Tom he come and saved me from a lynching, but he made a mess out of everything else. Me and my friend was fixing to leave for Mexico or somewheres, anywheres, just so's we was away from here, but I got sick with the janders. Now, all of a sudden, he's dead." I took a deep breath. "Got dynymited."

"Oh! Last night! I HEARD it!" Her voice was like a sad little girl's. "Is that his vest? That's blood on it, isn't it?"

I don't never cry. But I was crying.

"Oh, Hucky!" She put her arm around me and kissed me again. She was crying, too. "Look! We're HERE!" The buggy was stopping. I ain't even noticed we been moving. "It's where I live. Come in for some real 'buckles coffee and Dorie's butterscot cookies."

Whilst Becky was giving the driver some money, I crawled out and wiped my eyes and seen that Wyndy been following us on horseback. He did not look a happy man. "Tom hired him to watch me," I says. "He don't give up easy." She waved at him and invited him in. He hollers out from a ways off on his horse that, no, Finn's got to go back to the camp. NOW! Becky shrugged and took my hand and led me in, put the latch on the door.

It was the loveliest place I seen since I

come west. There was curtains on the windows and pictures on the walls and a cast-iron stove with a big new-fashioned porcelain tub behind it and soft chairs with crocheted doilies on them like in Tom's aunt's house. "Old Dorie likes a homey place," Becky says, stoking up the fire in the wood stove. She poured water in a painted tin coffee pot and set it on.

"Dorie?"

"Hunky Dorie. She's my business partner. She fixed up this house for us because of all the fat boys here in Leed, but we're looking for a bigger place where we can hire in more girls. And the fat boys are too tight with their money. Can you imagine? They want to KEEP it! So, we been to Stonewall to look around, Hillyo, Camp Crook, all the new shantytowns." When the water was a-biling, she throwed in a handful a coffee and took the pot off the fire. "Today Dorie's over in a new town on Rapid Crick. There's a lot of quick money in the Hills right now, but you have to grab it as it goes flying past, and it helps if you're where it first sets off." She poured me a cup a thick barefoot coffee through a silver tea strainer, and laid some cookies on a little tin plate with painted flowers on it. It was the best coffee I ever tasted. "For me, these mining shantytowns are too wild and scary," she says, then thumbed some snuff up her nose. "I'd like to be in a civiler place like Cheyenne or Abileen or even here in Leed, but Hunky Dorie loves excitement and hates the law. She says the law don't mainly favor the profession. And the miners at least are grateful, while the fat boys think they own you."

"Is Tom one a the fat boys?"

"He's around. They say he and some other bandits have partnered up, and they mean to grab it all. He pretends he doesn't see me. Or maybe he's not pretending." She sneezed and rubbed her nose. "I was never able to make out how you two got to be friends. He doesn't have any others. Just only you."

"I don't know nuther. I warn't nobody, just a dumb leather-headed loafer sleeping on the streets. I never done the things everybody else was doing like church or school. They said I warn't sivilized. But then Tom took me like a pard. That changed everything. All them stories Tom likes to tell, the Sarah Sod ones with the jeanies? It was like that. So, when he asked me to light out for the Territory with him, there warn't nothing else I wanted to do. Scouting out here with Tom was the most amazing life I could ever imagine. I wished it would last on forever."

"But then I come along," she says. A kind of sadfulness slid across her face, but then she smiled and says, "Scouts is what me and Dorie are now. It's why I was over in Deadwood Gulch. We're not scouting for Indians and robbers, though. We're looking for stupid horny boys with little bags of gold dust around their scrawny sunburnt necks." She giggled sweetly, just like she always done as a schoolgirl, then sniffed. "When's the last time you had a bath, Mr. Huckleberry Finn? By looks and smell, I'd judge at least a month or more."

"It's been some time. Me and my horse used to wash up regular in the crick, but the horse is gone and the crick shore is full of tetchy gold panners who don't tolerate nobody stirring things around."

"I'll hot up some water."

"Well . . . I ain't partial to baths . . ." She was still Tom's woman. I was thinking about Coyote and Snake Woman, and where all that ended up.

"Come on, we're like family, Hucky. I got to take CARE of you!" She put a big kettle on the stove and throwed in some wintergreen leaves. Then she took off her frock and hung it on a wall peg. She warn't so skinny like before and she was adding on a second chin, but she was still lovely and round in her frilly white underclothes. I don't know what to say, so I says it must be awful, trying to get in and out a them things in a hurry, and she laughs and says she DON'T get in and out, and she showed me how all the main bits opened up with pearl buttons and cloth hinges. I hain't never seen nothing like it, and says so. She sighed and smiled. "It was my embroidered pantalettes that got Tom so agitated back when we were still in school together," she says. "He was desperate to get them down and see what was under them, and he begged me to let him do that, but it didn't seem right. Until we were dying in Injun Joe's cave, and then he did it without asking. Now get out of those old rags. The water's near hot."

I didn't appear to have no polite choice, so I took my clothes off and crawled into the fancy porcelain tub. "You got the haunches, Hucky, of a wild dog," she says. "And you got an off complexion all over." She hung my traps over the back of a chair next the stove to dry them out, asking if I'd been wearing those britches since I come out West. "All that buckskin in the crotch, it's what makes them smell so pretty." When I was settled, she poured the heated water over me and put another kettle on. Then she commenced to lather me up with a cotton cloth and a handful a soft soap that stunk like lavender. "You ever been in love, Hucky?"

"Once."

"Did it make you feel wonderful?"

"I ain't never been in so much trouble. Had to run away without my boots on."

"Oh, Hucky, you're SO romantic! Maybe what you need is to get married."

"Done that. When I was living with the tribe, I found myself hitched to a native woman without no nose named Kiwi. She learnt me some things, so I warn't such a dumb fool with a woman, and I felt sorry for her, but I didn't like her. She didn't do nothing for my loneliness neither. So when she got fed up and moved out, I reckoned that part was over, I didn't have to do no more marrying."

Becky laughed. "You married a squaw!"

"Well, they don't like to be called that. I had to learn that the hard way. Kiwi had a punch could floor a man."

"Kiwi. Does that translate to something?"

"Probably. She had a longer name I couldn't never remember. But they all grinned and snorted when anybody announced it, so I was afeard to ask."

I told Becky all about them giving me a love potion and what it done to a body and how it somehow worked on the whole tribe at the same time, and she unloosed her little-girl laugh and says, "Are you making this up, Hucky?"

"Maybe."

Wyndy was banging on the door and calling out my name and damning degenrates and fornycators, but we didn't pay him no mind. The second kettleful was ready, so Becky poured it over me. "I'm reminded that back home," she says as she poured, "the locust trees'll be in bloom."

"You still think of it like home?"

"Only when I'm away from it." She set the empty kettle on the back of the stove, peeled out of her underclothes, and snuggled down into the warm water beside me. "Tom has all your treasure money, you know. He talked my pappy out of it, saying he was bringing it out to you. I don't suppose you've ever seen it."

"No. Don't matter."

"Tom always said giving money to you was just a waste."

"He's mostly right. Your pap probably says the same."

"Pappy's not doing well. His mind's jellying up. The village idiot is smarter'n him nowadays. He still thinks Tom is the prince of princes. Tom couldn't stand him and cussed him behind his back, calling him a pompous old fart, and sometimes to his face when he seemed blanked out. Tom never ever got his law degree. He was too impatient. And he didn't really need it. He's smarter'n most lawyers anyways. He took one of my pappy's diplomas and doctored it up and, next thing I knew, he was gone. He'd got tired of me right away. He liked Amy Lawrence better and saw more of her than me, though he had to pay for it with her. He said I was boring in bed and scared me with the things he wanted me to do. Now I do them with everybody." She took my hand and squeezed it. "But you know what? I don't specially like the life I've got, but I think I'd like housewifing Tom even less."

"Life don't rarely turn out like you think it might," I says.

"No, that's right. I'm hoping Tom's don't turn out like HE thinks it might," she says with a wicked little grin. "I've hired me a real lawyer, a client who favors the rough stuff in bed and on the street, too, and we are going after Tom's gold. I still got the marriage license. Either he shares up or we'll expose what a fraud and liar he is.

When all them claims he's granted are shown to be worthless, the poor boy will have his hands full, without he does what I say."

"He told me a story one night about killing his own pap. It happened after he left you and he was out here scouting on his own. He says he found the old man over in Baker City, a sick muddled-up drunk, worse off'n a beggar. Tom was shamed of him. When he told his pap that his mam had died, and desperate poor, too, the old fellow busted out bawling and blubbering, and Tom was so disgusted, he shot him."

"He told ME about killing his pa, too. It was on our wedding night up in Minnysota, when we were both wide awake, and still grabbing at each other by candlelight, and he told me the story to fill in the recess gaps. Says it was while you two were scouting somewheres down south and you got set upon by a gang of snarly bandits. You got scared and ran away, but he stood his ground, he said, and it was a dreadful battle, but he somehow managed to kill them all. When he took their masks off was when he discovered that the bandit chief was his own pa. He was carrying a tintype of Tom's ma in his breast pocket, and the bullet he'd killed his pa with went clean through her nose. Which story you think was true?"

"My Lakota friend would a said both at the same time."

She laughed, sighed. "You were born melancholic, Hucky. Me, I've had to grow into it."

Wyndy was standing over us, wailing about sin. "I must've left the back door open," Becky says. "Shut up, Wyndy. Take your clothes off and come on in. It'll raise the water level." Wyndy never stopped preaching, but he done what she told him to do. It was getting crowded, but me and Wyndy was both pretty skinny, and Becky had a way of making a body feel comfortable.

Chapter XXIX

After her water-bath, Becky wanted to take an air-bath, which she says a famous French doctor specially sejested as a wholesome practice for young ladies of a sensitive nature like herself. The sun finally come out so she allowed she'd take her air-bath out-of-doors, and she invited us to join her and maybe have a picnic or a mud-fight. But Wyndy says he had to get back and take me with him, so we put our clothes on and clumb up on his horse. She come out, all plump and rosy, to start her air-bath, and I says we might not see each other again for a time. Without Eeteh, I didn't know where I'd go or what I'd do, but General Hard Ass was a-coming, and I had to get somewheres he couldn't find me. If I need money, Becky says I better not take any off of Tom, even if he tried to give me some, because he'll just chase me down and say I stole it. "That boy don't give nothing away without he calculates how to get it back again." She says she'll go get some of her own to give me as a bone voyage, but I told her there warn't nothing I needed except somewheres to go. I says I might try to get back to St. Petersburg and go look up Amy Lawrence, and she says don't you dare.

The slow jog back to the Gulch took less'n an hour, but it was mighty uncomfortable on the backend of Wyndy's horse, and me and the horse had to listen the whole time to Wyndy whining religious songs about sinners and what awful things land on them in this world and in others. I'd been sinning up a storm, so I reckoned Wyndy's singing was one a them awful things and I had to bear it, though it warn't fair to the horse. The sun was a-blazing away so bright it dazzled my eyes, but the ground below was still wet and soggy, slow going for the horse.

We'd just reached one a the hills leading into the camp, when we was set upon by a crowd a wagons and animals and people coming up t'other way in a mighty hurry, Caleb and Oren among them, yelling that Cap'n Patch and his pals had took over the Gulch and was unloosing a rain of terror. "Don't GO there!"

"But where's TOM?" Wyndy cries out.

"The Cap'n says his scouting party was

ambushed by the red-skins!"

"They're all DEAD!"

"The Cap'n has pointed hisself mayor, sheriff, tax collector and judge!"

"They been stringin' people up by threesomes every thirty minutes!"

"They got Molly! He's NEXT! The Cap'n's mad about what he done to him and wants to lop off both a Molly's legs with his cutless'n THEN hang him!"

"Who they ain't hangin', they're FLOGGIN'!"

"The whores is gettin' flogged NEKKID! The Cap'n is layin' it on the pore things personal!"

"They jest got here and don't know what the heck's happening!"

"They got nuthin on ME! I been here a month and I don't know nuther!"

There was more desperate crowds heeling it up our way. Looked like the whole camp might be emptying out. But just then the picture-taker come a-galloping in from the opposite direction, hauling all his apparatuses. "THE AMAZ'N TOM SAWYER'S A-COMIN'!" he shouted as he clopped past. "THE SIVILIZER OF THE WEST!"

And sure enough, there he was, riding towards us in white pants and shiny boots, chest bare, his cremson bandanna tied round his head, long curly hair gathered up in a knot behind. A black skull-and-crossbones flag was a-flying from Storm's pommel like from a ship's mast, and there was a cutless slapping at Tom's side. Bear rode right behind him, looking mostly like himself.

Tom stopped long enough to give the picture-taker time to set up his camera down at the camp and to order everybody up here not to shoot, no matter what happens. "Just don't get in HIS way, or MINE! Bear's got orders to shoot ANYBODY that butts in or raires a gun! TELL EVERYBODY!" Then he snatched Eeteh's vest out a my hands, and he and Bear galloped away. We chased after them, fast as we could, but we knowed he'd wait for us. We was his audience.

Three poor fellows was a-dangling from the gallows as we come riding in. Molly was up on the platform, next in line, along with that twangy fiddle-player and a Chinese fellow who'd been selling grilled beefsteaks and fried rabbits in the street, which everybody judged was really hammered buffalo hide and mud rats. The fiddler was the gent who serenaded me on the gallows with a whiny song about jumping off into the other world, but he warn't singing it now, without his teary whimpering were such a song.

The stubby yaller-whiskered tavern-keeper and his toothless pal Mule Teeth was holding Doc Molligan up, and Cap'n Patch was standing over him with his cutless raired high. The Cap'n was wearing the bear-claw neckless the tribe give me and I give to Zeb, and the neckless and the blood spattered on him give him a most savage look. The army drummer in the goggles and black derby was playing a drumroll. Molly's left leg was already chopped off below the knee, the blood tied off above it, and the Cap'n was taking aim at the other one. Molly's eyes was crossed with fear or drunkness or most probably both. When the Cap'n seen the picture-taker setting up his camera, he stopped still for a moment, blade in the air, looking like he warn't sure whether to hold his pose, whack off Molly's other leg, or bust out a there.

The emigrants who hadn't run off was cheering Cap'n Patch, just like they'd cheered Tom, but now they started cheering Tom again as he come galloping in on Storm, Eeteh's raggedy vest flapping behind him, black jack a-flutter from Storm's pommel. "AARRRGH!" Tom roared from deep in his throat, and whushed his cutless round in the air. "AVAST, ye filthy bilge rat!

Prepare to DIE!"

Cap'n Patch only grinned in a mean bloody-face gold-tooth way, the loops in his ears glinting in the sun. He dropped his cutless, ca'mly hauled out his horse-pistols, aimed them both at Tom, and fired. Little flags popped out the barrels that said BANG! and GOT YOU! Yaller whiskers and Mule Teeth dropped Molly and cut. The Cap'n rolled down off of the platform to follow them, but now there warn't no way through the whooping crowd. He backed up against the gallows like a snarly trapped rat, rocking unsteady on his pegleg. Tom sprung off of his horse and stepped up to the Cap'n through the gawkers and poked at his chest with the curved point of his cutless blade. "Man your weapon, you scurvy one-eyed dog!" he growled down deep in his chest. "Or be ye too afeard?"

It took Cap'n Patch a moment to cipher out Tom's intentions. Then he grabbed up the cutless where it had fell and spun round on his peg to face Tom. He growled like a mad bear, holding his cutless out with both hands. Tom grinned and growled back, and swung at the Cap'n. The Cap'n jerked his cutless up to meet the blow and there was a powerful clash of steel, and Tom grinned again. The Cap'n took a swing at him, his blade swishing through the air, Tom jumping back and clattering his cutless against the Cap'n's.

And now the battle begun in earnest. There was a grand battering of steel on steel, Tom and the Cap'n a-growling and a-grunting, ducking and swinging, their hairknots flying. The emigrants was all yowling, nor else standing spillbounded with their jaws gapping like in Tom's Sarah Sod stories.

Then all of a sudden Cap'n Patch stumbled on his wooden leg and fell into the mud! He was at Tom's mercy! But Tom backed off, used his cutless blade to bat the Cap'n's weapon over where he could reach it, waited till he was up on his peg and foot again, and then they went at each other like before. First, one of them was near killing t'other, then it was t'other way around. People was whooping and screaming. Tom and the Cap'n was staggering about in the mud, cussing, flailing, their blades flashing about. Both of them was leaking blood variously. Sometimes they slapped down into the mud, but they always sprung up again with cutlesses clanging and with throaty growls.

Then Tom fell and lost his cutless. The Cap'n growled and grinned his gold-tooth grin and stood over Tom. Tom reached for his cutless and the Cap'n kicked it further away, stomped on Tom's arm, raired up his own blade in both hands. People was reaching for their weapons. My own hands was twitching. But Bear fired off a shot into the air, so we all done just like Tom says, even though things was going badly for him. People was scared. I was scared. The Cap'n drawed an X on Tom's chest with his cutless blade, then set to plunge it in where the lines crossed. It was all over for Tom! People cried out. Even Bear looked nervious and uncertain. But all of a sudden Tom twisted and grabbed the Cap'n's ankle with his free hand and upended him, snaggled his cutless back out a the mud, wiped it off. The Cap'n, covered now in mud and blood, scrambled to his foot and peg, took up his cutless again, and unloosed a mighty swing, just as Tom's own blade sliced clean through his neck. There warn't no change in the Cap'n's expression. It was like the blade had passed straight through without touching him, the way magicians do it in the circus sideshows. He still had a snarl on his face and was gripping his cutless with both hands. Then his head dropped off. The headless body took two steps and fell over, laying on the cutless.

At first, nobody says a word. We was all staring at the head, laying in the mud, its one eye still blinking. It seemed to be grinning, but it probably warn't. Then they all commenced to roar and shout out Tom's name. The picture-taker come over and took a photograph of Tom, all smeared with mud and blood, with his boot on the headless body and holding the head up by its hair-knot. Zeb's bear-claw neckless fell off into the mud and Tom picked it up, lifted it high like a trophy. The picture-taker took another photograph. "Prepare the Cap'n for burial," Tom declares. "And save the wooden leg for Doc Molligan. He's going to need it."

CHAPTER XXX

"Patch warn't smart enough to practice proper like I told him," Tom says, "but he had a natural talent." We'd just been to the Cap'n's funeral and the burying of the dozen emigrants he'd hung before Tom got there. Wyndy was doing the preaching, which was probably still going on. Tom had draped the Cap'n's coffin with his pirate flag, though he says he might go dig it up later, he hates to lose it. The box was too small and the Cap'n's head had to be set between his legs like it was being born there. The gold ear loops was gone, and his mouthful a gold teeth, too. A body couldn't hardly reckonize him. Bear had made a wooden grave marker that said CAP'N PATCH. CUTHROTE PIRATE. HE HAD STILE. Tom says he's going to have a proper gravestone carved out of Black Hills granite. The others was all buried together in a deep hole. They learnt the first names of four a them and made one name out a the four.

We was setting on the raised wooden sidewalk a-front of the claims office eating little wrens, finches, and bluebirds, sparrows and sapsuckers, grilled up for us by the grateful Chinese cookie Tom rescued from a hanging, who was also famous for buffalo-hide steaks and fried mud-rats. These birds was so small, they was skewered six at a time and held over the fire to burn the feathers off and roast the nubble of meat, then dipped in a sauce of honeyberries, chokecherries, and molasses, toasted again so's to blacken the molasses, and finally et entire, heads, bones, feet, and all. The emigrants seemed to need molasses in and on everything, and it was mostly what you tasted. Lakota cooking's a sight better. I was missing it.

I asked Tom about the twelve people who got hung before he turned up, couldn't he have hurried up and maybe saved a few? Tom, chomping the birds between his teeth, says he done what he could, but it warn't no consequence, they was all probably guilty of one hanging offense or nuther, just like the rest of us. Tom's teeth was still strong and mostly all there. I calculated that before I was forty I wouldn't have none, so, with the teeth I had left, I chawed the wee crispy creturs more cautious and slow. "It don't matter, Huck. It really don't. It was only the end a their stories, which probably warn't exceeding good ones anyways. Ourn may be better, but they'll end, too, and probably just as nonnamous."

Tom had took a bath in the crick and washed his wounds afterwards with whisky. He was still bare-chested, oozing blood from the X the Cap'n had drawed there, but, like Becky, he also seemed to judge that air-baths was good for a body, and says he don't want to leave the wounds to fester inside a shirt or bandages. Folks was still crowding round the gallows, telling each other about what they seen. They turned and hoorayed Tom from time to time, and he smiled like a bishop and waved back at them.

"But our stories ain't over yet, Hucky," he says, using a tiny bird's leg bone for a toothpick. He'd already et a couple a dozen birds, and he might a et more but the neck gristle was getting in his teeth. "We got a monstrous big day a-rolling up next month, the first sinteenery of the American Revolution! It'll be a hundred years to the day since our rapscallion founding fathers let rip their Declaration and kicked all them royalist butts OUT a here! With their get-up-and-go owdaciousness, them young scoundrels got theirselves planted forever into the history books."

Old Deadwood was down in the street in his union suit, bouncing about, popping his fob watch open and snapping it shut. His union suit was more or less the color a the street. He spied Tom and come a-running towards him, his limbs flying in all directions, and then he seen me and scrambled away again, the trap door of his union suit flapping.

"And now, a hundred years on, where can the sivilizing consequences of such get-up-and-go Americaness be most best seen? Why, right here in the Gulch, Hucky! We ARE America, clean to the bone! This is where the wonderfullest nation the world has ever seen is getting born! I BELIEVE that! It'll be GREAT! A new land of freedom and progress and brotherhood! A perfect new Jerusalem right here on earth! And you and me are PART of it! It's US that's making it happen! That being so, we are obleeged to throw the best damn sinteenery party in the nation, which these Territories is directly going to be a natural part of! They call us outlaws because they say we're on tribal land, so we got to show our amaz'n American PATRIOTICS! These lands is rightfully OURN and we're going to set up a Liberty Pole and raise the American flag on it to PROVE it! I aim to have a parade and fireworks and rifle squads banging away all through the night so's Sitting Bull and Crazy Horse and all their dumb savages can hear it plain. Maybe we can even run a circus. I can rescue back your horse from the injuns and you can show off your bareback riding and your shooting and roping. They say Wild Bill is on his way here. If he gets here in time, maybe we can get him to do some fancy pistol tricks. I can't manage all that by myself. I need you to help me, pard!"

I told General Hard Ass a stretcher about Wild Bill so's to save Tongo. If them two turned up here at the same time, I was in even more desperater trouble, if that was possible. "You got all them friends you come with. Ask them. Ask Bear."

"Bear ain't got over the pison arrow jimjams. He's out hugging trees again right now. And the others ain't friends. I'm making them rich. When I can't do that, they'll find somebody else. It ain't like you'n me, Hucky. We're real pards. We can count on us, no matter what." The cookie had brung us bowls of wild razberries in fresh cow milk, still warm from the udder. Tom lifted his bowl to his mouth, et it all down. "First of all," he says, licking his moustaches off, "we need the best shooter in the Hills to lead our new Black Hills Brigade, and I allow that should oughter be you."

"LISTEN to me, Tom! General Hard Ass is left Fort Lincoln by now, and him and his army probably ain't a day away from here. If he comes here and finds me, he HANGS me. I GOT to GO!"

"Confound it, Huck, you shouldn't never've got in trouble with that general in the first place."

"Couldn't help it. He asked me to do things I warn't able to do. I just ain't fitten for the army life."

"All right, but keep your britches on. I know that jackanapes personal. His vixenish young wife has him wrapt round her little finger. He got court-martialed because he couldn't stay away from her, the dog, and if I'd been persecuting him, he'd a wound up on the end of a rope. He's a lecher and a crinimal. But I can manage the bugger."

"All your generals is the same to me. Ain't a one a them wouldn't want to hang me, and with every right to go and do it. I don't NEED to keep on living, but if I WANT to, I got to get clear of them all."

"Hang it all, Hucky, it's just too dangersome. A white man alone don't stand a chance out there, specially now the Sioux War's hotted up."

"I know it. I do wish I had somebody to travel with, but I don't, so I ain't got no choice."

"Well, it's too bad about your Lakota friend, but, honest, Huck, I didn't have nothing to do with that. Peewee got killed, too. I loved Peewee like a brother and I'm mighty afflicted by what happened. Nobody had no idea your friend was in there. You should a told us. But you can't go now. Here, me'n you are together, and together we can lick anyTHING and anyBODY. It just don't make no sense to go off on your lonesome and get scalped."

"I been out here on my lonesome for a stretch now. I got learnt a few western trades I can follow, and I can palaver a bit with some a the tribes. There's a couple a fur trappers you and me used to know down a-near the Indian Territory. If I can get that far, maybe I can ride with them."

"But you're going to be one a the richest men in the WORLD! You can BUY the blamed general! You can't believe how RICH we are, Hucky! You're my pard, I'm sharing EVERYTHING with you, just like we always done."

"Being rich don't work for me, Tom."

"That's plain stupid," he says, getting mad.

"Give it to Becky or Deadwood."

"You don't give Deadwood money now. He don't even know what it is. You just take care of him. I'm doing that. And I don't need to give nothing to Becky, she's grabbing all she wants. She's aiming to turn the whole Gulch against me, if I don't do like she says."

"What are you going to do?"

"Well, the Gulch is a dangersome place. If she ain't careful, she may have an accident."

The Chinaman cookie brung us some whisky. Tom drank his down the same furisome way he chawed up the burnt birds. I passed him my glass. He looked me over. "You're still yallerer than our cookie. Ain't the janders over yet?"

"Comes and goes. I feel dog-tired all the time."

"Well, that's another reason you can't go. You ain't healthy enough." He drank down my whisky and rose up, causing a stir out in the street. "Come along now. I got a surprise for you."

As we stepped down off of the raised sidewalk, Tom was surrounded by grateful survivors of Cap'n Patch's rain of terror.

Some of them slapped his bare back or punched his arm, while others took off their hats and bowed their heads at him like he was the Awmighty. One a the new prostytutes who'd got horsewhipped by Eyepatch come over and give Tom a hug and kissed the X on his chest and says she'll pray for him every night at bedtime, even if that's at six in the morning. He was welcome to visit her any time at no charge once her awful wounds has healed, or even before if he wanted to see what that horrible pirate man done to her complexion.

Deadwood come staggering and loping towards us, his broke jaw set on a lopsided grin. Then he seen me with his crossed eyes and fell over in the mud in his anxiousness to get away. "That old sourdough has a new yarn about how he got that way," Tom says as we slopped along. "He says whilst he was taking a squat in the woods, there was a giant powder explosion that near busted his eardrums, and drove the shit right back up his arsehole. Says he ain't had no relief since. The blast throwed him all the way here into the street, where this stinking muck saved his life. It was the dynymite done all the bone-twisting, he says. Falling into the mud was like landing on a pile a feathers."

"Glad to hear it's good for something. Sure ain't no joy in tracking round in it."

"We'll have to lay in some brick streets," Tom says. He had lots of plans like that. Gas lamps on poles. Hitching posts. A newspaper. Stables to get the animals off the street. Tom can't get up and NOT go. We passed a new brewery which he says he had some money in. "Also I've cleaned up the old whisky-maker's copper worms and pot, so's to try to still up a fresh batch from that yist mash you rescued. You got to admit, Huck, the Gulch is a better place now'n it ever was before."

Remembering what Becky told me, I asked him whatever become a my treasure money that I left with the judge, and he says, "I got it with me. Just tell me when you want it."

"I'll take it now, then. See if I can't buy me a train ticket to Mexico."

"Trains don't go there. And anyways I AIN'T giving it to you to run away on. Look, here we are."

Where Tom had fetched me to was a place on a muddy hill slope overlooking the Gulch where the foundations for a house was being laid. "I'm building a fifteen-room mansion here, Huck. Ain't nothing like it ever seen back in St. Petersburg. It'll have colored glass windows and giant mirrors in rosewood frames, canopy beds with the finest horsehair mattresses and feather pillows, crystal shandy-leers and Paris wallpaper and China spittoons, even a most splendid bathroom with a French bathtub and a modern water closet like the one the Queen of England does her business on. I got a claim on nearly all Deadwood Gulch. People have to buy their lots from me, so I can pick and choose who my neighbors is. And I'm picking you, Huck! On that lot right there next to mine, I'm building a house just for you! It'll have everything you need, even a barn out back for your horse and an ice box to keep your beer cold and a big bed for entertaining the ladies in! Four at a time if you like! I'll find you some so's you don't get lonesome!"

"Can't afford nothing like that."

"One a the world's richest men can afford whatever he wants, dang it. Anyways, I'm giving it to you free."

"I thought when we left St. Pete we was running away from all this sivilizing."

Tom looked awful disappointed. He looked like he always done back home when I didn't answer him proper. It ain't no use to talk to a numskull like you, he'd say. If I was as ignorant as you, Huck, I wouldn't let on. I probably shouldn't a said what I said about his house. It made me feel bad after all he was trying to do for me. But when I tried to thank him and say I was sorry, I couldn't find the words for it.

Instead, I left Tom with all his worshippers and hiked up to the rubble that once was a bat cave to say my good-byes to Eeteh. I let out a couple a owl hoots and listened with all my ears for an answer, but it was dead silent. A powerful sadfulness come over me. The Gulch warn't tolerable for me no more, but I didn't know where else to go or what to do. The trails all led to one fort or nuther, and the general had pals in all of them. Tom had found the things I'd stowed under my cot to travel with and took them all. I didn't even have a horse. Tom had hung a lot of emigrants and some a them had horses I could borrow, but they warn't none a them Tongos nor not even Jacksons.

It warn't long before Tom fetched up, toting along his rifle, as I reckoned he might. The light was fading into one a those long summer twilights. "Wyndell says you was up here," he says. He had his shirt on again and he handled me Eeteh's bloody vest, saying he thought I might be wanting to bury it up here with Eeteh's remainders. I says there warn't no advantage in burying nothing that only needs a wash, and Tom grinned and nodded at that. "Here, I also brung you the bear-claws that was round the Cap'n's neck."

"I got that neckless from the tribe," I says. "Maybe they liked me less'n I judged they did. They said it was for good luck and I give it to old Zeb, and you seen what it done for me'n him. Now your Cap'n's lost his head. I sejest you don't keep the neckless yourself nuther, but pass it on to General Hard Ass for me, since you know him so good."

He grunted, looking around. "I thought I heard an owl up here."

"There's an old hoot owl lives in the crotch a that old Ponderosa over there," I lied.

Tom took aim and fired and a darkness left the crotch and a big old bird come crashing down, wings beating at the air. "Well, it won't hoot no more," he says, but he sounded disappointed. I reckoned Tom was as surprised as I was. It just showed, some stretchers can turn out true. "Becky's turning mean, Hucky," he says. "I just found out she's trying to take the mansion away from me and it ain't even builded yet! She wants to use it for a dad-blamed WHOREhouse! So I'm on my way back to the claim to talk it over with my consortium. I mainly clumb up here to tell you that. Wyndy'll be looking after you. Whatever you want, just let him know. When I get back, we'll talk more about our plans for the sinteenery." It was like he hadn't heard a thing.

I give Tom time to clear out and then, while there was still enough light in the sky to see by, I stumbled back down the hill to our empty tent, feeling as condamned as when I was on the gallows with a rope round my neck. Couldn't stay. Couldn't go. Never felt so desperate ornery and low down.

Peewee's pards was still plasser mining down crickside. They warn't just only swirling gravels round in a pan now, they'd contrived up an amazing rig of waterwheels and pumps, ditches and dams, flumes and sluce boxes. All for a few specks a trouble.

Wyndy was posted outside the front flap like usual. He was into one of his mistical fits, so he must a been chawing or smoking something local. Talking with him was like talking with a wound-up music box. "The end is a-coming!" he was chanting in a singsong voice, his glazed-over eyes aimed up at the dimming sky. "The light's a-going out! Repent! Repent! Whilst still you can!"

I tore half a thigh off of the remainders of a young elk spitted over the fire and took it in the tent with me. I reckoned I was well enough to wash it down with samples from Tom's new brewery which was setting about, so I laid down with the elk thigh and the beer and set to worrying over my perdicament. I only had a few hours before General Hard Ass might show up. I had to decide now what I was going to do. Maybe I should just give myself over to the general, I thought, and let him end my miserableness. I tried to think what Coyote would do or say, but then I remembered he warn't no more, he was just a bunch of exploded new worlds scattered around out in the sky. Of course, he never WAS, but I knowed what I meant. I needed his advice and I warn't going to get it. Whilst I was dreaming away about the Coyote who warn't there, I seemed to see Snake grinning in a corner. But maybe not a corner in the tent, maybe a corner in that house Tom was a-building, nestling in the foundations. Snake laughed and says I'm a saphead, a numskull. I could hear the ghost of Coyote somewheres afar off, arguing with him. He was hooting at Snake like an owl, playing the fool. I heard the hoot again. Far away. Then again. I was wide awake. Warn't Coyote! It was Eeteh!

CHAPTER XXXI

Outside the tent, Wyndell was still wailing along about the Pocky Lips. He says everything was a-going to end by fire, nor else by floods, he couldn't make up his mind. I pulled Eeteh's ruined buckskin vest over my shirt, packed up in a saddlebag what was left of the roasted elk, a bottle of Tom's whisky, and what traps and tinware and ammunition I could grab up, and slung it over my shoulder, my rifle and revolvers, too, took up a candle lantern and pocketed some matches and extra candles. Wyndy was most likely staring half-blind at the starry sky and I could foot it right past him, but I couldn't resk him following me, so I used my old way of sneaking into circuses, squeezing out betwixt tent stakes at the back.

It was a long ways to where the hoots was coming from, a different direction and further up into the Hills. The yaller janders didn't make it no easier, but at least, once I got clear a the camp, I could hoot back to let him know I was coming. I followed the rattling rain-swoll crick, keeping my head down. Owls warn't much for eating, but that didn't stop people from shooting at them. When you got a gun, you use it on whatever chances by. It was a dangersome place at night, busy with drunks, thieves, and murderers, and they all had guns. A body could hear gunshots and cussing right up to the dawn racket, when the sawing, hammering, and shouting got too noisy to hear nothing else.

It was ever so lonely out along the crick in the dark and it got more lonelier the further a body tracked it, but Eeteh's hoots cheered up the empty night. I was moving fast as I could towards them. If it warn't for the janders and the darkness, I'd a been heeling it flat out. When I seen other lanterns in the hills moving through the trees like lightning bugs, I allowed I could light my own from time to time to show Eeteh where I was.

Where I was was a most peculiar and unnatural place, and the further I got from the mining camp, the peculiarer it become. It didn't seem like a place so much as a kind of time with stuff in it, stuff that kept on changing whenever a body looked t'other away. I can't say where such scary thoughts come from, they warn't common to me, maybe it was only because I was alone and afraid, but they made me wonder if that warn't why folks fancied gold so much. Gold didn't have no time lodged in it, it was just only what it was. But though it was a dead thing, the deadest thing of all, it acted like it was the livest thing of all, changing everything and everybody, and that was ever so peculiar, and scary, too. Living in the Gulch was like living in a wizzerd's den.

After about an hour, the hoots started getting clearer. He warn't fur away. And the closer I got to him, the less stupid and spooky my thoughts was. But then, all of a sudden, an emigrant in a dark suit and crumpled derby come sliding out a the woods straight into my lantern light! Just when I was thinking about wizzerds! I fell back and raised my rifle. I didn't want to shoot nobody, but there warn't nothing going to stop me reaching Eeteh. He throwed off the derby and called out my Lakota name. It WAS Eeteh! It was the splendidest sight that ever was! I run to him and give him a hug and he give me a hug. Didn't nuther of us want to let go. It was like we was hanging on to life itself. "I was sure you was dead!" I says.

"Me, too!" he says. "I think I am dead!" And he took my lantern and led me, limping, further along the crick and up through the pines. We passed his horse Heyokha along the way, hobbled and hid in the bushes. He loosed a noisy load as we clumb past. Eeteh's pied Clown. Trying to be funny. Thunder Dreamer.

We reached another cave. The new one warn't so roomy as the one back in the Gulch, but there warn't no bats and it was in a lonesomer place behind boulders where we could keep the lantern lit. I give Eeteh his vest and set down against the cave wall, wore out from all the walking and climbing, nor else just from the janders.

Eeteh stepped out a the emigrant clothes, dressing down to his headband, breechcloth, and moccasins. His body was favorably bruised and tore up, and parts was still bleeding. He held up the bloody tatters of his vest and studied about it, then put it on.

I opened up the mochila and brung out the elk meat and whisky and tinware. I still hadn't got back a proper appetite for whisky, but I allowed it was the right time to have a nip or two. Eeteh sprinkled some on the worst of his wounds, whooping as he done so, then took a deep grateful drink from the bottle. He had collected nuts and berries and dug up some bitter potatoes, which we et raw with the roasted meat. It was the most amazing dinner I could ever remember, and I says so, and he looked up at me through the black tangle hanging down over his face, his dark eyes a-glitter in the candlelight like he might a been crying, and says the same.

I told him about what I seen at the robbers' cave after the explosion, about Peewee and all the dead bats, and he says he was sorry about the bats. It was night time, maybe most a the bats was already out having breakfast. He says he was in the cave earlier that day when they come to plant the explosives. He tried to crawl out like always at the back, but the opening was already blocked off with dynymite. He says my friend knowed all about that cave, he'd made a study of it. All the other ways in and out that Eeteh knowed was also triggered to blow up. He was trapped.

He finally struck a narrow crack that he couldn't squeeze through — he put his hands up to show how skinny it was — but he was able to open it up bigger with a heavy sharp stone. It was slow work and he calculated there was only minutes before the dynymite went off. He worried his stone hammerings might shiver through the cave and SET it off. It was dark inside the cave and growing dark outside, but he couldn't light a lamp without showing up the opening he'd made to anybody scouting by.

When he could poke his head through and fetch it back in again, he spread his buckskin vest for a carpet and took everything off down to his hide. He was in a most terrible hurry. He tossed his rifle and breechcloth and moccasins through the hole, clamped his knife in his teeth, and pushed his arms and head and shoulders through. He reckoned if they made it, the rest would follow. But it warn't so. He got stuck halfway. He says it was the scaredest moment of his life. He couldn't go back and he couldn't go forwards. It took some desperate shoves to scrape on through. He says it was worse'n the tribe's stupid Sun Dances for cutting a body up. He grabbed up his things and was barely started down the hill when everything blowed up. He throwed himself behind boulders and trees, but he still got hit by flying rock. He don't remember getting on down the hill and away from there, but somehow he done it.

He woke up in the dark with the knife still betwixt his teeth and hurting all over. He didn't know where he was. He could hear water trickling noisily over stones, so he reckoned he must be down a-near the crick, without that sound was his blood trickling over his bones. He could also hear two men jawing. They was discussing about some gold dust they just stole off of a man they killed. Mostly they was disappointed. It warn't pay enough for all their trouble. The robber life was a hard life, they said. But they'd heard the blast and says maybe they should crawl up and see if anything blowed up that was worth hiving. They passed by only an arm's length away from where Eeteh was hid in some bushes, too scared to breathe. His head was worth more'n what was carried in most miners' scrotum bags of gold dust, and robbers don't mind about taking heads off if there's bounty money in it, even if heads was a generl vexation to tote around.

When they was gone, Eeteh slid along where they'd come from and struck a body. He could hear some wolves close by, prowling around, whining in their soft hungry way. He had to hurry not to become their supper. He was mostly naked, easy to see, easy to kill, so to cover himself up, he borrowed the dead man's black pants and jacket. The hat was bonus and might fool people who he really was. I says it sure fooled me. The man's boots was off and cut up and throwed away. Probably the robbers was looking for money hid in them. When the man fell, he'd fell on his kerosene lantern. Eeteh showed me the bullet holes in the back of the black jacket and how it was burnt in front, then he tossed everything into the darkness.

We et and drank and jawed on into the night round the candlelight. We felt comfortabler than since the days we was helping out old Zeb. I told him about the changes in the Gulch and everything that'd happened, and about Cap'n Patch and how he lost his head, and Eeteh told all about after he escaped from the robbers' cave. He says at first he hid in an abandoned one-room log cabin in the hills up above the crick, but it turned out to be the hideout for a bandit gang, so, after a bad night scrouched down in awful pain behind a woodpile, he had to move on. Whilst hiding, he couldn't send out hoots, but he heard mine sometimes, weak and far off. Then he didn't hear me no more. He didn't think we'd ever see each other again. He thought he was going to die.

I says I couldn't send out hoots, because I had a lookout dogging me all day and all night. He says he knows about that, the Cheyenne braves who'd moved in with the tribe was watching him close, too. It was mainly why he run away when they all went off to war. He was afraid a the plans they had for him. He tried to tell them funny stories, but they didn't have no sense a humor. And, last he seen, things warn't going so good for Tongo neither. The others said he was a devilish and vengeful cretur. They wanted to kill him, but some judged he was a spirit horse and bad things might happen to them if they did. But they probably killed him anyways, Eeteh says. If Tongo got stubborn when they all rode west, he wouldn't a give them no choice.

I'd made up my mind I warn't going back to the Gulch. Nothing to go back for. So, we talked about Mexico. Eeteh says he heard tell them Mexicans warn't exceeding friendly. I says as long as you ain't got nothing to steal, they're the most friendliest people I ever met. They sing and joke like that's the common way a body talks, and they love whisky like everybody else, but they give you some if they got any extra. They're clever with a knife, though, even when they're drunk. You can't take your eyes off of them. Eeteh says some a them is Indian bounty hunters, and I says that's right, but he was just another Mexican now like the rest of them, warn't he? No, he don't speak their jabber, he says, and I says that, well, his tongue got cut out by the dang Apaches, didn't it? And he laughed and rolled up his tongue and grunted, and I grunted back, and we both laughed together and took another swallow of the whisky.

Talk about Mexico drawed us back to the main hitch in our plans. We couldn't go nowheres if I didn't have a horse. Eeteh says he seen some wild ones close by where the tribe was camped before they went west, and they maybe didn't take all their broke-in horses with them, so we could start there. Also there might be some food and blankets and other things left behind we could borrow for our travels.

We was too excited to sleep, so we decided to leave the Gulch and go there straight away, riding double on Eeteh's pinto. Eeteh put the emigrant clothes on again to hide himself and we slid down out a the cave with our traps to where Heyokha was hobbled. Heyokha warn't all that happy about the extra freight, but he seemed as keen as us to leave the Gulch behind, and stumbled along, wagging his croup, without no complaint.

It would likely be raining by morning, but for now the sky was bright with the same mad scatter a stars Jim and me seen back on the Big River, or stars just like them, so we didn't even need the lantern lit. Whilst we was moseying along, Eeteh told me a Snake story. Coyote warn't in it, he was dead and gone, scattered all around the sky. Eeteh pointed up at parts of him. The rest a the stars, he says, was mica dust. He says Snake was the cleverest cretur a body ever knowed. Most people admired him for how smart he was, but not all the world. Some a them was missing Coyote. Life warn't so hard or dangersome when Coyote was around. That's what some was thinking, though nobody says it out loud. And back then it warn't so dreadful gloomy. Coyote made them laugh. Mouse pipes up timidly and asks if they remembered the story about Coyote's talking member? Everybody was grinning. Mouse was grinning. Snake's forked tongue darted out and sweeped Mouse up, then he spitted out his remainders. Nobody was grinning now. Snake was a serene cretur, but he never tolerated no distractions. Some a Snake's pards says that's a good thing. It's what was wrong in Coyote's time. Argufying all the time about nothing, making stupid jokes. Nobody argufied or joked with Snake's pards, nor not with Snake nuther.

I wanted to hear the story about Coyote's

talking member, but all Eeteh's stories was about Snake now. I says they ain't so funny like before, and Eeteh says he can't help it, he only tells true stories. He says Snake maybe warn't so good for laughs like Coyote, but he could be kind and generous, specially to his friends. He set up Lizard in a new tepee next to his own and sent him various ladies to company him there. When Lizard complained that Bee stung him on his tail for only helping himself to some a Bee's honey, Snake went over to the hive to stomp him. But he warn't home, so Snake stomped Bee's family instead. Losing all his family like that made Bee mad, and he flew into Snake's mouth to sting him mortally in the throat, but he didn't get past Snake's teeth. Snake, chomping, says he wished Bee tasted more like the honey he used to make. Eeteh says it's a story children get told about not losing your temper.

We had to stop under an overhang for a morning storm to pass, so it was already noontime when we finally reached the tribe's old camp. Eeteh went ahead to be sure none a the families warn't still living there, but the camp was empty, they was all gone together. The camp set in a sweet spot in a broad grassy valley in the Hills alongside of a crick. The only broke-in horse we could find was an arthritic old nag with cracked heels and eye ulcers. But we seen a couple a wild stallions less'n a mile away and we set about calculating how we could catch one. Eeteh knowed where the tribe stored dried corn and other grains we could offer up like bait, and he dug some out so's I could judge for myself. He found some desecrated fruit that we et and a couple of old ruined lodge covers we could use to tarpolin off the rain.

Eeteh showed me a big eagle pit and how it worked. It had a cover made a poles crossed together like bootlaces and covered over with brush and grass, which was now mostly dry and blowing away. A dead rabbit or other cretur was laid on the cover, Eeteh says, and the hunter kneeled in the pit under the cover till an eagle come down to chaw on it. The hunter had to wait till he could catch the eagle from behind and grab both his legs at the same time and tie him up without getting pecked or clawed to death. The eagle always fought like crazy and sometimes, if the hunter warn't strong enough or fast enough, he got hurt and the bird flew away. Eeteh smiled sheepish and showed me the scars on his arm. He lifted the cover to show me the pit, and there was Tongo!

They had trussed him up and throwed him in there and left him to starve to death, probably too afraid of him to kill him right out. He raired his big head when he heard me shout, then fell back again. Eeteh, cussing his cousins, jumped down into the pit and cut Tongo's bonds with his knife, but the horse was too weak to stand, or even try. I was already in the pit with him, holding his head. He warn't nothing but hide and bones. His hoofs moved like they was trying to write something in the dirt under him. "Water!" I says, still holding his head in my lap, and Eeteh sprung out a the pit. "And bring some a that corn!"

CHAPTER XXXII

For a while, it looked like Tongo warn't going to live long. He couldn't drink nor eat nothing at all. His breathing warn't steady, and he showed all his teeth like dead horses done. I had to hold his jaws open and dribble water down his throat, careful not to drown him. I grinded up the dried corn into a paste and mixed it with crick water and spooned that into him, too, cautious and slow. Grains was richer for him than grass, I knowed that from my Pony days, so whenever Eeteh found some barley, pine nuts, or sunflower seeds, I mashed them in as well. It was so good, I added in some blueberries and wild bird eggs and cooked it into a flapjack for me and Eeteh. I slept curled up in the eagle pit with Tongo and give him a little to drink and eat every hour or so, and him and me mumbled together through the night. Eeteh kept watch outside best he could, but most nights he joined us, saying he was lonesome and scared a the wolves. We could hear them out there, roaming round together and howling in their woesome way.

The tribe had been living in a prime spot alongside of a crick at the foot of a woodsy hill full of berries and nuts and small animals scampering round. Eeteh brung back marmots and possums and wild turkeys he hunted for us, a pile a wild rice he harvested in the backwaters, and some timpsila, squash and sweet potatoes. There was honey, too, which Eeteh says Bee give him without him having to stomp nuther him nor his family, on account of it was the moon of the strong flow and there was a-plenty for everybody. Tongo always did have a sweet tooth and seemed to like it when I mixed in a little honey with the corn-mash. It went good on our flapjacks, too.

We was all alone and afeard, but we et well and lived a mostly peaceful life and slowly we got comfortabler. Eeteh's gashly wounds crusted over, my yallerness begun to fade like fence paint in the sun, and, when we took the cover off of the pit, Tongo was able to get up on his feet again and look out over the edge, though he was still wobbledy, and pretty soon laid back down again.

Eeteh went on telling stories. He says he couldn't stop himself, it was a kind of sickness. If it WAS a sickness — him telling stories, me listening — it was a sickness we'd both die of, because warn't nuther of us going to stop.

Eeteh says Snake was mighty clever, but when Coyote's pard Fox got sentenced to have his head chopped off for telling Snake to his face he warn't nothing but a mean low-down bully, everybody rised up and chased Snake out, and Lizard, too, taking bites out a their backsides as they run. I was glad to see them go, and I says so. Eeteh nodded and says all stories is sad stories, but not all the time.

After Snake got throwed over, Eeteh says, they was shut of a cruel boss, but nobody knowed what to do next. Snake always told them what to do and that was that, but now some wanted one thing, some another, they couldn't agree on nothing. They hollered out for help from the Great Spirits, but they didn't get no answer. They needed someone to make them laugh, too. They'd forgot how. They remembered all Coyote's jokes and tricks and stories and told them over again, but they warn't funny no more. That was the worse thing. There warn't NOTHING funny no more. It was something only

Coyote could furnish out. I asked Eeteh if he might ever come back. Eeteh pointed up at the sky and shook his head and says it looked to him like Coyote was gone forever.

There was one morning we thought we was ALL gone forever. We just been considering we might stay right where we was for a spell longer, till Tongo got stronger. There warn't nobody a-bothring us and life was easy. Eeteh was right at home now that everybody else was gone, and it suited me, too, though Tom and the Gulch warn't fur enough away. We reckoned we could maybe at least see out the summer, and make ourselves well enough for our long travels southards.

But then General Hard Ass and his boys come a-storming through.

Eeteh was out hunting and seen them raising dust off to the north. Looked like the whole blamed calvary. Eeteh was out a breath when he come galloping back to camp to tell me. They warn't shoving along very fast, Eeteh says, but they knowed where they was going. They was all in blue and spread out like a single blue eagle, the general at the beak, flying in low and steady like attacking armies do.

Tongo still warn't fit to leave the pit, so we quick slung all our goods and rags into it, dragged the cover over the hole, and loaded it over with tore-up bushes and other rubbage. We knocked down our meat spit, tossed an old lodge-skin over the ashes of the fire we'd cooked on, and scuffed up the ground where we might a left a trace. Eeteh jumped up on Heyokha and says to climb on, but I couldn't. I had to stay with Tongo. Eeteh wanted to stay then, too, but he had to hide Heyokha. The bluecoats shot enemy horses, it was a rule they had. Fact is, they shot just about anything that moved, he couldn't resk it. He says if things start to go wrong, he'll fire some shots to distract the soldiers away. I says they'll just chase him down and kill him, he should try to get away while he can, but I knowed he wouldn't. I crawled down into the pit to hide with Tongo, and Eeteh went heeling it up into the woods fast as old Thunder Dreamer could trot.

I watched the horizon from under the pit cover, holding on to Tongo, feeling aloner than since the day they hanged me. We didn't have to wait long. In they come at full gallop with terrible shouts and guns a-blazing, sad-eyed General Hard Ass out front in his slouch hat and buckskins, silver buckles, cremson tie, and shiny boots, his sword pointed high. He looked like he was trying to copy Tom Sawyer, but couldn't grow proper face hair, his moustaches drooping down like his spirit was a-leaking out his nose, stead of bristling up ear to ear like Tom's.

As they drawed closer, I slunk down in the shadows, got the rifle and both pistols ready to fire. I s'posed I should probably shoot Tongo and me first, but I didn't think I could do that, so I'd have to try some tricks and then let the general and his troopers shoot us both.

The pounding and roaring all around us died away when the calvary seen the tribe warn't in the camp no more, and they cussed the sneaky heathen cowards and fired off some shots into the air, because they had to shoot something, even if it was only the sky. They was mighty excited and mighty disappointed. There warn't even nothing to burn nor steal. Then, there was a loud burst a gunfire and hallooing like they'd struck something all of a sudden to shoot at. I hoped it warn't Eeteh.

There was some soldiers standing on the pit cover over our heads, complaining that the general's Lakota scout was from this mob a savages, he should a knowed they was already pushed off. He was a sneaky bummer, they didn't trust him. They reckoned Hard Ass would hang him for leading them here, and good riddance. Others was a-grumbling about the generals, how they was losing the war because of their stupidness, but some was saying back that losing a battle or two warn't losing a war. Them heathen Sooks warn't smart enough or brave enough or decent enough to keep on whupping white men like they been doing. Also their guns warn't as good.

Me and Tongo was alone under their feet in the eagle pit, and Tongo was all a-tremble. I was shushing him quiet in his ear and stroking his neck to try to ca'm him. Some a the soldiers up above was talking about getting a move on now to the Yallerstone River where the war was going, whilst others was saying there warn't no damn hurry, the war could wait for them. The quartermaster'll borrow them a bottle a bark juice from the larder if they take up a collection for him. They mostly yayed that idea and says they was plumb played out after this dreadful battle, they should make camp right here and rest up for a night.

"We could roast up that hoss," one of them says.

Tongo couldn't hold back. He let a sudden loud snort like he was disgusted by what he was hearing. I took up my pistols. I reckoned we was done for. "Did you snort at me, you ole faht?" asked one of the soldiers above us.

"So what if I did, bluebelly?"

"Watch yer tongue, butternut, or I'll stomp you like the ugly old cootie you ah!" They was beginning to push each other around and I was scared they might come crashing in on us. "Every day you suit up in blue, grayback, you gimme the screamers."

"How ye think I feel, sap-haid, ridin' longside of Yankee shee-it like you-all?"

It sounded like they begun rassling. Somebody with a deep voice come and ordered them to get back on their horses, the company was moving out, but they kept cussing and crashing around. Dust was falling in on us, and I was afraid the cover'd give way. There was more yelling, then the sound of rifle butts whacking skulls, and at last, after some grunts and cussing, I could hear the horses finally moving on. I peeked out. The soldiers was all slowly parading away, two of them slumped out over their horses, tied to their saddles.

What I seen next was Eeteh's wicked brother. My heart jumped up. He was hung back and still poking around. He kicked at the ruined spit and the dead ashes. He looked over at our pit where we was hiding, and come slowly towards us, toting his rifle. I cocked mine. I could probably shoot him first, but as soon as I done it, I'd have the whole consounded calvary interested in me. I didn't know WHAT to do. General Hard Ass done it for me. He shouted for his scout to get back on his horse, dammit, they was pulling out. Eeteh's brother stood there a moment, trying to peek in where we was, but the general took his revolver out and pointed at his head. He cocked it. Orders was orders, and Eeteh's brother was already in trouble for leading them all to a deserted camp. He mounted his horse, squinting back my way with a mean grin, and joined the others.

When they was all gone at last, I pushed the pit cover away and crawled out, and pretty soon Eeteh come creeping down out a the hills on Heyokha. The poor old nag with the cracked heels was laying down by the crick, shot up a hundred times or more. "We got to go where the war ain't," I says, and Eeteh nodded.

The first thing we had to do was help Tongo out a the pit. Every day he was stronger, but he warn't never going to be strong enough to jump out a that hole. We dug up earth and built a step a foot or so high in half the pit, stood him up on it, then built another step a foot higher in t'other half, and moved him over on it. We didn't have no proper shovel nor cart, only Eeteh's knife, our tin plates and cups, and our shirts for humping the dirt to the pit. It was distressid hard work and was going to take a million moons.

Emigrant miners was beginning to swarm up at the crick shore now, too, looking in the water for glittery traces. I found some wood and staked a claim, though I misdoubted nobody would take it seriously. Eeteh put on his black emigrant clothes with the derby tipped down low, and set on the edge of the eagle pit with his rifle on his knees. I fired my guns a few times to chase off the peskier ones.

Then I spied a gnarly old miner with a shovel and a pan and a bottle he attended to regular. I went over and told him we was looking for a partner with a shovel, and he was happy to obleege. He says his name was Shadrack and he was from Ohio where he'd been a farmer mostly till the grasshoppers et him out. I knowed Tom would a somehow got him to pay for the chance to shovel up the steps in the pit, but I was grateful just to have the shovel, and mostly let Shadrack lay off. Him and Eeteh nodded at each other without saying nothing, and Shadrack went down to the water with his pan to poke around. He didn't find no gold, but he catched a big fish, which he shared with his partners.

Me and Eeteh built the third step on top of the first one, and then, taking turns, the fourth, fifth, and sixth, and from there Tongo was able to climb out and look around. He warn't too impressed. He stumbled down to the crick for a long drink and then he come and laid down again, but he et the mash I made for him and generly made himself at home. He spent a few days walking about slowly like he was customing himself to the idea.

But then one day, all of a sudden Tongo shook his whole body like wet dogs do and broke into a slow trot. He circled round us a few times, snorting and wheezing — and the next second, he was galloping away! I called out to him, but he never even turned round. My chest felt like it had got kicked. I should a picketed him. But if he was of a mind to go, a picket wouldn't a stopped him. I was afraid he was going back to the wild and I'd never see him again. But Eeteh only says to wait. An hour went by, two hours, night come. I couldn't sleep for fretting. And then finally, at dawn, there he was, pounding towards us, splashing through the crick, looking his old self.

I was ever so glad to have him back. I fed him some corn-mash with honey and talked to him about how happy I was and stroked the sweat off of his neck. I didn't know how fur he'd traveled, though I judged he'd been running fast as he could, ever since he galloped away. But he still seemed lively. He bowed his neck a couple of times and snorted. Eeteh throwed a soft piece of old lodge-skin over him and cinched it. He made a thong out a strips from his ruined buckskin vest and, finally, after tossing his head around in protest, Tongo let us loop it over his jaw for a bridle. I kicked off my boots and clumb aboard. He was quivering like something was about to bust inside him — and then all of a sudden we was off!

Chapter XXXIII

We ripped up and down them hills just like the first time, running all day through chopped-down forests and lonely shanty-towns and cricks lined with raggedy prospectors, till, just as the bloody-red sunball was sinking out a-front of us, we come to the end of the Hills and struck out on a broad grassy plain with a swelled-up river churning through it. We passed wagon trains and log cabins and tepees and herds of cattle and horses. "Look! It's the Pony Express!" somebody shouted out. "No, it ain't! That beardy coot ain't no boy!"

Tongo favored running towards the setting sun to see if he could beat it to the horizon. Evenings did stretch out this time a year and seemed to give him a chance, but the sun was only teasing. It got there first like always and the night growed dark. The river valley deepened under ridges and bluffs all round, and up ahead, I could see big fires a-blazing up and a war party of dancing braves blowing war whistles and yipping like coyotes like they was getting ready for a friendly massacre, nor else they was having a holiday. It was exactly where I didn't want to go, and I leaned back and tugged most desperately on the buckskin thong, but Tongo he charged right into the middle of them and they all fell back like they was seeing a ghost. They WAS seeing a ghost! It was Eeteh's brothers and cousins, the ones who'd thronged Tongo into the pit to die, and here he was, come back to ha'nt them! They dropped their weapons and let loose a great warbling. They was wild-eyed and bloodied up and showing off scalps that they held up for us to see.

The tribe wailed out for us to stay and I let go one hand and give them a wave, but Tongo was already on a tear again, racing back by night the way he come by day, across the plain under the moon and stars and back up into the Hills again, just as the dawn beyond begun to turn them into silly-wets. Stead of going to where Eeteh was, though, I seen he was striking straight for the mining camp in the Gulch. I tried to guide him away from there with my knees and by jerking on the thong, but his mind was clean made up. He was the willfullest cretur I ever knowed. I was being delivered up to Tom and his pals, and there warn't nothing I could do to stop him.

It was early morning when we rode into the mining camp. We hain't stopped running since yesterday. The muddy street was packed with people, but Tongo galloped right through them, knocking down food stalls and tool racks and beer tents and sending citizens skaddling for their lives. Old cross-eyed Deadwood COULDN'T run nor even WALK, and when I seen him bumbling along cripple-crablike in his union suit and talking to himself, I was afeard for him. But Tongo jumped right OVER him whilst he had his nose down, consulting his fob watch. The picture-taker warn't so lucky. He was trying to set up his camera, and Tongo, hammering straight ahead, sent him on a flying belly-flop into the mud, his camera tromped by the horse's hoofs.

Tongo left the ground all of a sudden and up we rose onto the raised wooden sidewalk, the loafers setting in chairs up there leaping off into the mud not to get killed or worse. Tongo pranced down the boardwalk, stepping high as if to bang it louder, and neighed like he was blowing a trumpet. Tom busted out a the claims office as we passed it, a fat seegar poking out under his moustaches, Caleb and Bear right behind him. He says something to them and they all three went a-running.

Then off we jumped at t'other end, me most desperately hugging Tongo's neck, my heels flying. Tongo went galloping through the screaming and yowling crowd again, heading down crickside. Shots was ringing out behind us. I hadn't no cause to s'pose this was going to end well. When we passed Tom's big tent, I did wish we could stop to pick up a couple a bottles a whisky and a hambone off one a the wild pigs a-roasting on the spit, but Tongo he was in a mighty hurry. We splashed through the crick, knocking over plasser miners and sluce boxes, and kept right on going.

When at length we reached the old Lakota camp, Eeteh was a-waiting for us by the filled-up eagle pit, dressed in the dead miner's raggedy black clothes. Everything was packed already and loadened onto Heyokha. I slid off of Tongo, my knees feeling warped and custardy, my hands raw from gripping onto the thong. Eeteh says he was wondering where I'd went, and I says I was wondering the same thing. I told him about racing all the way to the sunset and finding the tribe, bloodied up from scalp harvesting, then tearing back at dawn to the

Hills and dancing on the wooden sidewalk, but I says I was mostly just hanging on, not able to get down off of Tongo's back without massacring myself.

Tongo was thirsty and hungry and wheezing like a fat man, so I took the thong out of his mouth and uncinched the lodge cover. Whilst he went down to the shore to drink and stir up the waters round old Shadrack, patiently panning away, I mashed up some corn and pine nuts and honey, and had a quick chaw myself. I was ever so hungry. Tongo come back and nuzzled me and et up the corn-mash and whinnied like he was happy all over. Then he turned and trotted away, his head high, tail swopping the air. By and by, he broke into an easy run. The lodge-skin flew off of him. It was the sadfullest thing I ever seen, that tattered pelt raising up as he galloped away, and falling with a plop like a period after a sentence. This time, I knowed, Tongo warn't a-coming back.

Even as I was watching him disappear into the timber, Tom come riding in on Storm. He was wearing his white hat and white gloves and the red bandanna round his throat, so he warn't Tom so much as Tom's fancy of Tom. "You and your horse is under arrest, Finn," he says. "Your assault on our town was a most reckless and unsivilized act." Tom's pals rode in behind him whilst he was unloosing his declarations, Caleb and Wyndell, Oren, Bear, Pegleg Molly, and fifteen or twenty others, including toothless Mule Teeth and his fat yaller-whiskered boss who used to be a judge, but was now promoted to saloonkeeper. Eeteh was standing alongside of his pinto, and now he pulled his black derby brim down over his eyes and stepped around behind him, peeking out at Tom over Heyokha's withers. "I judge it's most likely a hanging offense for you and we'll have to shoot your crinimal horse, but first we'll give you both a fair trial like always."

"The crinimal horse ain't here no more," I says. Tom's posse was all carrying guns, except for the lantern-jawed picture-taker, who was just arriving on foot in his mucky frock coat, but without no camera, looking mud-faced and grumpy. The Amaz'n Tom Sawyer didn't have nobody to take his picture today, though he still set his saddle straight up with his hat on like in the photograph the picture-taker showed me. Probably he couldn't help himself. He gazed around like he suspicioned we was hiding the horse somewheres. "Can't say where he's took off to," I says. I was carrying my rifle in one hand like a pistol and had my finger on the trigger in case anyone drawed. Tom seen that, and I hoped the others did, too. "I reckon he was plumb sick a the Gulch and the people in it and run away in disgust."

Caleb was sore offended at that and, bellowing out some cusswords, come galloping at me with his Colt drawed. I whipped up my rifle, but Tom swung his and knocked Caleb off of his horse. He hit the ground hard and his orange too-pay fell off and his gun went off, making everybody duck. Then they all laughed. The laughing raised Caleb's dander even higher up, and he stalked away, shaking his too-pay at them and sending everybody to hell.

"We believe in the law here in Deadwood Gulch," Tom says after him. "It ain't let us down yet." Tom looked like he was grinning, but it might a just been the way his moustaches curled up from his mouth to his ears. He turned back to me. "But you have, pard. No matter what I done for you, it warn't never enough. You're the most leather-headed dispreciative saphead I ever struck. It ain't my druthers to hang a pard, but you can't say you don't deserve it. You got no respect for the law nor not your old pard nuther. You're running away from the grandest idea what's ever been thought up by the human species just on accounta you ain't got the guts to stay and defend it. You're a coward and a traiter. You and that dark ugly varmint in the derby hiding behind the horse. Ain't that your rogue injun pal?" I didn't say it warn't, and Tom says, "How the heck did he get out a the cave?"

"He didn't. It's his ghost. You killed him. That's the suit they buried him in. Most folks can't see a ghost. I'm surprised at you having the knack."

"Must be my guilty conscience acting up." Tom stared hard and long at Eeteh. A number of curious plasser miners, new arrived, was a-gathering round. What they seen was a couple of poor scruffy tramps like theirselves, a handsome hero in a white hat, a posse of mostly ignorant townsfolk, and a powerful lot of guns. "He's an even worse coward and traiter'n you, turning against his own tribe and running off with a low-down white man, just when they need him to fight and die for his people."

I judged we was safe so long as Tom kept talking. Talking too much was a weakness the boy had, who didn't have many. I knowed Tom was hurting and I was sorry, but I was hurting, too. And I was worried about Eeteh. Any one a them pesky rascals could shoot him without no concern about the law. They could even collect a big bounty. I had to keep an eye on everybody at the same time and hope I'd be fast enough.

"If the main crinimal ain't available," Tom says from high up on Storm, "I guess you'll have to do, Finn. We're building a new jail and we can guest you in it, leastways till that general who's chasing you comes. I just got a message from him. He's on his way here to settle up with you. Hard to tell which of us is a-going to hang you first."

"I s'pose I ain't got much choice."

"Your one choice all along's been to stay right here. But you turned it down. I'm mighty disappointed. I told you we could handle that bugger of a general. Now I want you for myself. After the general's sent packing, we'll decide what we're going to do with you. We KNOW what we're going to do with your injun pal there. He was born a vilent crinimal, it was in his papoose bones. He's just fitten for our gallows, and for his like there ain't no appeal, nor not no room in the jailhouse nuther." He nodded to his posse. It was the signal for them to raise their guns and point them at us. "Throw down your weapons," Tom says. "NOW!"

It was hard to say where they come from, but when Tom says "now," the tribe appeared all around us, dressed in splendid feathered headdresses and toothy necklesses, pieces of silver, beaded jackets hung with shells and tinkling metal. Led by Eeteh's war-chief brother, they come riding in from all sides in a slow stately manner, meloncholical and most dignified, with their hands raised to say they was only wanting peace. Their hair was braided with julery and fur. Even their ankles had fur and silver bracelets on them. The chiefs in their war bonnets warn't mostly carrying weapons where a body could see, but all the braves was. Some had bows and arrows, some had rifles, some only quirts, lances and stone mallets, but they all looked mighty dangersome. They was mostly bare-chested and painted up for battle and had bunches of red eagle feathers in their hair, one each for who they killed.

Tom seen he was overnumbered and raised his paw in a peace reply, glaring at me. His posse'd shrunk together, and they all lowered their weapons because Tom told them to.

Eeteh took off his derby and went to talk with the chiefs. They all laughed and pointed at the clothes he was wearing. He turned round and showed them the bullet holes in the back, and they laughed again. I heard them ask about Ne Tongo, and Eeteh pointed off towards the woods. They nodded and muttered betwixt theirselves. Eeteh's brother signaled to one of the braves, and the brave led out a handsome speckled sorrel. Eeteh took the thong and thanked his brother in a formal way, then led the horse over to me. He was a gift, Eeteh says. He belonged to a very great warrior who was killed at the Greasy Grass River. The horse was very brave.

It was a beautiful gift. I says so in sign language with both hands, and told them in Lakota, best I could, the same thing.

General Long Hair also lost his curls there, Eeteh whispers to me. "They show you bluecoat scalps." My jaw gapped. Who I most feared in the world warn't IN it no more! My ducking and running was over! I couldn't hardly believe it! But I was sorry for him, too. He probably warn't planning to leave it so sudden.

"Thank your brother, Eeteh," I says, "but ask him please to don't show no scalps."

Eeteh returned to the chief, they jawed a bit more, Eeteh pointed at the posse, and his brother nodded. When Eeteh come back, he says his brother told him we should go now.

"Why're they helping us?"

"Ne Tongo spirit horse. God dog. Help win Long Hair war. You Tongo friend. All night they follow you here."

The sorrel was already wearing a cinched pelt, so I kicked off my boots and swung up. I walked him around in a circle, feeling mighty comfortable. He moved easy and proud and already felt like part a me. Eeteh says the horse's name is Waktay, but I could change it. "Tell him I am calling him Rain," I says, stroking his neck. "For him."

"Maghazhu," Eeteh says, and his brother looked quietly pleased and nodded.

Tom handled his rifle to Bear and come sauntering over on Storm, cocksure as ever. There was the click of weapons getting ready. Some was raised and pointed at him. I held up my hand to stop anybody shooting, but Tom didn't seem to pay no mind. "It don't have to end like this, Hucky," he says. He warn't staring down on me no more. It felt more natural.

"We're pards, Tom. There warn't no call to try and get me hung."

"I know it. I shouldn't a done it that way. You know it don't mean nothing, Hucky. I wouldn't a never done you no harm. I only needed for you to stay, and I was trying to make that happen anyhow I could. Keeping you penned up in jail a week seemed like one good way."

"Like your lie about the general. General Hard Ass ain't sending out messages, Tom. He got killed yesterday."

Tom probably don't know that, but he didn't even blink. "Then you got no reason to leave, Huck. You and me can get up that circus you sejested. Your injun friend can be in it. We can try it out on the sinteenery, and then take it all through the Territory and the States. The sinteenery's just a week away. You can leastways stay that long. It'll be the bulliest thing ever, and you and me can ride in it together!"

"You're my pard, Tom, always was. But it ain't tolerable here for me no more. If you want to ride together again, come along with us now."

Tom smiled like he might be tempted. "I think I read a story about that," he says. "It was about two brothers."

"Great, Tom. Let's live it."

"I think one a the brothers got killed by t'other one. An accident. You'd best stay here with me, Hucky."

I seen it warn't no use. I smiled back at him and says, "Good-bye, Tom."

"Aw shucks, Hucky." He set back on Storm, looking low-downer'n I ever seen him. Even his moustaches seemed to droop. "Well, all right, we can save the gallows for your next crime, you damn muggins! Soon enough you'll be back here making a fool a yourself again!"

I turned my back on him and walked Rain over to Eeteh, now setting on Heyokha, his rumpled derby back on over his headband.

"HUCKY!" Tom called out. I reached for my rifle and looked back over my shoulder. He'd found his old face again. He'd took his hat off. There was a twinkle in his eyes and an easy grin on his moustachioed face. "It ain't going to be much fun here without you, pard," he says. "But if Becky takes that house away, I'll build another one. Come back and live in it whenever you want. Bring your injun pal if you like." He raised his hand to me and I raised mine. "And be careful, Hucky! I'll miss you!" Then he turned back to his posse to lead them away towards their camp, his bald spot gleaming like it was polished, big wart-nosed Bear riding at the rear to make sure nobody got out a line.

I watched him go. I was going to miss him, too. But I warn't noway ever coming back to the Gulch.

Chapter XXXIV

The tribe says they wanted to walk a mile or two with us to be sure there warn't no trouble. First, I stopped down by the crick shore, and says to Shadrack that my Mexican friend was homesick, so me and him was lighting out for his old Mexico home. We'd sell him our claim for whatever whisky he had left. He still ain't found no glitter down at the shore, but he was a good fellow and he give us the mostly empty whisky bottle and some jerky as well, and says, "Adios, amigos."

The tribe was relaxed now and laughing amongst theirselves, and when we'd got a hill or two between us and the camp, they seen their job was done and begun peeling off. Eeteh says something that made everybody snort and laugh in their deadpan way, and when they said good-bye, Eeteh's brother give him a little money pouch, so's we could buy some food and tobacco and maybe a skillet and blankets and shoes for the horses.

We headed south towards the old wore-down emigrants' trail, which I reckoned might be more safer for Eeteh, though it warn't easy to hide there. Maybe we could see if Nookie's little sod cabin was still there and nobody in it, and rest up for a few days.

Whilst we was poking along under the sun, Eeteh says that when Snake thronged Coyote's sliced-up carcass into the sky, he missed one part. His talking member.

"Yay!" I says, and I laughed. Coyote was back! "It could still talk without the rest of him? Don't it need a brain to think with?"

Eeteh says Coyote never really had a separate brain. He thought with ALL his body parts, most SPECIALLY his member. That was what made it possible for him to change into so many different creturs. When he changed into a lark, he didn't even HAVE a member, not so's a body could see, so before he got chopped up, he was lucky Snake Woman made him change into a snake who has TWO. That is, he WAS lucky, till both of them begun fighting with each other.

I asked him, laughing, how Coyote moved around now he ain't got no feet. Like a worm? Eeteh sighed and says I ain't never understood proper how stories work, but if I had to know, he borrowed his cousin Fox who was happy to sport a couple extras. They didn't give Fox no pleasure, but they made him popular with the ladies, and give him some new ideas. I says I was glad I asked because I felt more comfortable now with Coyote's talking member, or members, but how did Snake miss them when he was filling up the sky? When Coyote was still a snake, Eeteh says, he was worried about Snake's tricks, so he hid his members in the end of his tail. He was a pisonous snake, and Snake judged the pison was low down in the tail and warn't the right thing for making new worlds, so he throwed it away.

"He should a burnt it," I says, and Eeteh sighed again and shook his head and says, if he done that, how could he be telling this story about what happened next?

I says I'm sorry and won't bust in on him again, and I asked him what DID happen next?

He says that Coyote's talking members warn't having much fun living on Fox's body because Fox always favored his own member when it come to the main part. They sometimes felt like nothing more'n advertisings for it. So they decided to collect some limbs and organs and other bits from their friends and make a new body out a them. Fox didn't care because the novelness was wore off and Coyote's members had took to shouting out rude sejestions to the ladies, most ruining Fox's fun. So they made a new cretur out a parts borrowed from Whooping Crane, Prairie Dog, Mountain Goat, Rainbow Trout, Turkey Vulture, Jack Rabbit, and Porkypine.

"That must a been something to see!" I says. "A cretur with two members, joined up from a crane, prairie dog, goat and trout, plain stops me cold in my tracks, never mind the rest!"

Eeteh says he thought I warn't going to bust in no more. I says again I was sorry, and I promised to keep my mouth shut, but I only wanted to know which parts come from which creturs so's I could picture it, and whether or not they missed them when Coyote borrowed them. Eeteh says he's really glad he didn't try to tell me about Coyote in the Land of the Dead.

"Ain't that a story about afterlife soul creturs? I thought you don't take no stock in souls."

Eeteh sighed and says that's just what he means.

I was plumb lost. I reckoned we could start over around the camp fire tonight with them two talking members fighting, which also must be something to see. Eeteh hain't said whether they was rassling or boxing or fighting any which way like boys do.

For now, I says how amazing it was it all turned out like it done.

Eeteh says he was amazed, too, so he asked Coyote about it. I didn't ask him if he meant Coyote or his talking members. Coyote puzzled it out, Eeteh says, and what he finally says was, it was a pretty good story and stories was like that.

"It was only a story?"

"Story never ONLY, Hahza. YOUR story."

"That warn't exactly what Coyote told me."

"What? Coyote talk to you?"

"Yep. It was whilst we was galloping across the plains and into the hills last night. Somehow he'd crawled up on Tongo's croup and was riding behind me. I dasn't turn round, fast as we was going, so I don't know whether it was all of Coyote nor only his member, or members. Besides, it was pitch dark and I wouldn't a seen nothing if I COULD turn round, though it most seemed like he was setting on my shoulder."

"Hah! Then it is COYOTE story?"

"More his'n mine. If there's a few stretchers in it, I ain't to blame. I was surprised he'd talk to me who warn't even a native, but he says don't NOBODY own him, and I says that's good, because don't nobody own me nuther. He warn't convinced a that and says him and Tongo was going to make me prove it. And that's just what they done."

I was afeard Eeteh'd be angry I smouched Coyote from him, but he was laughing. What he says is, it must a been Raven who'd flew up and landed on my shoulder. I must of felt his little feet. Raven was a trickster like Coyote, he says, and a considerable fraud and liar. It was easy to mix them up. Both Coyote's talking members was bigger'n better than his'n, so Raven offered to fly up into the sky to gather up all Coyote's body parts in trade for one of the members. Coyote had a spare, so he done that, but when he changed himself back together again, he found he only had half a member, and no head. Maybe Raven had forgot his head behind like he said, or maybe he'd played another trick. No matter. Coyote didn't have no head, and that considerably disadvantaged him. Raven had the other half a member and says if Coyote give him his half, he'll fly back out and collect his head.

I was lost again. I didn't know if both halfs of Coyote's member was still talking, and, if nuther of them warn't, then who was, since Coyote himself didn't have no head. It was like I'd left my own head somewheres and had fell backwards into the night. Eeteh had plain enough won Coyote back, and I let him. There was a crick down below us in the twilight without no prospectors on it, where we could probably fish up a supper. Best to make camp, I says to Eeteh, and muddytate on Coyote's misfortunes over the last of Shadrack's whisky, and my pard yayed that.

THE END. YOURS TRULY, HUCK FINN.

ACKNOWLEDGMENTS

Thanks to Larry McCaffery, Stéphane Vanderhaeghe, Bernard Hoepffner, John Glusman, Georges Borchardt, and Pilar for good cheer and helpful reads.

The employees of Thorndike Press hope you have enjoyed this Large Print book. All our Thorndike, Wheeler, and Kennebec Large Print titles are designed for easy reading, and all our books are made to last. Other Thorndike Press Large Print books are available at your library, through selected bookstores, or directly from us.

For information about titles, please call:

(800) 223-1244

or visit our Web site at:

http://gale.cengage.com/thorndike

To share your comments, please write:

Publisher
Thorndike Press
10 Water St., Suite 310
Waterville, ME 04901